Be Mine

Be Mine

A FRANK BASCOMBE NOVEL

Richard Ford

ecc●

An Imprint of HarperCollins*Publishers*

FIRST EDITION

Designed by Angie Boutin

Title page image © NikhomTreeVector/shutterstock

Library and Archives Canada Cataloguing in Publication information is available upon request.

ISBN 978-0-006-169208-6
ISBN 978-1-4434-7042-1 (Canada)

23 24 25 26 27 LBC 5 4 3 2 1

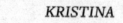

KRISTINA

Be Mine

HAPPINESS

Lately, I've begun to think more than I used to about happiness. This is not an idle consideration at any time in life; but it is a high-dollar bonus topic for me—b. 1945—approaching my stipulated biblical allotment.

Being an historical Presbyterian (not-attending, not-believing, like most Presbyterians), I've passed easily through life observing a version of happiness old Knox himself might've approved— walking the fine line between the twinned injunctions that say: "whatever doesn't kill you makes you stronger" and "happiness is whatever is not bludgeoning *unhappiness*." The second being more Augustinian—though all these complex systems get you to the same mystery: "Do what, now?"

This median path has worked fairly well through most situations life has flung my way. A gradual, sometimes unnoticed succession through time without anything great happening, though nothing unsurvivable and most of it quite okay. The grievous death of my first son (I have one other). Divorce (twice!). I've had cancer, my parents have died. My first wife has also died. I've been shot in the chest with an AR-15 and nearly died myself, but improbably didn't. I've lived through hurricanes and what some might say was depression (it was mild if it was depression at all). Nothing, however, has sent me spiraling to the bottom, so that cashing in my own chips seemed like a good idea. Much quite good contemporary literature, which I read in bed and—if I angle the page right—is all about just such matters, with happiness ever elusive but still the goal.

And yet. I'm not sure if happiness is the most important state for us all to aspire to. (There are statistics on these subjects, graduate degrees, fields of study offering grants, a think tank at UCLA.) Happiness apparently declines in most adults through their '30s and '40s, bottoming out in the early '50s, then sometimes starting up again in the '70s—though it's not a sure thing. Knowing what you fear in life may be a more useful measure and skill set. When asked by an interviewer, "Do you feel you could've been happier in life," the poet Larkin said, "No, not without being someone else." Thus, purely on average, I would say I've been happy. Happy enough, at least, to be Frank Bascombe and not someone else. And until late days that has been more than satisfactory for getting along.

Recently, however, since my surviving son, Paul Bascombe, who's 47, became sick and presenting well-distinguished symptoms of ALS (Lou Gehrig's disease—though there's speculation the Iron Horse really didn't have it but had something else), the subject of happiness has required more of my attention.

FOR THE LAST EIGHTEEN MONTHS I HAVE HELD A PART-TIME job at House Whisperers, in Haddam, New Jersey, where I live a solitary, senior, house-and-library-card-holder's life. House Whisperers is a boutique realty entity nestled within a larger, vertically integrated realty entity owned outright by my former employee Mike Mahoney, from my—and our—roaring '90s house-seller days on the Jersey Shore. A certified Tibetan—he long ago changed his name from Lobsang Dhargey to "something more Irish"—Mike got seriously rich by noticing a new market of well-financed Tibetan investors itchy to buy distressed New Jersey beach property left behind by the latest hurricane. (Getting rich almost always involves recognizing a market before the other guy, though who knew Tibetans had that kind of liquidity, or how they came by it?)

From selling distressed beach holdings, Mike moved swiftly using his newfound asset position to leveraging the purchase of hundreds of once-regular family homes—in Topeka, Ashtabula, Cedar Rapids, and Caruthersville, Georgia—residences which had become problematic for their owners due to tax liens, deferred maintenance, owner-infirmity, fixed-income woes, unpaid alimony, etc. These houses he fixed—and still fixes—up on the cheap using outsourced construction crews, assigning their upkeep to maintenance companies he owns, then securitizes the buildings into widgets he sells as shares on the Tokyo exchange to anybody (often other Tibetans) ready to take a risk. After which he rents them—sometimes back to their prior owners. Every bit of this shenanigan is perfectly legal following "the lost decade of housing," when the banking sector went prospecting for richer seams. HSP, Mike's umbrella company is called. Himalayan Solutions Partners. (There are no partners.)

House Whisperers, where I nominally work, is Mike's separate vest-pocket "niche" project whereby he locates and services high-end home-buyer clients who for their own reasons desire complete, BPSS-level anonymity when purchasing a home. There are plenty of people at all stages of the purchase process, right up to and past the point of sale, who simply don't want the world to know their beeswax: people who want to buy a house then never live in it, visit it, or even go inside; people who want a house for Grampa Beppo until he "passes" and the will clears probate. Or people who want to buy a house to actually *live* in, but are famous rock stars, disgraced politicians or Russian dissidents who don't like publicity or for a clamor to be made. House Whisperers reaches out to this market for a hefty fee. (I'm not talking here about people in the witness protection program or convicted weenie-wavers who can't find refuge in the general population. These cases are handled by government agencies and don't involve our type of clients.)

I, years ago, let my own realtor's ticket lapse, but I have been willing to come on board with Mike to jolt myself awake and out of my house in the aftermath of divorce and my second wife, Sally Caldwell, deciding to dedicate her life to one of service by counseling the grieving on distant shores (where a whole lot of grieving presumably goes on). She has recently taken orders as a lay nun, so a happy reconfiguring of our married life is likely not in sight.

Our small House Whisperers' office occupies second-floor space on Haddam Square above Hulett's shoes, across from the August Inn. My job there is really only a semi-job, not the gig economy, but not exactly not. I do little more, in truth, than answer the phone and pass along private contact info to our agency higher-ups. My minimal duties, however, afford as one of their side-attractions the chance to dispense granular, ground-level, real-time real-estate intel to people who've misunderstood our internet grille, which states we are "Confidential Consultants Offering Unique Home-Buying Strategies To An Uncommon Clientele." Citizens who (incorrectly) believe this describes *them,* routinely call me up seeking the lowdown on the commonest nuts-and-bolts real estate quandaries, which I'm only too happy to help them resolve based on years of experience: "How" (for instance) "does a reverse mortgage really work, and at age 92 with co-morbidities, should I jump into one?" No. "What's the downside on Chinese drywall for my mother-in-law apartment?" Lawsuits await. "Where's the breakeven for the fixer-upper I'm about to drop on the rental market but that needs new soffits?" When was it ever not a landlord's market? Make money by spending money.

Most of this information you can get out of the *New York Times*. Only people don't want to be bothered—which is why the rest of us have jobs. Plus, most citizens, even in high-end Haddam, don't read newspapers anyway.

Mike Mahoney, my would-be boss, is as ever a semi-lovable, quasi-honest entrepreneurial dynamo who believes that in all of his money-making forays he's being natively "responsive" to the suffering of others by relieving them of their encumbrances— their homes—all of it in accordance with some Dharmic dictum found in a bardo somewhere. I am sympathetic to him if only because he risks his skinny Tibetan ass on longshots and wins. And yet. On my shady block of Wilson Lane, the old ether of true residence has all but burned off now—as with many close-in neighborhoods across the land—leaving the door ajar to absentee owners, private-equity snap-ups, Airbnbs and executive apartments, where, before, citizen pharmacists, teachers, librarians and seminary profs paid the taxes and rightly took pride. It's rare anymore to know who lives next door to you. If you died in one of these not-quite domiciles, no wreaths would appear on the door, no pastor call, no neighbors would show up with a hot dish. In my day, I marketed these houses like flapjacks. But always to humans who wanted to live in them, raise children, celebrate birthdays and holidays, get divorced. And die—mostly happy.

LAST OCTOBER, AS I SAT AT MY HOUSE WHISPERER'S DESK LOOK-
ing out the window onto the Boro Green, where two young girls
in gym shorts were hanging banners for Oktoberfest, something
quite unusual happened to me. Entirely without knocking, across
the threshold of my tiny office walked my mother, who as far as
I knew had been dead fifty-six years. Not my actual mother. But
her twin, if all those years hadn't intervened, and if my mother
had had a twin—which she didn't.

From behind my desk I must've gaped like a drunk man.
My mouth may actually have fallen open. I heeled my chair
backwards in alarm, since I felt I was possibly having a stroke.
"You don't look very happy to see me," my mother said—or the
woman who looked like her the last time I saw her alive. 1965.
This person gazed at me mock seriously, then smiled an enig-
matic smile. She was sixty (near my mother's age when she died)
and possessed my mother's complex mirthful face and dense silver hair done in a pageboy, as well as her pert little features that
made her seem vivacious and onto whatever foolishness you were
advertising.

"I'm sorry," I said, reclaiming a relieved smile. "Not many
people come in without appointments. You remind me of someone I loved very much who died a long time ago." These words I
blurted as might happen in a dream.

"Uh-oh, *that* old story," the woman said, skeptically. "Well,
I'm not your ex-wife Delores, or your second wife, if that's who
I look like. My husband would get a kick outa you. I'm looking for the dentist's office. Dr. Calderon. I may have come in
the wrong entry. They got the signs all screwed up by the shoe
store." She opened a glittering regiment of choppers. "These are
brand-new implants," she said. "I'm transitioning back to a real
dentist."

"Okay." Calderon had been my dentist for 35 years, should've retired a decade ago but doesn't have anything better to do. I hadn't visited him in a while and needed a crown redo. "He's in number twelve. Back down to the street and turn left. It's the next entry *beyond* the shoe store." I reoffered her my recovered smile, but my heart was pounding.

"What happens in *here*," the woman said, looking around. "What's a house whisperer? Are you a private detective?"

"No. Real estate," I said.

"Oh, okay." She raveled her mouth. "Cute name. So who was it I look so much like?"

"My mother." I didn't want to admit it. Who knows why?

"Oooo. Really? That's *so* sweet. Does it make you happy to see her again? Me, I mean. Sometimes I see deceased people in my dreams. It always thrills me. For a while anyway."

"Well, yes," I said. "It does." It did.

"See, you can defeat death just by dreaming. My mom's still alive, and she's a terror. Still in Manalapan. Does her own shopping. Drives her little Kia. I don't see her, but my sister does."

"That's good."

"Oh, well," my mother said. "We don't get to choose our parents, do we? They don't choose us, either. So. It works out."

"No, we don't. I mean I guess it does."

"We probably wouldn't choose the same ones, would we?" My mother was in my little office, speaking these words to me. I might very well have lost consciousness or started baying.

"I don't know," I said.

"Yeeees, you do. But I *get* it," the woman said. "I . . . get it. You're real busy. You have a blessed day. Okay? Meanwhile I'm at the dentist. What's your name?"

"Frank," I said. I started to say just "Bascombe."

"Okay, Frank. Try to remember the kind of September." With those words—one of which was my name—my mother walked out the door, closed it behind her and was gone. Like a ghost.

———

THIS WAS AS MUCH AS IT TOOK TO INSERT "HAPPINESS" INTO MY brain, where it had not been for a long time. Old people—I'm seventy-four—can quit thinking about being happy altogether (the way the frog in the saucepan doesn't think about the water slowly getting hot until it's time for frog soup). If anyone had *asked* me if I was happy, I'd have said, "Absolutely. Happy as they come. Money in the bank." But if that same person had asked what *makes* me so happy, or what does happy *feel* like, I might've had a harder time. Happy wasn't part of my everyday *lexis* the way a hundred happy-neutral signifiers were (such as, I still hear well; my tires are properly rotated; no one's robbed me so far today).

Here, though, was my "mother" saying to me, "You don't look happy" (to see me). And, "Are you happy to see your mother?" I was, it just didn't show. Often, when I have a new picture taken at the DMV, the woman behind the camera says, "Give us a big smile, Mr. Bascombe, so the cops won't arrest you." I always have to say, "I thought I *was* smiling."

When my actual mother was dying in an early-days hospice facility in Skokie, and I was a junior at Michigan, riding the New York Central to visit her on weekends—the chagrin of seeing her sunken and denatured was immense—she one day, out of her morphine haze just snapped awake with me standing beside her bed, full of dread and awe. I was not certain she knew I was me, and literally staggered back in alarm. Her dark eyes were rounded and staring up as if she saw a specter, her nostrils flared as if breathing brimstone billows, her lips flattened together in ferocious, marshalled effort. She all at once shouted out

at me, "I only have one thing to say to you, buster!" "What is it?"
I said, trembling, scared shitless and full of dismay. I might even
have shouted back at her, I was so terrified. "Are you *happy?*"
she said accusingly. "Your father was a very happy man. He was
a fantastic golfer. Are you?" She didn't mean was I a fantastic
golfer (I'm not a golfer at all), but was I happy? It seemed the
most important thing in the world to her at that incomparable
moment—important enough to bring her back from oblivion
to put the question to me directly. (She died the next day after lunch.) "You *must* be," she said terrifyingly. "It's everything.
You *must* be happy." "I am," I said, quaking—though I might've
said, "Okay, then I *am*," as in, "If you want me to be, I will be."
I was lying. I was anything but happy. My mother was dying in
front of me—a momentous and bad thing; I wasn't doing well in
school; I had no girlfriend or any hope for one; I was anticipating
entering the Marines after graduation to escape my life by fighting in Asia. What was there to be happy about? There were other
things I might've said to her, querulous, young-man things like
"What do you mean by happy?" "Why would you ask me *that?*"
"I'm not really sure." But she was on her deathbed, so I said yes.

"Good. I'm so glad," my mother said. "I was hoping you
were. I've been worried sick about it. Now. Let me get some
sleep. I have a long way to go."

Which she didn't. She fell back almost lifeless into her pillow. I'm not sure she spoke to me again, although supposedly
we never forget people's last words spoken only to us. But I may
have. It was a long time ago.

———◆———

ANOTHER SIGNIFICANT OCCURRENCE, LIBERATING HAPPINESS
from cold storage and inserting it into the forefront of my brain,

came at an event last summer. In June, I decided to attend a reunion of the Gulf Pines Military Academy (Lonesome Pines) class of '63, on the frowsy Gulf Coast of Mississippi. Our get-togethers had formerly been held on the old parade grounds. But in the past decade and a half—during which the school was sold to a religious cult, then resold, then razed to make way for a casino parking lot—our convenings have taken place on the oak-shaded grounds of Jefferson Davis's ancestral home, which was itself blown to matchsticks by Hurricane Katrina, though most of the big oaks, doggedly hanging onto their Spanish moss, were spared. I've attended these reunions a few times over the years and have always gone away feeling perplexed but half elated. Per-plexed because most of my classmates were hard-core dipshits, and encountering them years on, in their muted, undemonstra-tive, heavy-footed, slightly antagonistic, often dilapidated states, served only to attest that exceeding one's beginnings was entirely a matter of dumb luck. Many of our classmates had gone off to Vietnam and come home bemused, spiritually-wizened, prema-turely timeworn (those who hadn't been blown to smithereens or *half* blown to smithereens). Most of us had been scattered by fate out across the continent to become John Deere salesmen, gym teachers, male nurses, abstract metal sculptors in Hayden Lake, or, like me, a real estate specialist in New Jersey. A few had managed to make a mint using native wizardry fueled largely by defeat and anger. But these were the ones I didn't talk to since their life story is the only story they know.

On the upbeat side, I felt it might be invigorating to square up and shake hands with a few of these fellow wayfarers—none of whom I really remembered—if only because of a book review I'd read in the *New York Times*. This was a review of a novel by a famous female writer with three names, a novel that followed the life of a character who'd lost all long-term memory (which could seem like a blessing, but not in this book). What the reviewer said about the novel had struck a resonant chime in my brain. She seemed to like the novel in a grudging way, and to substantiate her liking it, wrote: "What kind of person can we say we are if we lack the ability to string together a cohesive personal narrative?" This was meant to be praise.

Everything's, of course, a narrative these days. And I didn't particularly give a shit about mine. It's widely acknowledged that people live longer and stay happier the more stuff they can forget or ignore. Plus, my view of my personal narrative wouldn't agree with most other people's views of it—my two ex-wives, and my two surviving children, who may believe they're, in part, victims of "my narrative." Unlike the character in the novel, I was happy to turn loose much of my narrative, since it often kept me awake at night and made me unhappy.

But the reunion invitation came coincidentally just at the moment I'd picked up the *Book Review*. (Our reasons for going to reunions never represent our best selves.) And on a perverse whim I decided that if I flew down in steamy late August, postured around Jeff Davis's shaded lawn in the blazing heat, mingled, bumped elbows, clapped shoulders, talked out of my chest, nodded and guffawed, even shed a tear with all the former dipshits, I might actually come away with a reflected and clearer sense of "what kind of person I was" as my narrative neared its finish line. (I also acknowledge this may have been a disguised excuse to get out of Haddam in the summer dog days, when our realty business goes into a sleep mode.)

Fewer and fewer old classmates attend these dreary functions. This one was number fifty-six, and even fewer of our original cadre were there—just the smattering who live nearby or in New Orleans or Pensacola: people who had nothing else to do on a summer Saturday and didn't want to sit home and watch baseball on TV. Long metal folding tables with blue-and-white butcher paper (the school colors) had been set up. Plenty of folding chairs were supplied because a lot of us can't stand for long. Someone had shelled out money for lite fare—chilled shrimp, warm slaw, spud salad and watermelon. Plus a long corrugated tub of iced brewskis. There were maybe thirty of our bunch from a class of seventy. Nothing outsized was planned—just two hours of consuming the grub, maybe talk to someone (but not necessarily), down a beer or two, wander over to the Gulf Shores Casino across the highway, play the slots for an hour, then disappear.

And what I thought we'd all do was precisely what we all did: edgily surveil each other, make halting eye contact, then pull away; belly forth with a hand out, then fade again, nod, half smile, fake a laugh, try to work out who somebody was and how they'd survived the time since our 50th (which I'd attended and enjoyed because my wife Sally had come along and declared it and all my classmates to be "a hoot"). Words—very few—were found and uttered. Departures from life were noddingly conceded. Compliments and congenialities were sparingly sown about—how one "looked," what another had suffered and recovered well-enough from; where another's kids now called home, when one's wife had died (my first one only two years ago). No politics were risked, no talk of whatever war was being fought, nothing sexual or even semi-jocular ventured. The prospects of the Ole Miss and LSU and Bama squads were fleetingly, unemotionally broached. The food vanished first. Then the beer. Then so did we all—without my having learned anything about my narrative or what kind of person I was except I didn't feel I was much like any of them, which I'd suspected anyway.

All save for one exchange—a strange, unexpected, and revelatory *almost*-conversation I had with Pug Minokur, once of

Ferriday, Louisiana, hometown of the old cousin-schtupping hillbilly Jerry Lee, and a tough town on its best day. Pug—easily recognizable because he hadn't changed a jot—was standing by a big live oak all by his lonesome, beer in hand, clad in a pair of dopey tan walking shorts, an open-collar white shirt, long dingleberry-black-nylon socks and white patent leather slip-ons. To me, he seemed stranded and in need of someone to penetrate his isolation, offer up a word, save the moment since the festivities were by then drawing to an end. Pug's expression was without animation. Only, when he saw me, his eyes lit up and he smiled as if ready to share some innocuous fellow feeling before trudging off home. And I possessed the very ball we could get rolling, if briefly. Lifetimes ago, in the dimness of 1961, Pug had been the star on the Gulf Pines Fighting Seamen basketball team. A five-ten, shifty, streak-shooting hard-nosed point guard, Pug could've eventually gone over to Baton Rouge and started as a Tiger freshman, except for his penchant for breaking into suburban houses and stealing items he had no use for and which he instantly threw in the Mississippi River—before he got caught. Misfortune landed Pug not on the glittering road to LSU, but into Lonesome Pines, where a lot of the cadet corps were budding felons given a last chance by a juvenile judge who didn't want to go to the trouble of incarcerating them or sending them off to die in a combat zone. As an alienated, sports-inept townie who boarded-in, I for a brief moment fantasized my chance at school success to be (unaccountably) winning a place on the basketball team. I was nearly six feet—which was my only basketball aptitude. I was sadly slow-footed, foul-prone and clumsy, couldn't jump above my high-tops, and couldn't make the simplest layup or close-in jumper. However, I proved useful, along with a couple of other "oafs" as "dummy team" members. We were never allowed to play in actual games, only—by Shug

Borthwick, the old Seamen coach—to be stationed in vaguely basketball stances on the practice court, spots opposing players would occupy in real contests, and then do nothing but be driven around, shot over, screened and occasionally knocked flat by anybody on the varsity who decided that might be fun. Pug was our captain—a dashing, menacing figure in school blues wearing a brazen #1 on his jersey. He had never spoken to me and apparently saw no reason to. Once he had flashed past me in my frozen pick-setter's stance near the baseline and managed to elbow me savagely in the sternum—hard enough to make me fear he'd bruised my heart. This was deeply humiliating. I, of course, did my best to display no emotion, give no satisfaction away, suck it up, absorb Pug's best shot and say nothing. Though secretly I wanted to crawl away and die, never suit up again or see a basketball.

The next day, though, while my dummy team was "practicing," which meant rebounding and feeding ball after ball to the varsity heroes who were busy perfecting their two-handers and hook shots, and couldn't possibly get balls for themselves, Pug came up to me and said, "Charlie" (he thought my name was Charlie), "I think you should stick it out. You're tall enough and plenty tough enough. If you work hard on your fundamentals over the summer, you can earn a spot on the big team next year. I'll put in a word with Coach if you want me to." "I'd really like that, Pug," I said cravenly, "you're a great player." "I know," Pug said. "But we all have greatness in us, Charlie. I'm sure you do." And that was that.

Nothing—I can say it still without doubt—had ever meant as much to me as these few unwarranted, in all likelihood insincere words of semi-praise. Pug walked away—I watched—went straight over and said some possibly similar words to Coach Borthwick. Both of them turned to look at me snaring rebounds and trying not to get hit in the head. I believed Pug had done what he'd said he'd do. Next year, possibly, I could be living, thriving, excelling on a whole new plane of existence (because there was no doubt that through the summer I would work my bones to sawdust on the fundamentals, whatever they were). This new life would be glamorized not by dummy team mortifica-tions (dummy uniforms did not even have numbers) but by a whole new metric of points scored and real rebounds collected— not the way I'd been fielding them, like a fucking automaton.

That none of this ever occurred, that by the time next sea-son came around I'd become a neophyte sports scribe on the *Poop Deck*, the school newspaper, and never spoke another word to Pug Minokur (though I wrote about him as if he was Bob Cousey), never shot another basket except with my two sons on different backboards in different towns, at different stages of life—none of that mattered a tinker's tootle. I'd heard what I'd heard. An oath had been sworn. My future had been lined out for basketball glory—should I desire it. Which, as it happened, I didn't. Pug Minokur had come through when it counted. He was a giant, as tough and agile as they came, owned the heart of a warrior, but could still stoop to help another boy when that boy needed a word of fellowship and bucking up. Even if it was total bullshit.

These were sentiments I never expressed to Pug in those raddled days. I was embarrassed not to have "come out" the fol-lowing year and to have chosen noncontact play on the *Poop Deck*. Pug never seemed to notice me or recognize me again (Ole Charlie). We'd had our one shining moment and would have no more.

Until the reunion.

It was clearly Pug I spied, in spite of years: same scrunched forehead, same out-of-date flattop and undersized chin, as if that part of his face had been economized-on by his maker. A boy with Pug's features would once have been deemed "cute" by a high school girl who wanted credit for going out with a sports giant. But as a seventy-four-year-old retired Safelite assistant store manager from Bastrop, Pug looked only like a sad little redneck porch jockey who used to have a lot of friends.

But I was not going to let such an unpromising affect deter me. If my goal in coming to this half-ass reunion was to certify something preservable about myself, then memorialize it ("Bascombe wasn't so bad, or not all *that* bad, anyway"), this would be my chance to do the right thing. Justice delayed but not denied for all eternity.

I made my way across the sweltering St. Augustine to where Pug was leaned against one of the survivor oaks. His expression had already changed. He was now staring into some eternity, features undisturbed, his creased and shiny knees slightly bent below the hem of his walking shorts and above his socks, as if for balance. His eyes fixed on me as I approached, yet seemed not to include me. His can of Schlitz had not risen toward his lips, only hung at his side.

"Pug?" I said, extending a hand in his direction. "Franky Bascombe. I was your biggest fan back in '61. I saw you play for Birmingham Lutheran in '64 when you ran Huntsville Normal out of their building and poured in thirty." He'd eventually played—and starred—for some dink-ass sub-division-three school, then went in the Navy.

Pug's small, dark bullet eyes registered now and held me, as if I was someone speaking from a distance but possibly not to him. He did not shake my hand, so I withdrew it.

Pug was never a person of words. The ones he'd spoken to me when he'd said I should stick it out, hone my skills because we all contained greatness, etc.—words I was here to commemorate as a small but crucial life-changer for me and that I appreciated to this moment—these were the only words Pug ever spoke to me, though I'd devoted thousands to him in print.

"I've got something I want to thank you for, Pug," I said. Pug's real name was Rodney Jr. He looked much more like a Rodney Jr. now—in his high-waisted shorts, black socks and little strip mall haircut. I still knew something about white southerners; that Pug's uncommunicative, wall-you-out stare was his "Pug look." It was how Pug *was*; it was the face he greeted the world with since the cheering had stopped and all that was left was replacing cracked windshields and going home to supper for all the years down the line. Were he to speak, he might put in peril the smidgen that was left of the old Pug. Which was not what I wanted. "I'm probably overstepping my boundaries here, Pug," I quickly said, with a shoe-salesman's grin—ready to retreat. It was brutally hot. I was sweating rivers through my madras shirt, though Pug was seemingly not hot at all. Something kept him cool. The Gulf out across Highway 90 was baked and gray and densified like mud. Far out, tiny swimmers' heads were bobbing. A confederate flag hung lank against a dismal pole where the old, traitorous president's former estate had stood.

"You have to understand," Pug said calmly, as if he and I'd been gabbing like magpies about tempered-tinted window treatments so you don't roast on your vacation drive down to Weeki Wachee.

"What is it, Pug?" He was looking straight at me, face soft and pliant and full of some emotion he'd abandoned his usual noncommunicator's self to try to express. And of course, I saw then. Realized. Understood. Fool, fool, fool. Me.

"I'm really happy," Pug said and smiled, revealing his little, ranked, square discolored teeth. His dark eyes shone. I'd said nothing of significance and would not now. "It's been a wonderful, wonderful life, Franky" (not Charlie), Pug said. "And all of you shouldn't have gone to this trouble. I have . . ." He stopped and looked hard at me as if I'd interrupted him. His eyes blinked; his little mouth formed a semblance of a smile. He nodded. "I get it," Pug said, like the woman who looked like my mother would say to me six weeks later. "I get it." Pug looked amazed. "That little bitty clock doesn't work unless you plug it in, does it?" he said. "So . . ." Which was the totality of what Pug and I would be allotted that day. Or ever. I'd thanked him—for a life of memories. I took his amazingly soft, amazingly small and once skillful hand—his shooting hand—and gave it a gentle pumping for old times' sake. A teenage boy—his grandson, a young Pugster—was right then coming up to us, speaking soft words, which Pug didn't reply to. He nodded at me. Then the two of them walked away together toward where the cars were all parked in the griddling sun.

About which there's little more to say. How does an idea, long dormant, revive and parade its bright banner into life as a fully renewed goal? To be happy—before the gray curtain comes down. Or at least to consider why you're not, if you're not. And whether it's worth the bother to worry about. Which I contend it is. It *is* worth worrying about—though I'm certain of little else. But to go out the door, as my mother knew and as even Pug Minokur "knew" (if he knew anything), and not bother with being happy is to give life less than its full due. Which, after all, is what we're here for. To give life its full due, no matter what kind of person we are. Or am I wrong?

PART I

ONE

Rochester, Minnesota. Blear season of the Lupercal. Saints, bloody martyrs and sacrifice. Promise of fertile Spring in the frozen heart of winter. Valentine's Day, three days hence.

I'm driving with my son Paul Bascombe to the Comanche Mall for the Tuesday noon matinée at the Northern Lights Octoplex. The defroster is huffing, wipers whapping. It's snowing like Anchorage. Paul stares out, saying little. His right hand, I believe, may be trembling and also his knees inside his sweatpants. We have not taken in a matinée together since he was a sweet but disorderly twelve-year-old. As said, he is now forty-seven and not well.

Today's movie excursion, however, signals for me a positivist, nostalgic reprise of my own long-ago Saturdays in the chilled, funked dark of the old Bay View Biloxi, bingeing candy through four features, four shorts, six cartoons and a talent show. Then staggering, cotton-eyed, out into the queasy-hot coastal late day, feeling life could never again be this good. Possibly I was right.

Schedulers at Naldo Exhibitors (home offices, Mendota)— eight screens rarely showing films anyone would pay to see— are today offering up a feast of "Cupid's Week Specials" to lure shut-ins and old nostalgics out into the bruising cold and into otherwise vacant seats. My son is more or less a shut-in. I, the old nostalgic. Though I don't believe nostalgia to be my core worldview.

Screen eight is of minimal interest to me but appeals to my son, who claims to "love" *The St. Valentine's Day Massacre*, the Roger Corman splatter-rama from '67, which he considers "a riot and a classic." He also wants to stay for *Picnic at Hanging Rock* on screen six—the title he finds "interesting," though neither of us knows anything about it except that it's Australian and may have a Valentine's tie-in. Because of our daily need to consume time, he is willing to impose it on me. In this way he is not so different from when he was twelve.

Outside, at the intersection of South Broadway and State Highway 14, it is five below and sky-less, a big Alberta Clipper slinging ice needles and buckshot snow, causing my Civic to quake under its blusters. Minnesotans take this all in stride. "It's a dry cold," "we dress for it," "we were born driving on ice," "it can always get worse." As a decades-long Jerseyite, only here now to escort my son through his experimental ALS protocol at Mayo, I'm most at home in the meliorative, mid-seaboard succession— one season barely distinguishable from the next. In New Jersey no one talks about the weather—floating along within it like goldfish. Minnesota though, you have to give credit to. It takes freezing people's asses as serious business.

Today is commencing a high-stress/high-priority week for my son—and me. We have been in Rochester at the Clinic for two months, since before Christmas, while he's been enrolled in an experimental drug study—a Phase 1 "regenerative trial" in the Department of Neurology—which I don't understand very well but which his doctors colorfully refer to as "Medical Pioneers at the Borders of Science." His particular drug sports a bombastic name that sounds like "Cyclotron," which, once inside his body, allows his doctors to isolate and study crucial things (proteins) and eliminate crucial others having to do with why *his* disease progresses when other people's don't. Not much is known about what disposes a person to ALS, only what happens when you get it, so that if the study finds *nothing*, that will be *something*. His "treatment" is guaranteed not to save him or even make him better since his diagnosis has come too late (a good reason not to get involved). His entry evaluation indexed him as "high-qualified" for being studied, and even before we were out of the office, he'd announced he was *in*. "It's my legacy," he said, back in my car, though he believes, as I do, that legacies are a crock of shit. His ALS variant is brain-related, not spine-related, and therefore is quicker about its dirty business. His degree of neuro-degeneration was already far along at diagnosis, though he could live for years. Most patients have symptoms for longer than they know. Paul, in fact, until his workup, thought (and hoped) he had Lyme disease.

In the Clinic with his "team"—doctors, nurses, therapists, masseuses, counselors, facilitators, minders, all provided by his Mayo study—Paul has jettisoned his life-long exterior of screwy-inscrutable inwardness. In the books I've read, this conversion to extrovert has its own clinical moniker—"idiopathic self-objectification." Suffering a fierce and always fatal disease has, these books argue, offered him a special self, and "freed" him—I'm not sure *from* or *for* what: possibly not to worry about the rest of his life. To me, and for the good, he seems not so much possessed *by* his "situation" as in possession *of it*, become its living exponent and barker. With his care team, he's as jovial as a game-show host, regaling them with his unique views on everything. (We all have to have a team now.) They refer to him as "Handsome" or "Professor Bascombe" or "Lover Boy," while

Paul refers to ALS as "Al's" (as in Al's bar), and death as "acing the final," "buying the farm," "purchasing the real estate" or just his "magic number" (as in "my magic number is six months at best"). He's also of late become regrettably preoccupied by the life and music of the pint-size cockney songster Anthony Newley, who's been dead for thirty years. When we're alone, he can and will peel off unnerving karaoke renditions of "There's No Such Thing as Love," "The Candy Man," and "Who Can I Turn To?"—". . . with yew on a nyew dah-aye"—which I put up with but often have to make him stop. "It stabilizes me," he says, "to channel a persona who's (or was) not dying." His doctors insist it's good for him. Music Assisted Relaxation. It just sometimes drives me crazy.

Paul doesn't, in fact, think of himself as a patient, a sufferer or a living statistic, but as an amateur "scientist" objectifying a defective body that happens to be his—all for the benefit of unnamed others. Like a car that's broken but can still be driven. More than once he's observed to me he was "surprised" it was taking him this long to die. Though statistically it's not.

I have so far not observed him to exhibit much fear of death's approach. He seems more intrigued than concerned. (I, in fact, envy the peerlessness of his experience without envying the experience, itself.) Occasionally he expresses misgivings about suffering—what I most fear for him. Though sometimes I think that my son enduring an extravagantly fatal disease has not so much to do with death (unusual man that he is) but with seizing an opportunity to perform a difficult trick extremely well—a magic trick—that can only be performed once. Someone who did *not* know him might say he was coming to grips with life by preparing for a good death, as the Buddhists say: the white and red essences meeting at the heart. But I can say with certainty that he is all about a *good life* and not one jot about a good death (whatever that could be). In my solitary-silent moments, I do not cherish the thought that my son's fatal disease may be one of his life's high points, and sometimes ask myself: Have his forty-seven breathing years added up to enough of life? I know the standard answer. Though my heart's answer is (strange, for a man who never hopes), I hope so. It is merely unfortunate that his good life will not now be a very long one.

———◆———

THIS VALENTINE'S WEEK IS OF SUCH HIGH EMOTIONAL PORTENT because tomorrow at ten I am driving Paul to the Clinic for the last of his scheduled visits—the "Medical Pioneers Borders of Science Appreciation Meet & Greet," where the Pioneers in the drug study (there were originally eight Pioneers, but one was lost) will be neurologically welcomed, thanked, celebrated, flattered, given a gift, then sent away for "long-term follow-up" by the doctors. It is an unwieldy "graduation," since he's dying. (No one's supposed to say he's dying, though he of course does, and so do I, in order that living have a chance to compete in real time with its enemy on a level playing field.) Paul is dogged in his enthusiasm for the Pioneers. Though in a father's way, I worry that in him flickers an ineradicable hope that *something* in his two-month study will be miraculously unearthed such that *something, something, something* can be done to *something something else* and the worst *something* be avoided—which it won't. I fear this forecastable failure—the fate of us all—will set loose in him a great, honking, spirituo-psychic crash-in which will sink him. And me as well. Doctors are skilled at dispensing unhappy news, and have perfected "delivery strategies" taught at Hopkins and Yale, allowing them to avert their gaze when the world goes ass-up for the patient. But as his caregiver, I must defend him against such plummets. Though I happen to believe there's plenty to be said for a robust state of denial about many things— death being high on the list.

I have thus devised as a coping strategy, for Paul and me to embark after tomorrow's "coming-out" upon a semi-epic, driving trip westward. Latter-day Lewises and latter-day Clarks, spiriting out across wintry Minnesota, and beyond to prairied South Dakota, all the way to Mount Rushmore (where I myself visited, with my parents, in 1954), an improbable destination, improbably embarked on in the heart of winter, but possibly one Paul will find "hilarious" and capable of dousing his dreads and dismays that nothing can be done for him. It is the best I can do—the art of the saved moment being the only art I'm even halfway accomplished at, and even though I don't know what we do afterward. Come back to here? Drive to New Jersey? Fly to the Seychelles? He is so far skeptical about such a trip, and about me, and about most everything since these are likely his last choosings. Yet I would save my son from any harm I could, even if I can't finally outwit the worst.

———◆———

TRAFFIC NEARING OUR TURN INTO THE COMANCHE MALL IS bump 'n' stop, bump 'n' go. We are stalled on Rochester's crowded "miracle mile," though no one's honking. Minnesotans are self-conscious about their horns, whereas we Jerseyites consider horns to be musical instruments. Yellow-flashing salt trucks are clogging things up ahead, plus the cops have someone pulled over, not giving a rat's ass about blocking the box, their blue-blinking cruisers leaving us all stacked in front of Babies R Us. Paul and I are behind a pickup, which seems to be full of broken hockey sticks. Being newcomers to town, I've allowed for extra time.

Paul has so far not passed the morning well—struggling with his shirt buttons and teeth-brushing, teetering like a vaude-villian on a tightrope when he wobbled to the car, and taking too long in the bathroom. (I had to knock twice, which made him growl through the door, "I'm taking a dump, it's not that easy.") We were up early so he could attend his Clinic exit interview with Dr. Oakes, his neurologist (grinning, freckle-faced, redheaded semi beauty from Menominee, schooled at Stanford). Paul's final infusion was yesterday, and every Tuesday—today—he's invited in to "review his experiences": How things feel in his body, how he's tolerating the Riluzole he takes to slow his disease onset (it blurs his vision, makes his heart beat fast, and he pisses more—but doesn't get better), and how he's seeing life-in-general (better than I am). On his Clinic days he routinely strives to project a robust well-being, likes to "doll up" as if he and Dr. Oakes are having a date. This morning at home, though, his voice was "thinner" and higher-pitched, symptomology Dr. O will have noticed, noted and remarked on, though Paul hasn't mentioned anything to me. At his stage of disease progress—middle stage—his voice box muscles are fading because nerves in his brain are dying. One day he will simply stop talking. And at some point, *all* muscles will cease translating messages from his brain—even though his brain will valiantly continue sending them. After which he will—to all but the philosophically inclined—cease to "be." This is a subject we haven't been successful in broaching, but will need to try soon.

After ten minutes of gridlock, we are turned into the Co-manche Mall parking lot, which is vaster than most towns' corporate limits, and where it's snowing beebees. Plows are banging—cars and pedestrians skittering away from the flash-ing, pinging, scraping panzers spewing snow, dozing shopping carts, lost merchandise, compact cars, pets and children out to the snow Matterhorn behind Sears, where it'll stay frozen 'til summer. Snowplows rule this latitude, the bearded-burly meth-enflamed drivers granting lenience to no one.

The Northern Lights Octoplex, where we're headed, is on the mall backside beyond a towering Scheels hunting-&-fishing pagoda and a defunct Penneys. Paul has his metal tripod cane—more practical for the snow than his walker, though his walker is better at keeping him from stumbling and breaking his face, which he almost did this morning. Cold for some reason doesn't bother him the way it bothers me, though he is approaching the frontier between when he *can* walk and when he won't walk again. For many ALS-sufferers this can signal the dark passage from an already-assaulted estimation of themselves to something worse. I'm not sure how he will tolerate this. He is hard to calculate.

In the car, he has Anthony Newley going on his iPhone, which he "wears" in a goofy sequined plastic belt holster—Bluetooth earbuds in. He is staring silently at the mall tundra as if from an airplane. Something in his conversation with Dr. Oakes this morning has left him abstracted. Doctors of terminal patients must be doughty truth-tellers, respecting a sacred bond of candor with those they assist out of life. Except, of course, they can't win. Any untenanted word, an "and" instead of a "but," the wrong placement of a "very" or a "possibly" or an "in my view," and the well-adjusted sarcoma sufferer or kidney transplanter goes flailing off into unreachable despond. All progress abandoned. I will try to ask him about this if a moment presents, though typically he admits nothing.

On our drive to the mall, his only moments of animation have been when we passed his two favorite commercial establishments—Little Pharma Drug and Free Will Dry Cleaners. Both caused him to look appraisingly at me as we went by, as if we savored a secret but must not speak of it. For all of life, our father-son discourse has been encoded and elliptical—sustained, on-topic converse being simply not our way. Sometimes to the point of silence. It cannot be that unusual.

Free Will cleaners had red hearts swagged across its window and the stenciled words "Lint Free or Dye," which pleased him.

"Do you happen to know," he asked, without taking his ear appliances out, "the most common men's trouser size."

"I don't," I said, minding the traffic and snow.

"Thirty-four regular." He took in an unexpressive breath and let it out. I could hear a Tony Newley song buzzing in his ears. He said nothing else.

When Paul was in St. Jehoshaphat's in Connecticut (his name for the second-rate prep school his mother and I put him in) and well on his way to a life of unusualness, she and I had him in and out of numberless therapists' offices, testing institutes and holistic Maine summer camps, assessing whether he was locked in some syndrome or spectrum or "osis" and could be helped by whatever ministering-to might've been available in the long-ago '80s. He didn't "blend." He was cheerful and polite but didn't make (many) friends. His career goal was to be a ventriloquist. He didn't care about sports. He was left-handed. He stuttered. He exhibited vague rotating symptoms of Tourette's, OCD, possibly attention deficit. Nothing was deemed clinically "wrong." His IQ was a respectable 112 (better than mine and his mother's, but well below his sister's). He wasn't harming himself or others, didn't masturbate excessively, wasn't fascinated by fire, wasn't failing school. His behavior—often standing smiling Cheshire-like at things that weren't funny to anybody else—was, in Dr. Wolfgang Stopler's view, "not really *that* weird," given divorce, his brother's death, puberty's onslaught. His mother and I didn't agree with this diagnosis, but took solace that we'd made an effort, and that there was not much else we could do—since we liked him and didn't want to do much more anyway. Let him live his life. We didn't know someday he'd have ALS.

The other thing Paul said this morning as we were encountering mall traffic, snow peppering the windshield like gravel, was, "How do you feel about missing Vietnam?"

I had to turn to look at him. "Do what?"

"How do you feel about missing Vietnam?" His nose was running. He wiped it with his sleeve and fingered the silver stud he's had implanted in his left earlobe since he's been at Mayo.

"Why the hell are you asking me that?"

"I just wondered." Tick-tocking his head back and forth to Anthony Newley in both ears.

Paul was wearing his "sick suit." Gray sweats, generous around the ass so as not to further impede his already impeded mobility. He'd changed clothes after his exit interview (when he'd worn a button-down Brooks Oxford, a cranberry V-neck, chinos and Chinese Weejuns—all to impress Dr. Oakes. This was my exact uniform in the Sigma Chi house in Ann Arbor, circa 1964, and pretty much my current caregiver's mufti). Paul has added poundage since being diagnosed and now has a soft, *rounded* affect. He's always worn glasses and has been losing hair for a decade, which makes him resemble the old porn-pone Larry Flynt—not a good look. He has short, warty fingers and, since determined to be ill, has developed a refrigerator-interior skin tone, and sometimes exudes a tangy metal smell, possibly from his medication. He's always curled his tongue up inside his mouth, extending the gray-pink underpart past his lips—which I identify as exertion. In the car beside me, in his Kansas City Chiefs red, hooded, long-boy Super-Bowl parka over his sweats, his special Swiss shoes designed for Al's patients, and knitted mittens his mother made for him when he was a teen, he looked like a papoose.

"Is that what's going on in your brain? You're thinking about Vietnam?"

"Yeah."

"I'm *happy* I missed Vietnam." Wipers were noisily swatting snow. "You wouldn't be here if I hadn't. You could be a little Vietnamese boy."

I knew he loved this idea but didn't answer.

"Has it been like a barrier?" Paul thinks (sometimes obsessively) in terms of barriers; reluctances in ourselves that prevent us from doing all the dynamic things we want to do: Play the harmonica. Juggle. Do a backflip off the high board. None of which he could ever do. All achievement, to him, requires crossing thresholds that are painful. For instance, he is in fact a fair-to-poor ventriloquist, owns a professional-grade dummy with orange hair, a loud, checked hacking jacket, and stupid googly blue eyes. "Otto"—who he's brought along with us to Minnesota. *Learning* ventriloquism, which he did in high school, required powerful internal barriers be exceeded. It took him years, though he still moves his lips to make Otto talk—which he's aware of. His sister thinks Otto's creepy and won't tolerate the sight of him. Which makes Paul delirious.

"It hasn't been a barrier for me at all," I answered about Vietnam. The blue police flasher was flicking through the snow swarming the windshield. Some poor Somali was surrendering his license through his window as we inched past. "I didn't *choose* not to go to Vietnam," I said. "I got sick and was discharged. The Marines didn't want me. I felt sorry at the time but not for long. The war was terrible. You were born the year it ended."

"I just wondered if it created a syndrome like mine."

"Like yours? What's yours? You don't have a syndrome. You've got something else."

"Right." His heavy pink tongue became visible, denoting new exertion.

"Do you mean like *survivor's* guilt?" I said.

"I don't know. No. Survivor's guilt's bullshit." He asked me a week ago what was the modern equivalent of "the invisible man"—another of his movie favorites. Claude Rains, Gloria Stuart, et al. I didn't know. "An AI's survivor," he said. "Someone who doesn't exist." His mouth had wrinkled, then he looked away.

"Look," I said irritably as we passed the police cruiser, "missing getting blown up in Vietnam hasn't prevented *anything*. Okay? I've done everything I've wanted to do. Including being here now. Right?" He didn't like it when I got annoyed with him.

"Yeah."

"And if I live longer than you do—which I might not—I won't feel guilty about that either." This he liked, since outliving him is almost a certainty.

"So. Are you like glad I'm here?" Inside his Chiefs parka, he fattened his cheeks since he knew my answer required artfulness. It was his way of "self-locating," which the doctors say he should do.

"Yes and also no," I said. "I'm not glad you're *right* here. In Rochester. I wish we were on a beach in the Maldives. But otherwise, yes. I'm glad you're here. I'm glad I'm here. I'm glad you're alive. I mostly always have been."

"Okay." He stared ahead, tongue still slightly extruded. Yes and no answers are his favorites.

"This, by the way," I said, still irritated, "is completely idiotic, okay? I love you." It's never a bad idea to include these words in case he might think being sick is a barrier to love. I wasn't sure he heard me with his Bluetooth in.

"That's good," he said. "You can't let that genie out of the bottle though, Lawrence." He is on guard against all sentimentalities, being patronized, any melodrama or matters of the heart—which he hates and can be cruel about. Since we've been at Mayo he has begun calling me Lawrence, for Lawrence Nightingale.

"It's a cunning stunt," I say to end this.

"Yeah. You said it," he said, and looked back out into the snowy, congested traffic.

⸺

BY THE TIME WE'RE INTO A DISABLED SLOT AND CAN STRUGGLE through sputtering snow to the mall's west entrance—Paul, employing his cane with difficulty—all chances of seeing a movie are ended. A protest is underway at the inside entrance to the Octoplex. A line of noisy exhorters—mostly women in down parkas, a couple of RC priests, a chubby man in a pink cupid body suit with little wings, a few seniors in leisure attire and one or two school-age girls—has linked arms in a human chain across the theatre's doors and ticket window, barring all entry. Including ours. We have virtual tickets bought online, but the protestors are barricading everything, jigging placards up and down, waving and shouting. VALENTINES MEANS SPOUSAL ABUSE TO ME, VALENTINES DEMEANS WOMEN AND LOVE, MY HEART IS ALREADY BROKEN, VALENTINE SURVIVOR, CUPID SUCKS. A frowning white-haired woman in a bright orange snow parka and wielding a bullhorn is getting a chant going. VILE, MYSOGYNIST CRAP, one sign declares, referring, I suppose to *The Valentine's Day Massacre*, which isn't all that wrong, though I don't recall any women being machine-gunned, only Mick hooligans who'd be gunned down anyway.

Paul and I are stopped at the periphery of bundled-up spectators, who seem amused but not involved. "I guess you can protest two goats fucking if you want to," someone observes.

"What's this happy horseshit?" Paul growls, glasses fogged by the interior mall weather. In his long-boy coat and red balaclava and weaving on his tripod, he looks like a grizzled street person—which has been his look since he's been sick. "Everybody's a fuckin' survivor," he says.

"Let me see about this."

"Yeah. I've got your back, Lawrence." Almost losing his balance on his cane.

A weedy-looking young man in a white shirt and string tie stands behind the blocked, glass cinema doors, talking through a gap to a uniformed security guard. Protesters are picking up the chant, goofing and smiling at one another, arms joined as if they were with Dr. King and Harry Belafonte on the Pettus Bridge, instead of being annoying morons in a shopping mall. Minnesotans aren't supposed to demonstrate. "Undemonstrative" is the state motto.

"We've got tickets to the one-ten *Massacre*," I shout into the gap, to be heard. This kid's white shirt has a red *N* Naldo crest, meant to look like the "Harvard Club." I'm thinking he is the manager.

"They have a permit for an hour," the kid shouts and nods with a giddy grin, as if all this was entertainment to him. The high school kids behind the candy concession and the popcorn bin are pointing at the fat little cupid kicking up his legs like a Rockette.

"When's their hour up?" I look around to Paul, wavering on his cane, legs trembling, balaclava off, hair askew. He is fit to be tied, sweltering in his parka, lips curling, calling the protesters, I'm sure, "spazzes" and "morons" and "butt-licks."

"Go get some coffee at Starbucks," the manager says through the door gap. "It'll be over in a half hour." He's enjoying this and doesn't give two shits about the movie or us.

I scan down the Comanche Mall concourse, receding into smeary yellow light above moving shoppers. No Starbucks is in sight. Navigating a suburban shopping mall with a disabled son is nothing I've done before or care to do.

"Will you hold the movie?" I shout through the glass. Noise is raucous behind me. I wonder if the glass is bulletproof.

"Whatever," the kid says, like he's talking underwater. "Take a walk." By which he means "Take a hike." We are all but defeated.

WE WALK—OR TRY TO. COMANCHE MALL AT ONE P.M. IS ONLY half full, though it would feel the same if it was empty. Shopping malls all emit the same climate of endgame up and down their semi-cavernous expanses. (They were never meant to be places where people felt they belonged.) The mealy light emanates from nowhere. Air is a warm-cool temperature found only here, and riding it is a cotton candy aroma, like at a state fair. "When You Wish Upon a Star" sung by a cricket is being piped in on top of everything.

We turn a corner at Urban Outfitters, and in that instant the protesters become inaudible. There's still no Starbucks. Though there *is* GNP. A Foot Locker. A Caribou Coffee. A Nordic Shop. A sunglasses kiosk. Minnesota-style pizza. Tattoos and piercings. Exotic Pets. Thousand Lakes Dialysis. Decorative Concrete. Twin Cities Optometrists. The Gap. And a Marine Corps recruiting storefront with two blue-trousered leathernecks drowsily staring out at the mall traffic from behind clean desks.

The Marines have taped a Valentine's message to their window: "Give Her What She's Never Had . . . Semper Fi!"

Paul, having called the demonstrators pussies and douche-bags, doesn't seem to mind being here, and is gawking at everything with interest. In this way he is the best-adjusted desperately sick person imaginable. Having Al's means that things not working out or fitting together right is no big deal to him.

Years ago, for a desperate moment I taught English at overly precious Berkshire College, in Massachusetts, while simultaneously trying to manage (1) my son Ralph Bascombe dying of Reye's at age nine and (2) my wife divorcing me because I couldn't manage number one right. I used to challenge my classes of smirking little Aristotles with brain twisters. (I knew nothing to *teach* them except how to be me.) "What does 'mean' mean?" I would ask them, my mouth tightly pinched. "What do you people think you're saying when you say you *understand* something?" "What are you *really* doing when you *make sense* of anything?" I'd overheard them burbling these very expressions as I strolled alongside them across the campus diag every day: "What's the *meaning* of the white whale?" "I don't *understand* my roommate. She's from Utah." "I can't *make sense* of one word goofy old Professor so-and-so says . . ." To me, their teacher, knowing what the words you used actually signified didn't seem to ask too much. All these words were, in fact, pertinent to *my* life at that time. How did I *understand* that my firstborn son has died? Did it *make sense* that a person I love would cast me away? Such words, I felt, should be cornerstones of any first-rate education.

My students, of course, had zero interest and simply sat stonily at their desks staring at me. They wanted class over so they could get back out onto the college lawn and resume their conversations about screwing and sports.

What I wanted them to know, though, was that *understanding, making sense,* knowing the *meaning* of anything had to do with fitting together loose pieces of life that don't fit together, then making a new whole out of the newly unified shards. The white whale meant what you could marshal evidence and make it mean. This was what all scientific discoveries, all philosophy, all great novels do—I believed. Making sense is everlastingly a process of jiggering and re-jiggering and re-re-rejiggering. It's by nature provisional, and pretty soon you trade it in on something better. It's all "on the way," old Heidegger would say. Though it turned out, I wasn't around long enough to tell them that last important part.

For Paul, the skills of fitting together the unfittable—of understanding, meaning, and making sense—are lessons he's learned like a catechist since being diagnosed. Whereas for me, his being faced with onrushing death makes *no* sense, is starkly meaningless and not one iota understandable. I often find myself awake at night, feeling that *I* might be dying in synchronicity with him. (This apparently happens.) Though I trust it is not the case, since when I ask myself at that hour *what am I doing* (a good question to pose in all situations) my answer is: I'm here seeking to make living steal a march on dying, remaining alive so that at the moment my son leaves life behind, he will not feel alone. That is as much sense as I can make.

Here in the mall's human flow, Paul is now having a harder time with basic ambulation and has begun making gruff grunting sounds, his tongue pooched out with strain. He has not been walking so well this week, and I take his parka to carry—underneath which he's wearing his blue "Cornhole IS America" sweatshirt, revealing his new belly expanse. The two of us fit well in a mall. Though as in many public places now—and for perfectly supportable reasons—I feel someone from somewhere may be about to shoot at me.

"Do you ever feel like life's passing insanely quickly?" Paul asks. We've stopped, allowing foot traffic to eddy around us. He has his sly eyes going. "Insanely" is one of his words. "He's insanely jealous." "I'm insanely hungry." "It's insanely hot in Africa." Though no answer really answers—like was I sorry I missed Vietnam.

"No," I say. "Is it passing fast for *you*?"

"I have outrage fatigue," he says, deadpan. I hear him breathe in deeply.

"Did Dr. Oakes say something you didn't like hearing this morning?" Mall patrons' eyes are finding us then darting away. In Minnesota apparently one doesn't often see two adults speaking to each other in public.

"Like what?" he says.

"I don't know. I wasn't there."

"Like medical errors are the third largest cause of death after cancer and heart disease? Or that she won't marry me because she's already married? We didn't get that far." He raises his globey, thin-thatched head and smiles evilly. He is barely five-nine, and I am holding him up. His spectacles catch a sequin of tarnished mall light. He is Larry Flynt—a studious Larry Flynt in glasses. "Do you think Dr. Oakes dreams about me? I'm such a fucking hunk."

"I'm sure she does."

"Do you think she feels sorry for me?" His tongue is again showing, as if to help him stay balanced.

"I don't know. No."

He looks away, wanting me to disappear but I can't. "Do you think there are there any Comanches in here?" His voice is thinner and has "climbed" to a slightly higher register. Around us many passersby resemble him—people in wheelchairs, humping oxygen tanks, staggering behind walkers, talking through throat disks, bopping along on crutches, wearing surgical masks. The mall is like a hospital where sick is normal. He, however, I fear is in danger of swan-diving forward in the middle of everything.

I say, "Maybe we should sit down a moment."

"Yeah. Okay," he says hauntingly.

The Starbucks has come into sight but too far away. We need to sit *now*. Without much trouble I maneuver us out of the flow and into two empty seats in "Montparnasse in Minnesota," a mall-side "outdoor" bistro with wire-backed chairs, white tile floors, cheerful waitstaffers in white aprons, speaking in made-up French accents. Paul plops down in a heap, gripping his cane like an oldster.

A twitchy young waitress with bobbed hair, puce lips and a pierced cheek appears instantly. She asks tartly if we'd like to "or-dere zum-zing." She is from the Marais of Owatonna. I say we're only resting and smile hopefully. She frisks a little sashay I'd love to see in some other setting, and moués her astonishing lips. "Bien sûr, messieurs. When-eh-vare. Aht yur sur-vees." Off she goes to the paying customers.

Paul is exhausted, but again starts gawking around as if something's agitating him. It is on his "context therapist's" schedule that we two "share" difficult conversations—what we're going to miss in life once we die; how we'll look when we're dead; what we think we might find on "the other side." We could possibly attempt this now. Though in one of the Al's pamphlets Mayo provides (I've read many), loved ones are cautioned not to be "too take-charge" in an effort to be *genuine*. Paul, for his part, resists anyone but his doctors asking him "how he is." I can stand not to know until he feels like telling me.

I detect, though, what's agitating him. Across the half-crowded concourse are two bona fide, blondie Minnesota babes—a buxom Gudrun and a pouty Astrid, both involved with filling pink balloons in the shape of valentine hearts, outside The Word Is Your Oyster Christian bookshop. They're employing an air cylinder and having the time of their lives making it go "sheeee-uuuuuh" as each balloon fattens. One of the Marine recruiters has been eyeing them and has abandoned his post to come over and insert something Marine-ish and naughtily suggestive into their inflating work. The girls are loving it but pretending they're not.

This is what's deviling my son. Proximity to beautiful women always works deranging effects on him. From his prep-school days, the presence of female splendor made him stammer, then fall morbidly silent, then start blabbing whatever was rocketing kaleidoscopic inside his brain—his foreign coin collection, the history of the Enfield rifle, geometrical enigmas in Cheops at Giza—until his classmates just drifted away confused. *More* trips to shrinks. More whopper checks issued. More diagnoses of normality, although with concessions that our son might not follow a conventional life course.

The recruiter, who's a steel-rod-thin, square-headed, hollow-cheeked, arrow-spine type with a chest paved with ribbons and a sleeve full of chevrons, is a sergeant major—rarest of rare breeds, bravest of brave, toughest of tough—an apparent participant in every campaign since Antietam. He is older than he looks, but the balloon girls are amazed by him (though wary—for good reason). The sarge major is doing what Marines are trained to do: project outer invincibility concealing a (false) empathetic soul, who'll give you the rogering of your life then not stay around for the emotional tallying up. A certain kind of midwestern girl can't say no to this.

It's too much, though, for Paul, who's shifting back and forth in his wire chair and making discomforted sounds. His fingers are fidgeting. He darts a hawkish look to me, then back across at the threesome who couldn't be less aware of him if he was made of air. "I'm worried about the movie. I don't want to miss the credits because of a bunch of ass-wipes," he says. His mouth forms a tongue lump under his lower lip. His eyes behind his glasses fix on me accusingly. I am expected to remedy something I can't remedy.

"The manager said he'd hold it for us," I say. "Do you want to talk about our trip tomorrow?" My optimist's cobbled-up winter expedition to Mount Rushmore, meant to head off a giant willies attack following tomorrow's Medical Pioneers reception.

"Yeah-no." Paul looks away quickly. He's observed that Minnesotans say "yeah-no" to everything, which proves they're limp-dicks. The pink wingèd cupid from the protest line comes mincing past in the crowd, waving a spangly wand and carrying a placard that has a red valentine heart with a black thumbs-down inside it. The sarge major motions the two balloon honeys to have a look. They smile and shake their heads. Possibly the protest is breaking up, and we'll still have a chance to enjoy our massacre. "Do you think about Ann a lot?" Ann—his mother, who died two years ago in a "care community" in Haddam, where he visited her, and I did, too. She and I had been divorced 37 years, but Paul always wished we weren't and felt many things in his life would've been better if we hadn't. Which would've been true for all of us. It is a subject he brings up often. Valentine's week is the anniversary of her death.

"Sure. I think about your mother all the time." I do not refer to her as my "wife" or my "ex-wife" and never as Ann. "I think about *every* important thing I ever did and every important person I ever knew pretty much every day. Don't you do that?"

He does not enjoy having questions returned as questions. "What do you think about her?" Behind his lenses his slate eyes wander away from me, but are intent. His mouth is loose and damp—his tongue finally relaxed. "Do you wish you and she'd gotten married again?" His voice is thin and tired-sounding.

"No," I say. "Yeah-no" would be more accurate. When Ann was living a comfortable, Parkinsonian retiree's life in her "community," out the Haddam Great Road, we made one half-hearted stab at love's renewal, as a credit for time served. I'd had a mini-stroke, a global amnesia episode and a small and newly observed hole detected in my heart (which she said was no surprise to her). We were a perfect impaired pair, she said. We embarked on a poorly advised trip to visit my parents' graves in Illinois and Iowa. She never met them and felt, therefore, I didn't honor them sufficiently. It was shortly after she found out she had myeloma and wouldn't be around long. We went so far as to make a try at late-life lovemaking in a Best Western in Davenport *on* a davenport, the doing of which turned out to be like scientists in laboratory gloves moving radioactive test tubes around inside hermetically sealed glass boxes. We joked about it later, but not in Davenport.

End of story. Ann expired before we had a chance to do more than agree that if we got remarried, Paul and his sister would be outraged for the life we'd deprived them of by staying divorced. These were our substitute words for "I love you."

At the sad end of Ann's life—and this *is* the end of the love story—I was the only stand-by she could stand to be around for more than five minutes, which might've been how our long-marriage-that-never-happened would've turned out. You can't generally fix things at the end. Though Paul routinely takes everything between his mother and me to heart.

"Listen, son," I say and put my elbows on the marble tabletop like a cop. "I guess I cared more for your mother than I loved her. And she cared less for me than she did when we were young. Okay?" I need to re-chart our course here, since it's heading us toward an argument I don't have the heart for in a mall at 1:30 in the afternoon, and would ruin our movie if we get to see it.

"That's not true!" He is suddenly enlivened, tapping the soft, fleshy side of his left hand on the table. In his "Cornhole IS America" sweatshirt he looks preposterous. "When I visited her out there in that shithole where she lived," (The Adult Community at Carnage Hill) "she said, 'I love your father. I don't know why he doesn't do the right thing and marry me before I die or *he* does.'" Paul's mouth wrinkles and goes perplexed—a way I've often seen him look. It is his default look, or *was* before he got sick. Though he is not angry. At the end of the day (an expression I hate), what's to be angry about?

"She never said that to me," I say softly.

"She wanted you to say it to *her*. Didn't you want to?"

"Maybe a little," I say. "I just never did."

"Okay," he says. "Well . . ." He's ceased tapping, is willing to let our conversation lapse as arbitrarily as it began. Possibly something difficult has been resolved. Though we have not talked about our trip. Which I wish we had.

Sergeant Major (I'm calling him) "Gunnerson," I notice, is now making his way through the flow of shoppers toward us. He is a soldered piece of human fighting machinery—blue trousers, red stripes, mitered haircut, oak-jawed. He is staring straight at me—enough that I brace up in my chair, ready to receive a blow I apparently have coming. Only he carries right past into the interior of Montparnasse in Minnesota—on a mission to requisition coffee for his brother Marine back at the storefront. Everything's a beach assault, even at the mall.

Paul has said nothing more than "Well . . ." Words about his lost mother have moved him more than they've moved me. I am guilty, as ever, of withholding. This time from the deceased.

"We'd better see about our movie," I say and smile at him.

He looks away into the van of Tuesday pre-Valentine's shoppers, searching for the two balloon babes, who are no longer to be seen. One more minor heartbreak, late in life.

———

THE NORTHERN LIGHTS OCTOPLEX, WHEN WE ARRIVE BACK TO where paying customers go in, is shadowy inside and looks closed, all protesters vanished. Not even their crap is left on the concourse floor. Lights are dimmed at the candy and popcorn concessions. A statue of P. Bunyan lurks in the gloom, bearded, plaid-shirted, smiling maniacally toward the front doors. The ticket girl is gone from her booth, its miniature Times Square crawl still streaming movie times in green. We are on the wrong side of history here.

In the rear of the lobby the theatre manager is corraling velvet ropes and silver stanchions into a storage room beside the Men's. I tap the glass with a quarter, but he pretends I'm not here, which is correct. My son stands in the middle of the empty concourse watching me, weaving resentfully on his cane. He's put back on his Kanzcity Chiefs coat. I tap harder—at least to score a rain check or better yet a refund. An explanation would be enough.

"Yeah. They're shut," a voice says. It is the security guard I've seen chatting up the manager through the glass—not that long ago. Long enough, though, for all our plans to go south.

"He said he'd hold it and start again . . ." (referring to the numb-nuts manager moogling around inside). ". . . We bought tickets."

The guard's gold nameplate proclaims he is "Knutsen" (probably "Ka-noot-sun"). Officer Knutsen—a thick-headed, mustachioed second son of old Norway. Undoubtedly an ex–city cop grown too porky to do the job. (These are always the ones who shoot you.) His security issue is the same cop paraphernalia he wore on the force—big gun, cuffs, Taser, pepper spray, shoulder mic—just cheaper versions. Gold oak leaves on his epaulettes announce he is a "major."

"I guess there was a bomb threat. Ya gotta expect that now." Major Knutsen talks while holding his breath and nodding, trying to look concerned but isn't. "Who'd want to go to a movie in this weather, anyway?" Apparently the blizzard outside blows right into the movie theatre. He thumbs his cop belt and gives it a tug-up over his belly, then gargles his throat, releasing the aroma of his lunch. He has the smallest possible blue eyes.

"My son really wanted to go. We bought tickets," I say again. Talking to this man is the equivalent of addressing a vending machine.

"Zat yur son?" Major Knutsen casts a chilly eye at Paul—by himself, hair askew, sour-faced in his Chiefs garb. Paul gives me a small, cruel smile indicating he likes it that I'm talking to Major Knutsen. This is what I *should* be doing for not getting us in the movie.

"He loves movies."

"You bet." Major Knutsen nods, referencing whatever class of humanoid Paul presents as. He's seen it all, could tell me things I wouldn't believe. He's not going to say anything about my son.

Few people are going in and out the mall entrance. The action is down at the Starbucks and the Applebee's. Andy is now singing to all shoppers "*Hot-diggity, dog-ziggity, BOOM*" with a calliope accompaniment.

"Okay. So, we good now?" Major Knutsen sniffs the way cops sniff. "I seen you tapping the glass, there. I just wondered . . ."

"Sorry? Oh, sure, We're good," I say. I look at Paul who mouths words that say "Get us the fuck outa here." He may be hurting from too long on his feet. I *am* good. Completely. Even without a movie. I smile at Officer Knutsen, who means well but is not used to being smiled at. *Hot-diggity, dog-ziggity* . . .

"O-*kay*," he says but doesn't move.

"O-*kay*," I say. "Thanks."

"T'swhat we're here for." He shifts his weight, pauses, then starts away down the concourse where the more interesting people are. He speaks an all-clear into his shoulder mic. "That's a 24" . . . or some such. He has a nice, lilting swinging gait, almost dainty. No doubt he is an excellent dancer.

Our day's not gone at all the way I wanted it to. Like many days in this exceptional winter. But we are off again. Paul and I. Movieless.

TWO

How my son and I became medical pilgrims in a far-north third-tier midwestern city is a story possibly worth relating, since like many worthwhile stories—including those of the great masters—it affirms the ageless wisdom which says that when you seek to give god a good belly-laugh, tell her your plans.

Not that my plans last October, when Paul was diagnosed, were all that enterprising. I was "working" at House Whisperers four hours a day, trying to convince myself I was doing something and not nothing. My job primarily entails facilitating private meetings between high-roller home-buyer prospects and Miss Evelyn Snowman, LLB, our "client counselor"—a former FBI counterintelligence specialist (this turns out to be perfect for real-estate work). Evelyn's job is to meet clients—in my office (I'm never present; moneybags like this kind of cointelpro folderol)—interview them, be interviewed *by* them, vet and profile them. Then if all checks out, offer them virtual tours of likely properties, and after that, actual ultra-private in-person viewings. If all *that* works out, she takes matters from offer to counter-offer, to negotiation, to up-front money, to contract, on through to closing—all without snooping neighbors getting wise, causing a stink and obtaining restraining orders because the house next door is being sold to Faisal el Akbar, former Kuwaiti security head, or the niece of Idi Amin, who's enrolling at the seminary, hoping for a fresh start. I could perform *my* part of this work from home, like the rest of the world. But my employer Mr. Mahoney likes the "heritage" brick-and-mortar feel of a desk, a window, a customer chair, a waste basket and handset. Which is fine with me since that's how I sold houses in my day, and even if Mike doesn't understand that "heritage" is nothing but a gimmick.

Haddam, New Jersey, wasn't always so skittish about who gets to live there. Until 2016, citizens could be confident it'd be mostly well-heeled white men. When Ann and I arrived in the seventies, only Stalin's daughter lived down our block on Hoving Road—the sole celebrity curio in town. We'd see her walking her Pomeranians past our house every day and letting them shit on our lawn as if she owned it. Gone now are those days— casualties of the housing boom, the housing crash, Hurricane Sandy, multiculturalism, 9/11, the rise of the right, ISIS, the Taliban and broadband—and far beyond my powers to alter.

Last October, Ann had been dead two years. My second wife, Sally Caldwell, had matriculated into lay-nun-grief-counselor training in either Switzerland or Swaziland, from where she occasionally called me late at night, half-looped, to tell me I was a "luminous" man but never seemed to need her and never "gave" enough. Which was why she preferred grieving people whose language she didn't speak. (These people apparently give a lot.) I actually *did* need her, and would be happy if she'd come back today. Only I thought—and still think—that defeating need is the secret to being in love, and that most of the time "giving" was code for people wanting you to care more than they do.

Neither of my children lived with me. My daughter, Clarissa Bascombe (age 45), is in Scottsdale, where she owns and runs a chain of prestige boarding and grooming kennels with her committed life-partner, Cookie Lippincott, who has inherited dough and doesn't try to control her. Paul had moved to Haddam from KC in the last painful months of his mother's life, to "be with her," then stayed on. I've visited him in his scratchy-moldy third-floor "studio" in a converted old-family mansion on Humbert Street—which was depressing. Though before he got sick, he apparently considered my house to be his anyway.

Paul, inside of a month, found a job online as an "associate" in the theological seminary's "human logistics" detail. Which means outsourced security, like Major Knutsen, only without a gun, cuffs, plastic restraints, nunchucks, pepper spray or a Taser—just a badge patch, an official shirt, an earpiece, a chin mic and a smile. "We're eyes-on-the-ground *only*," Paul told me in my living room, watching the evening news, when I hinted it seemed unusual. "Everything low-impact," he said in his official, human logistics voice. "Not police *or* security. We never use those words. We're *a presence*, per se."

It turns out there are just as many gropings, stalkings, leerings, male-noticings, genital exposures and inappropriate thoughts—plus the standard break-ins, assaults, larcenies, crimes against property and nature—at the best religious institutions as there are at Columbia and Mount Holyoke. It's all hushed up, Paul told me confidentially. Which reminded me of my youthful Ann Arbor days, when demoralized farm kids from Bad Axe and the Soo (plus the predictable homesick Chinese) "flew" off their dorm roofs after midnight, free forever from organic chemistry and their term paper on *The Magic Mountain*. Hearses quietly crept out of campus before light—as if suicide was catching (which it may be).

Still. I had a hard time picturing my unusual son as a digit on the hand appended to the long arm of the law. Though when he would sometimes ride his bike over after his "shift," still in his mint-green "work shirt" ready for a beer and a free meal, he assured me in a grave, chin-down way that human logistics (HL) was a transformational field, and he regretted wasting precious years writing dopey greeting cards at Hallmark, then later running a garden supply/rent-to-own in Kansas City, all of which he now looked on as "tail-chasing." (I'd always thought they were fine jobs and been happy he was in Kansas City doing them.)

Human logistics, Paul felt and even in his present, diminished circumstance still feels, is the vocation he was born for, given his knack for small-scale conflict resolution, being a good listener, not easily angered and "basically liking people." None of which I've noticed is true of him. The pitfall, he said, is once you "grow" in your job, the company (Gormles Logistics 3.1 Innovations) wants to boot you up to supervision, which didn't match his skill set. I've told him my own life had followed a similar uncompassed course, that I'd never completely "found myself"— except in the mirror every morning. Einstein, I assured him, longed to be a butcher but got sidetracked into relativity because as a Jew he couldn't get in the butcher's union. At least, I felt, my son didn't get a library science degree or go to culinary school.

It's not, in fact, the worst outcome for one's children to come home—assuming they don't move into your house, eat every meal at your table, share your toilet, fill up the garbage cans and live in front of your TV.

Haddam has always sheltered oddments like Paul, strangies you get used to seeing hanging around the Post Office or the newspaper kiosk, or at back tables in the library, reading *China Today* or *Lancet* and laughing about things only they know. These people wear the same clothes day-in, day-out, always appear fiercely *involved* in something, though in fact they're doing nothing, since in an hour you see them involved in the same thing a block away. They are (or were) the love-child son or moody eldest daughter of some ex–New Jersey governor, long deceased, or the sallow, hollow-eyed offspring of some Swiss seminarian, who's moved on. These aren't the people who buy bump stocks or take up positions in a bell tower and rain terror upon an innocent world. They're the watery *presences* at the periphery of yours and everyone else's sight line, awaiting nothing, seemingly friendless (though not always), harming nothing and no one, growing old as you grow old, and who repair *somewhere* at night to sleep. It's possible to think people like this don't have lives full of expectancy and small triumphs. But they do.

Paul Bascombe is (or, was) such an outlier—only more self-directed. Until his Al's diagnosis, he held down a job, maintained a small crew of unusual friends he played chess, read Robert Heinlein and Philip K. Dick, probably listened to and discussed Anthony Newley with, and did things together on computers. True, he is not married—though he was briefly once, in the '90s, to a nice, intelligent if also strange girl from Cheboygan in the upper Lower Peninsula (no kids). At some point "something happened," and she became no longer in the picture and wasn't replaced. I asked twice when he was running the garden supply, but he only said it was a long story, and I wouldn't understand—which was probably true. In fact, he may not be a man with a skill set that matches matrimony.

Admittedly, my son Paul Bascombe's life has not been a life of achievement—no bestsellers notched, no software patents granted, no trophies or touchdowns or even identifiable themes, other than the theme of himself. He never quite "caught on" was his mother's view at the end. Though in my view he has merely lived the *somehow* life I and others live, and seemed okay about it until his illness. He of course is beneficiary to a fat trust fund from his deceased mother, which his sister administers

(I'm deemed too old for that, but perfect for shepherding him through Mayo). So, even though he will die young, he will likely never be destitute or live in a cardboard box or be warehoused in a nut hatch—no matter how eccentric he survives to be. One might wish he would live at least a partway more conventional life, rise through the ranks at Gormles, be picked for top man in human logistics, marry a Polish widow named Blaczyowski from Wall Township, buy a house in Lakewood and eventually retire to Jupiter—the town in Florida, not the planet. But there's no promise such a life would make him happy, and—as with many—might indeed have turned him sullen and glum, which is not his nature. Though none of this will happen now.

THE WEEK AFTER HALLOWEEN LAST FALL, I EMBARKED UPON A melancholy journey which could be said to have led me all the way to Rochester. Ann, in her will but also face-to-face when she was dying, instructed that half her cremated self be buried in the Haddam Cemetery beside our son, Ralph Bascombe, who would now be fifty-one and a famous physicist at Caltech, or a lyric poet, or an oboe prodigy. There's a plot reserved there for me and also space for Paul and Clarissa, should the spirit move us.

Ann's other half she wanted scattered into Ives Lake in the forested fastness of the Huron Mountain Club in the Michigan UP, where she'd spent girlhood summers, and later we'd vacationed as a family when we *were* one. She had occasionally still "gone up," stayed in the ancestral cottage, sailed her Starfish, toasted weenies and woogled whoever was squiring her around at the time. I am persona non grata there, due to personal shortcomings none of the old oligarch club-members would ever have been guilty of.

Neither of our two children possessed the least willingness to perform this doleful duty. (Neither did I, but I'd said I would.) It proved impossible to get permission from the HMC's supreme soviet for a private interment—"against all the rules." So the Tuesday after Halloween, I flew alone from Newark to Detroit, and on to Marquette, with Ann's ashes in a quart Ziploc bag, packed inside a Delta toiletries kit. In Marquette I rented a Lincoln Navigator and drove west toward Big Bay, checked into the Comfort Inn, and next morning drove out to the HMC's imposing rustic main gate. It was already frosty and leaves were down. I was concerned there'd be armed guards in the woods patrolling for poachers, so I continued on to the west side of the great impoundment (31 square miles), found a notch in the woods and angled the Navigator down into some dry alders. With the parcel in my pocket, dressed in boots, my Kara Koram and blue U of M watch cap, I stalked off into the forest, following instincts I didn't have, but soon found a stream running north. There was cold sun, and the wind was up and biting. The stream led me to a bog I skirted round. And when I reached the other side, I felt a hollowing-out of sounds and glimpsed open space upwards in the bare limbs, which I took to be blue autumn sky over water. And soon enough—1,000 feet on—there was Ives Lake, lapping languid against the rocky western shoreline, beyond a stand of tamaracks. I was breathless—my heart pumping hard, my face chilled, my gloveless hands stiff and red and skint. I'd been all but running through the woods as if something or someone was chasing me.

I had no clear plans for the completion of my mission. I'd brought two boiled eggs and a piece of link sausage from the Comfort Inn's continental breakfast. I'd also bought a half-pint of Stoli at a party store. These would be my sacraments. The lake spread cold and alien in front of me, its far shore two miles across, walled by woods like where I was. No humans were in sight. The tamaracks glowed through the primordial pines and firs, nearby where decades past Ann and Ralph and Clarissa and Paul—and I—had idylled as a family unit, swum, canoed, sailed, built fires, sung songs and roasted our own weenies deep into the cool summer nights. No one would spy me here, I thought— ghost of blither times. I sat down on a log facing the lake. I brought the eggs out of my pocket, peeled the shells into a hole I dug with my heel, and ate both, plus the smoky link which was exquisite. I took a searing toss of vodka and washed it all down. Wind stirred the surface of the lake, bringing forward a strong fishy smell. Wood smoke rode in from someplace possibly not far away, but I didn't care. I sat on my log like a bear and waggled my booted feet and warmed my hands in my pockets and waited. And then, at no appointed moment, I took the Ziploc out of its holder. Wind over the lake was against me, but nearby a spit of weedy-muddy land extended into the tilting water—a mini- peninsula. Ziploc in hand, I stepped forth onto the muddy flat and into the breeze. A spotter plane flying low would've seen me. I walked twenty yards farther onto the mud spit, where I could turn my back to the wind and have water in front of me. Carefully I opened the plastic zipper, stepped three feet into the shallows, took off my M cap, turned the bag over and let its grainy contents sift out, where for a moment the ashes made a cloud then a soot stain on the water's surface, then separated and drifted, began to settle and simply disappeared. "'And some there be which had no memorial . . .'" I recited from memory. I had looked these phrases up in Ecclesiasticus, using my mother's old King James. "'. . . who are perished as though they had never been, and are become as though they had never been, and their children after them.'"

"Not your fate, my darling darling," I said to the breezes.

"Not your fate. Not today." I then packed my vodka, put away the empty Ziploc and walked back through the woods at a more leisurely pace, all alone.

———◆———

WHEN I REACHED THE MARQUETTE AIRPORT THAT AFTERNOON I was, not surprisingly, in the fragilest and complexest of spirits: I'd done precisely what I'd come to do—which had a solid core of *good* within it. And I'd also done precisely what I'd come to do—which was the sorrowful est, sorrowful-est thing. Yet as I hurried down the concourse to my gate, there suddenly settled upon me—not at all expected—a question. A question anyone would concede was timely, given where I'd just been and what I'd just done and given my stage in life. Late and unaccompanied.

Namely. What now to do? Again.

This was in my middle days of thinking about happiness. I read for the blind on WHAD two hours a week. I did my bit for House Whisperers. I saw my son occasionally but not often. I checked books out of the library, watched movies and football on TV, occasionally drove out to the Red Man Club but rarely fished. Even *I* could understand such a tepid existence was not giving life its full due. Not what my mother meant on her death-bed all those years ago. Much more like Pug Minokur in his walking shorts.

The year previous, I'd had a TIA, though nothing had turned up worrisome. (I took a statin.) The microscopic pin hole had been detected in my heart at Haddam MC, but wasn't considered serious enough for blood thinners (a relief in the erectile department). I owned a blood pressure cuff but didn't use it. I had cataracts in both eyes but noticed nothing. I saw vitreous swimmers from a cudgel-stick injury in my Marine training in the

'60s, and experienced occasional morning bouts of vertigo—for which I employed corrective routines you only want to perform alone. Sometimes my heart would pound, sometimes my feet burned. My fingernails grew like a corpse. These were the ineluctable *facts of life* that make fantasies of "a clean bill of health," and being "young for your age" as laughable as a goat show.

However, I slept fairly well—was always young in my dreams. I had no one "in my life," and felt possibly I would never again. (I could've stood a candidate or two.) But I still thought about love and its good neighbor, sex, in vivid particulars and without ambiguity or conflict—just no longer as a stakeholder. For a while after I came back from my Lonesome Pines reunion, I gave a thought to travel. Though the problem with travel is eventually you *arrive*—with your old self lagging behind a few hours or nights or days, and finally catching up with all the same shit on his mind—at which point all you can do is travel on to someplace else.

For a week I thought about signing up at the seminary for a class in the Old Testament. I'd never gotten past the *begat*s and always suspected the rest wasn't worth reading. I printed out a brochure for a singles' cruise up the inner passage to Ketchikan, at the conclusion of which (in my daydream) I would charm a middle-age Canuck divorcée, fall in love and lust, and be ready to up-stakes in NJ, drive to her place in Kamloops, where we'd run a B&B and I'd become a Canadian. I thought of many things: the Red Cross, umpire school, driving a school bus. Accomplishment (of some kind), I felt, was the font of happiness, whereas irrelevance and shadowy loneliness were worse than two packs of Luckies a day. Yet by the week of my journey to return my lost wife to Michigan, I hadn't discerned my pathway forward.

Why do we not do things? It is a far richer question than why we *do*.

———◆———

TWO DAYS, HOWEVER, BEFORE MY FLIGHT TO MARQUETTE, I was in my House Whisperer's office, thinking of nothing more than what lay immediately in front of me. I'd been on a call with a onetime member of the Divorced Men's Club (now disbanded), Carter "Knot-head" Knott—who's eighty—regarding the disposition of a time-share his sister "Glad" owned in Destin, which he was itching to sell now that she'd croaked. ("You take a mauling with these pieces of shit. Walk away. Let the bastards sue you. They won't.") I was musing out my window at a hornet on the glass that had just sensed the season was changing, when through my customers' door, exactly the way my "mother" had, in walked my employer, Mr. Mahoney—a happy sight on any day.

Mike has become round and burnished with success and self-authentication. Gone, are our lean and mean tiger years on the Shore when we stacked 'em deep and sold 'em never very cheap. I'd sold him the business following the '08 bottom-out, and he'd instantly pivoted to hurricane-distressed homes and made gazillions. "Tenacious Tibetan Scales Real Estate Everests," *The Asbury Press* gloatingly reported.

Mike likes to pop in unannounced at his various real-estate entities—his house-maintenance entity, his sales entity, his rental entity, his bullpen of foreclosure goons dotted around New Jersey. Seventy percent of Mike's employees are family members—all of them terrified of being sent back to Lhasa. Stopping to see me, though, is always a treat. We're old conspirators from the same crimes. I like him immensely.

"Woop! Okay! I caught you! Again!" His head was in my doorway—small, fierce eyes behind tinted designer specs. I'd seen his Flying Spur circle the Green when I was on the phone with Carter Knott. He employs his nephew as his driver.

"I was just putting these big checks back in the safe," I said. It's our regular Bud 'n' Lou. I'm the larcenous clerk. He's the tyrannical but heart-of-gold boss. He doesn't understand all of this, which makes it better. Mike's once dense-black monk's hair has gone brittle and is missing patches. He dyes it even blacker, making his head a bit of checkerboard. He also sports a tidy spare tire to commemorate his financial wizardry. This day he was attired in his version of Friday business casual—tan velour tracksuit with gold piping and loads of zippers. Midget-size gold Air Jordans with silver laces—possibly real silver. Mike owns an online clothing distributorship in Karachi and has recycled his divorced Tibetan wife, Sheela, to oversee it. The tracksuit was likely an own-brand. He's rich as Nebuchadnezzar, almost certainly a felon, but as much an American as Thomas Jefferson. Naturally he's a Republican, though he doesn't like Trump.

We rarely talk business anymore, but he never stops by for no reason. Once inside my office, he walked to the window, stuffed his hands into his tracksuit pockets (his short arms are now thick as sausages) and stared down at the Green and the fancy-shops arcade—thinking no doubt he should buy it all, put me in charge, open an Izod or a Patagonia, eventually cash it out to rich Arabs, then do it again in five years. His is a mind never idle, though I like picturing him long ago as a small Tibetan boy in a magenta skirt, a funny hat and sandals.

"I have a fantastic idea." Mike was speaking to the window as if he was rehearsing.

"All ears, here," I said.

His rounded cranium tilted slightly to determine whether I was making fun of him, which I do sometimes. He is a man of strict linear calculations, warm-natured but not innately mirthful. He'd make a good Christian.

"Hear me out, Frank." He stepped away from the streaming-in afternoon light and took a seat in the customer's chair, where multimillion-dollar home conveyances were routinely sealed. He exuded his usual tiny rich-man's eagerness. "I've found a new undetected market your son can absolutely get a foothold in." His eyes snapped behind his gold-rims. He hunched forward, tiny Air Jordans barely connecting chair to floor. Mike's English is steeped in '70s bidnus lingo, from the days when he earned his spurs as an up-start telemarketing chieftain in Carteret. Taking a "floor" (in something). "Getting in on the backside" (of something). "Popping your cherry in the secondaries." Balance sheet, working capital, escrow all used as metaphors. I was trying not to smile and rile him up. He continued, "This was in *Real Estate Forward*. Okay?" A fringe industry-journal produced in Pakistan that he reads online. "Clients have to know everything today, Frank. Okay? Not just the house they're buying, but the whole goddamned neighborhood." Mike's face wizened in business intensity. He likes to curse. "They'll pay for pre-sale research no agent gives a shit about because bad news jeopardizes the sale. Right?"

"Right," I said.

"So. Your rich client wants to know if the guy across the street has a felony record, okay? Or if the little boy three houses up has learning disabilities he got from the water supply. Neighbors aren't normal anymore, Frank. You have to put 'em under the microscope. It's not like when we started." Mike's face went grave. A pearl of elder spittle had developed in his left mouth corner. He sniffed, inhaling the sweet bouquet of unexpected money. When Mike talks business he entirely loses his accent. "This is a biiig, fertile, unrecognized market here, Frank. I can launch it as a web service. We can open into the connecting office." (He owns the building.) "HSP'll take fifteen percent as a finder's. You and Paul take over and pocket the rest. You buy me out when you're flush. We call it 'Local Knowledge Solutions.' You'll get rich and move to Bimini." His eyes snapped again. Mike found it troubling that my son hadn't risen higher in the world. He envisioned Paul—minus his green Gormles shirt and ventriloquist's dummy—as a fresh untapped resource. (I knew better.) Mike featured Paul poring over stacks of printouts, scouring court filings, logging gum-shoe computer miles and coming up with "hits" about some neighbor's wife's missionary uncle who has leprosy but lives on the third floor where no one sees him, and how that choice bit of news could take "half a mil off asking" on a barn-board contemporary two blocks down and keep somebody out of a negligence suit. Mike believed Paul and me being partners in a no-ceiling growth field would allow me to stop worrying about my son (which I didn't used to do) while securing the stability of my legacy. Tibetans think this way.

"Paul won't do that." I smiled apologetically, which I knew would irritate him.

"Why not!" Mike's little bullet fists whapped the customer's chair arms. "What am I? Some little beige putz?" Co-workers in his phone-bank days had called him that, then lived to regret it when he bought the company. "You have to *order* him to do it!" Mike whipped a bright-orange silk handkerchief from his pants pocket and gave his mouth a swipe, erasing the spit button he'd sensed was there. From a second pocket he produced a silver dispenser-canister and gave his tongue a spritz—which I understood was diversionary behavior for not getting his way.

"He likes his human logistics work," I said and clasped my hands prayerfully on my desktop. "I can't tell him what to do. He's not a Tibetan. It's good of you to think of him, though."

"It's *not* good of me. He's idiotic." Mike believed human logistics was like having a career as a crossing guard.

"Well . . ." I, of course, didn't want to go into business with my son any more than I wanted to be a Canadian or drive a school bus.

"Speak to him! Tell him!" Suddenly scanning around the sides of his chair as though there might be things on the floor threatening his next movement. Mike and I were not happy arguing. From somewhere out in the Boro of Haddam, I heard fireworks going off, whistling and popping in the calm autumnal heavens. Absolutely against all ordinances. The richer a town becomes, the more its citizens feel compelled to shoot off fireworks.

"I'll see him next week. I'll bring it up," I said. "He'll appreciate it. He admires you." Not true. Paul actually thought Mike was "strange."

"I just want to open doors for people, Frank." Mike was tapping both hands nervously on his chair arms. Republicans all believe they want to open doors for people, but only as long as they get to go in first.

"You're a great man, Senator."

Mike was now nodding for no reason, not knowing exactly how to perform his next little man's move. Possibly a sniff of nostalgia had tempered his exuberance. Nostalgia for the old life, when everything he did worked out. If he failed at something—even this—it made him sad.

I stood right up then. Mike was a flagrant and reflexive hugger. It had begun when he got stinking rich. He was so grateful, grateful, grateful for everything America allowed him. The chance to "give back," to pay dues, to put the shoe on the other foot. Buppety. Bup. I wasn't stepping around the desk. I didn't want to be hugged in my own office.

"Did you bet the Eagles this Sunday?" he said, standing, his velour lounging garments falling flawlessly into place. He owned a skybox at Lincoln Financial and was football crazy.

He'd invited me many times. But I preferred TV, which is what football is made for.

"They made a big mistake at quarterback, is the way I see it," I said, glad to move into sports. Firmer ground than my son.

"They looked a giftèd horse in the wazoo, is what I think," Mike said.

"Something like that," I said. "They're pretty interesting, though."

"I tried to buy a piece of the team. Just a crumb!" He widened his little eyes and beamed at the splendor of it all. A minority owner from Tibet. "They told me they'd call me. Ha!"

"We know what that means." I gave him our old wisenheimer nod. Nostalgia was now sucked from the room. Gone.

"Ha!" His eyes fired, his feet began jittering with happy new enthusiasm. "'Fuck you, Charley.' *That's* what it means! They're a bunch of old fucking white guys. I don't blame 'em."

"Fuck you and the Lama you rode in on, right?" I said. It was one of our oldest. "I miss you, Don Miguel."

"Ha!" This all made him happy now. "Me, too," he said. "Talk to your putzburger son."

"I will," I said. And he was away, out the door, down the stairs to his Bentley and off back to Red Bank. A good deed done—or almost.

———◆———

WHEN I REACHED THE DELTA GATE IN MARQUETTE—HAVING stabilized to a fugue state of grief mixed with low-grade aspiration regarding timely questions relevant to what *now* for me, or what *ever*—the waiting area was a-thrive with activity. The Northern Michigan University Fighting Bull-Bats were a day away from playing the archrival, Wisconsin–Eau Claire Anvil

Heads in a pigskin contest to decide the Peckerwood League Championship and who would bring home the Old Oaken Slop-pot and go on to the Clinker Bowl in Duluth on New Year's day, when the fate of the world would be decided.

The Anvil Head squad was just de-planing. Pep-band members were crowding into the gate area—they'd come on a different plane—shiny instruments in hand, all in purple and gold. A "spirit squad" of substantial Wisconsin beauties with purple and gold pom-poms was conferencing in front of the band, looking slightly put-upon. The tall Ichabod dairy-farmer drum major with his mace and polished knee boots, stood sufferingly eyeing the girls, wishing one could be his on the flight back to cheesehead land.

I'd begun reconsidering a trip to Ketchikan, trusting that doing the wrong thing that you don't know is wrong, is better than doing nothing because you fear a worse error. (It's the classic old person's quandary, usually decided in favor of doing nothing.) I'd decided, as well, that on arrival to Haddam I was going to sit my son Paul down—we were scheduled for the KC–Chargers game on Sunday—and raise the matter of Mike's offer of ground-floor purchase with solid upside, plus minimum exposure in a dynamic one-off industry which might on its face seem like a hare-brained gimmick but because it was Mike's gimmick, was guaranteed to make somebody rich—since Mike's schemes always made *somebody* rich.

At some signal the pep band instruments all sprang up. The pom-pom girls scurried into a loose rank in front of the band, agitating their pom-poms and smiling as trumpets blasted the overture to "Fanfare for the Common Man." A small contingent of Anvil-Head boosters had ridden with the team and were now arrayed, holding signs saying "A-Head Nation," "Swat the Bats" and "Go Anvils." It was all in the best possible school fervor. Anvil-Head players promptly began emerging from the jet-way—wide, lumbering, strangely-graceful galoots sporting headphones, carrying playbooks, suited in gold ties and purple sports coats—most of them Black, but not all. They looked sleepy and slightly vexed by the hubbub.

Which was the precise moment my phone started binging. Area code 480.

My daughter, Clarissa. Calling from the Valley of the Sun. Although just as likely from the Ardennes. Or Finland. Or Tierra del Fuego. She and her wife travel a lot.

I gave a thought to not answering, as I often do when my daughter calls. My plane could be arriving. (It wasn't.) I had to take a leak. (I didn't, although I usually do.) I left my phone in my luggage. (I hadn't.) These were excuses I could've given. Instead I answered.

"Where are you?" Clarissa said, followed by lead brick silence. Why did she need to know where I was? My stomach brought forth a high-pitched, low-decibel *scurleee* noise, sourced from the pastie I'd eaten in the Pastie Kioski in Negaunee on the way to the airport from the Huron Mountain Club that morning.

"I'm in Marquette. Michigan," I said. Interring your mother's remains. Incurring pie-crust remorse. Wishing I was someone else. I didn't say any of these. Lesbians, as far as I can tell, never believe anything men say.

"Have you even spoken to your son?"

"Not in a couple of weeks," I said. For some reason I felt short of breath. "He's coming over for the Chiefs and Chargers Sunday. I'm making . . ." I was about to say "meatloaf." Instead I said, "Why?" The Anvil Heads were mostly off the plane. The booster contingent was already straying away. Music had dwindled to a hymnal rendering of the alma mater.

"Haven't you noticed his symptoms? He's tissue-y. He doesn't want to tell you, he thinks you'll get mad at him. He doesn't trust you. You're really an awful man. He fell down when I had him at Sanford Weill this week. It was pathetic. He's afraid he's going to lose his idiot security-guard job. You don't even *try* to take care of him."

"I *don't* take care of him," I said. "*He* takes care of him. What the fuck are you talking about? Tissue-y. What's that?" The red-coated Delta agent behind the check-in pursed her lips and pretended not to notice, but was clearly thinking through her security-profile checklist: *Older white male speaking profanely, exhibiting agitation, shouting into phone. Possibly off meds. Potentially armed.* My plane *was* arriving. Waiting first-class passengers had coalesced into a clutch, stealing guarded looks at the economy-ticket holders as if ill feelings might surface. I was in row 20. The back.

Clarissa had forgotten to include what she was talking about. Again the leaded phone silence. I pushed my Samsung against my ear and fingered the other ear to mute the waiting-area announcements. On Clarissa's end I heard her say to someone— not me, but in annoyance, "Just tell her I'll have to call her back. We charge for that service. This isn't a charity."

"What?" she said, returning to me—in the Marquette airport, in a swarm of thickening apprehension. "Oh. He has ALS. I'm surprised it's me who has to tell you. Do you even know what that is?" Something—something metal—tapped against her phone. "Stop that!" she said to someone or some creature. "We can't use that."

"*What* is it?" I said. I'd heard what she'd said. My son had ALS. I needed to hear it again. My son has ALS. My son has ALS. Say it three times, and it won't be true. "Of course I know what it is. It's Lou Gehrig's disease."

"Whatever. He called me three weeks ago, when I was on the Cape. He said he had some weird symptoms. Maybe he had Lyme disease, since we'd lived in Connecticut a hundred years ago. It's how his mind works. Cookie and I were with some Harvard people on their Hinckley. And one of our friends' friends—Greta something—is a neurologist at Brigham's. Nut-case said his legs had been trembling, and his hands were weak, and he felt clumsy. Greta said I should have him evaluated. She knew someone at Sanford Weill. She called right from the boat. And that was it."

It. It. It.

"What do you mean? *What* was *it*?" My knees—I was standing now, had inched away from other passengers—had ice needles in them and were also trembling. "What happened?"

"I flew down. Two weeks ago? Paul came up on the train. We went up to Sanford Weill on 68th. He seemed fine. We got right in. Greta's friend—Doctor Bendo, if you can believe that. He did an MRI and some blood tests. Stuck needles in Paul's muscles for nerve output. Very painful, I guess. Though Paul seemed not to think so. They asked him a lot of questions and got him to walk back and forth, checked his balance and a lot of other stuff. It wasn't good. The doctor said he's probably had it for a while. Which is typical. He may already have dysphagia."

"What's that?" It. It.

"Trouble swallowing. Has he suffered some big trauma in the last year? Sometimes—it's in the literature—patients report that. It's just speculation."

"I don't know. No."

Clarissa had also forgotten about me being an awful man who didn't take care of his son. She could have been relating this all to her Harvard friends on their fucking Hinckley over golden goblets of Montrachet.

". . . fasciculations," she said.

"What? They're what?"

"Trembling. In his legs. He was always a klutz."

"I don't know."

"He feels fine. He says stupid stuff, which is stupid because he's *not* stupid. He went right back to work. His job. What's that about?"

"He likes it. I don't know," I said.

"Naturally."

"Naturally what?"

"He—this Bendo—thinks he may have the bad kind. Of ALS. The fast-progressing kind. It starts in your brain instead of your spine. It controls breathing, among other things." Wherever Clarissa was, dogs started barking a torrent. Then, as if a heavy door had been shut, the sound ceased. She said nothing for a moment. "Sorry, I'm out at the kennels." Anvil Head players were drifting down the concourse toward baggage claim. The pep band was stowing their instruments.

I said, "What's supposed to happen now?"

"He's going to get worse. Possibly pretty fast. His nerves are dying. He won't be able to be a security guard. That's for sure. He's really become a blowhard. Have you noticed that?"

"He's happy. He's a mainstream citizen. It brings out the blowhard in people."

"Mm-hm," his sister said. "I . . ."

"You what?"

"Nothing." Silence. "I talked to Cookie. We can fly him out here. There's a Mayo here. Her father donated a whole wing. We'll have him re-evaluated. I've made some calls. We know people."

"*I'm* going to take care of him," I heard myself say into my pathetic little phone. Passengers were exiting another flight.

Smiling, tan-skinned people in flowered beach attire, straw hats and leis. They'd been in Oahu and were back in the UP now, ready to yuk it up. My heart began whompety-whompetying, my knees going from ice to water, my stomach experiencing pains south of the beltline. I ached for a pit-stop.

"That's a non-starter," Clarissa said coldly. "You're too old."

"You don't even *like* him." I said this too loudly. "And he loves you. You act like I'm a hundred years old. I'm not too old."

"You're seventy-four whatever."

"I'm seventy-four whatever. Exactly. Paul's my son. If he's going to die, I'll take care of him. I love him. He's not a pet." Die. I'd said that.

"Fuck you, Frank. You're an idiot. It's all about you, isn't it?"

"No. It's not about me. It's not about you, either. Why'd you call me now instead of two weeks ago?"

"He said he'd tell you. He was afraid you'd be—whatever. Like he'd failed some stupid test. I don't know. I can do more for him than you can." Her voice had become wobbly, struggling and throaty. "I don't want to talk to you now. I'm upset. Paul's dying."

"I'm sorry. No, he's not."

"Mmmm-huh. Okay. You know about it now. We'll talk some other time. Call him. Or talk to him. I don't know." An audible suspiration left my daughter, trying to reclaim her breath and her all-important authority. "If he hasn't told you, that means he's afraid."

"I understand." Ker-ter-whump, ker-ter-whump. Skeewer-aaallll. My poor besieged belly with the killer pastie inside. There's never an ideal moment for these sorts of detonations. De-planed Michiganders were streaming past, guffawing about theirs being "good leis."

"I just . . ." Clarissa began, then stopped.

"I know," I said. I didn't know. I was *her* father, too. It wasn't that hard to be, following initial hostilities.

"He probably won't die tomorrow," she said in a bargaining tone, all but inaudible across the miles.

"I'll start with that," I said. "Thank you. I love you."

"Yeah, sure. Okay. I'm not mad at you. I'm just mad about this." She breathed in as hard as she'd been breathing out a moment before. "He doesn't need this."

"I know. I . . ." I think I meant to say thank you again. But the line went empty. I thought she'd said something else, but I couldn't be sure.

———

FROM THE DELTA LOUNGE IN DETROIT, IN A SWIVET OF PANIC, I got on the phone to Dr. Catherine Flaherty, recently stepped down as head of endocrinology at Scripps La Jolla. Catherine. Light of my life, fire of my loins. Here was a long story, as there is for everything if you survive.

Since 1983, Catherine (who's 60) and I have never totally been out of touch. And since Sally's departure, she and I have spoken a time or two with a circling, half suppressed fragrance of possibility scent-able down the cyberlines. The fifteen years that separated us at the beginning, when she was twenty-something and I was thirty eight, are not the years that separate us now—a fact I observe but don't mention. I'd seen her in the flesh only twice since we came back from "being in France together" in '84—both times at the Century Club, once when she was speaking to a pituitary gathering, and once when she was getting divorced. Each time I was nearly undone by how much she hadn't changed by age forty-whatever—still a tall, strapping Dartmouth rowing-team co-captain. Same long Boston incisors.

Same ironical Beacon Hill brogue from her old man; same honied hair—not blunted and doctorish; the same petal-perfect skin and delectable runner's calves. Both times I was immured in my own imponderables—children (of course), realty enterprises on the Shore. And, damningly—a failure to seize the moment anyone *would* seize if he had a brain: Leave it all and take her away. Catherine, naturally, was nose-down to her own life's di-*few*-cultees: her big doctor career, her divorce, her causes, other suitors hanging round her door whom she never took seriously. (Such women are never alone.) There'd been tacit acknowledgement of something still astir between us, but agreement that this was only natural. Its time had come. And gone. An unnecessarily gloomy view, I thought, since a positive-gradualist approach can often pay dividends. Sometimes the reason we don't do things is because we're patient.

From Detroit, when I told her semi-coherently what little I knew about Paul's situation, she seemed glad to hear from me, was completely ready to step in and seemed to know all that was required. She, for starters, wasn't satisfied with the evaluation at Cornell. ("Cursory at best. This is much too serious.") These first-rate specialists only trust their own—their own nurses, techs, phlebotomists, scanners, pipettes, blood pressure cuffs, etc. Medicine, in most ways, is not a science *or* an art, but a guildish freemasonry extending back to black mysteries and necromancy. I'm okay with it.

A Doctor Karl Pomfret, Catherine said, had recently transitioned from La Jolla "up to Mayo-Rochester" (my own alma mater—I was there with my ailing prostate in 2000; I still have the sweatshirt and the mug). His "remit" (Catherine now used these Englishy-Frenchy words—"remit," "easy-peasy," "prinking." *Tranche* and *carte blanche* as verbs), his remit was neuro-degenerative disorders. He'd been brought in to conduct large-scale trials having to do with "motor neurons that work well," and to find out what genetic material they contain that could prove "interesting" about the ones that "go wonky." There was "simply" nobody better. They had "trained" (like gymnasts or kickboxers) together at Hopkins ("different shops"), had briefly dated (". . . a joke—I always called him Pommes Frites"). This Pomfret was now married to a happy, plump Swedish woman who adored life in Minnesota because it reminded her of Norr-botten. She—Catherine—would "ring up" Karl and "have Paul seen" as soon as I could get him out there. Easy-peasy. Cornell was, of course, "absolutely first-rate, don't get me wrong, but it isn't Mayo, if you know what I mean." I did.

"So?" Catherine said. One box ticked. Next? "You again. What do *you* have to say for yourself, young man?" I imagined I heard the crashing, sudsing cold Pacific thundering onto ada-mantine rocks somewhere below where she might've been sitting, under a pergola, sunning her bronzed, tattoo-less extremities, possibly topless (just for home), drinking a smoothie you have to send "to the islands" to get the best fruit for. "So is Sally gone still . . . ? Where was it she went?" I was half dazed by the ease and dispatch with which she'd gotten my son "sorted" and headed down the best-practices chute toward renewed neuro-degenerative well-being.

"Chechnya," I said. "There's grief to go around there. I'll probably never see her again." She didn't know Sally Caldwell, had never met my children, which didn't bother her. She and Sally shared a crispness of outlook and would probably have liked each other. Which would not have worked out favorably for me.

"Are you having any fun, Frank?" A German tour group, all with yellow plastic shoulder-strap travel-agent bags and passports strung to their necks, began skittering out of the lounge, looking stunned, as if they'd missed their flight announcement and were now marooned in Detroit, not speaking Michigan. President Trump's swollen, eyes-bulging face filled the TV screen behind the honor bar, doing his pooch-lipped, arms-folded Mussolini. I couldn't take my eyes off him—tuberous limbs, prognathous jaw, looking in all directions at once, seeking approval but not finding enough.

"I've been trying to think of a way to *have* some fun," I said cravenly. "How would you like it if I flew out there?" I shocked myself.

"My goodness." A sultry land breeze wafted past her phone. I could breathe eucalyptus and passion-flower. "I don't know. What would we do together?"

"I'd work that out." My remit. "I could arrive with a surprise."

"Probably not *that* surprising. I know your surprises." She chuckled about that and took a sip of her smoothie or whatever it was. "Uhm." She made that noise. "My friends are all old-time Republicans out here. I don't think you're a Republican, are you, Frank?"

"Not yet," I said. "I still subscribe to the big tent."

"Well then, I couldn't take you to the La Jolla Club. People would have heart attacks. They've never met anybody like you."

A first registered taint of reluctance. Though it might have been the opposite. Age often makes reluctance and acceptance indistinguishable, since the outcomes can be the same. I didn't want to come on strong in case there could be a chance for later. Age also makes the long game the only game in town.

"How's your own body? Your doctor's inquiring."

"Tip-top," I said. I was startled by her job-interview directness—familiar from our first encounter when I was working for a sports magazine in 1983, and she was a Dartmouth intern, age 22—a fraught period; I was recently divorced and a walking-talking sponge of existential gloom I was confident I'd completely disguised. I was not about to reveal my TIA, my global amnesia, my hole in the heart, my carotid plaque buildup, my cataracts, my morning struggles with vertigo—all of which could forecast diverse "issues" of which I was fearful and expectant. Tip-top, tip-top, tip-top. "How's yours?"

"Fine. Some little-girl things. I'm okay. So, are you thinking you've missed something important in life?" A sound I heard meant she'd stood up and stepped to a stone belvedere from which to gaze out onto the sea's shimmering panorama.

"I've missed *you*. I've been reading Heidegger. The body's indifferent to him. We're all questioners, choosers and self-producers."

"Mmmm. Wasn't he a Nazi?"

"Not about everything," I said. "He thought a lot about human existence."

Catherine performed an intake of breath, indicating boredom. I don't know why I had to say that. It was 9 a.m. where she was. Noon in Detroit, an hour from where I went to college, met young Ann Dykstra, set a course that would somehow lead me to here, on the phone in the Sky Club with a woman 15 years my junior who couldn't possibly be interested in anything I'd say. "Did you write down Karl Pomfret's name and contact info. His office'll call you. Okay, sweetheart?" *Sweetheart*. I was still that. Possibly Catherine might enjoy a cruise to Ketchikan.

"Okay," I said, too loud. "Thank you."

Catherine cleared her throat in a doctorish way. "I've joined the Catholics, by the way. My father would be gobsmacked—though *he* was one 'til he married my mother. That'll probably change your view about coming out here. You could go to Mass with me. Or, you could stay home and read Heidegger."

"I've always loved you," I said spasmically. "I don't care."

"What don't you not care about?" Ignoring the love part.

"If you're a mackerel snapper or a Mormon."

She cleared her throat again, as if she was about to say something else, then didn't. I could hear a dove coo where she was—at the belvedere commanding the sea, under the pergola, beside the bird-of-paradise, amid the eucalyptus. The ocean breeze crooned through the empty space.

"So, can I come out there and see you? Sometime? You're really what I've missed. Or who."

"Oh, I don't know. I'd have some house-cleaning chores to take care of." The current goodly swain—out with the old, in with the older.

"That's okay." Better than okay.

"And you have your son, who I'm sorry about. I really am."

Boom-bang. Boomety-bang! I'd been aware of my son's dire predicament all of one hour and was now planning an errant flight to La Jolla on a mission of love not mercy. What was wrong with me? Possibly nothing.

"I'm really glad you called." Catherine's voice was liquid and suddenly jolly and skeptical at the same time, the way I remembered it when she was a girl.

"I can't wait to see you." I suddenly realized I was in the wrong concourse and would need to hotfoot it. But I wanted to stay in Detroit, city of broken automotive dreams, maunder moonily on to Catherine 'til the cows came home.

"Bye," she said, still amused.

"Bye," I said. "Bye." I said it again and possibly once more.

Which was the note upon which we ended.

———

KARL POMFRET CALLED THE NEXT AFTERNOON WHEN I'D GOT-
ten home—unexpressive and formal in doctor-phone-prissiness,
as if he didn't like speaking to other humans, or as if something
in Catherine's gilded voice had let certain cats out of certain
bags, causing the reopening of certain seams of longing we both
knew well. I was empathetic toward him. He'd lost out. He, not
so empathetic to me.

I could relate to him almost nothing of use about my son's
condition. The Cornell doctors had suspected but not formally
concluded, etc.; possibly "the bad kind"; to meet him he seemed
fine. All info came via his sister, which I knew was not real info.
I wouldn't see him myself until Sunday for the Chiefs and Chargers. Catherine had said, etc., etc., etc. . . .

Pomfret asked me if "nerve conductor tests" had been performed. I said I thought so. He said nerve-death diseases were
actually many illnesses that often passed under one name. Like
cancer. (I said I'd had that, had been to Mayo, which seemed not
to interest him.) He asked me if the word Hisayama had been
used. Not to me. He asked if I had noticed anything unusual
about Paul's mobility, dexterity, his musculature, his posture. I
said Paul was a klutzburger, an "unusual" boy (I said "boy") on
his best afternoon, so one might not immediately notice. Which
I hadn't. I hadn't really seen him that much—the last of these
words causing me to feel a chest-emptying whir of insufficiency,
conceivably culpable, even jail-able. I hadn't known he *had anything* before yesterday. How do you know something before you
know it? As when Uncle Malachy suddenly falls dead, but minutes ago was sitting, eating a piece of lemon sponge cake in the
kitchen.

"Has your son said anything to you about this, Mr. Bascombe?" Pomfret didn't seem to be writing anything down.

When you achieve Mayo-grade competency you've seen and heard 10,000 iterations of one thing. The same flaws in all phases of god's handiwork. What was there to write down?

"No. He spoke to his sister. She took him to Sanford Weill, I guess." I was becoming one of those mealy-mouths who say "I guess" at the end of every utterance, instead of "Yeah! You better fuckin' believe it."

Pomfret breathed a labored sigh into the receiver, as if he was wearing a surgical mask. "Okay," he said. "Can he get to Rochester? Where are you, Mr. Bascombe? Or where's your son?"

"*Here!*" As if I'd just waked up. "In central Jersey. Where we live. *He* lives."

"How old is Paul?"

"Forty-seven."

There was a pause during which I finally heard the tapping of keys on a computer. I'd conjured a mental portrait of Dr. Pomfret. Small, too angular, short coarse hair, rivets for eyes, a runner, possibly a sculler with his own lightweight craft, who lived, breathed, ate and slept motor neuron death. I couldn't see how these qualities could get him to first base with Dr. Flaherty. I was also suspicious of a trace of der Rheinland in his consonants. Or, worse, Switzerland.

"Mr. Bascombe, who'll be accompanying your son out to Mayo?" Tap, tap, tap.

"Me. I will. Do you know how long he might be there?"

"It depents," Herr Bascombe. Ja, ja, ja. More tapping. "Ven vee ee-fal-u-ate yur son, ve might haf more tings to talk about, dependink on vhat vee see. Is all right?" Tap, tap, tap, tap, tap, tap, tap. "Wunderbar, wunderbar."

"Sure. It is. It's great." I was suddenly jittery, as if I was talking to an undertaker. I longed to say: "If you take Paul into your experimental study, can you fix him and send him back to being a human logistics associate, where he was so happy?" That had not been my life's goal for my son, but now it was.

"Okay," Pomfret said. "I've sent this off. You'll hear from my appointment nurse, Miss Boykin. We'll get you in at the earliest."

"Get *Paul* in."

"Get *Paul* in." (Ja, ja) "Just be calm. We'll take good care of Paul."

"Okay. Okay. Thanks."

A momentary pause. "If you talk to Kate, give her my best regards."

"Who's Kate?"

"Catherine. Dr. Flaherty. We were at Hopkins together. I had a sneaker for her in those days."

"A sneaker. You did?"

"She wasn't interested in doctors, though. Had her sights on the big bucks. And got 'em."

True enough. Her ex-husband Gilles was a Lazard Frères freebooter, owned his own volcanic island in the Indian Ocean and attended the Sorbonne. They were, naturally, "still friends."

"Where'd you two get acquainted?" Pomfret said. "Were you her teacher?"

"Yeah," I said for no reason but to deceive him.

"High school?"

"Yeah. In Dedham, Mass. We were the Dedham Doornails. I taught her to read Chaucer in Chinese."

"Oh. Okay. Great." Something where Pomfret was made a *thunk* noise. "We'll be in touch very soon."

"Great," I said. "It's all great. It's really great. It really is. Thank you."

We ended things.

THREE

Embarking on our Mount Rushmore trip entails, for complicated reasons, the imminent renting of an RV (about which more later). And with our Valentine's movie now a write-off, today—Tuesday—offers me the chance to secure such a vehicle and be primed and ready should Paul's spirits rise to our adventure tomorrow. Plus, with just a jot more time, I can look to my own private needs in ways that will also become clear.

I do not, it should be said, find it at all hard to feel at home in Rochester. Most days, I get on well. My employer, Mr. Mahoney, through his Himalayan Solutions entity, and with his dedication to lessening the suffering of others, has loaned to Paul and me, for our Mayo stay, one of his securitized "homes," which dot the nation and possibly soon the globe, and which suits us completely. Our loaner house sits in a comfortable, older, close-in neighborhood, minutes from the Clinic, a street of mostly-still-nice '20s, '30s and '40s stick-built and brick-and-stucco abodes, slowly relaxing into the Midwestern motley of "mixed use"— remnant elms, uncertain curbings, roots elbowing through sidewalk cracks—all in obvious need of civic repurposing.

Mixed use has never borne a negative charge for me. Residing across the street, as we now do, from an acupuncture studio, where previously a urologist lived a century (and died) in his white-brick Colonial, or down the block from the Abyssinian deaf church which occupies a former shoe salesman's Tudor fourplex, preserves, in my view, the best of urban randomness. I have not inquired about Paul's views of living here while his life pares down to arch necessities—ambulation, swallowing, talking, breathing. But as with many things, his feelings are likely to be congruent with mine. Qualified assent.

Once every week, in the seven weeks since we arrived, Paul and I have driven from our medical-pilgrim digs on New Bemidji Street, eastward out Minnesota 14, to where the rich cropland takes up, the terrain begins to delve, and where we can achieve a profitable vista from a height of land. (It is not far here from the federal medical facility where Sheik Omar, Lyndon LaRouche, and the Unabomber have all been afforded state-of-the-art health care at public expense.)

When I have the car turned around and pulled to the shoulder by the Shriners' Adopt-a-Highway sign—keeping the motor and heater going—we are allowed to gaze down upon Rochester much as a gathering army would. It's good to take a cartographer's view of the places we abide—no matter how long we intend to abide there. One of the genuine if few advantages to traveling by air (which we didn't do when we came out in December) is seeing a locale as if you approached an island and can take in its entirety before you put a foot down. Aerial vistas provide important data we might never obtain if we rode in on a mule like Johnny Appleseed, facing rearwards. I remember the first time I flew into the Crescent City of New Orleans and could see, below me, the heart of that gaudy, bruised metropolis arrayed precarious along the great river's epic turn toward the Gulf. Right away I knew that underlying all that went on there was a sense of denial, burning like fever, and of self-willed recklessness and possibly mania. These were its totems.

All cities and towns survive and flourish by orienting human behavior to a loosely construed and made-up *idea*—e.g., self-willed recklessness—in order that succeeding inhabitants not suffer from confounding randomness. Most ideas and institutions we hold dear and even deem iconic are as contrived as the Watts Towers, Miss Liberty and Babe the Blue Ox.

I personally have never minded a low-grade sensation of randomness and have sought, as much as convenient, to keep randomness nourished. Living as I do, with my son—whose life is now hard-wired toward ALS life (and death), yet who's often at a loss for precisely what to *do* next—I am often at a loss for exactly how to *be at all*, which feeling I take to be the essence of randomness and not always a bad thing, in moderation. In this way, Paul and I have achieved a kind of complementary tolerance between what to do and how to be—which has served us well thus far.

From our high-ground perch, peering down, it is not that easy to see why Rochester—the town—should be here at all, or what its totems are, beyond the intricate and monumental Clinic. Possibly Indians once lived here, now long forgotten by most. Or conceivably it stands at the intersection of ancient pioneer trading routes, also lost from memory. As such it is one of those dots on the map where, when innocent citizens are gunned down outside a suburban CVS, other citizens line up fast to say, "These things don't happen *here*." As if *here* made a place.

As with most cities, Rochester's often chosen (unclear by whom) as one of the "best towns to live in America." Yet it does not seem to me a true civic *entity*—not quite—only a labyrinthine, humming, amoeba-ish and provisional *designation* for human housing and traffic, with businesses sprouting like dandelions. When I've chatted with my son's care team, most of them convey to me they'd be just as happy if the *town* of Rochester could be moved away so all that's left was nothing but Mayo, Mayo, and more Mayo—bravely, savingly devoted to illness (or, if you like, to boundless good health) and in need of nothing else and no one.

Which is why Paul's and my drives for the purpose of contemplating the topography, manner and tendency of all we can see are of value: to be able to say in spite of all, "*Yes*, this is space adequate for doing whatever we think we're doing. *There* is a small river. *That* direction we face is west. The Twin Cities are *that* way (out of sight, but unmissable). *There*, are major arteries. *There*, the first-tier suburbs, the second and third. That colossus of glass and steel in the middle ground, red beacons beaconing, white steam billowing from hidden stacks, a helicopter just settling down—*that* is the Clinic where everything happening is of the utmost import. And that space of leafless maples, elms and oaks just beyond, is where our house sits, barely visible beside a large blue spruce. And all beyond *that* is prairie. Expanding and expanding." Randomness, in other words, is fine in whatever portions you can stand it. But at some point it's good, possibly necessary, to set your own coordinates.

With this in mind, I have tried in our weeks of occupancy—and in case Paul were suddenly to feel panicky that we're nowhere at all (randomness at its worse)—to promote an atmosphere of "really living" in Rochester. Early on I subscribed to the *Post Bulletin*, opened a checking account at the robber baron Wells Fargo, signed up for library cards in both our names, enrolled us in a coffee club "points" membership, and joined the Y in case we decide to work out. I've rented a PO box. I've anointed a dry cleaner (Free Will), a car repair (Babbitt's Mostly Mufflers), a drugstore (Little Pharma), plus sussed out the Octoplex, which

unfortunately failed us today. Short of joining the Zion Lutherans, setting out nasturtiums and registering to vote, I've done
all I can to solidify an idea of "normal life" for us, so we're not
constantly peeking around the sides of things to confront life's
shuddering advances. Possibly this is what the poet meant when
he said, ". . . There is another world, but it is in this world."

And so, when I put my head to the pillow at night and out my
window see past the spooky-empty limbs to the Clinic looming
and ominous three blocks away, like a great spaceship humming
at all hours, a darkened white sky behind, thousands of yellow-
lit windows waiting as the air ambulance descends, I don't in the
moments before I pronounce my peace mantra and sleep finds
me, worry much. I read in the newspaper that Minnesota boasts
the highest "stay rate" in the entire Great Lakes region. A perfect *anywhere for anybody anytime.* A longed-for balance of randomness and non-insistent *hereness.* So that when all is said and
done—which will one day be said and done—it may even be a
suitable *here* for me. A last grab at happiness.

EVEN BEFORE PAUL AND I CAN EXIT THE COMANCHE MALL LOT,
he has required I drive him "home," and right in the car gone
to his iPhone, called Mayo Integrative Enhancement, and arranged for an at-home, one-on-one stretch, strengthen and
meditate session—this afternoon—with his favorite therapist,
Miss Wanda Stiffler, RN, MPT. (The Clinic has made this
service available as part of his study.) Nurse Wanda is a horsey,
jolly, 40-ish bottle-blond, a rough-handed, Marlboro-smoking
miner's daughter from Biwabik, Minnesota, who sings in an all-
female polka band where she imitates a trumpet using her lips,
and when she is in our house, puts Paul through punishing paces

in behalf of restoring top-notch physical and mental health—
which doesn't really work. (For these interludes I am never invited.) Wanda came down to the Cities for her nurse's degree
after 9/11, got channeled into "neuro-degenerative," for which
she has a genius, then got hired by Mayo before she could make
it back to Biwabik. After which, somehow twenty years went by.
Every week Wanda shows up at our house wearing pink scrubs,
squeegee nurse shoes and piled-up hair, smelling of cigarettes
and winking at me when I let her in. "Su. Howz-uh-pee-shunt-
dewin-tuh-dee?" ("So, how's our patient doing today?") I've
seen the "Don't Tread on Me" coiled-snake sticker on her Jetta
parked on the street—which titillates Paul since he's never met
such a person and likes pretending being around her is dangerous. He's also mentioned—because he can't bear *not* to mention
it—that Nurse Wanda might be coaxed into a complimentary
"fister" if he plays his cards right. To which I've explained he
could immediately lose his Clinic privileges, be blacklisted as a
disabled pervert, and end up the only Al's patient in the Rochester city jail. I'm sure Wanda would just laugh, give him a poke
in the shoulder, a squinty Biwabik evil eye, and possibly a "you-
guyz. Gimme a breek-okee . . ." Though it's not inconceivable
she might decide to oblige.

Paul also this afternoon has re-enrolled in a Clinic-sponsored
ALS "sharers webinar" (words he relishes) in which ALS patients
from all over everywhere (Kiev to Encino), in various stages of
affliction, rehash their life stories to a computer screen full of
other patients' faces and, in the process, "revealing context" is
provided for the isolation and helplessness ALS sufferers almost
all fall victim to no matter if Mother Teresa and Jonas Salk were
looking after them.

I have not sat in on these sessions, but ALS webinars can't
be much different from AA meetings: perfect if you're the one

doing the confessing, but returns diminish when you're sitting silently fuming about how none of this shit matches *your situation*, and planning all you're going to say when it's *your* turn, while pretending to listen, "be supportive," and not seem angry when how can you *not* be.

Paul has been "reported" (twice) for making his fellow ALS sufferers "uneasy" with his personal views. Making others uneasy isn't supposed to happen, since ALS patients are already uncomfortable enough. One of the web moderators suggested via my "patient support portal" that Paul not log in *quite* so often and opt instead for a tele-course in meditation. Though if he elects to attend, again it's understood he should remember that everybody's experience of devastating neuro-degenerative disease is not uniform. (Paul, I think, is not as empathetic as he might be.) He told one group of webinar sharers—many of whom are immobilized, belted into space-age motorized wheel-chairs, frowning at their screens, unable to express how grate-ful they are except in robot voices—that to him the experience of "finding out" he had this dread disease was like being in an airplane and realizing the engine had gone silent, and just being up there waiting for gravity to take over and the plunge to com-mence. "It wasn't all that bad," he told them. "I sorta enjoyed it. It felt authentic." It was after this that he was invited to attend less regularly. Today he's being given a second chance, following a promise to participate less and be more collegial. He's eager to try. I'm not sure why.

Though I will say this in my son's defense—he, whom I look to each day now, whose meals I struggle to cook, whose jokes I struggle to laugh at, whose private often alarming furies I of-ten overhear, whose farts and BMs I sniff, whose sleep I nightly monitor for signs of continued life, whose clothes I wash, whose hostilities I fend off, whose faltering gait I steady, whose falls I (try to) catch but often can't, whose persistent life I wonder at more and more, until I think *I* will vanish when he vanishes—I will say that when one is dying, one's life is not *like* others' lives, even those who may be dying in the same room or on the same screen. Web facilitators want us to believe everything is sharable; misery likes company, etc. But in these weeks we've been alone together, joined unwillingly at the heart, I believe Paul has done his best, yet is also passing through all of it alone, even with me here—maybe especially with me here. A great man said that everybody knows what light is, but it is difficult to *say* what light is. This goes double ditto when the subject is not light but darkness.

Consequently, I understand why private nurses torture old widows, and starve and stick pins in the toes of comatose millionaires. Caregivers all get a snootful. Dying makes the nondying feel excluded and shabby, since dying's struggle is like no other. Long ago, when I was a doomed-to-fail scribbler of mid-century American short stories of the sort that showed up in *The New Yorker*, written by John Cheever and John Updike (mine never did even once), I practiced the "rule" taught me in my writing course at Michigan, which stipulated that inserting a death into a fragile short story was never permitted, since death must have importance proportional to the life that's ended, and short stories, my teacher believed, weren't good at relating the vastness of human life. This was the novel's province. And since I wasn't particularly good at instilling outsize importance to characters in *any* form, my fate was settled. But now, since I've had of late more and more business with both big "D" *and* little "d" death, I've concluded my teacher's rule was wrong. It isn't life that's well-nigh unfathomable and in need of amplification and more light. For life, there's plenty of data to work with since we all have one. It's *death* that's the profound mystery and the real story. Think about it—as I often do, listening to my son's breathing through each night's pre-eminent hours, able to participate only by thinking I am dying alongside him. Strangely, I've never felt I have less in common with him than in these days and weeks of his evanescence. Even though I can say I know him much better, I have never had less a "relationship," never been more in the dark about how he thinks and feels about things. It is not so different from contemplating outer space, which we try to conjure but really can't. As dank old Heidegger puts it, only a full awareness of death (which you only get one way) makes one able to appreciate the fullness and mystery of being. Boolah, boolah.

IT'S NOW TEN PAST TWO IN THE CENTRAL TIME ZONE. THE threatened Alberta clipper from the morning has sagged south, and snow has ceased. Late-winter sun is painful off the passing windshields as I drive out 52 North to A Fool's Paradise RV Rentals. It's still frigid as Nome, but plenty of Rochesterites are heading to the Cities for a pre-Valentine's dinner. I wish I were.

There are now fewer than two hours of useable daylight available to me here at forty-four degrees north latitude. I have never been a proficient time manager. Though as my son's caregiver I'm called upon to manage time in such a way as to seem *not* to manage it—since diurnal time matters little to him and yet is precious. Paul will soon be in Nurse Wanda's neurodegeneratively capable hands—'til four—then in his sufferingsouls webinar 'til 5:30 (unless he's booted out). At which point it'll be dark as midnight, and he and I can switch on the news, order a pizza, and I can try again to sell him on the Mount Rushmore trip, after which we'll close down the day in the living room with a game of cornhole, which Paul plays from his wheel-chair and was never very good at to begin with, but now is hope-less even with his good left arm, spraying the bags all over as if that was the point. I believe, in truth, he only plays to have a chance to say cornhole over and over.

For years, Paul has cultivated a wish (rich and variegated) that he and I together rent an RV and travel to all the towns in America with names he considers hilarious and thus requiring a visit. Whynot, Mississippi. Stinking Springs, New Mexico. Cheat Falls, West Virginia. Cape Flattery, Washington. Froid, Montana. Sopchoppy, Florida. Horseheads, New York. Ending up in Carefree, AZ, where he can buy a "tiny house" and live forever. There are a great many of these towns when you go look-ing for them.

When he learned the dire extent of his illness and we'd ar-rived in Rochester to begin his experimental study, he began to advocate again for our long-postponed trip, which he calls the Flying Dutchman Tour and believes Al's was invented for, since once you get to the end, there's nothing there. All's in the ride, not the arrival. It is half fantasy and mostly for laughs, like many things that go on in his head which he seems to take se-riously. Nonetheless he has found a used RV rental in the *Post Bulletin*. And we can "embark," he believes, the minute his Bor-ders of Science Medical Pioneers Meet & Greet is over (tomor-row) and strike out for Stinking Springs, which has namesakes in three adjoining states—Utah, Wyoming, and Colorado, with two for good measure in New Mexico and California. All of which makes him happy.

I unwillingly must play the bad cop here and have told Paul such an expedition is a no-go. For one thing, it would take us the rest of our already shortened lives. Second, he's not up to it, and neither am I. Getting him around is already problematic—

which he acknowledges. And such a voyage could spell disaster—broken down on a wintry Wyoming snowscape, beyond cell service, leagues from medical care, poorly clothed, weak and with no survival skills.

My substitute Mount Rushmore plan boasts, on the other hand, simplicity, brevity and common sense as selling points. Rent the RV at the place he wants—A Fool's Paradise—a roadside emporium we've visited once and where one finds for-sale-or-rent golf carts, septic tanks, porta-potties, snowmobiles, cherry pickers, enormous American flags, blank grave monuments, waterslide parts and an array of 25 used RVs set out in rows in the frozen snow. Paul can choose whichever RV rig he wants. And the minute his Medical Pioneer event's over, we can load up and set off for Mount Rushmore in South Dakota, making stops at whatever loony sights we find (I've done online researches). There's the "World's Only Corn Palace" in Mitchell, SD, where my parents stopped off in our sole transcontinental junket in 1954, and of which I have good memories. There's Elvis's Harley—on display in Murdo. There are any number of dinosaur parks. There's Wall Drug. A tractor museum. A genuine Crow Indian reservation. A Minuteman Missile National Historic Site in Philip. Plus the Badlands. Ending south of Rapid City at the site of the four presidents' visages, hammered into a mountain like Stone-Age marionettes. "Tells the story of the entire nation," Rushmore.gov says. "It's what it means to be an American," etc. It's not Cheat Falls or Stinking Springs, but for outlandishness it's in the ballpark, and best of all it can be accomplished in +/- three days, weather permitting. I do all the driving.

So far, Paul's remained noncommittal, not liking that it's my idea instead of his, as if I'm taking over and tricking him into something inappropriately serious. Dying is the last of his life's great escapades and the last he would want to undertake with ill-fitting spirits. In this way he aspires to be full of life more than anyone I know—death being nothing you'd think could ever befall him.

And yet. I must be cautious that our trip doesn't morph into the emblem of his entire, foreshortened life. One more thing to flee from. In as much as there aren't many chances left to do things right.

As I said, we've already made one prospecting visit to A Fool's Paradise—last week. Paul, struggling on his tripod, in his Chiefs parka, wobbling heavy-footed through the snowy ranks of rent-able rigs, gawking inside many of these beasts, followed along by the owner, Mr. Engvall (Pete, an enormous African-American in a Minnesota Gophers hoodie, who might've played tackle for the maroon and gold). Paul told him we were here "interviewing rigs" and declared a preference for the older C-type vintage campers (he knows these terms), bargy old clunkers bolted onto truck chassis, not conspicuously road-worthy. "Authenticity," Paul announced, was again the gold standard. The one he liked best was an old beige behemoth with a faded aqua ocean wave on its side, and "Windbreaker" painted-on long ago in red, the whole outfit fastened onto a red Dodge 1500 with Florida plates—the green and white ones with the oranges. On the rear window a translucent sticker read "In Loving Memory of Norm Cepeda."

I stood by on the snowpack in freezing temps, late-winter gloom descending under the lot's strung-up lights, while Paul strained to see inside (he couldn't manage the metal steps but didn't want help). Mr. Engvall shined a giant flashlight into the interior.

"Awesome. Fucking awesome," Paul said, then glared around at me as if I was discouraging something, which I had no thought of doing. "It's all built-in inside," he said, shuffling around below the open doorway. "Everything's accessible. Space is the limiting factor—but not really." He flashed around at me again. "Don't you think it's fuckin' great?"

"I do," I said. "It's great. Awesome's the word. Are you okay with how old it is?"

"They don't make these units anymore. I prefer 'em," Pete Engvall said. He was a tall, broad-shouldered, wide-body with dead, protuberant eyes and a bulwark forehead. His wife, he'd said, was an oncology nurse at the Clinic. Her father, Gunnar—a man with a literary bent—founded the RV business in '68, and he—Pete—had had the idea to add the golf carts, the cherry pickers, the flags, etc. He was tired of it now, had purchased a prefab home in Arizona. He wanted to buy a franchise. Possibly a Jiffy Lube or a donut shop.

"I should own this," Paul said, regarding the Windbreaker admiringly. "Drive it to Alaska and stay there."

"You can drive it to Alaska. If you want to," Pete Engvall said. "You can *own* it. I'll make you two a good deal."

"With my girlfriend, Cheryl, not him." Meaning me. I didn't know about Cheryl. Paul is close to the vest about his love interests, as if he wasn't supposed to have any. I would've liked to hear more. Possibly she could've been brought on board for the trip. If she existed.

"O-*kay*," Pete Engvall said and gave me a wry who's-he-kiddin' smile.

Paul looked at me—again threateningly. His upper lip bore ice from his nose, and his smudged glasses had slipped forward. It was ten degrees and murky dark on the lot. He was gripping the chrome handhold on the Windbreaker's side panel. We'd reached some sort of impasse, as if all we could do was stare at things.

"Who's this Norm Cepeda?" Paul said.

"Yeah. No. Couldn't tell ya," Pete Engvall said, pulling his Gophers hoodie lower over his forehead and stoving his big gloved hands together for warmth. "I guess he died. Down in Florida. His daughter lives in Red Wing. I bought it off her." I of course could only think of the old San Francisco firsty and Cooperstown enshrinee, Orlando "Cha-cha" Cepeda—an all-timer as well as an ex–dope smuggler in his native Ponce, PR. Engvall might've known about him, but Paul wouldn't.

"*Windbreaker*," Paul said, speculatively. "That's a riot. Ppptt-tttp." He made a wet fart noise with his lips and leered at me.

"I guess," Engvall said. "Can't blame me. I didn't name it. I just rent 'em."

"Ppptttttp. Stroke of genius." Paul made his fart noise once more. After which we started back to the car, no decision being made about anything.

ON OUR RIDE BACK TO TOWN, A LOW WHITE CLOUD-SKY BLOCK-ing the winter moon, Paul fell into a funk—possibly over the Flying Dutchman being a no-go. We were heading for Minne-sota Pizza across the river.

"I won't be able to drive that piece of shit," he said about the Windbreaker. "We waited too long now."

"Sure you can," I said. "I'll pull us off on a country road in South Dakota and hand you the reins. You can do it. Farm kids drive when they're four."

"I'm not four. Age isn't a state of mind." He shot his eyes narrowly toward me to see if I was in on this. "It needs to have one of those lifts to get me in."

"I'll hire a mule team."

He fell mute as we turned off 52 onto 2nd, which took us to South Broadway, from which we could cross the river to our pizza place. Early-evening February traffic was dense and slowing, headlights igniting the road ice. "Soooo saaad," Paul said. "Something we could do together. Did you know Lou Gehrig spoke German to his parents?"

"I did know that."

"He went to Columbia. He didn't finish."

"He didn't need to." Something smelled musty inside the car. His clothes. His knees were jinking. I thought he might be feeling bad and wanted to forget our pizza. "Who's Cheryl?"

"A reference librarian at home." In a high-pitched, put-on hysterical falsetto, he said, "She sees me for who I really am. Or was once. I'll never get laid now."

"Are you hurting?"

"Two football fields." Meaning he wasn't feeling that bad. Five football fields was serious. "That guy Engvall. How come he's Black? He's a dunce."

"I don't think he's a dunce. He's Black because the lord made him that way. Same for you. He just has a Norwegian name."

"Fur, fur, fur, that's what Midwesterners say when they mean *for*. He said that. Fur, fur, fur. Same *fur* you. I'm here *fur* the kielbasy."

"He liked you," I said.

"Did you explain I was sick? Pete. Pete. Petey. Pete. Peter. Pete."

"You're not *sick* sick," I said. "You're something else."

"And vhat vould *that* be," he said in his Bela Lugosi voice. "Vhat! Ptray tell vould you zay zhat *I am*? Don't speak in Hungarian. You'll haf only vun chance to answer."

"You're a douchebag. Do you want to go to Mount Rushmore with me in the Windbreaker?"

"You were probably going anyway." He looked out into the hissing evening traffic. His right hand was trembling. "Did you know trained dogs can smell Al's? They use them in Canada at all ports of entry. For quarantine."

"Just tell me when you make up your mind about going. Okay?"

"Did you ever imagine you'd live this long, Lawrence?"

"No. I really didn't."

"Your life hasn't been hard enough. Do you ever think that?"

"There's still time for it to get harder." Which I knew would shut him up. It almost did.

"Ooooo yeah," he said. "You got dat right."

After which we went on to dinner.

———

A FOOL'S PARADISE, AS I DRIVE INTO THE LOT TODAY, SEEMS smaller in the freezing afternoon light than a week ago. Its string of bulbs on the highway frontage isn't lit—only a crappy sign-on-wheels sits parked in the roadside snow, advertising "Big Valentine's Bargains." Unclear what these might be. The RVs extend back into a snowy scrub field like boats at anchor, all with this morning's snow shining on their windshields. Far in the back are piles of last season's Christmas trees and a corrugated Quonset where all things weather-sensitive are stored. An American flag as big as Utah hangs on a pole in front. It is a blasted place. Nothing seems to be going on.

The office cabin is off to the left with a car at the side and smoke curling from a metal chimney. I hadn't noticed the next-door neighbors are a GUNZ shop, and an ADULT OUTLET with "toys" and "risky" videos for sale. Customer cars are parked in front of both. It is choice commercial acreage. In a year a Best Buy or a Trader Joe's could be up—Pete Engvall and his wife off to Tempe.

I'm only here to get a closer look at the Windbreaker—to determine its suitability for our trip and the weather, and to fill out the paperwork to be ready for tomorrow, if Paul agrees. A decision about *something* seems called for.

Pete Engvall is not here, it turns out. Instead, his cute, petite Mayo oncology-nurse wife is behind the owner's desk when I step in out of the butchering cold, to where it's a blast furnace indoors—a fierce little Jotul in the corner, the heat source. In her pink Clinic scrubs, she is as wiry-blondie-hawkish as Pete is a stolid slab of obsidian. She, though—Krista (her little desk plaque says)—is undoubtably glad to miss a morning of jabbing needles in people and filling them full of toxins to make them well.

"Oh, he's out at the lake," Krista says, when I say I'm looking for Mr. Engvall, shaking her head at the scandal of it. "Put that boy in an ice hut with a bottle of schnapps and some cheap cigars, and don't look for him 'til dark. It's good, though. The winter can take a toll on you." The wall behind her contains a big fake-looking stuffed muskellunge (a whole stuffed mallard duck in its mouth) above a small gallery of framed star-quality photos. Pete in shorts holding a similar fish, on a dock on a lake in summer. Pete—thinner in Army camos, a laughing-tongue T-shirt and a green beret—grinning with his M16, beside an armored personnel carrier. Krista, also in desert fatigues (flak jacket, sidearm, helmet), smiling into the sun from the open flap of a tent. Gorgeous but lethal. On both sides, on framed green velvet, are medals and ribbons these citizen warriors have brought home. The best America has to offer. I expect to see a signed glossy of 'W' Bush, grinning with plundered authority. But there isn't one. There is, though, a framed realty license above a photo of Krista in front of an Edina office. They are no doubt moderate Republicans. Nervous about taxes and America's standing, but not bothered if an immigrant buys A Fool's Paradise and replaces it with a Chili's.

"My son and I looked at an RV to rent a week ago," I say. "Mr. Engvall showed it to us. I just want to have a second look in the daylight." I nod to portray total transparency. Republicans often suspect you're trying to cheat them even if they know you.

"Go for it!" Krista says, beaming. "You head right on out there. I'll give you the keys. Which one is it?"

"It's one of the oldies. It's the Windbreaker."

"Vintages are the best," she says, swiveling round to a wall box I hadn't noticed, which when opened reveals rows of hooks hung with keys. "What's the license?"

"I don't know. It's from Florida."

"Florida?" She casts a surprised smile back over her shoulder as if something was naughty about Florida. "We oughta be down *there* today, shouldn't we?"

"We should," I say.

"I'm in maxillary-oncology at the Clinic, and there's a Mayo in Jacksonville. I go down there to teach the nurses sometimes. But I'm partial to this one. They're all good, though."

"My son's being treated here." More like *studied*, like a gerbil.

"Great," Krista says, nose in the key box. I'm already sweating in my Kara Koram and wool cap. "They'll fix him up," she says into the box. "What's he got?"

"I hope so." No reason to tell everything.

"Here. Key, key, key, key, where are you, you stinker? Ah! Okay. Florida. Right where I couldn't find you, right in front of me." She swivels back, holding up a key fob in the shape of a day-glo pink fish, as if she was holding a mouse by its tail. "Two thousand eleven Dodge Ram 1500 club cab. Which has a little back seat," not getting up, reaching the key across her desk, where there's an open copy of *Elle*. "It's on Valentine's special. Twenty percent off if you keep it a week."

"I might not," I say.

"Whatever." She winks, shakes her head in mock surprise. She doesn't renounce her good spirits easily. "I didn't hear you say what your son has."

"He has ALS."

"Oh, wow!" Her pretty, sparkling face grows diagnostic and serious. Only full awareness of death makes one able to appreciate the fullness and mystery of being. "*Thaaat's* a biggy. I'll give you the 20 off." She swivels to close the key cupboard. "Pete had a daughter when I met him." Her back is to me. "*And* a wife. We met in the Army. Iraq numero uno. Both of us Minnesotans. Never intended it to go anywhere." She turns and smiles at me glamorously from behind the desk. "Then Janelle got killed. A school shooting in St. Cloud—way before the Red Lake one. His marriage didn't survive *that*. One day he just called up down here." Her tongue point makes a tour around her cheek to certify emotion. "Out in the gloom you can usually find some lights on."

"I guessed you two'd been married forever." They could hardly be more unlikely.

"In dog's years we have." Krista rolls her eyes. "Feels like it sometimes. Mr. . . . ?"

"Bascombe. Frank."

"Frank Bascombe. All-American name. I don't suppose you're looking for a house to buy."

"Not right now, no."

"I do a little of everything." She points up to her realtor's license without looking at it. "What's your son's name?" She's giving me her 'truly interested smile,' offered to all wayward souls needing consolation, including Pete Engvall. It is a wonderful smile.

"Paul."

"I bet *he's* a card."

"That's exactly what he is."

"And I'm sure you love him."

"I do." I should leave this instant. But I don't.

"Go check out your RV, Frank. Then come back and we'll dicker."

It's the old realtor's rib-tickler from when jokes were legal. 'Bring your wife in and we'll dick 'er.' Gone forever.

"Okay," I say. "I will." And I'm quick out the door back into the frozen world.

———

OUT ACROSS THE HARD SNOW UNDER THE ENORMOUS FLAG, THE office heat has rendered me light-headed, sweaty hands icy, cold going down into my chest, as I pass cherry pickers, an embankment of piled plastic and concrete septics, five new Ski-Doos, a collection of reconditioned porta-potties with different names. "Thrones of Minnesota." "We're #2." "Bide-o-wee." Paul would love this. The golf carts, more big flags, the grave monuments, possibly a tank, some surface-to-air missiles and a mini-sub are all stored in the Quonset in case the coming election goes sideways—which it might. It's colder out here amid the paraphernalia and the ordnance. High in the frozen blue a Delta commuter etches a clean white scar across the empty sphere.

The Windbreaker is no trouble to find back where the lot becomes field. Like everything else seen twice, it's assumed a more human scale—friendlier and more shipshape. I will have no trouble piloting it. I make a cursory entry-up into the camper box, where the air is dead and refrigeratorish and propane-smelling—and colder. Window light leaking in does nothing to make things cozy. Inside, I identify only one would-be bed—a Formica bench that doubles as a settee and also as a table, but you could sleep on it. Possibly there's a second bed disguised as something else, but I don't see it. The "kitchen" is only two pony-size electric rings on a pony-size particle-board surface. The head is across from the outside door, so users must renounce privacy. The floor is white-flecked blue linoleum, and the whole inside is finished in a pale asylum brown that's not really a color.

The Windbreaker is, in other words, nothing close to a 2-man rig; especially if one man is constantly banging into things and in increasing need of assistance. The only convenience is it'd be impossible to fall all the way down once you got in. Though if you succeeded in falling, you'd need EMS help to get up and out. These aspects of RV life Paul hasn't thought through. My Honda would be worlds better but would have no Flying Dutch-man affiliation.

But if later tonight, during our cornhole match, I reveal to him the Windbreaker is only a one-man deal—lonely souls on lonely missions—he could easily nix my whole project. One more illustration of why we don't do what we don't do. Clearly it is not essential that we rent this piece of crap and drive it to Mount Rushmore. But approaching the theater of lasts, it seems critical to try to make this work, since I'm running out of ideas for what we can do after tomorrow. We could stand pat. But we mustn't stand pat.

My feet are now two ice ingots. I clamber back down onto the frozen turf. Most of the other RVs, in daylight, are newer and nicer and have names like "Interceptor," "Monarch," "Molester." American recreational nomenclature. Though they lack the authenticity Paul requires.

I go round and with my key open the Dodge's driver door and climb up and in, where it's even more freezing and stiff, my living breath instantly misting the windshield. It reeks of cigarettes, and there are Dos Equis cans and paper trash on the floor. But it is not truly uncomfortable to be in behind the big steering wheel. The leather seats are spacious, front and even the back, the instrumentation newish and curved like a fighter jet. All is compact and expansive at once. I have never sat in such a machine.

For some reason, I open the glove box, expecting to find I don't know what. A pistol? A treasure map? A severed hand? Here are papers, documents, an owner's guide, a box of Life-Styles in assorted shades and flavors—one is missing. Here is an official order to appear in Osceola County Court on May 4th, 2012, issued to a Lorenza Amelia Cepeda. Here is mail to "Señora Cepeda," who once apparently lived in Kenansville, and does not open letters from an M. Jeffers, in Lake Wales, or from the Kenansville public defender, or from the Osceola County Department of child welfare, or from the Granite State Life Insurance Company of Concord, NH 03301. Where Señora Cepeda might be today, only god knows. Red Wing? I silently wish her clearer sailing and return her papers to the box where she left them.

I use my key to give the big Dodge a cold crank. It can't have been turned over recently unless Pete Engvall makes rounds to keep the batteries up, which I doubt. What, I wish I knew, would 1500 stand for? The big mill, though, after several T. rex metal-on-metal noises (no oil at the top, sleepy lifters, a solenoid doing whatever . . .), somehow fires off. The radio blasts on, as does the defrost—Arctic air singeing my face. It's clamorous and nerve-shattering and slightly terrifying for an instant, before

I get things turned off, and the motor begins issuing clickety-clickety noises, then calms to a rumblous idle. I give the engine a couple of revs, drop the lever into "D", the transmission clunks, and the wheels lurch, splitting ice under the tires. It is an intimidating but empowering, ultra-American-made-to-be-simple sensation to awaken such a beast, but one I believe I can handle, possibly even like. Pete Engvall can get it warmed up for us tomorrow, fill the reservoirs, check the vitals, clean it up. There's a 4-wheel knob—how hard can that be to operate? We can buy an air sanitizer and turn everything coconut, which will thrill my son. I'll only need to persuade Paul not to venture into the camper where he'll freeze to death or damage himself. A Best Western or a Hilton Garden will best address all our human needs. None of this is different from selling a house, where you substitute the house you *have* for the house the client thinks he wants. An optimist, I've read, is a person who believes the inevitable is what's supposed to happen.

———

WHEN I TRAMP BACK ACROSS TO THE OFFICE, NURSE KRISTA HAS her coat on for her three p.m. Clinic shift. Her yellow Smart car is idling outside. Her winter garb over her scrubs is a pink down vest and pink bunny-fur booties. They know how to dress for the weather. Doubtless there are no-nonsense undergarments involved.

She is still in buoyant spirits, which she probably is every day—her oncology patients keen for her arrival, loving it that she's an Iraq vet, loving it that she's so cute *and* good *and* skillful. I love it as well, though it is baking in here.

"Pete the mighty fisherman hasn't bothered to call in," she

says, blue eyes sparkling merrily. "Toooo much fun out there freezing his little black buns off. I need to close 'er down, here, Frank. How'd you like it?"

"It's good. We'll take it." Agreeing to all. I'll be lucky not to get a headache in here. I'm slightly out of breath, as if something was exciting me.

"O-*kay*!" Krista says, hunting for her office keys.

"Can you let Mr. Engvall know I'll pick the truck up tomorrow around noon. If he'd service and clean it and warm it up. I'll do the paperwork when I get here with my son." There's also the matter of the promised Valentine 20 percent. Though it's enough just to be back here in close quarters with Krista— Army nurse.

"Petey'll prolly give it to you for nothing, when I tell him about your son. Which'll be circa two a.m., when we have our Drambuie, once I get home from work. He's not a champeen sleeper since his daughter died. His brain gets full of stuff. Which is why he goes fishin'." She widens her eyes to imply that's not all that happens at two a.m., which I'm happy to know, if true.

"That's not necessary," I say—about the freebie, though I won't say no.

"Do you have a wife someplace, Frank?" Krista's going about shutting the vents on the Jotul, which is making the place a kiln. She is now all business. "I mean, you know, to look after your son." She stands up straight, her pixie features bearing profound nurse impartiality. Women are incalculable in all that they can supply, then take away in the span of one heartbeat.

"I've got wives in a couple of places. Not one that's here."

"I get it. At least *you're* here, though," Krista says. Krista and Pete. Solid. Grateful. Optimistic. Plausibly interracial. Faith-based in all likelihood, but private about it. "I got to get 'er going here," she says. "I'll tell Mr. Nibs you'll be here at noon tomorrow. He'll have that old Windbreaker hot to trot." Nothing about the name seems amusing to her. Minnesotans think different things are funny.

"Okay," I say. "That's great." And we are done. Quickly. Krista and me. She might as well be Pete.

"Ready to face the elephants?" Krista's pulling on bunny-fur gloves. It's her daily funny-boner for her Clinic patients, no matter the dire elephants that lie ahead for them.

"All ready," I say, holding back the door—and am off, crucial issues settled. Half of tomorrow's project sealed if not yet signed and delivered. If only my son will say yes.

———•———

PHASE TWO OF MY AFTERNOON'S ANTICIPATIONS WILL BENEFIT from comment as I head north through Rochester's commercial fringe (a Microtel, a giant Kia dealer, a marooned Verizon store). Sun has already tucked into the western tree lines, and shadows fall sideways onto the highway. Most Minnesota drivers have their brights on at three p.m.—narrowing the chances of interacting with a deer as exurbia thins and farm acreage takes over. All around would be blanketed by genetically altered corn if all around weren't blanketed in snow.

Spending most all of one's waking hours with someone who's dying—even if that someone is your son—*should* demand at least *some* attention to one's own prerogatives. (Liberal do-gooders of course would disagree.) The week we arrived—just before Christmas—I attended the optional "new caregivers" colloquium in a sustainably oak-paneled, ultra-nonaggressive Mayo conference room, where I and other Al's family units were gloomily assembled. Most of the other family members seemed more wretched than I was, but all pretended to be chatty and upbeat so as not to start howling and teeth-gnashing about all that can't be done for the someone they love. My role, for reasons I can't explain, fell to offering myself as the positivist everyman, taking in all views, nodding, making quips, writing salient "thoughts" into a moleskin notebook, squinting, posing unnecessary questions that inevitably began with "I see . . ." "I see. So body vigilance actually *can* play a role . . . ?" Other families may have suspected I was a Mayo shill, but were glad to have me there to resent, instead of themselves—or, worse, their unlucky loved ones. Grief, Sally Caldwell told me before she flew the coop, can be a paradox.

In session one (I lasted for two) our facilitator, Miss Duling, a sharp, petite, green-eyed lady in her '70s—like me—in an orange-flowered dress, with a doily of white hair and a Mayo name tag that said "Compassion Consultant" on her red jacket, told our group we were all to "Take care of *ourselves* as well as our afflicted member. Don't be an extension"—a conspirator's smile—"of the someone else's dying. This can be a form of," (You guessed it.) "sublimated selfishness." "Try to use time for personal betterment. Set goals in the present—though it may seem odd to set goals with someone who won't be around. Goals, of course, need not be long-range. Demote the importance of the past. It's your life, too." She even quoted that scrofulous old faker Faulkner (I was the only family member who recognized him) when she said, "There is no *was*. There is only *is*." I wrote a lot of this down but so far have not done much to apply the lessons.

On this late sun-lost Tuesday afternoon—very much in Miss Duling's good, self-preservative spirit—I'm making my way in a hurry out to Vietnam-Minnesota Hospitality. The name doesn't immediately declare itself as a massage establishment, but it *is*, occupying a spacious prosperous-looking white-clapboard Minnesota farm-family house (once, the Pieter Amdahl Organic Dairy) off Highway 52 North on Provender Road, prominent on a hill above the corn rows, midway between Rochester and Zumbrota. As I grow older, less and less seems incongruous.

I came upon VMH the week Paul and I arrived, while browsing through the *Post Bulletin*'s "services" section, for a place to get my headlights re-aligned. The VMH ad said, "Vietnamese Massage Specialty. Women and Men Welcome. Locally Owned. Friendly. Reliable. Safe."

It may or may not go without saying, but I have never before patronized a massage establishment. As close as I came was once, in the Marines, visiting a cathouse called El Burro in Ensenada—my only "sex trade" exposure. (Why all six of us didn't die of the black death only god can explain.) On the outskirts of Haddam, far down Route 1 toward Trenton, there have always been strip-mall storefronts with signs advertising "spas" and "full service massage," which everyone knew the deal about. Several times, Divorced Men's Club members let it slip they'd "partaken"—usually in the throes of poisonous divorce or spousal-death bereavement. They admitted finding these visits surprisingly "just the thing" to uncap the pressures and stresses of modern post-marital life. Though they were typically skimpy on details. Was it a real massage? Was it a quicky? Was it the whole nine yards with all the Thanksgiving trimmings? (Information you burned to know but out of manly delicacy never asked.) "Okay, Bascombe, just go on out there. See what you think. You make of it what you make of it." Wink, wink. One member, Flip Baxter, even gave me a gift certificate for Christmas, a card that bore pink lotus-flower filigree along the bottom, and that you could get punched every visit. Like Starbucks.

I never went. Though not out of any sense that going was wrong. I don't believe it's wrong. It's not the world's oldest profession—next to politics—because it fails to serve a vital human need. Most acts that carry ethical stigma need to be periodically re-evaluated.

The reason I never "partook" was, of course, simple fear. Fear I'd get mugged and left dead in a dumpster. Fear I'd venture in, lose my nerve, get confused, then not know how to get out (like a fun house). Fear that though all these establishments are nominally *run* by Asians, they're actually *owned* by Union County Italians in cahoots with the cops. Such places must "agree" to be occasionally raided, and all customers—judges, Sunday school teachers, gastroenterologists, prison guards, farriers, furriers and realtors—herded out, shirt-less and wild-haired in a miserable perp walk, then hauled off for processing in West Windsor. Later they're turned loose to go home and silently commit seppuku in the hot tub.

Why we don't do what we don't do is also often for a good reason.

I will admit that once, on a drive home from Pete Lorenzo's spaghetti slinger in Trenton, I took a jug handle at Province Line Road, swung back south down Highway 1, and pulled into the lot of Little Saigon Tulip Massage, between Bennie's Grinders and an out-of-business RadioShack. This was when Sally Caldwell had first departed for Chechnya, and I was feeling dull and desperate and in need of what I decided was "company."

The storefront (there were pink lights on upstairs) was as ordinary as a shoe repair, only with thick blackout curtains masking the windows and a red neon sign that said "Massage—Open." It was past dusk, a humid July, New Jersey Friday evening. Locusts were humming. Traffic on Route 1 teemed northward. A couple of darkened cars were parked in front. Nothing seemed overtly libidinal, though I knew $80 (which I happened to have in my pocket) would get me anything I wanted. I could easily *just do it*, I thought, as a blameless alternative to doing nothing. Many must do it for that reason—like joining the Navy.

As I sat there, socketed in my Crown Vic in the vernal darkness, the front door of the Little Saigon Tulip opened (behind it was another light-suppressing curtain) and out stepped two enormously fat men—young men, it seemed to me. Men in their twenties. They could've been twins. They weren't laughing or staggering drunk or even animated or talking. Just stolidly exiting the place as if they'd stopped by to pay for some half soles. Nothing about watching them from the darkened cockpit of my car seemed strange or erotically charged. In fact, it felt encouraging that these two had someplace to go to have their own human needs attended to, as unoffending as their human needs probably were. A simple massage, in all likelihood.

This was, for me, an ideal outcome to having turned around, come back, given the whole enterprise a once-over, then deciding against it. I felt no sense of superiority; only separateness—which I felt anyway. When the two big boys, who'd come together, fitted themselves into their Explorer, backed around and eased out into the lights-blazing traffic flow of Route 1, I followed behind them like a squad car, right into the southbound lane, their two round heads silhouetted in the front seat. I could tell they'd begun talking as they headed toward Trenton. I, however, made the right at McGinty Lane and took the long back way up to Haddam, feeling less desperate and dull, and actually, unexpectedly upbeat. It doesn't take much, it turns out, to improve one's attitude.

Vietnam-Minnesota Hospitality, it should first be said, is nothing like Little Saigon Tulip. For one thing it's in Minnesota not New Jersey, which means it's on the other side of the moon. Second, I can drive out to VMH every week, sometimes twice, for an actual massage (though I'm not sure how "Vietnamese" these massages are except that apparently Vietnamese people give them). Third, VMH is truly family, not mafia-run. The owners, the Tran family from nearby Kiester, Minnesota, are fourth-generation Vietnamese arrivers, having escaped certain death in Saigon, in 1968, and are now as all-American as Betty Crocker. In Kiester, where grandfather Tran was "inserted" by our State Department in 1970, the Trans have much more than prospered; they've massively flourished in fifty years of small-town Minnesota habitation. They own the movie theater—the "Key" (for Kiester)—plus the town's only Shop 'n Save. They own a Motel 6 in Albert Lea, two Family Dollars across the line in Iowa. And more's in the works. All the kids and grandkids went to college or could've if they'd wanted to. Grandfather Tran's son Jeff attended Bowdoin and sits on the Faribault County planning commission. One extra-brainy cousin's an anesthesiologist at Mayo. They're all Zion Lutherans and moderate Democrats—having switched from Free Will Baptist and Republican in Reagan's first term. In my own seven weeks of temporary Minnesota residence, I've become a regular and satisfied VMH customer, relentlessly polite, a generous tipper—all but a *familiar*. I pay in greenbacks and am appreciated, respected and accepted as if I was from Minnesota (or Vietnam) myself.

That the Tran family owns Vietnam-Minnesota Hospitality, miles out in the boonies on the way to St. Paul, is nothing that's talked up in Kiester. Though nothing could be more straight-forward and seemly: A valued foreign asset with CIA ties is airlifted out of peril by a grateful America, gets implanted in the worst, most alien place imaginable (in terms of climate and social hierarchies), is generally expected to flounder and likely perish, yet manages—though the first years are admittedly hard—to become (more or less) accepted by the local burghers, rises gradually, eventually triumphing to become mayor or governor or senator (or president). It's not so different from the Andrew Carnegie or the Elizabeth Taylor origin stories. Or the Mike Mahoney saga in Red Bank.

Close-up, of course, little is ever truly simple. My more personal reason for pounding the eighteen miles out to Vietnam-Minnesota Hospitality, in all manner of weather and turbulent frames of mind, has been not that I so admire the Tran family's transit of Venus—though I do; but because I've unexpectedly fallen into something like love with one of the massage "attendants," someone who practices weekly, ardent, life-restoring exactions upon me in the big farmhouse—truly the most wholesome and normal thing in the world—and who, in certain dispositions of light and coquettish humor, seems to "love" me back. Which for me is a bounty.

Yes, yes, yes, yes, yes, yes, yes, yes, *yes!* "I know. *I know-I know.*" Much of life should have quotes around it.

My massage attendant Ms. Betty Duong Tran is the granddaughter of old Byron Lo Duc Tran, long deceased, venerated and imbedded CIA informant who landed in Kiester and made his fortune, etc., etc.

Betty is one of six daughters of Jeff Nguyen Tran (of Bowdoin and the Faribault planning board). At 34, she's earning her business BS at UM Rochester and has sights set for the hospitality industry. These and related subjects are what we mostly talk about while I'm having my massages, which take place in her "studio" upstairs in the previously-Amdahl farmhouse overlooking snow-frozen cornfields south toward Rochester. Inside, she's decorated her walls with a Kirby Puckett Minnesota Twins poster, an "Oof-dah" sign, several framed Ole and Lena cartoons and several romanticized color photos of the Mekong, the Thien Mu Pagoda and emerald rice fields; there's a healthy ficus plant, a wall-mounted defibrillator and a large live-action poster (signed) of yester-year tennis star Boris Becker levitating as he demolishes a ball into atoms with an expression of serene Teutonic resolve on his handsome Krautheimer mug. Plus, there's her laptop and a small Toshiba TV she keeps covered with a tea towel. None of these decor features do I inquire about. Betty herself was born in nearby Austin, Minnesota, and is not an immigrant. But that isn't to say life for her has been a holiday.

As she's working on me—I'm always naked with a red silk dragon drape—we also occasionally yak about her family's history and dauntless ascent, as well as about case studies in her capstone marketing course, focusing on Holiday Inn's controversial decision to re-brand and the time-arc needed for customer loyalty to re-consolidate following an initial period of wandering in the hospitality wilderness, while Hilton, Marriott, Wyndham and Hyatt saw welcome upticks in their market share. These are matters that absorb Betty and that I am semiconversant in because I'm a man who admires commerce. Her life's goal is not for the corporate boardroom—due to a late start in an ill-starred marriage to a Kiester plow-jockey and all-state hockey standout who moved them out to Mankato, where he had a scholarship and NHL aspirations, and somehow precious time got lost. By sheer fortitude, though, she made "a clean break" with Ingemur—no offspring—and was welcomed back into her Kiester family without prejudice. Her long-term career prospectus is to put her UMR degree to work in HR—some "full-service hospital group," or event-planning mega-chain—and try to make people's lot in life better in ways they would never expect. To her, this "sounds like a plan," a phrase I don't like, but I support her as wholeheartedly as our circumstances permit.

How driving out to Provender Road in late December led to a version of love is not that complicated. Love may be the most elusive and untrackable of dwarf galaxies when love is what you lack. But when love arrives and takes up residence on its own, or you take up residence in *it*, love is the most homespun human project—practically overlookable—which is why so many lose track and end up alone.

When my son Paul began his short-course experimental drug trials at Mayo—and we moved into our Mike-Mahoney-securitized home on New Bemidji Street where we now reside—I found myself suffering the completely predictable jimjams of immense, suffocating stress. All efforts at quasi-normal life were so far unavailing. I broxed a hole right through my second bicuspid, and my gums and hair began receding. I slept only fitfully. What good humor I managed was reserved for my son. Major stress, a Mayo caregiver site says, is like eating a Baconator every meal. The immune system betrays you right out to organ collapse. If three house moves are the psychic equivalent of a death, a son's diagnosis of ALS is equal to crashing your car into a wall day after day, with the outcome always the same.

In the last days of December, when Paul was in the Clinic long mornings, I was routinely stranded in the "Neuro" waiting lounge, reading Mayo publications provided free for patient families—pamphlets about the six warning signs of Alzheimer's, or the four warning signs of dengue, Guinea worm disease, African sleeping sickness, rabies and trichinosis. And, of course, depression, which I hadn't believed I had.

In the newspaper someone had left on the couch, I happened to see the boxed ad for Vietnam-Minnesota Hospitality. "Men and women WELCOME. Locally owned, safe . . ." etc. I can't say what about this homely little teaser—palm fronds forming an encircling bower—appealed to me as something I profoundly needed, given my fears of Mafiosi, perp walks and police dogs. But, surrounded by an anxiety-fogged Mayo waiting room full of dread-filled strangers facing fickle fate's dour predilections, I just decided Right! This is really good. In fact, this is excellent. I have to do this immediately, possibly sooner. It's a rationale that has ancient origins in the spirit-weariness that lurks in the strongest of us. And of course it can be the origin of the best decisions we ever make.

December 29th—a Thursday—was scrapingly, gaspingly, squeakingly cold. I arrived to Provender Road by appointment at ten a.m. Paul was in the Clinic being bee-hived. I rang the front doorbell at the big white house, which really *is* an iconic family-farm home place, left as it was the day the Amdahls moved away to Vadnais Heights in the Cities: handmade yellow brick silo out back, implement shop across the barnyard. A pole barn. A chicken house. Assorted animal pens and stablery on the downwind side, a hundred yards off a frozen pond with willows. Betty has said the elder Amdahls haven't spoken about their ancestral home being transfigured into a massage business by Asiatics old man Harmon Amdahl fought in the jungles of the Ia Drang to save the world either for or from. But to me it is all admirable, the bellwether of the new farm economy with an ethnic overlay—like it or don't.

I was admitted in on that cold morning by petite Betty Tran herself. I'd "drawn" her in the day's rotation, since she works early so she can attend her classes in the afternoon. There were no other vehicles outside, ten a.m. not being a popular hour for massages. Inside, the house was appointed just as the Amdahls had left it—all their "nice" eclectic veneer furnishings, plaid-upholstered couches with matching hassocks, wall-mounted flat-screens in every room, a many-chaired faux mahogany dining-room suite for Sundays, a world of hooked rugs, brocaded window curtains to keep the heat in, glass-topped coffee tables, glass animals with glass shepherds tending them, a porcelain bell set and a porcelain Black child fishing with his own porcelain pole. Plus a Bible in Norwegian, an old SAE pledge paddle, and a wall sampler stating that "All Who Wander Are Not Lost." Everything the prosperous third-generation Scandinavian-American farmhouse *should* contain. There was also a large, flocked, cheerfully lighted, ornamented and apparently permanent Christmas tree with a star on top.

From the entry I noticed pale light issuing from a back hall leading to a kitchen, where young women's happy voices, cups clinking and sink-water running made me feel not a stranger. This was not a retail experience I'd ever had.

Betty, on the other hand, was precisely who I'd hoped for. Diminutive, smiling, cheerful, with bobbed hair and darkly alert eyes. 4 feet, 10 inches, not a centimeter taller, with pert, friendly gestures that were welcoming yet confident, happy to look me in the eye and give me a slightly unsettling wink. She was dressed in a sky blue peignoir "shorty," possibly not much more than that—her work clothes. She had to have been freezing but seemed ready to get down to business—whatever business would be. I'd put down 200 bucks "deposit" on my Visa, but had no precise idea what I'd come for.

Betty took my down coat, which was as big as she was, and told me to leave my boots on the Welcome mat. I'd said my name ("Hi, I'm Frank"). "I'm Betty." She'd smiled, I'd have to say, demurely. "We can go upstairs to my studio, okay?" It was then I saw the stage set of farm-family furnishings, smelled the coffee from the back, heard women's tinkling voices. It wasn't so different from Mangum & Gayden Funeral Home in Haddam. It wouldn't have surprised me to see a casket with lilies and a gladiolus where the LG hung.

"So. How are *you*, Frank?" Betty was motioning me up the banistered stairs, at the top of which was no light.

"Really, really good," I said. I'd been nervous on the freezing door stoop, listening to the bell go ding-dong, nervous when Betty opened the door in her skimpy blue cover-up. But once in the warm inside air, my outer garments shed, shoes off, ascending to who knew where, I felt better than I'd felt in months. Possibly years. And so easy done! Unexpected, unexplained feelings of well-being, I knew, should never be questioned.

Up to a narrow lightless hallway. "Go right, now." She spoke in a nasally Minnesota twang which causes native Minnesotans to squint when they say certain words. She snapped on a salad-bowl ceiling globe, revealing a dark bathroom at the end of a hall. "And then go left," into what I took would be her "studio." I will admit at that moment to a trilling-trilling commencing high-up in my stomach, like an old phone vibrating, reaching outward to my lower coastals—not a sensation I'd experienced of late. If I'd tried to speak, I might well have spoken in a baby's voice. Although no fewer than one billion people (mostly men) were doing the very same thing I was doing at the very same moment all around the planet.

Fully athrill, I stepped forward into Betty's room. I was involuntarily smiling.

"O-kay!" Betty closed the door behind us. Inside was her massage table, a neatly made simple bed by the window, plus the defibrillator, Twins poster and the rest. There was also her school bookshelf, a framed color photo of a smiling teenage Betty in cheerleader gear, standing in an ice rink (on the actual ice) beside a tall, smiling, square-headed, fresh-faced man-boy on skates, wearing a Mankato State Mavericks hockey jersey. The redoubtable Ingemur. Who, of course, would still be in love with her. Though I wasn't here to do either hanky or panky.

"Here we are, Frank." Betty was handing me the silky red dragon drape. She rounded her dark eyes, which were perfect disks in a pool of perfect white. "Take off your clothes behind the screen, please." In the corner was a flimsy black imitation-bamboo privacy screen from Costco—not private enough to conceal all of me.

"How much do I leave on?" I said waveringly.

Betty was kneeling, pouring yellow liquid into a red-flowered saucer and igniting a fat candle on a tiny stand. Sandalwood—the aroma both my wives had approved for bathroom use, which lent it unwelcome associations.

"However you like." She had dialed up soft island-breezes music on her phone and looked around at me as if I was naked already, which was how I felt without being ready to be. Was this modesty? Premature buyer's remorse? Nothing had happened but a candle being lit. Conceivably this was as far as everything—and I—needed to go. Nothing was shameful. There were no templates for these visits. Everything in the room grew suddenly very quiet. "Are you okay?" Betty's narrow face took on a mock-serious frown, her forehead wrinkling, her pretty lower lip protruded, both hands on her bare thighs where she knelt on a little prayer rug.

"Sure. I think so," I lied. Outside her icy window a bare ginkgo stood visible. On its branches three fat crows began blatherous squawkings, raising their beaks like singing cartoon crows—as if they could see me taking my clothes off in front of a rank stranger. Ann had always liked this quality in me. My "modesty." When we were fresh and young, she'd remarked that I was "Courtly. A man with time-worn etiquettes long out of fashion, but badly needed." Like a lot of other things you think when you're first married: not quite true.

"Is there something I need to tell you first?" I said. I don't know what I could've meant. Pet allergies? A pacemaker? A wooden leg?

"Nope." Betty looked gravely at me as if I was exhibiting worrisome signs. "Are you nervous?"

"I didn't expect to be," I said, smiling ghoulishly. I was very warm and felt very large in her tiny room in my wool Bean socks, but still dressed. I felt I could easily stagger over and break a table. I wanted to sit and possibly not take my clothes off. A mental picture of flashers flashing across empty snowfields. Boots pounding on stairs. Timely use of the defibrillator.

"Maybe you should sit," Betty said. "Sit on my bed. I can make some tea for us. It'll calm you. Okay?"

"I'm calm. But okay." I sat meaningfully down on her hard little bed, while she began making tea over the candle flame. I felt astonishingly relieved, as if in these last moments I'd come close to dying.

Which is how everything with Betty Tran unpromisingly, desultorily, humiliatingly, unsuccessfully, if sweetly, commenced. Though it is not at all how it has turned out.

———•———

PRESENTLY, BETTY CLICKED OFF THE ISLAND-BREEZES MUSIC, went behind the bamboo curtain and retrieved a woolly tartan robe and put it on. We drank the tepid, tasteless tea and laughed about my becoming "flustered," which she said happened more than you'd think (mostly with younger men). She punched me on the shoulder when she told me that, as if I was now miraculously young. She asked me where I was from, and when I told her New Jersey she said she knew it was a beautiful place, and there were "seriously good" hospitals where her HR skills could land her a job, though she'd never been outside of Minnesota except for a trip to Fargo-Moorhead and one other time to Madison for a high school cheering workshop. Never to Vietnam, she said primly, though she hoped to go one day. I didn't and still don't know if she was exactly like or nothing like what anyone might expect a young, sexy, Vietnamese-American massage attendant to be. She was chatty, prone to laughing at herself and me—as if she'd known me for decades. She was capable of quite incisive and reflective comments about a variety of things, and a good listener ("I don't know why you'd say that, Frank," when I told her I was fairly sure I'd never get married again). She was interested in the story of my son and felt the savants at Mayo could probably "fix" him, since they'd fixed her father's hernia back in 1990. At the end of my hour, she told me the eleven-to-twelve slot was open if I wanted to stay. And because Paul was in the Clinic 'til past one, I forked over another 200, and she brewed more tea and produced from under her bed a tin box containing crisp, thin ginger-and-lemon cookies, which were the best thing I'd ever tasted, and will go to my grave, like Proust, with their dense, alien flavors haunting my lips. (These, she said, were for "special clients.") We talked about our divorces; we talked, but not too much, about House Whisperers (she didn't really understand, with good reason). We talked briefly about the Vietnam War, where I didn't fight and could therefore be fully cognizant of the moral wrongness of things done and not achieved. She told me about being married "way too young." And how that had slowed her progress, how her extended family out in Kiester were very tight-knit and loving and had "been there" for her, but hoped she'd be married soon and go wherever her husband took her—perhaps to the Cities, where there was opportunity. The massage business, she said, was a "holding pattern" until the entrepreneurial Tran family could obtain a Hampton Inn franchise and tear down the Amdahl house or better yet sell it and move it away. There was nothing shady or unseemly about a massage business, she believed, any more than a NAPA store, which it turned out her family also owned one of in Waseca. On we talked, sitting on her bed in her "studio," her legs crossed, cradling her tea mug, my back against the cold window sill, like two college roomies on the day before classes begin, when there's a good chance to get acquainted. Several times her cell phone rang—her ringtone was a bullfrog croaking—but each time she didn't answer it, suggesting this hour was all mine. Until it was straight-up noon and I had to "skedaddle." I, of course, had never gone to high school one day with a certifiable female— only with smirking, gimlet-eyed lay-abouts and misfit "men"— all white—at saltpeterish Lonesome Pines. But sitting, talking two hours with pretty, exciting, vivid, immensely likeable Betty was like a fantasy (I'm told) men my age frequently indulge: the high school girl you should've loved but for a thousand reasons didn't, yet dream you could still love now. Only *that* girl (if she isn't dead) is your own age, and you wouldn't give a second thought to loving her even if you could.

Betty Tran, though, *was* that girl, preserved in youth and winsomeness, sitting campfire-style on her narrow bed, laughing, winking, nudging, rolling her eyes, tartan-robed and nobody's fool, and, best of all *within my reach*. Not a fantasy but realer than real—at least it seemed that way to me that day.

At the end of our two hours I rose—not without help. ("Maybe next time we try a massage," she said, her eyes widened in mock surprise.) Again, I felt myself an oversized presence in her little room, though without being about to fall over. My back snarled at me, my knees, ankles, wrists, the nape of my neck where it connects with my lower cerebellum, plus something deep in my butt—all howled out. I'd been "sitting funny" for too long, then risen too fast. When I got full up, my heart made a profound kow-thunk, and my brain—which had felt renewed— again ran flashing to ambulances, gurneys hurried up stairways, me on the floor supine, dead-eyed with Betty kneeling beside, nodding, smiling, explaining to the EMS team, "He's fine. He's really happy. He wanted it this way." I did.

Except . . . for my poor son, waiting in Mayo Neuro with Al's, wondering where I was, while trying to comprehend all it did and didn't mean to say he was "still alive."

On reflection, it was not that "nothing" happened between Betty and me; or that "everything" happened. Nothing had *actually* happened. I simply felt terrific about whatever it was because all of it felt true of life—something Chekhov could've written about and given deep meaning to—the eventful non-event that manages to be everything.

"Can I come back another time?" I said with, I knew, a greedy, helpless grin (not, I hoped, a leer).

"Oh, sure," Betty said brightly, smoothing the chenille bed-spread where our bodies, sitting close to one another, had depressed its mitered perfection. "I like you," she said. Though she added, "I like most people."

"Me, too."

"You come any day." For the first time I detected the twitchy-clipped, sing-songy cadence of Asia or what I took to be Asia in her speech-music. It only made her more alluring.

"O-*kay*," I beamed. "I'll come back as soon as I can." Eager beaver, not the wisest strategy for anything.

"I'll give you a little kiss, then." Betty, in her tartan, which smelled of sandalwood and a far-away hint of sweat, stood on her pink-painted tippy-toes, held her small, delicate but forceful hands apart for me to enter their semi-embrace, and kissed me on my cheek. "There," she said. "Steal it with a kiss." (I knew what she meant.) Though if I didn't stagger back, it was only because I don't remember staggering back. I don't remember much after that, until I was in my Honda, barreling along frozen Provender

Road between the snow-white, mid-day fields of stubble, and discovered I was going eighty.

———

WHAT MUST I TELL YOU? THAT MY SON'S "SITUATION" AND MY impending survivorship have intensified and put a premium on the present? That I've reached the point in life at which no woman I'm ever going to be attracted to is ever going to be attracted to me—so the sky's the limit? That for much longer than my son's been sick, I've occasionally waked—as always, at 2:46 a.m., the precise hour of my birth—and wondered: How do you stand it, these dismal facts of life, *without* some durable fantasy or deception or dissembling? Or, on sunnier mornings, wondered if it isn't plausible to erect a narrative with a certain someone who doesn't need to understand me unless it's easy? Someone I talk to almost exclusively about the most mundane things? Who's not bothered that I don't "give" enough? Who has few opinions but many goals? Who doesn't need me to impress her except with courtesy and forbearance? Who may not think about me when I'm not in sight and never *ever* thinks of what I think about her? With whom I don't have "sex" per se, but certainly don't have nothing?

And here's the capper in Betty's case . . . And about which and who I might be completely deluded? Strike the bell loudly. I'm willing to be wrong if the reward for being wrong is a rich one.

"Love," admittedly, may not be the word our panel of experts would concur on. (They're a tough group.) But if they will concede that love may be what's left when everything that's *not* love is taken away, then I may have a case to make. It's at least worth the panel's consideration, when they convene in Chicago, to contrast my feelings for Betty Tran with the true love I experienced with my two wives for forty years—muddling along, chasing "authenticity" and "who gives what to whom and who only takes."

———·———

OF COURSE, I WAS BACK OUT PROVENDER ROAD TWO DAYS LATER. Paul had his first course of at-home therapies with Nurse Wanda—a bonus, since he's deemed to be a "good sport," which he only half-way is.

On my second visit things were different and would stay different right up to the later-than-usual appointment I'm driving to this afternoon.

I cannot say if Betty Tran is truly skillful at massage, only that she's nimble and authoritative, with quick, incisive, digital frications (she grunts and often giggles) as if she was following *some* established protocol. I know that shedding my clothes and emerging in the red drape and popping onto her table for Betty to exert upon me, seemed entirely something I *had* to do, and satisfied the directive of "setting goals in the present." Though Miss Duling would probably consider paying a young Asian-American woman 200 bucks to scale me like K2, then *apply* upon me ardently with oil-scented hands, knees, knuckles, heels, elbows, even her pretty forehead and chin, to be a case of sublimated selfishness. Though for me it was and still is a clear case of "There is no *was*. There is only *is*."

When I'm on Betty's table, splayed like a pike (my nakedness is of little interest to her), I experience the pure ecstasy of being not known and in charge of nothing. I also instantly quit thinking about death—mine or anybody's. Having your clothes off in the presence of a good-natured young woman while soothing tropical music plays can be incommensurably transporting. (Men are no longer allowed to say we simply *like* women—not without a lot of preconditions, disclaimers, NDAs and clarifiers requiring more time than we want to put in.) During these few weeks with Betty, I've realized that my susceptibility to mindless transport had been unwittingly switched off (age does this, too); while my late-life tendency to view myself in grainy, unflattering lights had been switched on too high. It's similar to turning on the camera in your phone and suddenly viewing your *self*—horse-faced, unsmiling, hollow-eyed, needing a shave—staring uncomprehendingly back like a criminal.

This deflating experience can actually bring on curdling sensations of personal fraudulence. A sense of imposture had *already* invaded my caregiving duties—an inner voice barking like a drill instructor: Bascombe! Yo! Dick-brain! You're never *all in* about anything, are you? Isn't there a program you can entirely *get with*? Must you always and only be environed by yourself? What do you *do* to actually *help* your son? Do you even wish he'd get well? Fraudulence gets built into daily existence like a knife blade sewn into a shirt.

Except. In these six-plus weeks since Betty entered my life and our relationship has so-to-say blossomed, feelings of fraudulence have gone into retreat. I've even become a more adroit, patient and sensitive caregiver to my son, though I'm not sure he knows it.

And there's more.

Needless to say, there are worlds about Betty Tran I don't know and never will. But these voids and the few facts she *has* revealed have taken on an enhanced significance. (Deep understanding of other humans is greatly over-rated.) As I've said, she considers her massage vocation to be a perfectly practical and upright way to finance her business degree and possibly find a husband. I don't know and don't ask anything about her other clients—how many there are or what the extent of her services might be. I definitely do not think of her as a sex worker, nor consider that I take advantage of her in any but the agreed-to ways. I know much about her family and some about her terminated marriage to Ingo. But I cannot say anything about how she "sees" me. If you told me that when she says she likes me (which she often says), she is merely venerating the elderly, I wouldn't be surprised and not completely disappointed. I only know for sure that when I arrive and later leave, I never feel recrimination or confusion, only a sense of betterment—which cannot be said of most human experiences.

Yet if the question must be asked about whether there is something serious between Betty Tran and me, my answer is President Clinton's, when asked a similar question about a love interest: It depends on what you mean by *is*.

Since things have begun to go forward (more than a month now), I have taken her on a small handful of "dates" for dinner. Her favorite is scampi, at the pricey Italian at the DoubleTree; and also to a Greek place she likes. This, in lieu of a massage (I still shell out the two hundred). I've given her my mobile number, which she has yet to use. And I have offered to write her job recommendations when the time comes. I even accompanied her—on Dr. King's birthday, a holiday her family reverences—out into the corn prairies to Kiester for a family dinner. I was not in my element, but was treated as an honored guest. Though from the tenor of her father's questions to me—about the future of brick-and-mortar retail and whether advertising will eventually transition to 100 percent online—I understood Betty had identified me as one of her business profs and not a client.

On our dinner dates we laugh, and Betty dilates about school challenges and what it was like to be married to a hockey star, and where she hopes someday to live and whether there'll be room in life for children. I talk about Paul, who comes out sounding complex and interesting, and about having been a sportswriter and even covering hockey before she was born, and a bunch of other stuff I embroider upon about the real-estate business being a life of service—which interests her because of the HR angles. Inside my still-frozen car in the DoubleTree parking structure, we've kissed and embraced sweetly a time or two, and Betty has once (I might've misheard it) said she loved me after I said I loved her. And though I'm confident she doesn't see me as matrimonial material, I have more than once lain in bed, my son asleep behind the wall, and fantasized about Betty and me pursuing a simple, garden-variety life in Eden Prairie or Anoka, where she would put her marketing degree to work for Marriott, and we could travel to Hue and the Mekong, but also to Venice and Paris and sparkling places she dreams about, and all would be jolly. I've read in a magazine while in the car-repair waiting room, that in making choices of life-partners, contemporary women are looking to maximize the "Michelan-gelo effect"—engaging in acts of "mutual sculpting" with which to realize goals of self-expansion while accumulating knowledge and absorbing another person into one's self. This isn't anything I'd be good at. I don't have enough time in life remaining. Plus, I have a son with ALS whose care I'm often stealing time from. It's pointless, therefore, to entertain these Technicolor fantasies any longer than it takes to fall asleep.

Massage, however, continues to be the core of what's be-tween us. Sometimes Betty, for reasons I never anticipate, will completely undress for our sessions. Just some spritely spirit in-habits or leaves her. I don't pretend not to notice, but neither do I comment—again as if naked and clothed were distinctions without a difference. She is regulation pretty, not a knockout.

Undressed, she is as tiny as she seems clothed, but unexpectedly curvy and fleshy where you wouldn't expect. (She has virtually no behind, which I don't much like.) Thankfully, she has no tattoos or piercings other than pinpoint rubyish studs in her tight little ears. She has an arrow-fletch scar in the corner of her left eye from a high school cheering mishap, and some adolescent pimples up into her hairline. But she is otherwise without obvious blemish. In the last two weeks she's dyed her short gamine bob as yellow as a daisy, the effect of which is she looks closer to seventeen than thirty-four. Truthfully, that Betty is Vietnamese is to me the least noticeable thing about her (I'm not good at detecting ethnic variances anyway; she could be Singaporean). Sometimes, though, when the lights are atmospherically low, the ocean music whooshing and all is warm and cozy, her agile, soft, assertive fingers will venture, I'm sure unintentionally, into my conducive zone—the back-of-her-hand, a brush-of-a-finger, a point-of-the-elbow—contact which in a more personal context would be beyond ignoring. At these moments I resolutely say nothing, even if it's clear I've registered. A time or two, I've uttered a groan or a sigh; perhaps I've flinched, or my eyes have shot open or closed with pleasure. Betty is typically noncommittal. "Okay, fine," she's said. Or "Um-huh." Or "Yes, yes." Though once she said, "Well, we see you're still alive." A frank tumescence can always be rationalized as part of overall-body response—like a charley horse, or a shiver when an elbow digs into my spine, setting off tremblers up and down. If you're *me*, though, you think, "Yes! What else *should* I be doing and feeling at this precise and dwindling moment in my life?" Even if Betty *is* only venerating the elderly for a fee, people *die* at my age (men especially; women can count on seventeen more years). And in the obits it never credits that "Bascombe had his last well-sourced, fully actualized erection two years or five years or ten years ago." Now is now. There is and only *is*.

I doubt, in any case, I'll ever try to expand the depth and range of Betty's and my relationship—if that's what it is. Either for fear she'd say "Forget it" and ruin everything, or that she'd say "Okay, yeah" and ruin everything. There are old doozies, I know, who get besotted that an attractive young woman such as Betty Tran rilly, rilly loves them, pines for them when they're not around, thinks of them constantly, dreams of them at night and in the early hours. I am not that big a doozie. In truth, it's problematic to imagine doing much more than we do—both on her table and in the front seat of my Civic inside the structure behind the DoubleTree. For passion to thrive, one must be able to envision it. And for me the sheer mechanical, logistical, strategical, interpersonal geometrics have already become remote. An early, now-deceased member of the Divorced Men's Club, a North Carolina classics professor retired from Rutgers, had made a frequent habit of romancing comely coeds far into his sixties. He remarked to me once over lunch that "Sex, Fr-uh-ank, wuz always so awk-wud. But it gets a lot mo-uh awk-wud at mah age. 'Nemo dat quod non habet.'" Which I went home and looked up, and found to mean "No one can give what he doesn't have." It might be a motto for my life. Both my wives would agree.

And yet, at the end of every session, when I'm lying languorous as a porch hound on the warm Naugahyde, the universe of the senses swirling about me and becoming for a few sparkling moments *my universe*, and Betty is already dressed and making tea, and no one is speaking—the sounds of the farmhouse softened, the cold snow-swept plains as distant as Coconut Island—I think that something in the sweet solemnity of her smiling, wondering face, as she looks over at me, our time now ending, is

again at least *like love*. And if not, it is surely one of the "unclas-
sified affections" I've read about. In her gaze is acknowledgment
that I have witnessed and agreed to certain incongruities in her,
and she has witnessed and agreed to some in me (though I think
of myself as the most congruent of men); and that this is our
laudable achievement—whether it means we have a relationship,
or it means nothing and I am like every other schmoe who pays
for what he came for, and at the end leaves happy. There might
be more laudable achievements over a longer existence. But for
me this is enough.

———————————•———————————

WHEN I PULL OFF PROVENDER ROAD INTO THE FARMYARD
Vietnam-Minnesota Hospitality uses as its customer lot, it's
four-thirty. Paul is now finished with nurse Stiffler and his webinar, and is home alone—which can be perilous. The sky in the
west is clear with red-green light burnishing distant house roofs.
Snow all around is dull and in shadows. Several specterish deer
stand in the field below the house. A good-sized waning moon
has paused in the east above the colors in the sky.

Lights in the Amdahl house are festive in twilight, as if the
Amdahls are back, staging their traditional Valentine's obser-
vance (though as Lutherans they'd be hesitant about too much
celebration). Small Japanese cars of the other massage attendants
are parked close to the barn, where my headlights find them.
One alien vehicle, a sleek red Vette, is parked where I usually
park—nosed into the pickets that boundary the front yard,
where stands the arms-out and leafless ginkgo I see from inside
Betty's room. I'm twelve minutes early and pull beside the Vette,
but at a discreet distance. When I kill my lights, someone—not
Betty—parts a living room curtain, leans close to the pane for

a scan of my car, then steps away. I feel, at this unaccustomed hour, a stranger here.

There's not time now—with Paul waiting and alone—for a usual session. I've booked the hour and made this late-day dash—light failing, hopes diminishing—just to cheer myself. When I called, an anonymous female voice (it is not so different from a hair salon) said I was in luck, Betty had an opening at four forty-five. She may no longer be the client draw she would once have been, and it's hard to believe she is overly dedicated, since she sometimes grows distracted while working on me, will stop for sometimes long moments and stare out the window at the empty expanse without speaking.

I have brought a valentine—though I don't know what Vietnamese think about Valentine's Day. Conceivably they buy in. I also have a wild-hare valentine thought—more than far-fetched—which is to invite Betty on Paul's and my trip tomorrow—an inspiring addition to the club cab's concise rear seating. It is a new and dense fantasy and obviously out of the question. I would, though, relish the pleasure of her company in circumstances exceeding the usual, while she escapes Minnesota and sees more of her native country. I could buy a room for her at a Hilton Garden. She could luxuriate in the shower with an abundance of towels, watch all 500 channels, sleep on starched sheets then eat the free breakfast for Honors members only. I could even pay a late-night visit—possibly chaste/possibly not— once Paul is bedded down. He could encounter Dad in a new light. Plus, once he'd set eyes on Betty, he could wow her with his voice-throwing techniques, talk granularly about human logistics, substantiate *himself* as the renaissance man he esteems himself to be, and not think about all he otherwise has to think about. She would like him, I'm sure.

My valentine, which I have under the visor, is one Paul would approve of. (There was only a picked-over selection at Walgreens.) It depicts a ten-gallon-hatted cowpoke strumming a guitar astride a skinny cayuse underneath a Pecos moon. His steed has pulled a quizzical look on his horse face, and is bending round to look back to his cowboy. The message reads, "Love, oh faithful love. Be mine on Valentine's Day!" I've written in ballpoint, "Can't wait to see you. Love, xoxoxoxo Frank," and snugged two hundred smacks into the envelope.

I've now been here five minutes, motor idling, heater gushing and the AM playing '70s oldies. I could already be comfortably inside the cozy living room, grazing old copies of *Progressive Farmer* instead of asphyxiating out here in this freeze box.

Though just as I shut 'er down, slip my valentine into my pocket and crack my door open, the farmhouse front door opens back and out steps someone I recognize. Sarge-Maje Gunnerson, still in his blue-dress trousers, wearing a bomber jacket, plus his white cover. Without a backward glance, he makes for the Vette in a crisp, arms-bent military jog, as if he hadn't expected it to be this cold. He doesn't look my way. I wait for him to squeeze in before I make my move. Once in, he's prompt about getting going. Headlights rotate up, illuminating the house. Ignition results in an impressive, glottal roar, then an inevitable vroom-vroom. He grinds into gear, swings backward, then just before the headlights sweep the driveway and me, the front door opens again and Betty Tran's face is there. She's smiling, waving a dainty hand, her slender arm bare, bobbling her head of bright yellow hair in a gesture she's performed for me other times. "Good-bye, good-bye. Come back, come back," words I "hear" as if they were booming through a PA. "Good-bye, good-bye. Come back, come back." Sergeant Major Gunnerson gives his horn a high school harry "beepety-beep-beep" (like the Road Runner). He has possibly not even seen her. His back bumper has a "Semper Fi" sticker. Give her what she's never had. In a squall of snow and gravel, he is quickly underway. I am left sitting with my envelope. "Be Mine on Valentine's Day."

FOUR

A nd now I'm late, I'm late, for a very important date. My son. At home. Alone too long, hazarding god knows what I could've-should've saved him from—a gas-jet left on and ignored. His jugular nicked in a bathroom fall. A seizure—these happen in ALS cases. Each time I'm late from VMH, or when Betty and I smooch it up in the car and lose track, I hurry back thinking how the charging documents will read. "Comes now defendant Bascombe, before the court, accused of abandoning handicapped son—toppled off the porch steps, attempting to signal neighbors, neck-broke, stiff as a plank." Crowd gasps. "Defendant pleads extenuating circumstances . . . imperative massage establishment visit, etc., etc."

Having your grown son likely-to-die-ahead-of-you is not at all what you think. Not "like" anything else. No fixed vocabulary, no Hallmark sentiments apply. When our son Ralph Bascombe was soon to die and *did* die, in 1979, his mother and I launched into a catacomb of dread—dread not so much in Ralph's behalf—who did all he could to make us feel better by resisting death for all he was worth and often saying things that were very funny. But dreading each other and ourselves. We simply couldn't forgive the failure to allay each other's pain—

which we'd promised to do in our marriage vows, and tried. It's why marriages where children die often crumble, as ours did. Though don't judge me 'til you're walking in my huaraches.

What pain did we not allay for each other? The pain of being left exposed to the fact that you are only, only, only helplessly yourself. The closest anyone can go with us to death, the poet tells us, is not very damn close. Paul's dilemma and mine may therefore, in fact, be un-uniteable.

———

DRIVING BACK AT 5:15, THE CITY STEEPS THE EVENING SKY OUT ahead with lemony pallor. End-of-day traffic blazes toward the commuter towns north of here. Oronoco. Pine Island. Zumbrota, where the LPNs, radiationists, the lab techs and third-tier Clinic staff call home—the mandarin docs all cloistered in gated, glass, stone & redwood vu-homes in the timbered, manicured hills, Porsches and Jaguars in the drive.

Paul has called twice—once I answered, once I didn't. When I didn't, his message (his voice worrisomely thinner) said, "Okay, Lawrence, no go with the abdominal snowwoman." (Nurse Stiffler.) "She threatened to cut my pecker off if I brought it into the conversation again. It's not the fall that hurts, it's the sudden stop at the end." Click.

Call #2 is in traffic, the taste of Betty's perfidy stinging in my nostrils. My son sounds sour and taxed. "Where the fuck *are* you?" Why does everyone need to know that? Does *where* you are determine what you'll say?

"I'm on the way home," I say. "I took a second look at the Windbreaker. It's a go if you're up for it." Winding up my voice to win over his bad mood and mine.

"A go at what?"

"At our Mount Rushmore trip tomorrow. The Corn Palace in Mitchell, South Dakota, where everyone's named Hansen and the land goes on forever. Remember?"

"Are you having another of your episodes?" my son says. "What's wrong with you, Lawrence?"

"I don't have episodes. Everything's great. Did things go bad at the webinar?"

"I was elected class president by a voice vote. Not all of them could talk, of course. Let's open up the phones and hear what our listeners have to say. Here's Lawrence in Lawrenceville. Why the long face, Larry?" Clatter-dee-clatter. He has dropped his phone. His right hand doesn't work the way it used to. I hope he hasn't swanned out of his wheelchair, which he uses in the house when he's tired.

"Are you okay, son?" Minnesota has laws against phone use when operating. Other drivers are giving me dagger stares. A man makes his hand into a phone, holds it to his ear, then turns it into a pistol and pretends to shoot me. His Cherokee has a Biden sticker.

More clatter-dee-clatter, then muffled effortful sounds. Then hoarse breathing. "I'm perfectly fine. If I go on talking I won't die. Turns out you can be dying and still make a contribution. I was a big hit." He means the webinar.

"Good." Edging into faster city traffic I need both hands. I punch the phone onto speaker to get my instrument out of sight.

More muffled noises. "When're you coming home? I'm wheelchair bound, you must by now be aware."

"Are you really all right?"

"You said that. I'm a dying man, Lawrence. I'm just not getting it done fast enough."

"Yeah. Sorry."

"Inspired by actual events, right? Today's Mom's un-anniversary. I don't want you to overlook it."

"I haven't. I didn't."

"You're a forgetful old cocksucker. Admit it."

"It lets me be there for *you*, though." One of his most hated new-age coinages—of which there are many. Silence invades the line. Paul has called to do precisely what we're doing. Take up a subject by not taking it up. "Do you want to go tomorrow?"

"I read online the most popular punctuation mark is the semicolon."

"That's pretty interesting."

"My favorite's the three-dot ellipsis. It's the most misunderstood."

"I see."

"Do you? You're on the fucking speakerphone. I can tell. Only assholes use speakerphones."

"I love you, Paul."

"Love you, love you, love you. Mean it." He hangs up.

———

BLOCKS FROM HOME, I AM ALREADY PERFORMING WHAT OLD people must become expert at—closing painful events out of mind. My dead wife's death anniversary. Betty's inopportunely timed session with Sarge Major Gunnerson—about which I feel queasily jilted. Many bad sensations would be tolerable if we didn't have to have words for them. Jilted. Nietzsche believed no happiness could be achieved through discourse (words). Silence for him was the maker's mark. *Un*happiness is a different matter.

Last November, when Paul and I convened our Sunday Chiefs and Chargers TV-dinner on my couch, the afternoon when I'd, in a course reversal, planned to initiate the subject of Mike Mahoney's can't-miss, get-rich deal—until I found out Paul was sick—I knew there would likely be a bottom-out moment when my son would disclose to me his diagnosis, after which god only knew what I would say or do. In fact, though, he almost forgot about it, so transfixed was he by the game. Just when the Chiefs' quarterback—lithe, darting number 15—was being disarticulated by two Charger goliaths (his red helmet actually popped off like it was his head) Paul looked absently over to me as I was finishing my vodka-lime and considering another. "By the way," he said. I'd noticed his right hand was unsteady. The first I'd observed it. "I've got this nerve thing. I guess Clary told you." He furrowed his brows behind his glasses, sighed, then resumed bemused attention to the game.

"She did," I answered. "I'm on top of it. We're driving out to Mayo in Minnesota to get you re-evaluated. If you want to."

"Sure. Okay. Super. I'll take a leave at work. They owe me." Eye contact not required.

A "nerve thing." "Take a leave at work." We knew what we knew—or some of it. It was only *his* business before that moment. It was ours now. The old double bind of who should feel betrayed—him, for me going over his head and making Mayo plans; me, for not being considered a sympathetic person to talk to. We didn't choose that route. We didn't talk about Mike's get-rich-quick scheme either.

The only way to know what Betty Tran thinks—about me or anything—would of course be to *ask* her using words, which would then make heart-rendingly clear there's *no* way to know. No best word there, either. If there *is* a next week, the best I can do is drive back to Vietnam-Minnesota Hospitality and pay for a massage as if nothing was amiss (since maybe there isn't). The business of business is always business—'til it's not fun anymore.

Winding through darkened Rochester resident streets, I feel a chaotic urge to dial up Dr. Flaherty in La Jolla, on the (thin) pretext of 1. Discussing my son's journey into illness; 2. Conversing with her about how *I* am; 3. Asking how *she* is; 4. Inquiring whether there might be a through-line for us at some time to be determined, possibly soon. All subjects I'd rather take up under a pergola where linnets and hummingbirds vie for nectar and a tray of martinis awaits. This, though, will do.

I pull to the curb to make such a call. On both sides of the street (10th Street NW) on snow-crusted lawns silvered from lighted front windows, yard signage is fairly evenly arrayed. Trump–Biden. Hard to know which bunch I'd rather run afoul of—a mob of shrieking, sandaled liberals waving blue security blankets, or a stampede of tattooed muscle-bound yokels with AR-15s and redacted copies of the constitution. A tall, rangy, frowning woman in a muu-muu comes to the front window of her house, where I've stopped at the curb, and takes a gander at me. A teenage boy wearing a white shirt and a tie and eating something, steps in beside her. They speak to someone offstage, a husband, just sat down with a beer for the early news. The porch light snaps on—Halloween pumpkins and skeletons still occupy the steps from last fall. The front door does not open, which isn't to say it won't. A car-window conversation with an out-of-sorts husband is not something I need to experience at this moment. My duty lies ahead, not alas in La Jolla. As has become normal in this sad period of anticipation, nothing's to do but doing it. I stow my phone and ease away.

PAUL'S AND MY AMENITIES ON NEW BEMIDJI STREET ARE NOT neighborhood-standard, and as such represent the winds-of-change in how real property is valued, held, used, thought and dreamed about by Americans living their only lives in real time.

"New Bemidji Street" in fact doesn't exist. It is the name Paul and I have given to 171 11th Avenue NW because we both believe residential streets deserve bona fide names. Our Mike Mahoney house, a classic "big-ranch-on-a-slab," is notably out-of-keeping with the older varietal residential preferences—Sears' craftsmen, Dutch barns, etc. Sited on a prized double lot, it was custom-built in the '80s by a celebrated Texas cardiologist "rock star" brought up from Baylor Med to lead the Clinic's repair-or-remove department, and who didn't give a rat's ass if his dream house fit in, since he thought the old-style midwestern houses should be razed so the street could look more like Houston. The story goes, he wore rattlesnake cowboy boots, a wide Stetson, carried a nickel-plated handgun, smoked Cohibas and drove a Maserati, and quickly made everyone at the Clinic loathe him, at which point he shoved off back to Texas, marooning his Mexican wife to deal with his mess.

Mike's company bought the house from its elderly second-generation owners, the Kalbfleisches, who'd grown weary of mortgage payments and upkeep and longed to downsize to Siesta Key. Solid and Texas-size (4001 sq. ft.), it's a one-level, has handicap features ("death-ready") and everything inside works. It also contains *all* the Kalbfleisches' furnishings—their parents' and baby pictures, their attic cumulus, drawers of underwear, hot-water bottles, electric bills, lawn-care receipts, their Beloit '59 yearbook—even their grade reports, diplomas, and marriage license. You'd think people would treasure these most intimate possessions. But you'd be wrong. Normally, Mike's Himalayan Partners' crews would chuck all this waddage into a dumpster and speed-remodel the house into an executive rental. Paul's and my sudden housing need in December came along just as Mike's people were showing the Kalbfleisches the door. We've been happy to put up with their clutter.

Most in-town neighborhoods contain these late-arriving eye-sores all abutters would be happy to see burned down and something more "appropriate" put up. Eight minutes to the Clinic on foot (which Paul can't manage now), it boasts a three-car garage out of the snowplow's way, a short front walk where I get occasional exercise shoveling, a double-sized living room for Paul and me to play cornhole on our mostly unoccupied nights, and a humongous Sony with all the channels. For years, I joked about "ranches" while I was flogging them in the New Jersey low-country. But I've made my peace now. Chipped-marble roofs, crank-out windows, ill-lit hallways leading to ill-lit bed-rooms, pink-and-blue bath decor, all-electric floorboard heating, louvered closets and drywall . . . When all's said and done, I don't have to own it. Though Mike's assured me I *could*—with a valued-employee discount—while he commodifies my house in Haddam.

When I turn down New Bemidji Street, aiming for the big blue spruce outside our house, I'm parched for a drink, ready for whatever Paul has to regale me with. Except . . . wig-wag, wig-wag, wig-wag. A red hook-and-ladder and a boxy Rochester FD command vehicle, both with red flashers flashing, have the street in front of my house blocked. A swarm of blue police lights is strobing helter-skelter up and down the pavement, cruisers up onto front yards and sidewalks, a shadowy army of helmeted, body-armored cops, some in haz-mats and toting weaponry, has established positions on car hoods, on the snowy ground, behind trees, in the bucket of the hook-and-ladder, eyes and weapons trained on the facade of the stucco duplex next door to the acu-puncture studio across my street. A bank of kliegs worthy of Grauman's Chinese is illuminating the duplex's front door. I've assumed this house was vacant. A Century 21 yard sign is half-over in the snow, beside a "Hate Doesn't Live Here" placard.

My heart makes a flutter deep in its cavity. My thighs and feet go chill. It's only 5:30, but dark as three a.m. Where is my 47-year-old son who can't walk good and thinks all the wrong things are funny? Easy pickins' for the cops. Though in perfect truth I trust Paul not to be out wobbling about, spouting professional savvy and insight based on his human logistics experience. For one thing, it's too cold.

I pull to the curb—our house is farther down. Neighbors are in the yards despite the cold—people I've never seen. Lights in houses are on. Other neighbors are inside gawking at whatever this is—something not good. A small, dangerous looking, gray tank-like contraption is being maneuvered toward the front of the klieg-lit duplex. Something dramatic is clearly set to happen or *has* happened—possibly something violent or disastrous or preposterous or all four together. A bomb defusing. A dope lab take-down. A fugitive brought to justice right in my neighborhood.

Only, if everything's ready to crescendo, why are the neighbors lounging around, gaping and in harm's way? Sawhorse barricades are in place at both extents of the operation—which is all being video'd by the cops. I get out into the cold night. Three citizens are standing on the half-dark sidewalk, arms folded like jurors, taking in the whole scene. All are in snowmobile suits. One, in a plaid Elmer Fudd cap, I make out is a female—short and round and securely padded.

"What gives?" I say—an expression I haven't uttered since military school when it meant something dirty. The fire trucks are making deep, throbbing, "grrrr-ing" sounds, setting the night air stinging. A voice, possibly a police higher-up, also a woman, begins speaking loudly into a bullhorn, "Okay. Extraction team.

Stand by." None of these curb-siders have spoken to me, though they carry on with each other. "This'll be good," the woman in the Elmer Fudd says.

"They oughta sell tickets for this shit," one of the men says. Because of their balaclavas, I can't make out which man speaks.

"Frickin' tax dollars. Hard at frickin' work," the other man answers.

"Is this all legit?" I say, trying again. I am standing beside them but clearly not of them.

All at once, from nowhere but the night, a helicopter—a sleek and lethal, wasp-avenger—materializes at treetops, focusing a much intenser white light onto the duplex and scene unfolding in front of it. All activity below is briefly paralyzed. A scanner radio in one of the fire vehicles pops into life. "Roger that, eighty-seven. We've got the hee-lo now. Stand by." It is the woman again, a husky voice of unassailable police self-assurance.

One of the three beside me takes out a flip phone and begins speaking. They are obviously Minnesotans, since they haven't acknowledged me.

"I can't hear a goddamn thing." It's the female. She is having to shout. "There's a helicopter up my butt. We're freezing our onions off. If this was real, we'd all be . . . What? No. How do I know? Give her the whole glassful and see how she looks. What? No. You dimwit. Be glad you're not out here where *we* are. Later." Her phone disappears into her snowmobile pocket. "Cri-mo-fuckin-nently," she says.

"What'd she say?" one of the men asks over the chopper noise.

"What does she *ever* say?" the woman answers loudly. "Boo-hoo-hoo, it's not my fault. Sound familiar? She's *your* daughter."

"Maybe Trump's in there," the other man shouts.

"He's way too smart."

"Oh, yeah. I guess so."

The female commander, using her bullhorn under the helicopter thwap, shouts out, "Okay, okay. Bring her out *now*!" A SWAT pod, who've been unseen behind the mini-tank vehicle, suddenly rushes forth in a tight crouching single file, toy-like weapons to shoulder, making straight for the front door of the duplex, prepared apparently to breach the door as if it wasn't a door. And in two seconds this is precisely what happens, the SWATs disappearing straight inside—all six at once. Instantly there's shouting and swearing, muffled by the helicopter, but coming apparently from inside the house. There's then a loud *boom*, and the duplex's front windows spray outward, followed by more shouting. "Police, police! Get down! Get down! Get. The. Fuck. *Down!*" The lady bullhorn commander starts shouting again. "All right. Get her out! Get her out!" Through the shattered duplex door-space come three SWATs charging forward, a young Black woman in a flak vest being held by all three officers, boosting her under her arms, her legs and feet running in air to keep up with the giant men conveying her to, I guess, safety. This has all happened in thirty seconds. What I haven't noticed before is that there is a trampoline in the front yard of the duplex. Whose?

"Well. La-dee-fuckin'-*dah*," one of the snowmobile men says. Neighbors down the block and closer to the action start applauding and woo-hooing and whistling, while the extracted Black woman is whisked through the police line, past officers and firemen, past the light stanchions and vehicles, and deposited in the back of a dark sedan, whose blue roof flasher starts turning as it accelerates through the crowd up New Bemidji toward where, I don't know. The heelo, poised above everything, douses its spotlight, performs a slow, gainly rotation left, acquires altitude—I can make out the pilots—becomes quickly smaller, then disappears into the night. Neighbors are clapping for it, too. "Coulda left that one inside, if you ask me," one of the men beside me observes to his friends. They're already beginning to walk away. No one has spoken to me or even acknowledged my existence.

"If that was any of us," the other man says, "we'd be French toast . . ."

"*You'd* be. I wouldn't be," the woman answers.

"Yeah, you would. You'd be dead meat."

"I'm always for the victim," the woman says.

"We've noticed that," the other man says.

"Put a stove pipe up your skinny ass."

"Okay. I will. And then what happens?"

"Try it."

"What if I already did?"

The three of them are down the dark sidewalk. They are laughing. My guess is they don't ride snowmobiles, only dress the part.

"Two minutes. No casualties. Good job, hostage extractors," the female voice is saying calmly now through the bullhorn. Police and firemen are beginning to de-congregate. The sky—I gaze up to it—is as starry as a planetarium, promising colder temps tomorrow for Paul's and my departure. It's still early evening. A good night for an extraction.

There is, in fact, out here in the cold, with the ersatz crime scene closing like the circus leaving town, a surprisingly upbeat insider feel I appreciate—of things accomplished, if not perfectly. Two long firetrucks move off into the night, lights softly blinking. The kliegs are being dismantled. Firefighters in flame-gear are around having a laugh and a smoke. Neighbors have filtered back indoors. The street is resuming the familiar anonymity I like. I hear a motor—a chainsaw or a snowmobile—crank into life. Then another. Possibly a third. They scream out, then are distant. An upstairs light in the dark house in front of which I am standing clicks on. A man's heavy figure, fully clothed, passes the rectangle and doesn't reappear. Lilting snow begins sifting through trees out of the clear and starry sky. Minnesota can get snow out of a turnip.

———•———

THE GREAT, TEXAS-SIZE HOUSE IS SILENT WHEN I GET INSIDE its front door—not a bad sign, not a good sign for my son's well-being. Heat's turned up, all lights are blazing. The oversized living room, anchored at one end by a wide gas-log fireplace, has been set up for our cornhole competition—furniture repositioned by my son from his chair, cornhole stations with stacks of cornhole bags at the ready. The Kalbfleische furnishings—zebra-skin sectional, rattan rugs, chrome sling chairs, an Eames knockoff for the man of the house, some western cactus prints mixed in with Marya Kalbfleische's New England acrylic miniatures—portray a loveable, tatty hodgepodge no one would think twice about leaving behind. Bob Kalbfleische, in his prime, was in patient outreach at the Clinic; Marya, a visiting art teacher in the high schools. They bore no children, enjoyed travel, until Bob developed mentation deficits, and money became a thought.

The house—silent, too hot and splashily lit—feels clamorous to me. Police must experience this all the time—the teeming hyper-awareness of rooms to be entered, not knowing what's there. Paul, with his head in the oven. Paul, pendulous behind the bathroom door. I do what I can to make this not be unnerving.

I step through the dining room and hear the big Kenmore go kuh-*chunk* in the kitchen as its compressor kicks on. Something creaks in the house. A gunked odor floats through—vaguely gassy. Though when I enter the kitchen, here is a pizza, box-lid open, one triangle removed. Paul is slowly losing his sense of taste and craves for more and more exotic flavor combinations. This one, a "kitchen sink"—marked on top—seems to be pickles, cherries, anchovies and some kind of charred Spam Paul calls "chunder steak." I pry up a slice—I'm starving—give it a sniff, then put it back.

For a moment in the ticking kitchen, I enjoy a reverie that I can have a peaceful drink alone. Simultaneously I hear my son's voice back in his room, no doubt at his laptop where he maintains connectivity—increasingly attenuated—with the outside world. I hear him say loudly, as if he was talking to someone there. "Ha! You pulled that one outa your fat ass, didn't you?" Likely he is FaceTiming with his odd friends cohort, trading Tony Newley trivia. I am no longer worried. He is in his elephant.

I open the freezer for my liter of Stoli and pour three fat fingers into a National Park commemorative tumbler, frosting it as liquid hits the glass. My tumbler bears a color photograph of the Grand Canyon—tourists on a wooden platform gazing into the abyss. I raise a toast to the Kalbfleisches. Happy Floridians. Their tumbler collection does not include Mount Rushmore.

I give a thought, the Stoli instantly taking hold of me, to Paul's and my hoped-for trip tomorrow. Not the grand excursion I'd have chosen. Any father of any son would prefer para-sailing off the Eiger. Scuba-ing deep into the Blue Hole. Escapades we could afterwards claim to have had the time of our lives doing. Die happy. Not that anyone ever does die happy. The idea of choice in most things is of course a feathery lie of western philosophy. Selling houses lets you know it. *There*, humans regularly choose then unchoose, choose then regret choosing, choose then rechoose, resist choosing, then choose wrong and learn to like it. Choice usually isn't choice, only what you're left with. Paul, I know, would like a clearer view of his choices in his current predicament. On one of our weekly drives out Highway 14 to survey the city from a height, he recently said (shockingly) to me, "How old are you in heaven, do you think? Will I stay the age I am?"

"As opposed to what?" I said. We were watching the sun sink into the snowy prairie-scape, turning the sky fiery. I was, as I said, shocked.

"Don't be a prick."

"I didn't know you cared about things like that," I said.

"You can't control what you think," he said. "You *are* a prick."

"The afterlife's not my area of expertise. It's all a great mystery to me."

"A mystery's not the same as not knowing the answer. Forget it."

Another time, we were driving from the Rathskeller, his preferred Rochester dining-destination, where he orders schnitzel to be able to say "schnitzel."

"I feel like I'm getting smaller," he said. He wasn't smiling, his mouth part-way open, his tongue point on his dry lips.

"I'm sorry."

"I'm achieving my essential self, is what Dr. Oakes said."

"I've never thought I had one of those," I said, turning onto our street.

"It means embracing whatever you're doing at any given moment. It's really simple. You're just not very good at it."

"I guess you have to be there."

"You do," he said. "That's where I am. I'm *there*."

Often, when he's alone in these weeks we've been in Rochester, he'll careen into a futilist's rage—over new difficulties buttoning his shirt, squeezing toothpaste out of the tube, combing his hair into a comb-over for when he goes to the Clinic and wants to be handsome. In these moments he beats his temples (I believe)—which he also did as a child. I can hear him through the walls, his thinning voice, "Mo-ther-fuck-ing *tooth-paste*! I can choose to terminate you. Replace you with a fucking suppository."

I'm scared shitless when I hear these rantings, grateful not to be in his room with him and to feel more helpless than I already feel. I'm as stymied, of course, as he is about death, of being exiled from awareness (the thing we treasure more than love). Which is why in the middle of the night, confounded by such thoughts, my mind soars often to the solar system—*its* mysteries, logos and lexicon. Null infinity, event horizons, nebulas bright and dark—all the ways by which things we don't understand are consolingly contained by larger things we understand even less. Paul never (up to now) took life all that seriously, always kept a weather eye on its transitory character, its existence as bright embers tossed into the dark. And even though he is determined not to let Al's define him now, and to find and accept a practical vocation as a dying man, I sense he is still all over the map about death and has not had nearly enough of lived life. The fact that things end may be the most interesting quality about them; but it's different if it's you that's ending. Though, as in all things, I could easily be wrong.

———

WITH MY GRAND CANYON TUMBLER, I VENTURE DOWN THE carpeted hallway toward the bedrooms. The closest is mine, then Paul's; the third contains the Sony 65 where we watched Super Bowl LIV (KC ran away with it; #15 the MVP). The farthest contains Paul's laptop, by which he's in touch with Sri Lankans who play speed chess, and human logistics websites where visitors swap humorous stories about non-lethal restraint devices. He is a frequenter of chat rooms where people less sensitive than "these webinar pussies" trade hard-core AI's experience and outrage. Also sites about ventriloquism, Anthony Newley sightings, research into new fatal illnesses, body morphology, color blindness (he thinks he has it but doesn't), and hook-up services for people with not much time to live. "Should I be saving myself for something more *appropriate*?" he's asked me. I didn't have an answer.

Shadowy hallway photos here reveal the Kalbfleisches—side-by-side on a bridge that may be Pont Neuf. The happy couple at Machu Picchu. On skis atop some snowy mountain, smiling into a wintery sun. Bob is sober-faced in front of the Mayo Building—early career, from his full head of hair. Marya stands at an ornate fountain beside a woman who looks exactly like her—possibly her twin. Later, Bob, older in a hospital bed with Marya leaning in, both of them laughing. Vodka-numb, I understand that nothing about these photos tells the whole story of what it is to be a Kalbfleische. If I met them, I'm sure I'd like them and have things in common. Though *having* children makes most similarities moot.

When I peek around the door jamb, Paul is in his wheelchair asleep in front of his computer, with the ceiling light on. He's wearing the red-and-green-striped Marimekko bathrobe once owned by Marya Kalbfleische, and a baggy T-shirt that says "Complaints Dept." with a big red arrow pointing to his groin. He has many such shirts bought online. The "Glen Campbell Good-bye Tour" with a photo of Glen in sunnier days. "Drive German, Dress Italian, Kiss French." A vintage Chiefs jersey he's had for decades and believes is worth money. Plus a USMC one he bought in my honor—and against my wishes—in Cedar Falls, on our drive out in December.

Asleep in his chair, he looks depleted—big headphones and glasses on, head back (un-snoring), mouth agog, belly rising and subsiding. I see him this way often. Except for breathing, it's how I think he'll look when he's dead.

I sit on the edge of the guest-room bed—jaunty blue-and-white nautical coverlet—and silently observe my son, try to see all of him while he is still all here. Since I am so close-up to him in my daily maintenance I often do not see him well. When my mother died, in 1965 in Skokie, the evening before her burial, I visited the funeral home—Kresge's—to pay her a final call. Her casket was open in one of the smaller boudoirs. It had not been long since I'd seen her alive. When I stepped into the softly lit room and pulled up a folding chair to sit beside her, I felt suddenly and unexpectedly more alive than I'd felt in months. I was in despair that she was gone and I was alone forever (it seemed). I was in all likelihood headed to the jungles of Vietnam in a few months. I had nothing to be happy about. But sitting beside her empty presence I felt invigorated, my spirits gathered. It was no Jimmy Cagney moment in which I "talked" to my mother, promised her I'd do better, told her how beautiful she was (she wasn't, she was dead), committed myself to a life of kinder acts and selflessness. I don't know if I thought *anything*, profound or otherwise. But if I said I tingled all over that wouldn't be wrong. I didn't "see" anything new. I didn't decide to skip the next day's sad duties, drive to Grand Marais and hire out on an oar boat. Nothing was different. *I* wasn't different. I stood and looked down onto my mother's lifeless, rouged face. I noticed a small, pale scar in front of her left ear. I noticed that her strong nose made her look, in death, slightly like an eagle. Her mouth, closed tight by the embalmer's stitchery, had at its corners the shadow of a faint, naughty smile—which I guess had always been there but was never remarked. It cannot be that I saw my mother truly for the first time only when she was dead. But I saw her, I suppose you'd say, singly. Outside of any contexts but mine and death's. And I felt intensely alert and intensely attuned—to myself. And that was all.

The point being we ought not wait 'til it's too late to see the people we might think we see already.

Paul, in his wheelchair, breathes rhythmically, sighs, sniffs, huffs, his warty fingers flittering. Sometimes in sleep he laughs. I hear it through the walls. In his dreams, does he know he has a fatal disease? Are we only sick when we're awake? Is the joke on us?

What I feel though, watching him, is an undeniable sensation of negligence. My own. And fear. Fear that I have never afforded him his adult due, have placated him, under-rated him, sometimes forgotten him, as if he was not always plausible to me, being who he is: Fattish, balding, warty-fingered, not so empathetic, not a good listener, sometimes a bore and a bloviator—like numberless forty-seven-year-olds. These of course do not add up to defects. It is simply that now and then I think, *How can this man be my son?* Many fathers must experience this bafflement. It is *not* laudable.

I stand and take a step nearer. I mean to see what's on his table. His cell phone, which to my knowledge no one calls him on but the Clinic. A Mayo pamphlet about cataracts, which he suffers. His ALS Society diploma and ID card. A genealogy report which confirms him to be "English" and "Western European" (Dutch from his mother), also surprisingly French. Not what he'd hoped, which was at a minimum "some kind of African." Here is a printout listing significant people who've died in the past year. I. M. Pei. Diahann Carroll. Lee Iacocca. Claus von Bülow. Daryl Dragon. One of the Monkees. He's told me that when he considers dying, it interests him to know the company he'll be keeping. Here is a tube of hemorrhoid cream—he is a sufferer there, too. Here is today's *USA Today*, his favorite news source, brought by Nurse Wanda. Here is a black, sequined yarmulke, given him by one of his doctors for "days when being a Jew might help"—as close as he comes to being religious. Also, a printout from an online genetics lab in Texas that tells him about other diseases he can look forward to if he were to be alive.

In his chair beside me, my son farts a soft, fragrant hiss. A keeper. SBD. Air of elephant, he calls these. In sleep, he rolls his mealy tongue upwards in his mouth and makes a "hnuff" noise of—I suppose—pleasure. Here is his once-bitten pizza triangle nested on a folded scrap of paper onto which he's written something—notes I should read to keep up with him. Out on darkened, snowy, now-emptied New Bemidji Street, I hear the muffled bangety-bangety of the snowplow. He has possibly heard nothing of the "hostage extraction." The house ticks. It is six o'clock. I know very well where my child is. He is here, with me.

Here, also is his "suicide book." *To Be or Not To Be: What Is the Answer?* By a Dr. Romeo Hudspeth of SUNY Oneonta, Department of Philosophy and Human Ethics (I didn't know there were other kinds). Paul has ordered it on Amazon but to my knowledge not opened it. Though I have, on the sly. It is a compilation of capsule biographies of well-known suicides—Charles Boyer, Clover Adams, et al., a hundred total—plus details of their untimely deaths, followed by explanations of why each should've held off; (help was around the corner; things weren't really all that bad; tomorrow would've looked different; if only someone else had been there to talk to). It's hard to think of suicides having a syllabus.

Paul and I have talked only side-wise about suicide. Al's patients all think about it—with good reason—and sometimes are known to pull it off. My belief is that he will not, since it requires "a commitment" I don't think he has, and because, as I said, life still interests him. He's aware, though, he could reach a condition in which he might wish to "purchase the real estate" but not be able. He's wondered to me if I'd "do the honors" for him. To which I've said no, though truthfully that time would have to come for me to really know—which would not then be suicide, per se. He's told me about a friend at Hallmark who "did it." A gregarious, older Cuban-American woman who worked in the "care card department" (sympathy, new babies, wedding showers) not the humor department where the geniuses work. This woman, he said, simply got tired of writing goopy cards all day and pretending to "care" when she didn't really give a shit. She didn't inform a soul or pull a long face. One day she just stopped her car on the Heart of America Bridge and jumped in the Missouri River, leaving behind a note that said, "If you get out of life with one friend left, you're probably a kiss-ass."

I myself have long considered suicide to be a completely personal matter. Not always a weakness or a "disease" needing curing. For many, suicide must be as natural as booking a small-ship cruise to the Canaries—only you don't make it back to port. Dr. Hudspeth says it's usually better to wait if you *can* wait—like resisting a doughnut craving. Though it's also true that suicide experts are mostly people who haven't succeeded doing it themselves.

I have a friend in Haddam I occasionally go fishing with, whose mother, age 88, "took her own life," was declared dead, received a toe tag, rigor mortis well underway, the whole nine yards. Only by some chromosomal intransigence, she revived in the morgue and sat up talking about baseball. Once they'd let her out of the crazy ward (where my friend said she belonged) she fell in love with a younger man (68), moved to the Catskills, began making designer cheeses, and had the time of her life until she tried it again at 103—this time with success. Which leads me to believe there must be more to the idea of killing yourself than meets the eye—if you'd do it twice.

At 74, with a modest laundry list of ailments and sorrowing memories, I think of killing myself no less than once a day. Probably I, too, lack the nerve and would get balled up with practicalities and let the moment elude me. Which is probably why most people fail to kill themselves. Not that they wouldn't like to be dead. The small stuff just gets in their way. The bigger mystery, of course, is why more people choose to stay alive.

Reaching for Paul's page of notes underneath his wedge of "kitchen sink," I clumsily brush a key on his laptop, which brings his screen to life—like the heavens opening not when you want them to. I take a teetery step back, trying not to stumble, and get a strong whiff of Paul's sweats, his unwashed hair, the pizza and his sleeping breath. It is an *old-man* aroma.

On his screen, The Masters is on from last April. Tiger in his red muscle shirt and black assassin's cap, strong as a stevedore at age 43, striding the 18th with Joe-the-caddie lugging behind. Tiger is steely—ready to get this bullshit over with, salvage his 2-shot lead, collect another green jacket (and the 11.5 mil), embrace destiny, reburnish the image, tell the sportswriters to kiss his ass. It is one of *the* moments in golf history—up there with caddie Ouimet's 1913 Open victory and Sarazen's shot-heard-round-the-world. I didn't know my son liked golf.

Paul is staring at me when I happen to look down at him. He doesn't speak or blink or seem even to breathe, as if wherever he's just been he'd prefer not to leave.

"What're you doing?" His voice is a croak.

"Nothing," I say softly. I put my hand on his yielding shoulder, which causes him to groan. On the screen Tiger is already arms-aloft, putter brandished, garish grin of triumph on his un-handsome face. He, too, will soon be bald. "Does that hurt?" I say. Possibly Paul has taken the fall I feared. Left alone, unno-ticed. Negligence.

With his right hand crinkled he pulls his earphones down around his neck. "What?" I hear bzz-bzz-bzz-ing. Anthony Newley possibly but not recognizable. I hear the snowplow still going—the saddest of sounds. "My voice is weird, isn't it?" It *is*. Thinner and younger.

"I don't notice."

He stares silently at the screen. Tiger embracing young son, Charlie. "I was dreaming. You and me and Mom and Clary and Ralph were at Mount Rushmore."

"That's good. I've got that all arranged now." I don't want to talk about his dead mother. Mom.

He clears his throat. "I was stuttering in the dream. And I had a service dog who was Mr. Toby." Our loveable old Basset Hound from when he was little, and who got run over right in front of him. A day he's never forgotten.

"Okay."

"I used to stutter, didn't I?" He half looks around at me. I am beside and behind him, looking down onto his comb-over.

"You did a lot of things." From above him, I make out the faint cicatrix in the corner of his left eye beside his glasses' lens. A wound from thirty years ago, which left him with vitreous swimmers, astigmatism, thick glasses and cataracts (but not color blindness).

My son twaddles his fat fingers, hands resting on his gut and his Complaints Dept. shirt. Tiger is long-striding, cap in hand, up the ramp to Butler Cabin. All smiles. Win. Win. Win. Win. Win.

"Did you remember today's the anniversary?"

"You asked me that." He swivels his head around again. His color isn't wholesome, a little yellow and shineless in the poor bedroom light. His mother cannot see him, which is good. He may think so, too. He makes a soft humming in his throat. It is him being satisfied with this moment. His fingers twitter faster. "How was Nurse Stiffler?"

His lips evert in pleasure. "Great. She may not come back. Now that my study's over. She has bigger fish to fry." He loves saying this. "I've come into my own, I guess, Lawrence."

"You have. Grace under no observable pressure."

"Hmmh." He looks at his screen where a handsome sportscaster in a yellow jacket is soundlessly putting everything into perspective. The preposterous comeback. The brazen triumph. The glory of it. The poetry. Paul sighs in appreciation. Vodka quilts everything for me. I place two hands on his shiny black wheelchair handles. It's not seven yet. But I must get him to bed. "How about a cornhole?" he says. His eyes tighten with delight. Hilarity is his refuge.

"Rain check. Like your massacre movie."

"Oh. Great." He puts his earphones on the desktop, takes off his glasses and peers at the window where the room and we are reflected. Nothing else is going on. "I'm not so sure this bullshit meet and bleat in the morning's worth it. Are you? I'm a lot fitter than the other victims. I don't want to make 'em feel bad. It's easier in a webinar." He's referring to his Medical Pioneers reception at ten, which I wish he'd forgo, since I want us to be starting for Mount Rushmore. I say nothing, though, to preserve any chance of it happening. "Do you think they'll have paper tableclothes and sheet cake?"

This is a joke to him, I don't know why. "Yeah. And fruit punch and pecan sandies. You're the guest of honor."

"Turd in every punch bowl."

"Bride at every funeral. Plus a lovely gift."

"A watch with no numbers." He is remorseless.

"We can decide in the morning. Okay?"

"It'll be a hoot. Hoot-hoot. Hoot-hoot. Pppttt." He looks up and smiles evilly.

"Hoot hoot," I say. "Pppttt." I begin pulling him back from his crowded desk, and we are off to bed early.

———————

AT 11:08 I SIT STRAIGHT UP IN MY BED, LIKE THE DEAD IN Hardy's poem. When you go to bed at 7:30, night yawns ahead like a prison sentence. A copy of *Disgrace* is perched on my chest—I discovered it in the nightstand. The little reading-lamp beam burns down on its satiny white cover. When I reach to set it on the bed table, I see a sentence I've underlined. "With careful ceremony he gets to his knees and touches his forehead to the floor." I have the feeling I have done this very thing earlier in the night, in my sleep. Some obeisance having to do with Ann's death anniversary. Though I don't remember dreaming of her. I dreamed, instead, of searching for Paul inside a vast, empty airplane hangar where people are speaking German and riding around on Segways. This then shifted to looking for my car—the old Crown Vic—in a deserted parking structure that could've been in Ann Arbor. My goal as always is to forget my dreams as fast as possible, since they never reveal anything but what I know already. I'm aware of *why* I might've dreamed of Ann, but have no idea what it would signify—why I'd bow down.

I've waked up hungry as a lion—having forgotten to eat since lunch, when I had potted meat and Ritz crackers and delivered Paul to his therapy session. His "kitchen sink" is still out on the counter. But lights in the hall will wake me up—I leave them on so Paul won't fall when he visits the can. He's done this three times. Much of what I do is preserve him. For caregivers the world is a world of unfinished business.

I turn off my bed lamp and fumble in the side table for two fortune cookies scrounged from our last visit to Master Kong's, which I don't care for but Paul does. I free both from their wrappers and crunch them down with dregs of my vodka. They are tasty and stale and leave me satisfied without having to leave the bed. The ability to feel good when there's almost no good to feel is a talent right up there with the talent for surviving loss—which I also apparently possess, along with the skill of forgetting. When I played Little League, and we lived in Biloxi, I was once heart-searingly dropped from my team, Biloxi Flooring, for manifest lack of baseball skills. This was by far the darkest moment in my eleven-year-old life. No one got dropped. Ever. If you were no good, you simply never got to play. Rode the pine in your uniform, clutching your glove but never getting a chance. Inside our house, a shamrock-green Back Bay bungalow, I moped around for days, ashamed, future-less. My mother acted worried. My father had a talk with me about facing obstacles and the unfairness of the world, which I thought was a lot of bullshit. Then, on the third day of my exile, at our front door came a knock. It was Saturday morning. Our practice day. One of my teammates, Bill Anderson, was outside standing on the steps, holding his Wilson and his bat. He was our starting right fielder. As I stood there, craven, he told me he'd decided to go to a Christian renewal camp in Alabama and was quitting the team. A place was open for me if I wanted it. I should show up for practice that afternoon. I almost kissed him, though we shook hands like little grown-ups. It was the kindest thing anybody would ever do for me until Pug Minokur invited me to try out for the varsity at Lonesome Pines. Yes, I said. I would go. You bet. My heart swelled. Bill Anderson seemed to understand.

I went back to the kitchen and told my parents about this stroke of impossible luck. My father said to me, "I wouldn't go if it was me, Franky. I wouldn't give the sons of bitches the satisfaction." My mother looked down at her plate containing a pimento cheese sandwich. I knew she agreed with him. For them—prideful, Depression-worn—being asked to come back was a bigger insult than being sent away. I should feel worse than I already did.

But what I felt—and why I remember it now in my chilly room in Rochester, far away in life and time from Biloxi, summer of 1956—was, "Happy days are here again, the skies above are clear again." I went straight to my room, reclaimed my glove, my orange Biloxi Flooring 'BF' cap and cleats. I literally ran out past my parents, headed for the diamond, which was two blocks away, though practice wouldn't start until three. All thoughts of humiliation and cruel exclusion—which had caused me to question my very existence—had been routed by the chance to feel good about *something*. About anything. My parents never mentioned the matter again. My mother even came to a couple of games when I either didn't play or played badly. My father never came. I sensed he'd seen a weakness in me. I was a boy who didn't view the world in the severe ways he did. Which I didn't. It has always been my problem—spiritual insulation from too much bad and too much good. Both my wives have pointed this out as not an ideal way to live life. But it is how I'm "adapting," I believe, to my current lineup of dire requirements. It may be why I dreamed of Ann, and then forgot it.

In the dark now, feeling remarkably positive as cold seeps in my window, the savor of stale cookie and warm vodka on my tongue, I dig deeper into my bedside-table drawer for the package of Kools one of the Kalbfleisches has left behind. Plus, a book of matches with the imprimatur of the Hotel Allerton in Chicago. One of these ciggies—dry as kindling—I fasten to my lips, scrape a match, and in an instant am huffing a wad of hot menthol smoke, trying not to suck it down wrong, since it will set me to growlfing. I climb out of bed, feet-chilled, cold going up my pj legs, and walk to the barely open window, blowing a smoke funnel into the gap and out through the screen. It is a very good thing to smoke in the dark in one's pj's beside a cold window, beyond which a frozen world rests its weary bones for the next day's trials. I have never smoked, but it can't be such a bad thing at my age. There are few enough of these pleasures.

Outside, the street is not eventless. In the citrus-y sodium streetlamp glow, snowflakes are no longer falling, only glittering ice crystals hanging in the stillness. An idling police cruiser sits in front of the extraction duplex—the house and yard swaddled in crime-scene tape, the officer visible in the dashboard glow, looking at his phone. The ice rink across the street in Kutzky Park is misty and still lighted. Two skaters stand talking at center ice, leaning on their hockey sticks. Somewhere I hear muffled voices laughing. A distant generator is humming. An unfelt breeze chortles a roof vent on the house next door. A car girders down Bemidji Street on studded tires. On the sidewalk in front of the Abyssinian church, where the message board says "Worship on Facebook," a darkened male figure is taking a piss against a tree, the sight of which alerts the officer in his cruiser to switch on his blue light, causing the man to zip up and shuffle away into the park. Down the street, our neighbor, the immense, humming Clinic, presides like an ocean liner. "Come on! We'll fix you," it promises. "And if we can't, you won't mind."

I take another drag on my Kool, but inexpertly let smoke into the wrong passageway, causing me to gasp, gurgle, then a clap-shut of all sphincters, then a strangled breath for smoke to escape wherever it can inside me, leaving me seeing spots—chest aching, head swirling, minty vileness assailing my mouth. I am a fool. Again.

Finding my way back to bed, I take a last dribble of vodka to calm all. More and more of life seems remarkably like every other thing in life, now—at least to me. Illness like health, waking like sleep, glad like sorry, surprised like not much interested. This, too, is a feature of my age, I'm sure—or, as the saying goes, "of aging." I am aging. I have aged. I have come of age. I am agèd. I have reached a great age (but am not, myself, great).

So then my trusty peace mantra to beckon sleep's return. The peace of Paris. The peace bonus. The Peace Bridge. The Peace River. The Peace Garden State. Make peace not war. The end of art is peace. Justice of the peace. Peace officer. Peace pipe. Peace treaty. Peace. Peace. Peace. Peace. Peace. Peace. Peace. Peace. The peace that passeth understanding . . .

PART II

PART II

FIVE

Nine a.m., we are up—shit, shaved and showered—and about the day's vital business. Paul has required help with all. The things you think you'll loathe are often not things you mind at all. I don't mind, for instance, my caregiving duties. What else *should* I be doing? What else *would* I be doing? Sitting at my House Whisperers desk, staring out the window at leafless oaks and mulberries, wondering how I got all the way to *now* so fucking fast? All while my son fades away in his sister's care? Unthinkable.

Paul has dressed in his regulation Clinic-day ensemble—chinos, Oxford button-down, etc., from Brady's Dad 'n Lad at home—ignoring that it's nine degrees outside, with just enough light breeze to kill you. He's struggled with his tripod cane and opted for his "towel rack" walker, which is not what he wanted for his final Clinic appearance. I've given him his Riluzole, combed his hair into a best-practices baldy cover-up, shaved his face with my Norelco, helped brush his teeth, cleaned his glasses, applied Blistex to his lips, patted on English Leather, all after spreading ice-melt out front and starting the car to get it warm inside. I've fixed our breakfast, which he managed by himself. (Cream of Wheat—he likes the happy Black chef on the box, who's naturally being phased out.) While he was on the toilet, I've also packed two blue Michigan 'M' duffels with longies, heavy socks, sweaters, Bean pants, mukluks, gloves and balaclavas, plus his Chiefs parka and watch cap. I'm banking on a departure straight from the Clinic, and getting on the road to Mount Rushmore.

Paul has waked up buoyant to "hit the Meet & Greet," "pick up the hardware." But I'm aware he may be apprehensive—he hasn't said so—about how he will conduct himself when he no longer has his important work as a medical groundbreaker with doctors as his best pals, and only me to help make life be life for as long as it can be. I can't blame him.

In the car he's moody following difficulties managing the front steps using his walker, then getting situated into the Honda—which he calls my "Honda Ascetic." He's worn his new car coat from Kohl's and black rubbers over his Weejuns. He's not warm enough and is irascible about being cold, even in his Thinsulates and houndstooth Irish cap which makes him look prissy. "Only idiots get cold," he growls during the two-block drive to the Clinic. "Plus, I look like I'm dying." His knees are bumping—either from cold or fresh fasciculations. He's worse today—which could be from anxiety. Though with Al's what exactly causes what is rarely clear, just the outcome is never better for long.

WHEN I WOKE AT SEVEN—LATER THAN I WANTED—I HEARD Paul in the house clumping with his cane, talking to himself. "Put that right there. Just put that right there . . ." I feel he's safe when we're both inside, even if I can't see him. I'd been grinding my molars and had forgotten my night guard. I was also sore in my shoulders and thighs, which meant I hadn't slept peaceably.

Paul's scribbled notes filched last night were on my bed table. His handwriting, which he used to be vain about, now looks as if he'd clutched the pen like a dagger. We think what people write down in their private moments will always reveal crucial evidence of their innermost selves. Only, what goes on in anybody's head is rarely worth knowing. Paul's private notes said . . .

C's draft #32. Need RB
If you're a weatherman, does thunder scare you?
I stare at women's crotches. Too much!
Oswego. How many of these are there? Indian name?
Get a tattoo.
Is my munch big enough?
Re-useable things.

Nothing very enlightening—except that my son seems not much different from someone who's not gravely ill.

On my voicemail, which I listened to in bed as morning light returned, were two messages. One from Betty Tran. One from Sally Caldwell, calling in the middle of my night from wherever she was, often—but not this time—expressing uncertainty about the grieving process.

Betty's message was typical. "Frank. I think I saw you outside tonight. Why didn't you come in? I wanted to see you. Bye now." Her alluring little laugh, leaving me half heart-sick, but half-relieved.

Sally's message was more satisfying and more information-based than usual. "Hi there, sweetheart," she said. "I've just had lunch and am about to take a nap. I thought of you. It's almost Valentine's Day. Which you don't much like. I hope you're taking care of old Paul. It must be frozen in Minnesota. I remember the winters when I was in Chicago, and my kids were teeny tinies.

Brrrrr. I'm not suffering my usual failure of faith today, but I just realized that maybe there isn't ever anybody who's perfect for anybody else. I should've maybe understood that where you're concerned. I used to think of you as priestly, you'll remember, because you didn't seem to need anybody. I also said there was something hollow in you. I don't believe either one of those now. It's probably best you didn't pick up. I've had a glass of this unbelievably strong—'Koge,' they call it—it's like wine but not wine. I hope today's a good day for you. Happy Valentine's on Friday. I of course love you. Bye." Click.

Neither of these communiqués contained data immediately useful to my new morning's challenges.

———

THE MAYO CLINIC IS WHAT'S HAPPENING AT TEN O'CLOCK ON Wednesday, two days before Valentine's. Cars and hotel limos and taxis and vans and Ubers are waiting to off-load under the Gonda Building porte cochere. My son is apparently not the only one with medical issues today.

"Clinic" is standard middle-western understatement for what Mayo *really is*—a glistening, many-building'd, many-tiered, many-lobed, swarming colossus where, on any given day, thousands enter and thousands leave 200% confident that if there's a cure for them, this is where it lives, and they're smart sumbitches for being here. Hospitals mostly dispense dread. Here, no one goes away unsatisfied, even if they leave in a box. When I came in 2001 to have my prostate blasted with titanium—my daughter Clarissa making the crucial decisions—I arrived morbidly muddled, resigned I'd come all this way only to wither and die. But stepping into the "great atrium," murmurous with thronging humankind crossing and crisscrossing like the great trade routes of antiquity, eyes fastened where they needed to be going, all advancing with assurance—patients, loved ones, doctors, nurses, medical tourists, citizens in wheelchairs, on walkers, riding gurneys, hauling drip poles and leading service dogs—I could instantly see that prostate cancer was little more than a chicken-shit complaint I could easily get taken care of at the arrivals desk. So restorative was the Mayo *climate*, I was glad *something'd* gone wrong so I could get it fixed here. My son's prognosis, of course, is different.

Today, Paul and I do not check in as we usually do. We're VIPs this morning. A Mayo "concierge"—one of the greeters the Clinic provides for patient assistance—steps out the revolving doors into the stifling chill as if he knows my car. He's pushing a wheelchair and wearing a blue Mayo parka and a big, coffee-breath, come-on-in grin, as if he knows not only my car, but everything about both of us. These fellows are mostly 60-ish, jowly-jovial Rotarian types with hamburger laughs, ex-military or retirees out of the sheet metal trade, who'd otherwise be home with the wife watching TV.

"Here's trouble, heeeere's trouble." Our man starts right in with Paul, getting the car door opened since Paul's not able. He doesn't know us from Frederick Douglass but pretends he does, has our names and my plate number on a list. Burt Lister, his name tag says. Paul's right hand is clenching and curling, and he looks already defeated in his car coat and Irish cap.

"Here's your buddy," I say across the car seat. Paul swivels half around and gives me a fierce look. His glasses are fogged, his hands twittering. "Just take a breath." I set my hand on his shoulder. "This'll get over."

"What will?" he snaps. "The whole fuckin' nine yards?"

"We'll get on our way before you know it." I smile at him.

"Look out here, now, John Dillinger. We'll have to give you

the chair if you get frisky," Burt says loudly. He's smiling and goofing while he's getting Paul out and into the wheelchair. A blast of frozen winter crashes into the warm car interior through the open door. "Take hold of my bear's paw now, John, and *oouut yoo cooom*. Okay. I'll do it for you. Who's this guy show-furring you around? Is this your butler?"

"I'm his dad." Leaning toward the door.

"We all need a driver, don't we, Dad?" Burt's levering Paul out and onto his feet, then plopping him down into the extra-size Mayo chair, made (I've learned) by the same German company that made Messerschmitts. Someone's begun honking behind us. The drive-thru's spilling back. Pedestrians are on the move around us. "Just go park your chariot, Dad. I'll have Mr. Cupid inside the door. I'm sure he's got a joke for me. He's a corker."

Clutching the black-plastic chair arms, Paul is already agitated from being manhandled by a stranger. Up to now, he's been able to navigate the Clinic by himself; but not today. Which scares him. I smile, consider giving him a thumbs-up, but he isn't looking my way. He is looking at nothing.

"Will do," I say. The passenger door closes as Paul is maneuvered into the crowded building without ever looking back at me. I give him the thumbs-up anyway, to show the colors.

————◆————

MY PHONE'S BINGING WHEN I PULL INTO THE MAYO PARKING structure—signs reading FULL all the way to the top, where only a few cars are and all of wintery Rochester lies below and around. Not a bad place for a sandwich on a sunny summer day. The call is from Betty, which I impulsively answer—though I need to hurry back. She has been thinking of me, which is the best I can hope for. I should ask her to marry me. She'd have plenty of life left once I toddled off.

"Hi."

"Hi. I left you a message." We've rarely talked on the phone. I'm thrilled.

"It was too late to call back." A lie—but we're talking now. All around up here—Level D—are the tops of city buildings, pillowy steam clouds rising off, and close by the great Mayo medi-scape, teeming within. In the eastern distance, I can see the snowy rise of land from which Paul and I survey the city and gain new perspectives. It is a mole hill.

"Why didn't you come in? I saw you," Betty says plaintively. "I was waiting. We had an appointment. Okay?"

"I know. I'm sorry." No need to haul up Sarge-Major Gunnerson and his pathetic Vette.

Betty says something—a single word "yes"—to someone in the room with her or passing by in the hall. A cousin.

"I'll pay for the hour," I say. The wrong thing.

"Are you feeling all right? You could come now. I hear bad tension in your voice. Okay?"

"Okay," I say. "I'm at the Clinic with Paul. I can't come right now."

"My product-branding seminar canceled for Lincoln's birthday. I can see you later." Honest Abe, turning 211 today. I forgot.

"That'd really be swell. Thank you," I say. "I wish I could. Paul and I are driving to Mount Rushmore."

Betty says nothing. Possibly she's forgotten about Paul or doesn't believe he exists. She may not know about Mount Rushmore. "Would you marry me?" I say—because I can. I'm also ready to say, "I'll pay your school bills. We can buy a house in Wayzata. You can join a gym. We'll eat out every night." This scenario doesn't have Paul in it, of course.

Betty says, "Are you having a crisis?" As usual she doesn't say my name. It's possible she's never used it. I can't remember. But she would have to if we got married. At least once.

"Maybe," I say—about a crisis. "Not a big one."

"I wish you'd come now," Betty says sweetly. "I can help you."

"I'm on top of a parking structure. But I'm not jumping off. You didn't answer about marrying me. I'm serious."

"You're the second person to say that in two days." I hear female voices in the background. Dishes tinkling. She's in the kitchen in the Amdahls' house, making toast, networking on the phone.

"That's great," I say. Not for me.

"People are nice."

"That's great, too. You're a very nice girl. Woman, I mean."

"I'm going to marry somebody already," she says, sounding indifferent.

"Who?" Really? Well-endowed, be-ribboned Sarge-Major Gunnerson no doubt. Always faithful.

"He's a pharmacist in the Cities. He's Vietnamese. My sister's husband's brother." I hear clicking on a laptop. "He's from Cloquet."

"What's that? I mean where?"

"By Duluth. Up north. He has two children. His other wife died." Clickety-clickety.

"Is this a new plan?"

"Oh, no. Not a new plan," she says, distractedly. "I keep putting it off."

"What about your hospitality career? Don't you care about that?"

"Oh, sure. We'll move back up there. There's a Wyndham Suites with a water park in Duluth."

"I guess there's no chance of marrying me, then."

"You have your son. That's like a marriage." She giggles. "I wish you would come today."

"Me, too. I can't, though."

"Sometime later, then. Okay? Don't worry about the money."

"I won't worry about it," I say. "I have a valentine for you. I'll send it to you."

"Okay. You can put the money in. Two surprises."

"Two surprises. Right."

"So I see you." I still don't have a name.

"Yes. You'll see me."

"I really like you. Okay?"

"I really like you, too. Okay."

And that, alas—here, atop a parking structure—is the end of that.

———

I'M CHILLED TO THE GIZZARD BY THE TIME I'M INSIDE THE Gonda atrium entrance—the parking elevator has stopped working. Mayo petitioners are flooding in and out the revolving doors. Burt Lister has stationed Paul's chair too close to the sucking draft, where I don't want him to be. He's dying, but he could still get a chest cold.

In his car coat and tweed cap, Paul's gray eyes are sparkling, and his feet in their rubbers are jittery on his wheelchair clips. He is somehow, once again, where he belongs, braying and yorking with Burt about all the things they see eye to eye on. Burt owns a pick-your-own apple orchard in Oslo, Minnesota. Paul owned (with his sister's oversight) a yard 'n garden in KC, where he sold dwarf spruces and weeping cherries. Burt's a Packers fan but respects the prowess of the Chiefs. Burt is a lifelong curling athlete and sees good prospects for wheelchair curling as a

Special Olympics sport. Burt used to be a stutterer but overcame it. Paul has told him a stuttering joke, which they've been howling about.

"Burt rides a big Harley with a confederate flag on the bitch bar," Paul says.

Burt's nodding. "Not everybody understands the symbolism there, but plenty do." His big incisors catch a glint of light.

"I guess so," I say. Crowds are shifting past us out into the towering atrium around which many banked elevators are waiting. It's now 10:20. We're late.

Paul is staring at me goadingly. He's gotten important lowdown from Burt and wants me to know he knows I know he knows I know.

"Okay, Houston," Burt says. "Time to get Flash Gordon here up to 8E Neurology." Burt's releasing the chair brake, giving the wheels a turn and a jerk. "Feet up. We're blasting off here."

"Good stuff," Paul says, and we are away into the vast, living Mayo-opolis.

———

GONDA ATRIUM IS A LOFTY, BUZZING, LIGHT-SHOT SCANDINA-vian fishbowl, and we are three fish swimming through—Burt dedicatedly pushing, Paul in his car coat and Irish cap, me bringing up the rear, sore-collar-boned and achy-hipped from bad sleep, the result of nothing more than being alive. A massage would be good. Over in front of the great window—three stories of glass, outside which a tableau of frozen, morning Rochester street-life is in wintry relief—a barbershop group of red-jacketed oldsters is crooning "Edelweiss" and "Sunrise, Sunset," and nearer the elevators, the direction we're headed, a big happy Rosemary Clooney-looking woman in a pink dress is putting a service dog, a Labradoodle, through its paces while passersby grinningly spectate. Wide corridors lead unceasing foot traffic in all directions. One floor below us is the "subway," a great, tubular shopping arcade where loved ones of the sick, dying and recovering can purchase pizzas, chili dogs and hoagies, while browsing for Mayo-themed tchotchkes and mediocre Norwegian art to take back to Hibbing. It would be completely plausible to *reside* inside Mayo, like Quasimodo in Notre-Dame—and never have to die. Though as much as it's committed to the healing mysteries, Mayo is equally committed to people-moving by the multitudes, which produces an ether of kinetic, germ-free positivism all can breathe. Plus, mingled through the yearning hum is the synchronous chime of other languages and inflections, patients of all stripe and origin on their way *somewhere*, laughing self-deprecatingly, trying not to careen into others, someone sneezing and a perfect stranger without stopping saying "Gesundheit." Here is the feeling of relief and arrival, of things working out well-so-far. Sick is more than normal here—sick is good. Only a nitwit wouldn't love it. And, in my solidly secondary role, nothing at all is about me— a luxury I can't get enough of.

Burt has stopped twice to give patient-pedestrians elaborate directions to where they're going. Everyone carries papers for their next appointment and needs to arrive without their blood pressure blasting off. He tells two Buddhist monks how to get to TGI Friday's on the subway level. He points the way to the serenity chapel for an elderly farm couple—the man in can't-bust-'ems. A well-dressed new-arriver family is looking for the compassionate-care seminar I've attended. Burt, of course, is security *posing* as Samaritan. He's possibly packing, did tours in Tora Bora, and now is finding new ways to make a contribution in a part-time capacity. The feeling inside Mayo is that anyone

and everyone can walk in, sign up for a round of chemo or a cardiac catheterization and be back in the Cities for dinner. If they
sold condos here, I'd buy one.

Paul is now telling Burt he's got Al's and it isn't all that bad.
Burt is regaling Paul about the "winter run" his Harley club makes
up to the Boundary Waters. "Way too cold for the gals," Burt
says. "The rest of us take it in stride. A lot of ex-military. Yep."
"Cold's a clothing choice in my view," Paul says, stupefyingly.
"There you go," as Burt wheels him backwards into the big elevator up to Neuro and all that awaits there. Paul and I haven't talked
again about the Meet & Greet—where we're headed—whether
it's a productive idea. Which he must deem it to be, since we're
going. "I'd live in Mankato if they moved it to Delray Beach," a
woman—someone who isn't getting on our elevator because it's
too crowded—says to a woman inside with us. "Bye now." Smiling in as the door hisses closed. "Don't be gone too long."

Neurology is a beehive when Paul, Burt and I come off the
elevator. The wide waiting room, like an airport waiting room,
features rows of facing, semi-comfortable seating—most of it
occupied—non-aggressive paneling, tasteful, nearly-good plein
air wall art, and a long, crowded check-in desk staffed by good-
natured Minnesota gals who've worked at Mayo a million years
and wouldn't know what else to do with themselves. Clocks
above the check-in give the time in London, Tokyo, Moscow,
New York and Abu Dhabi. Periodically a nurse in scrubs appears
through a pair of swinging doors at the end of the room, and in
a clarion voice reads a patient's name off a clipboard. Instantly,
someone in one of the many chairs begins flagging a hand and
struggling up, shouting "Here!" "Hi! Say your name and birthday for me," the nurse says, leading him or her back through the
doors. "So I guess it's nippy out," the nurse is chirping, allaying
all concerns. "Where're you folks in from? Big Fork! That's a

ways! I guess they keep the roads open for the log trucks. Pretty much have to, don't they . . ." Doors swing closed.

Burt pushes Paul to the end of a chair row, then strides off to the check-in to let the admission women know we're here. We're getting the big-shot treatment due to Paul's status as graduating Medical Pioneer. The end of one life-phase, the commencement of a worse one. The ladies at the desk all know Burt and are laughing about something he's said, letting on he's a complete scandal. He's taken a swipe at his hair with a pocket comb on the way over. "Okay now look, you two," Burt says, back already, leaning hands-on-knees in front of us in his blue Mayo parka and black crepe-sole cop shoes. A minty aroma now is his personal atmosphere. Dense bristles sprout in his big ears. Nothing a woman would go for. "When you folks get all finished now . . ." Burt always speaks louder than he needs to, which causes waiting patients to look at us guardedly. "You just tell the gals at the check-in to beep me." (Somewhere under his coat is a beeper, along with security paraphernalia he and Paul have bonded over.) "I'll head right up here and take you back down. Piece of cake. Okay, Catahoula?" A Minnesota joke of some kind.

"Okay," I say. "Thanks. Piece of cake."

Burt reaches and gives Paul an assuring clomp on the knee. "You keep those dobbers up, Jack Dempsey. Hang in there."

"What does that mean?" Paul says. In his silly car coat and stupid Irish cap he is bedeviled. He wasn't here, and now he *is* here. Not the expected protocol. Burt is someone he now doesn't like all that much. Paul looks up at me, hectored. Burt's probably not a bad guy, confederate flag put to the side.

"We'll beep you," I say. "Thanks." Burt gives me a confidential wink, looks at Paul with patented pathos then heads back toward the elevators. He has a limp I hadn't seen before. Possibly he is a war hero.

Paul starts looking around irritably for someone to take responsibility for us and instruct us what to do. Across from us a pair of women in head-to-toe black burkas is chatting softly, while a scrawny Arab-looking man wearing a surgical mask, and who isn't talking to them, is conversing in English on a cell phone—which are verboten here. All around plenty of older couples, some with grandchildren, are conversing in hushed tones. Several people are in wheelchairs, some tubed up with oxygen valises. There are Asians in suits, Africans in dashikis and big headgear. There are half-camo'd veterans, a smattering of child patients with parents, a Catholic priest. A burly nun. Two heavy-set Texas boys in white hats and flashy boots. Two black-suited Hutterite men arrive together. A brawny Black athlete—possibly a gridiron star, in a tracksuit—with his glamorous white wife. It's the UN. Everybody's vulnerable to their personal mainframe needing re-booting by the best there is. Twice, when I've been waiting for Paul, I've seen celebrities pass through. Once, famed Mark Twain imposter, Hal Holbrook. Another time, Braves all-world swat-master Hank Aaron. Both strode in like they owned the place, went straight through the double doors without being called. My own satisfaction in these long winter weeks has been the elusive relief of doing only what I'm supposed to do and having no trouble doing it. It is a rarity in life. Even if today's visit is unusual.

Paul for a time does not speak, though I can tell he's becoming more irritated. Possibly belligerent—his regular response to anxiety. He doesn't like for only me to be here in charge of him. He wants for more authority than mine. His fingers are twitching, and he's taken off his cap, leaving hair follicles "stalked" on top with plenty of bald real estate exposed. He is as ever odd-looking.

While we wait, I skim today's *Post Bulletin* a prior occupant

has left on my chair. Here are separate stories of the same ra-
bid fox attacking a BMW 6-Series and being fought off by a
woman owner—a Miss Bingham—with an edging tool. There
is a moose loose on a golf course. Four snowmobilers have gone
through the ice on Bamber Lake. A shooting has occurred over
a Christmas toy left in a neighbor's driveway. A private Cessna
has landed (safely) on Interstate 90. As well as a longer story
naming Rochester as a town offering much to people already
here but not much to people who're arriving, and about whether
this is a good or a bad thing. (Good, I'd say.) As a Rochester
newcomer with an ingrained townie mind-set, I'm interested in
the upticks in breaking-and-enterings factored into the rise in
Spanish-speaking citizenry and whether numbers ever lie. Also,
the investigative story on water quality as a vector in Asperger's
incidence. And the "smell" on the new Jack Nicklaus course built
over the site of an old tannery. Most places' stories are like other
places' stories. Regional diversity being any longer a distinction
without a distinction. Which makes me again like Rochester
as a place one might live at some uncertain future time, since I
wouldn't be worried I was missing something somewhere else,
inasmuch as there *is* no somewhere else.

For a moment I doze (almost) in the warm susurrus of the
waiting area. "Well, when that defibrillator fires off, you goddamn well know about it," someone says behind me. Another
man is speaking in a fast-clip subcontinental accent about Air
India cancellations in Chicago. Someone is snoring. Someone
is talking about what a good actor Tom Cruise is. All of it as
The Carpenters are singing "Close to You" piped in from 1970.
"Waaaaaah..."

Without realizing it, I am watching a young and large Black
woman in a business-attire pantsuit—including a necktie—
exiting the double doors where patient summoning goes on. She

has a lustrous showgirl smile and is heading for us. Ducks on a pond. Possibly I have seen her before.

"Paul?" this large woman sings out disconcertingly even before she reaches where we're sitting, both of us locked in interpersonal remoteness. "Hiiiiee. Remember? Meeegan?" Other patients again look around—at her, then at us.

"Yeah." Paul speaks almost inaudibly from his wheelchair. His feet sheathed in black bad-weather rubbers start to fidget. I start to stand up, still achy in my shoulders. This woman is somehow Meegan?

"Don't-get-up, don't-get-up, Mr. Bascombe. Both of you sit right where you are." Paul has no choice. I *have* seen this man-suited, in all ways festively cheerful woman—without knowing her name—at the angst-clouded, first-week ALS family mixer where I made a target of loathing of myself with the other Al's loved ones. Her blue nameplate states she is "Meegan Stooks, MSW—Events Coordinator," a position not known to the US Department of Labor before 1997, but no doubt where a plus-size, extroverted Cleveland State grad with no animus for old sick white people can get her feet on the ground. "Okay. Look." Meegan has big hands, big feet, big rear carriage, perfectly white teeth. A solid six-footer with buzzed hair, a gold ear stud like Paul's silver one, boxy shoes and iron pantyhose. There is not a name for her skin color, but it is deeply dark and flawless and smooth and beautiful with unrevealed hues mixed in. She glows. In college she was the dorm favorite, relentlessly up-for-everything, knew all the songs, made straight-A's, mentored the shy girls, knew every player on every team—but never seemed to land one. In front of Paul and me she's exuding the best possible aroma—sweet vanilla with an understory of something orange. She is perfect for the Mayo Clinic. "We just want to celebrate you. Okay, Paul?" Meegan is imposingly, squarely in front of us, looking slightly startled. Her body all but makes a noise. "Make sure everything's how you want it." Something's vaguely southern in her voice. Possibly the Mississippi section of Ohio, guaranteeing she'll turn you into a pillar of salt if you cross her. White people think all Black people are from the south.

"What're we about to do here, Meegan," I say, summoning my face of sincere but amiable concern. "Paul's not up for too much celebrating." Paul has been looking around as if Meegan wasn't here, and now looks at me as if I'd suggested he was a known criminal.

"Oh, no. No-no," Meegan leans in over-animatedly. "Compleeeetly un-der-stood. We're on the same page, Mr. B. Paul's team just wants to say thanks for being an awesome colleague in the trial and being a pioneer, and give him a token of appreciation. Okay? Nothing in *the world* to worry about."

Mr. B.

"Okay, son?" I say.

"Yeah. Okay," Paul says.

"Are you sure?"

"Yeah."

"*Okay*, then," Meegan says. Straightening, head thrown back, Meegan gives Paul a sly "I've got your number" look. I expect her to wink at him. She is a dazzling specimen of young American womanhood. "We just need a couple quick questions answered." She produces from her inside suit pocket a slab of mobile phone, which she begins puzzling with, urging it to cooperate. Paul is staring up at her, having descended into a buffered gray zone. He has noticed her ear stud. "Okaaaay. Let's see." Meegan shakes her head, feigning frustration with stupid ole technology. She begins reading off the phone's screen. "Any food allergies, Paul? I think there's some sheet cake down there, and it may have peanuts in it. And there's some fruit punch."

"Where?" Paul says, his feet busy, his fingers too, on the hand-grips of his chair. Sheet cake is not lost on him.

"We're going right down that hallway there." Meegan shifts her gaze to the hall and the doors where patients disappear, and where Paul has gone every week for nearly two months. "We've got a really great multi-purpose room down there where everything's set up, and your team and a couple of the other pioneers are waiting. Everybody wants to see you. I don't blame them." She's typing-typing something onto her phone's screen while talking.

Paul has admitted nothing about allergies, which he doesn't have. He has cataracts and hemorrhoids, but apart from that only ALS. His eyes travel to the doors which automatically open, revealing the clarion-call woman in scrubs, consulting her clipboard. "Akmed Faisal Atiyeh!" Her call goes out into the crowded room. "Mr. or Ms. Atiyeh?" No one looks up. There is something mournful about it.

"Ok-aay," Meegan says, perusing her phone. Her hands are smooth and young and skilled, her fingernails ivory and immaculate. "Do you. Let's see. *Do you* mind if when we get in the room someone from public relations asks you some questions for the newsletter? Just some easy questions."

"What?" Paul licks his tongue around his mouth's 'O'. It is his signal of increased agitation. Something's disorienting him. This walloping woman. A change in routine. A mini-stroke.

"Well. I really don't *know!*" Meegan says. "Nothing intrusive. I think there'll be a photographer, too." She widens her flawlessly brown eyes. She's checking down at her phone, ticking boxes off a digital schedule only she can see. "Do you . . . do you think you'll need a wheelchair?" Her eyes find Paul seated in front of her *in* a wheelchair. He stares back at her.

"No."

"O-kay!" Meegan says. "Nope on wheelchair," without looking up. "Can you walk forty feet?"

Paul croaks, "I don't know."

"N-o-o-o-o problem." Click, click, click. She looks down at my son and smiles at him flirtatiously. "So! Are we ready to *pawty*? We've got this great gift for you, too."

"What is it?" Paul says.

"Oh, you'll see, Mr. Man. People want to make a fuss."

Paul looks up at me. His father. Beside him. I must help him. I'm not sure where to start.

"You okay with this, Paul?" is all I can say. Again.

"Okay," Paul says. "Okay yeah."

"Sure he is," Meegan says, snugging her phone away and checking her watch, a delicate gold bracelet sunk into her wrist at the end of her coat sleeve. "We can't hold this man down, can we? You come, too, Mr. B. Come right this way." She steps off surprisingly quickly, leaving us side by side in our chairs.

"I have to push him," I say, getting to my feet with unexpected difficulty, my shoulder making interior scraping noises no one but I can hear. I drop Paul's Irish cap into his lap. "You can look after your own cap, can't you?" He says nothing.

"Come right this way, you two." Meegan's already ten feet away, heading off but looking around to urge us along. "Okay," she says. "You've got a wheelchair. *I* see."

Other patients are again noticing us. (Two shitheads jumping the queue, glomming VIP status while we suffer. Always the way.)

I manage around behind Paul's chair. "Feet up out of the way," I say sternly. The clarion nurse is standing where we're headed. She smiles knowingly at Meegan, then brightly at us.

"Ejner Jensen," she calls out across the roomful of patients. What's happened to Mr. or Ms. Atiyeh? "Here. Ejner Jensen," someone shouts from the back. "I'm here."

"Come on this way, Dad," Meegan is exhorting. I am not—we are not—moving fast enough. She's smiling a coercive events-coordinator smile back to us. It's ten-thirty. Seven-thirty in Abu Dhabi. My feet feel leaded. The corridor ahead is a long thoroughfare of sleek, fluorescent-lit medical goings-on. Personnel in scrubs and white doctor coats, someone pushing a gurney with what might be a corpse on board. Two female nurses emerge from a room and begin running in the opposite direction from us. Two white-coats-of-color stroll along laughing. It is like the *long corridor* with the floaty curtains which the departing supposedly enter, and all the rest of us hope never to.

"It's number sixteen. Right up ahead," Meegan says, chivvying us. "Just on the right. Everything's all set." A couple of nurses are seen to go in this room—Dr. Oakes with them. Two more docs are behind them—one of them Dr. Pommes Frites, whom I've met only twice and who looks just as I pictured him—all talking on cell phones.

Number sixteen has a lozenge illuminated in green over its door, designating *in use*. I do not feel on sound footing here. I hate to say this is like a dream—since nothing is ever like a dream. But this corridor, abuzz, impersonal, baleful, is indeed the dream corridor of death, and I am pushing my son down it. Nothing's worth celebrating here, if you're him. Why do humans have to celebrate goddamn everything? Why is a funeral a "celebration of life"? Why are gloomy priests "celebrants"? Why are celebrities "celebrities"? What is it about people?

"I think we ought to get out of here right now, Paul, and drive straight to Mount Rushmore." I say this twenty feet before we reach room 16, where Meegan awaits, smiling like an undertaker. A woman in a wheelchair is just being rolled in, not in as good shape as Paul Bascombe, but a pioneer none the less. "I don't think this is a good idea." I cannot keep from saying this. "You don't need to be celebrated."

Paul has said nothing as we've proceeded down death's bright companionway. Just stared ahead. "Celebrated for being sick," he says, his fingers beating rat-a-tat-tats on his chair arms, feet bopping in their stirrups. "We can skip it."

"Okay-ay," Meegan is calling to us as I U-turn Paul around and thrust him and myself back toward the swinging doors and the sea of patient faces. The clarion nurse is summoning another pilgrim to his or her assigned hour. "Babiak. William Babiak." Come on down.

———

HURRYING US BACK ACROSS THE CROWD-STREAMING, SUN-SHOT atrium, I detect Burt Lister—parka'd, Arctic-gloved, capless now, chatting up a pair of nurses in pink scrubs, gilding their ears. This is why he bothers with the job—face time with the tomatoes, the wife safe at home.

I'm aiming us toward the revolving exit doors, hoping not to attract Burt's attention in case there's an Amber Alert— kidnapped by father, etc., in spite of best intentions. It's rare to know when enough is enough. Paul is again ogling around the medical agora, fastening onto a last snapshot memory. The octo- genarian barbershoppers at the end of the atrium have finished "If I Had a Hammer" to polite applause, and are tuning up for the Michigan fight song to win a smile from old Wolverines heading off to endoscopy and knee replacement. Paul swivels around and leers at me. He has his Irish topper back on and in his car coat looks like an elderly, bespectacled pawnbroker being taken for an outing by a nephew.

Burt unfortunately *does* spy us. At least he spies *someone* he kinda recognizes. The nurses have scurried off. He's alone beside a white-board by the elevator alcove. "Compassion Fatigue Seminar," a red arrow pointing downstairs. Crowds eddy between us—on crutches, walkers, in motorized chairs—everyone carrying documents, looking miniaturized. Burt surveys the throng like a prison guard, picking out someone to forcibly help. His gaze sweeps past us. I stare straight at him to make myself look unfamiliar. But his big face brightens. He cocks his head, raises both hands in a surrendering 'ain't it always the way' way. He then gives me the international double-selfer handclasp, native to Shriners, Rotarians and Kiwanians the world over. And just that fast we are past him—as the barbershoppers glide into "Hail! To the victors valiant, Hail! To the conquering heroes, Hail! Hail!"

"I have to piss like a Percheron," Paul growls, staring ahead, hunched as if in pain. It's the Riluzole. He has yet to piss his pants, that I know of, and is mortified by the prospect.

"I'm on it," I say and change course toward the Men's. Mayo has facilities everywhere. This, I believe, is a mission Paul can handle solo. "Can you manage it if I wheel you in and go get the car?"

He says, "This is what death's like. You piss all the time."

"I have some experience there," I say. I do. I still do. "You're not exactly dying."

"I'm *in*-exactly dying," he says. "Is that better? I think about death in grainier terms than you do, Lawrence."

I push him straight into the echoing, odorless Men's room and right up to and in front of the tier of metal urinals, spotless as an altar. No one else is in here. Paul's already twisting around, tongue out, as I get the lock clamped on his chair wheel so he can stand and not fall.

Once up, he turns his head with a grimace of dislike where I'm clutching the chair-back for him. Outside the pisser door, arrivers and leavers are noisily thronging. A dog is barking. Cell phones are ringing. The barbershop quartet has finished with "The Victors" and swooned into "Heartaches, har-har-har-takes, it doesn't matter how my heart aches."

"Take a hike, Lawrence." Paul's struggling with the zipper on his khakis, head down, knees against the urinal well, his cap in danger of falling in.

"Watch your cap."

"Watch my cap," he says. "Okay. I'll watch my cap. Will that help me piss?" He's not standing confidently.

"Maybe."

"Make yourself useful. Get the fuck outa here."

I wish to help him. It is the narrative of my life at this particular moment to help him. But I can't. He won't have it. I leave him to his awesome efforts and hope the best.

———◆———

EXTRICATING MY CAR FROM THE FRIGID PARKING STRUCTURE roof is far from a piece of cake. I have no idea where my ticket's gone, my conversation with Betty Tran having jangled it out of memory. As I rocket round and down the car-lined decks, I'm raging I'll have to pay the whole year for only an hour of parking. Though by a lucky stroke, a previous enraged customer has confronted the same ticket obstacle and plowed right on through the barrier arm, splintering it all over the snowy concrete—someone with bad news from cardiology and who's decided rules don't apply to him anymore.

When I turn into the 5-deep Clinic drive-thru, Paul is an effigy of all that's dismal. Marooned outside in the freezing cold in his chair, huffing stinging air, face grim as more arrivers and leavers push past him, something has gone not the way he's wanted. Conceivably a stir's been created, which is why he's *outside*.

His mouth is going before I can pull close enough to get out. A stream of invective. All his favorites. He raises both arms in the air as if someone had a gun on him, his mouth working and working. Someone else—a less good father—might just drive on.

I'm quickly out onto the gusty pavement, where you can't stop long or they'll arrest you. I begin wrangling my son and his chair toward the car door. Other cars are edging up. Someone in a van decides it's time to honk. Someone from Iowa.

"What happened?" I say. Paul's face is beetled in frozen fury. I'm pulling him up by both hands. He smells of English Leather and Blistex. "Just take a step. You walked to the car an hour ago." Only *I'm* now falling—backwards—into the car and about to pull Paul on top of me. People are noticing. Another one of the blue-parka'd Mayo concierges—not Burt Lister—is instantly there to help, grappling my sore shoulder with a big mitt, while keeping Paul steadied and upright with the other. We are two old battlers being parted by the ref.

"You two girls quit ballroom dancing too soon if you ask me," this tall man says with a smirk of easy effort. "Just slide yourself under my elbow here, and I'll guide junior right in." Our woe is his fun. His breath is making mealy clouds in front of me.

"Okay," I say. Suddenly I'm winded, but can still duck and back up until I'm out of the way, and can lean on the fender. I hear someone behind me say, "Oh, lord."

This large assisting man is the body double of old Vikes' head coach Bud Grant—never won a Super Bowl, beat polio, owned the hearts of Minnesotans everywhere even though he was from

Wisconsin. He is chewing Dentyne—which I didn't think they made anymore. His name tag says he is Fred Durkee.

"There you go, Mister," Bud Grant/Fred Durkee says, easing Paul sideways into the car seat, lifting his legs and inserting them as if they were breakable. "We minimize the damage, this way. Better get that seat belt on. You could have a wild ride with *this* guy." Me.

Paul has merely assented—not helped. It's possible he's noticed the Bud Grant resemblance.

"You good to drive, Pop?" Like Bud, Fred is tall-timber handsome, right into his '70s—crisp white hair, chisel-sharp, crinkle-eyed features, pie-plate hands. He gives ole Burt a run for his money upstairs with the admissions gals. Though in truth, he and Burt are the same person.

"I'm all set," I say. I'm breathing exhaust and need to get back in the car. I'm also grinning—not with glee or pleasure or gratitude—but the way people grin when they don't know what else to do. "Really grateful" is what I pathetically muster, possibly not loud enough in the engine rev and car honk for him to hear me. Pop.

Paul is staring out at me grimly.

"Try not to drive like they drive in New Jersey," big Fred says. "I went down there once. It was different." He's seen my license plate. He's waving to the van behind us. I need to get moving.

"Yeah. Okay." I am still grinning. A manly embrace or a fist bump is clearly out of bounds. "Really grateful" is all I say—again.

"Come back to see us. We'll be here," Fred Durkee says, beginning to wave cars around us.

And that is all we have time to say by way of good-bye.

SIX

Paul's pit-stop (he believes I abandoned him) has resulted in a sorrowful pants-soaking, for which nothing can be done in the car. As a prostate veteran I know these matters well and can sympathize. In Paul's case, in haste and clumsiness, he's also snagged the tender dew-lap of his pecker in his khakis' zipper, inflicting a paralyzing wound he's made worse by zippering *back* over the site—twice as painful—and loosing a freshet of blood he's tried to stopper with toilet paper, but which is still leaking.

"Some fat-ass attendant came in and saw me and asked if he could help or call someone." He's fuming in the car seat, fists balled, shoulders bunched, elbows into his sides, his face slightly waxen.

"Did you let him?" I am driving us.

"I told him I was fine. I got the wheelchair into the fucking disabled stall and wrapped my dick. It's not that big a deal. I've got dick to spare. It just hurt like shit."

"Do we need to do something? Find an urgent care?"

"Maybe a nurse could stitch me up." He closes his eyes to seek solace. "It's fine. Do I have to say it again?"

"Where're we headed?" I ask. I'm driving us toward New Bemidji Street, but am ready to strike off for A Fool's Paradise, take command of the Windbreaker and get us on the road. Our alternative is stay here, face blear facts in a blear nowhere, notime on Lincoln's birthday. Like all new graduates, he is released only back to the present.

"Aren't we going to Mount whatever and do fucking *something*? I don't know. I'm just along for the ride now. I missed my meet and greet."

"Do you want to go back?"

"What do you think my *great* gift was?"

"A free tire rotation. I don't know. How's your schwantz holding up?" This he will not be able to resist. Slumped in his seat like a sack of Irish potatoes, he averts his gaze as we cruise past our neighborhood blind man, tapping along the icy sidewalk hoping in his blind-man's sunglasses not to step off the edge of the world. Paul is working up a killer comeback, suppressing a wizened smile. This has been his way since he was thirteen—a skilled escape artist from life's drab everyday. Now, though, he is this age and sick and alone with me in Minnesota, bound for someplace he doesn't want to go. Jokes are hard to come by.

"You know what the message for the day is, Lawrence?" Looking straight ahead up wintry Bemidji Street.

"This better be good." We're stopped in front of our house. The neighbors have their recycling out, but ours is not.

Paul says, "There may actually *be* an excuse for elder abuse. There's new research on it at Ball State." His knees are jitterbugging. Possibly he's already happy.

"You need to work on that," I say.

"Shut up. What's the most popular body function? It's not as clear-cut as you think." He looks over, giving me the dead eye, his tongue working between his damp lips, his poor tired eyes trained on me behind his glasses.

"Hiccuping. I don't know." The blind man is catching up with us.

"Everybody says that. Try again."

"Farting. You fart all the time. You must like to."

"That's personal. I'll ask you again when we're in Nebraska."

"We're not going to Nebraska. It's South Dakota."

"Whatever. Same difference."

"Do you need anything in the house? I packed clothes for us."

"I wish I could be somewhere else today. Which is weird. Because I *am* somewhere else." He looks at me across the seat, a round face of despair and wonder.

"There're weirder things."

"Yeah, I know."

I wish, of course, I could whisk him away to a realer somewhere where all the jokes are hilarious and we could yuk it up like chimps—outposts far beyond us today. We are two alone together, bound for where we're bound for. Fools in a fools' paradise.

———•———

PAUL REQUIRES SEVERAL LAST-MINUTE TRIP ESSENTIALS. HIS laptop. A selection of his novelty sweatshirts ("I Can't See You If You Can't See Me;" "Genius at Wrok;" "That's Not Funny!"). He ditches his car coat, Irish topper and bloodied, pissed-on pants in favor of his Chiefs coat and cap, sweats and Swiss Al's footwear. He includes his new slick-slide cornhole bags (6 to the box). Also his thick "forecaster" book previewing the coming NFL draft—Kansas City looking to shore up the "O-line," plus the running back. He's also taking his red-velvet-lined impact case wherein he keeps his ventriloquist's dummy, Otto. (I'd hoped his depleted digital dexterities would make Otto a non-starter, but I'm wrong.) He also takes the new John Denver biography. Den-ver, he believes, was a "massive talent" in the firmament with Tony Newley and Ute Lemper, although nothing like either of them, "which is why he's outstanding." It's far too much crap for a three-day journey. But all is good if we get going. (I take only what's in my 'M' duffel, plus my pocket Heidegger, which puts me dead to sleep in five minutes, and is all I ask of it.)

By 11:30, Paul has attended to his, now, "minor wound." I've manufactured pastrami dagwoods, with horseradish, sweet pick-les, more anchovies, and stinky Limburger on pumpernickel—which Paul says he can't taste but wolfs down after I cut it for him. And by noon we're back in the Ascetic, heading to 52 North and A Fool's Paradise. Not altogether *so* remarkable—if one person doesn't have ALS, and the other person isn't the father.

————◆————

OUT ON COMMERCIAL 52, WEDNESDAY HAS BECOME A DAY OF cloudless heartbreaking Arctic sky, reminding me more than anything of summer. There's steady UPS and FedEx traffic toward the suburbs. An unusual number of cars are brandish-ing Trump stickers—the election, the impeachment, the whole nationwide Busby-Berkeley being nothing I can pay attention to now. When you're in charge of a failing son little else goes on.

I am, I admit, feeling a great tension-mitigation just by be-ing underway. And Paul, in the car, is resurgent. No mention of his men's room mishap, the passed-over meet & greet or his mother's death anniversary. His sister has called this morning as she knows his drug trial is finished. But I've determined not to talk to her today, since she wouldn't like our trip. She wants to move him to Scottsdale where he would do what, it's anybody's guess—though not better than he does with me, on the case 24-7.

Paul notes the passing valentine signage. He insists he never "worked" on valentine cards. They were an "excuse holiday" at Hallmark, he declares—an excuse to spend money on something idiotic. Valentine's has actually "lost ground as a holiday, demographically speaking," he says. Mostly only Republicans care about it. He speaks, for a time, about his recycling ideas, prioritizing the re-use of items normally thrown away. Ballpoint pen refills, Band-Aids, Q-tips, chewing gum, toothbrushes, maxi pads. Technology's catching up fast, he says. Soon nothing will be considered garbage.

And then we're there—A Fool's Paradise—the lot sheeny with ice and freshly plowed. A new message on the sign-on-wheels reminds drivers of the Valentine's sump pump, septic and American-flag specials—sturdy beacon of American can-do mercantile optimism, which promises that "you-don't-need-it-if-we-don't-have-it." The Adult Outlet and the Gunz store are doing big business—sex toys and AR-15s, a perfect valentine combo. The Windbreaker sits in front of the office cabin, thin smoke puttering from its dual pipes. Smoke's also puffing out the metal chimney. Krista's yellow Smart car sits to the side where it was yesterday.

"What's this place?" Paul says. He's only seen it here at night.

"It's where we're renting that noble steed there." (The Windbreaker.) "As per your wishes. How soon they forget."

"It looks different." He's peering out his window at the big red Dodge. The camper rig is a more faded aqua and beige hue than I remember. Bits of Windbreaker are tattered from long service. I haven't paid strictest attention to all aspects.

"We don't have to do this," I say.

"We've crossed a barrier now," he says, looking grave like Larry Flynt. "It's whether *you're* up to it."

"I'm up to it. I'm not the one with ALS. I'm ready." Only half true. I'm not sure what barrier we've crossed.

"Are *you* up to *me* having ALS?" He calls it what it is now. "Can you handle the gimp in South Dakota or wherever the fuck. I'm not half the man I used to be. There's a shadow hanging over me. Tony sings that."

"Haven't I been up to it so far?"

"No. I don't know. You're a weird fucker." He for some reason sighs, as if he's already bored with this conversation.

"What do you think *you* are?" I say, pulling us to a stop out front of the office.

"I'm perfectly normal. I'm the poster boy for death with dignity. I could do ads on TV. What could you do ads for?"

All-suffering fathers. I don't say that. "Nothing, I guess."

"Dick-heads on the dick-head channel hosted by Dick Clark." He smirks, pleased with himself.

"Is that your measure for things? What you can do a TV ad for?"

"Henceforth that's how you'll be judged. By me anyway."

"I'm fine with it."

"You're fine with everything," Paul says. "That's your whole problem. It means you're not fine with *anything*. A jack-of-no-trades. That's what Ann thought."

"You mean Ann your late mother?" Not my lucky day.

"She thought you'd be happier after she died because she reminded you of all your flaws."

"That's not true."

"Maybe I'm right. Maybe I'm wrong. Maybe I'll find a place in this world or never belong. You're a turd, in *my* book."

"Do you want to go back? I can drive us back to Haddam."

"So *what* can happen? *You* want to go back to New Jersey? I don't. I want to get on with this. See Mount Rushmore and die—that's my motto."

"We'll make it happen, then. The first part anyway."

"Yeah. Make it happen, Lawrence. You're tired of me, anyway."

"No, I'm not. I'm not tired of you at all. You're wrong." I shouldn't have to say it, but I do.

"Okay." He looks sadly out at the idling Windbreaker. "Do what you have to. I'll just be here waiting."

———

"I ASKED PETE IF WE'D SEE YOU AGAIN," KRISTA SAYS FROM HER business desk, the wall of martial photos, battle ribbons and the stuffed muskie-with-duck arrayed behind her. She saucers her eyes and smiles at me. Inside is again sweltering. A set of keys waits atop the rental papers I'm here to sign.

"I had to do some negotiating with my son."

"Yep. You learn to negotiate if you're a nurse. People come to the end, and they think they can negotiate *that*. Then I have to explain it to them. Where'd you say it was you were going?" She's not wearing her scrubs today but a plushy, green ski-bunny getup with white fur suspenders over a pink turtleneck. A fetching little package big Pete has negotiated for himself. She's pulled the rental documents over in front of her and pushed the keys toward me. I have not taken a seat.

"Mount Rushmore." I nod and smile for her approval.

"That's the one with the presidents?" She's writing this onto the agreement, in case we go someplace else and need to be apprehended. The *Elle* she was reading yesterday hasn't moved.

"It is," I say.

"Probably do better in the summer." She's writing and shaking her head. Her hands are small and without nail polish— forbidden for nurses. Her left hand has a plain gold band from fisherman Pete.

"We don't have a choice right now."

"It's your son, right?" She uses her ballpoint to scratch up into her blond "shag" nurse's hair. She is older than I thought yesterday. Tough, wrinkled hands give her away. Being a nurse has kept her trim. "What'd you say he's got? AIDS?"

"ALS." I almost say 'Al's.' I am nodding—for no reason.

"*Thaaaat's* not good."

"No. It isn't."

"Do you have A-A?" I think she means Triple-A. I do. Best hundred and thirty dollars you'll ever spend. Three visits in one year to slim-jim my Honda, once for the battery. "I do."

"And that *is* good—in *this* weather. The propane's all topped off. Potable water's good. It's fulla gas and anti-freeze. I cleaned it up with Lysol. Don't let your gas get below a quarter. Word to the wise."

"Perfect. Thank you." I could remain here all day with no better destination than this: Her beguiling presence, while my son cools his heels.

"Our phone number's on here. We'll be up in Mendota with my niece. But call us if you need to. Pete likes emergencies. He misses Iraq, *I* believe." She looks up with a warm, business-y smile and slides the paperwork over. "Sign your Jubilation T. Cornpone at the bottom there, Mister. I suppose you've got a driver's license."

"I do." Going for my billfold.

"Aaaand a-major-credit-card."

"Absolutely," handing both over. Krista opens her drawer, removes an old manual card-crusher she handles like a pro, getting my Visa settled on top and cranking across with ease. "I gave you the Valentine's special because of your son."

"Okay," I say. "That's great."

"We don't do insurance. You have to have your own."

"I do," I say. "Do you want to see it?"

"Naaa." She's looking my driver's license over. "You like it down in Nude Jersey?"

"I do," signing and dating the agreement and the receipt. "At least so far." I finger the keys with the pink Florida fish fob.

"Pete got discharged at Fort Dix. Isn't that in New Jersey, or is it Virginia?" She's fitting our agreement into a plastic folder with RV RENTALS written in black marker.

"It's Nude Jersey. I used to live not far from there."

"He didn't care for it. He loooves Minnesota. All the lakes. His father worked in the iron range. The only Colored they had. You don't need a sump pump, do you?"

"I don't."

She stands up. "I'll walk out with you. I want to meet this son of yours. Is he out there?" She is surprisingly solid-looking. A vet. Possibly a snowmobiler. A wrist-wrestler. A pint-sized Playmate. I take a fretful look out the window at Paul, mouth moving, looking altered as usual.

"I'm sure he'd like to meet *you*." Which is putting it mildly.

Outside in the sterilizing sunshine, all around is featureless and too bright: Highway 52 with its car-stream, the gun and sex shops, the lot full of septics, cherry-pickers, tombstones, ranks of RVs from which the idling Windbreaker has been selected— nothing has obvious relation to anything else, all features of the ineffable.

"So, is this our patient!" Krista calls out loudly in the knife-blade cold. She approaches the passenger-side window like a cop. Paul stares out at her looking skeptical and slightly annoyed. He has no idea who she is. A female of Krista's minor beauty would normally launch him into mile-a-minute yakking about re-useable Q-tips and John Denver. However, he can't get his window down since I've got the keys.

"Paul," I say helpfully from behind her. He's wearing his red sweatpants and a gray hoodie with "ALS Team Member" across his front.

"I guess he's not saying too much." Krista smiles through the glass. Paul's eyes shift to me. His lips pronounce more inaudible words. My ears are frozen. I need a cap and gloves. I hadn't planned to be outside long.

"He's not always a good communicator," I say.

Krista gives Paul the two-fingers-plus-a-thumb "I love you" sign through his window. He blinks at her. She waves a wiggle finger-wave with her other hand. "I'll show you where the spare is." She's walking us to the rear of the camper, where the Dodge is still patiently producing a gray-white stream of frost vapor. "It's right up here," she says, stepping around and pointing below the Norm Cepeda window—husband, brother, father of Lorenza, the inadequate parent and flight risk. The spare is encased in what, in my youth, was called a "continental kit." Apogee of high school automotive cool. We stand a moment staring at it, bracketed by rust to the Windbreaker's rear carriage.

"You think I could leave my car here a few days?" I say. Customers are driving in and driving out at the gun and sex businesses, inching back onto 52, eager to get home and put their purchases to use.

"Pull it around by my car and leave the keys. If you don't come back, Pete'll sell it for parts."

"Fair enough."

Krista looks up at me as if she's brought me back here in the frozen daylight to impart something important. I pray, pray, pray it's not a something about Paul that only nurses know and doctors don't get around to revealing because they're playing golf. Not the bon voyage I'm looking for. Krista stares straight at me, so that I notice she is ever-so-slightly cross-eyed. How did she get in the Army?

"Frank," she says, folding her arms saint-like across her front. At least she has my name right, re-noted on my Visa. "Are you spiritual?"

"I don't think so," I say. "Are you?"

"I am," she says, mimping her little rose mouth as if her words need to be paid intense attention to. "Not in a religious way. More like a fortune teller way. Which I don't really believe in. Do you?"

"I used to." Long ago, when my marriage to Ann had crashed and I was sunk deep into post-divorce dreaminess, I paid visits to a dusky "Mrs. Miller" in a little brick house on the side of Route 1, next to a Rusty Jones. Five dollars bought a look at my palm. "You're a good man at heart," Mrs. Miller always assured me. "I see a long life." "Things will brighten up for you." If I gave her more than 5, she would give me better news. In the fall, when I learned Paul had Al's I drove to her house, but it had been razed and replaced by an Islamic Centre, where no one was seeing a good future for the likes of me.

"I just want to tell you this, Frank." Re-alerting me with a serious, firm mouth as she clutches herself with her two arms. "I think something good's going to happen on this trip. I want to tell you that. You'll find something to make you feel rewarded. I don't always get a strong sense. But I get a very strong, positive one from you. I thought so when I met you yesterday. I told Pete last night. You just have to be sure you and Paul take a chance and do things you thought you'd never do."

"We've done that a lot recently. But okay."

"You met Pete."

"Yes." Paul pronounced him a dunce.

"I had this same feeling when him and I connected over in

Baghdad, Iraq. I thought I'd never see him again because he was married. But then after everything happened with Janelle, he came and found me at the Clinic, and the feeling was just as strong. Marrying him was certainly something I never thought I'd do. You know? And here we are." She nods at me wondrously. We're freezing out here in the truck fumes. Never, though, turn a deaf ear to good tidings. Not so high above us, small in the depthless blue, a helicopter—a heelo—red light flashing, shoots past, bound for the Clinic. "That's really it, Frank. You're freezing, and I'm yapping my whole life story." She widens her eyes and gives her head a jokey-smiley shake the way she did yesterday. Both her eyes look normal now, as if she'd shaken them straight.

"I'm glad to know this." Shudder, shudder.

"I'm Krista," she says, as if I didn't know. I'd also seen it on her realtor's license. "Krista and Pete Engvall. The odd couple."

"They're usually the best kind," I say. "I always thought I was perfect for the people I fell in love with. Maybe that's the problem."

"Could be you were," Krista says, "then Mr. Life has his say."

"He does. He's doing it now."

"There you go. By the way, I wouldn't try to sleep in this ole bucket if I was you. You'll freeze your sweet patooties off."

"Okay," I say. "It crossed my mind."

"It'd be okay in New Jersey. But here's where winter was invented."

"I noticed." Paul, I know, is watching through his side-mirror. He'll assume I'm up to something I'm far from up to. Krista is already half down the side of the Windbreaker. She gives another little finger-wave to Paul from outside his window. I believe he gives her one back. Partings are harder at my age. They traffic in finality. It is enough to say good-bye without saying good-bye.

SEVEN

Racketing along I-90, all of 44N/92W looks the same—glacial, white, vast as Melville's whale. Paul's symptoms are more noticeable to me now—as if I'd thought all we needed was to set off, and Al's would laughingly go away. Possibly it's being in a confined space, but he looks mangier and paler—tissue-y—his voice registered up. He's encountered difficulty getting his left earpiece in using his right hand, the fingers of which are balky and given to clenching like a CP sufferer—which in essence he is, only worse. He is *not* experiencing fasciculations—that I notice; but I believe his spinal nerves may be communicating less fluently with his muscles. Symptoms are never fully readable and often dangle the shiny object of improvement. He is thoroughly acquainted, though, with his disease's tricks and seems to take little notice. By the time he's dead, he'll be the world's greatest expert—as good as his doctors. And as helpless.

In my one, previously mentioned episode of global amnesia—I took the garbage out at home, in Haddam, then had no memory of taking the garbage out—my neurologist at Haddam Medical Arts, Dr. Cadwalader, told me, while showing me scans of my brain on his office computer, that during these fugues people go completely normally about their business, taking out the garbage, making love to their spouses, having teeth pulled, then only afterward discover they have no memory of it. Nobody around notices anything unusual while these events are occurring. The *patient* notices nothing—until later, when the time has to be accounted for and nothing's there. Taking the garbage out might've taken ten minutes but had simply been paved over. Not forgotten. Not misremembered. Just not there and never was. Cadwalader said these snafus are harmless, don't recur and don't even show up on brain pictures. The lost time can be five minutes or it can be an hour or a morning or even longer. It's never fun, and leaves most people shaken—which was my experience. (As always nowadays there's a website where people recount goofy things they didn't know they were doing until they couldn't find their Subaru or explain why the next-door neighbor's wife no longer speaks to them.) Today, though, larruping along with my son, vectored for Sioux Falls—a place I never expected would find us together—I wonder if these last three tumultuous months might just become one of those interstellar empty spots. Since, under the right conditions—or in the case of my son and me, under the very worst conditions—who of us wouldn't wish for it? To emerge through a misty glass to find we haven't brought all our bad stuff with us because there is no bad stuff anymore. Again, the poet wrote that there is another world, but it is in this world. Maybe *that's* what he had in mind.

For a while Paul has sat silent, belted in, staring out at the changeless Minnesota snowscape like a passenger in a club car, his phone and its ear-works unused in his lap, his face and mouth pinched as if he was distilling several lines of thought into one clear assay before speaking. We've stored our gear into the "living" compartment of the Windbreaker, where it's freezing, still as a tomb and dense with propane—nowhere a sane person would spend five minutes. Ever since he "loved it" a week ago, he's exhibited zero interest, as if a camper with an hilarious name was my idea. I suspect if we were striking off to Soddy-Daisy, Tennessee, or Two Dot, Montana, he'd be equally disengaged. Nevertheless, my plan is to drive us to Sioux Falls, put up in a stress-free Hilton Garden or Marriott and see how the world looks tomorrow.

Our big Ram, it turns out, is a sleek beast, jumping easily out and around the Interstate traffic. We ride high up, the big mirrors, the big steering wheel, dashboard and the big tires all conjoining for a military-like command. Previous drivers have logged 180 thousand doubtless highway miles. But there are few rattles and vibrations, and the ride is actually cushiony. Nothing about the camper box on behind makes me feel I'm being tail-gated by a runaway semi—which was my fear. Detroit may not build the best (leave that to the Axis powers and the Swedes), but it does good enough for America. Plus the heater'll "blow you right outa here." Krista has hung a fir-tree (not coconut) air freshener on the rearview, producing a treacly-minty stink. This, I tossed before we hit Stewartville. The Lysol has now taken charge and quashed the cigarette funk, leaving all nearly neutral-smelling.

Paul has noticed the gigantic, ghostly wind turbines which clutter the highway-side snowfields—thirty to a patch. Wind is the energy out here, since there's plenty of it. The great propel-lers swoop drowsily in whatever fractional breeze is stirring. I for one would hate to peer out my window to greet the day and find one of these whirly-gigs from Mars rotating in my yard. Better a small-footprint oil well.

"Some of 'em aren't even turning," Paul says. "Are they bro-ken?" Among the multitude, a few are motionless, while most circle soundlessly.

"They're not turned on," I say. "Somebody needs to plug them in."

He says nothing about this, watches in silence as blue-cold fields, where in summer corn would be high as an elephant's eye, glide past. "I'm strangely drawn to them, Lawrence," he says spookily to mock me. With his left hand he rubs at the sheen of ice laminating the inside of his window glass. "They're speaking to me, Lawrence. They're telling me something. They're measuring my life. You probably don't feel it, do you?"

"They're the liberals' view of the future," I say. A double-truck 18-wheeler rumbles past us, spewing snow and banging into the sun-blaze off the ice fields. We're doing a solid 73, where I'm comfortable.

"I guess you're voting for Trump," Paul says.

"Fucking A. And then some." This is one of our routines. We "play Republican," one-upping each other with things nobody in his right mind would take seriously. Making Greenland a state. Bombing Puerto Rico. Capital punishment for not carrying a sidearm. I'm better at it than he is. He's told me he voted for Obama both times, but I'm not sure he voted at all.

His arm-spasming—which has now stopped—has distracted him into silence. Since being diagnosed, Paul has been dedicated to casting himself as a person who does *not* have ALS, and with setting a good example. He's allowed himself to be video'd for the online newsletter at Haddam High, during which he told unfunny jokes, got Otto onto his lap to say sexually suggestive things, while he struggled not to move his lips. He blathered on about a trip he was planning to the Cornhole World Championship in South Carolina—after which he would "just see what happens with the Al's thing." "Dying Alum Chooses Brighter Side" was the headline. He declined other interviews.

Using only his left hand, he makes another stab at getting his Bluetooth in, cocking one mouth corner in a garish grin, his tongue-bottom urging out in the manner of the young Cassius Clay. Twice the earpiece falls out, causing him to mutter "piece of shit." The third time he gets it worked in with the heel of his right hand. "Small ear canals," he says. "By the way, Lawrence, there's not shit out here." Then he sinks back, closes his eyes and resumes listening to Ute Lemper sing "Alles Schwindel."

In truth, there isn't much of touristic value in southwestern Minnesota. The Hormel meatpacking plant in Austin, and the ancestral home of inventor Jacob Mud, who's credited with inventing the mudroom at his home in Luverne. The World's Only Corn Palace—open all year—in Mitchell, South Dakota, is our first port of call tomorrow. "Favorite of presidents, kings, prelates, movie stars and Emperor Haile Selassie"—the last I doubt. "Everything in your wildest dreams made out of corn." This has elements up Paul's alley—self-conscious inanity, latent juvenile sexual content and a "life in these United States" down-home garishness. Again, he is hard to predict—which can be good.

While he sleeps, I tune in to sports talk from Omaha, where there's a hot-stove about pitchers and catchers reporting to Bradenton, plus the prospects for "Husker Nation" starting spring drills with a new coach and a juco transfer at QB who's demanding playing time with the west coast offense. It is blissful to hear this news out upon the vast and vacant prairie. Nothing would make me happier than to see Mount Rushmore then head to Port St. Lucie, sit in the bleachers with Paul and take in the Mets and the Cards in the watery sunshine of early March. How far will such dreams take me? How far is square one from cloud nine?

At 5:30, we cross the South Dakota line and pass straight along the outskirts of Sioux Falls, cloaked in starless darkness— a tablecloth of lights and commerce, south-spreading and west, blue police flashers there and here across the grid, giant car cathedrals, miles of housing, unlit golf courses and streams of inching headlights. 171,000 (mostly Nordic) souls. Sioux Falls could be Birmingham.

We track its north quadrant, keeping on 90, only then I miss signage for the Hilton Garden and Denny's at exit 412, and have to get off and backtrack ten miles through Hartford, just as Paul is coming awake. We've come 237 miles. So far, nothing worse than a missed exit has threatened us.

"Where are we *now*?" He is hoarse, his earbuds in, looking out at the wash of lights that has become South Dakota. Far in the night a searchlight sweeps up and across the sky.

"This is Uranus. Anything you want to say to the citizens?" I am relieved to be here.

"What's here?"

"A Hilton. I'm going to get us a room. We can eat at Denny's." In my ages-ago sportswriter days, nothing was more welcome and welcoming than a Hilton (when they were real hotels). A tip-top taproom. A good central location, steps from the best steak house and the ballpark; often a lonely damsel in the lobby bar who'd let me buy her a sidecar, both pretending to be interested until it seemed one thing might lead to another, whereupon we'd call it quits. These encounters are not always what you think.

"Aren't we going to sleep in the camper or whatever?" Paul swivels his head stiffly around, as if assessing the Windbreaker out his window.

"You can freeze *your* ass off. It's six degrees." The dashboard thermometer certifies it. "I'll cut you out with the jaws of life in the morning." The jaws of life are one of his favored new-age innovations. The self-opening parachute, the touchless car wash and the waterless urinal are others.

"My legs are numb."

"You just sat too long in one position."

We're on the access road, heading toward the red-and-gold HILTON sign, safe refuge for weary travelers.

"What's going to happen?" He's tapping his knee as if to make it communicate. Fat snowflakes float through the darkness. The Interstate is now beside us and up. Sioux Falls is ahead again.

"When?" I ask.

He turns his face to me, his mouth partway open. His face is almost perfectly round. His glasses' reflection make him seem someone I don't quite know.

"I mean what's going to happen to me?" He takes in then releases a deep breath.

"Are we talking the long run?"

"The long run. The short run. The run of the mill. The run for the money. I don't know."

"I don't know either. Am I supposed to? I haven't done this before."

"Me either." He raises his chin as if to draw a better, unimpeded breath, then sighs again. His numb leg pulses. "I had a nice dream. I didn't want to wake up."

"What did you dream? Maybe I'll dream it."

"It's stupid." We're turning into the Hilton, where there are already many vehicles. It's possible we won't find a room, though it's not yet six. "I dreamed I was married to Candice Bergen, and Edgar Bergen was my father. You weren't there. Otto was there, and he was kind of half-real, and I could still work him. We lived in Hollywood, where I've never even been. Mother was there. It was Valentine's. I didn't have Al's. Remember she used to make valentines for us? She was doing that."

"Your mother loved Valentine's Day."

"It was weird, but it was good. Do you think Candice is a babe?"

"Absolutely. For sure." I pull us into a VIP slot, near the front door. We are not VIPs anymore, but there are no other close-in slots.

I turn off the ignition, and we sit then in the dark thinking about Candice as snow melts on the windshield. Inside the bright Hilton lobby, guests are walking about, holding cocktails, pulling suitcases, laughing and engaging in animated conversations with strangers about winter fuel costs and the weather. My vision of perfect happiness.

"Do you think I'm going to spend the rest of my life doing this?"

"What're we talking about here?"

Paul stares at the wall of lighted Hilton bedrooms in front of us, where other guests are in stages of dress and undress, watching TV from bed, talking on their phones, laughing at children. Some rooms are still dark. Possibly there's a chance for us. "Just stuff I don't want to be doing. Until you know . . ."

"I *don't* know."

"'Til the bug stops here."

I wait to speak. "Isn't this trip any fun?"

"No, it's good." Yeah-no. The entire human condition in two words. "What did mother think about me?"

"She always wanted you to hurry and grow up. I told her you already *were* grown up. You were like forty. She thought you were young for your age and could be difficult. She loved you. You're not difficult."

"She always treated me like I was a teenager. I never liked that. You do it, too."

"I'm sorry you think that. I don't think that. Nobody's young for their age, by the way. You're always how you're supposed to be."

"Do you think about dying all the time because of me?"

"I think about dying all the time because of *me*. It isn't so bad."

"What do you think? About being dead?"

"I think it's like a lightbulb going off," I say. "I hope it is anyway."

"It's not really plannable is it?"

"You're supposed to think of that as freeing. I've read all about it in a book." *Being and Time*, page 263. "You know, we're just taking this trip because we can. I thought you'd enjoy it." It is satisfying to talk with fewer subordinate clauses.

Someone, a small man in a white singlet undershirt, holding a beer, comes to his hotel-room window—his slender, blond wife behind him, pulling a dress over her head to get comfortable. They're in for the night. She is talking. He is peering out, giving his beer can a gentle shaking. His eyes seem to fall on us—though he can't see us. Our faces are in shadows. He says something to his wife, motions to our vehicle with his beer and laughs. It's the Florida plates. How far we've strayed from home. How we must like *this* weather.

"So, are we getting out?" Paul says, as if he's been waiting an hour.

"Sure. Let's get out."

"Don't think I don't know things, Lawrence. I do."

"I know. I'll just keep up the good work." I smile at my son. I know what he means. There will be still more to say in time.

I begin climbing out into the night.

ARRANGEMENTS AT THE HILTON GARDEN ARE EXACTLY AS hoped for. A "Premium" ground-level, wheelchair-accessible double not by the elevator, the ice machine or the pool, two free bottles of warm Dasani water, free breakfast and a complimentary *USA Today*. Room 122 is far down the east-west wing, almost to the exit sign, although a "church group" has rented the hotel's "Big Events" room for a retirement party and many guests have left their doors open, laughter and TV noise floating through the hallway, children running squealing, tag-team races up and down, their footfalls booming on the cheap floors, making sleep a concern. Paul shoves the luggage cart, which allows him to stay upright and go forward while I handle his chair. His right hand is curling in, and his footfalls are heavy and effortful. When we made the drive up from New Jersey in December he wasn't this way. We were just two guys—possibly gay—on a winter's wander. Now, he's impaired, and I am his minder. The little *Lord of the Flies* children eye us gravely as we pass. They assume he's a feeb. Though from being continuously scrutinized by swarms of doctors who view afflicted people like sheep bouncing over a stile, his sense of the god-awful about himself has been "contextualized"—not that he's stopped caring about how he's perceived. Nothing, though, would make *me* happier than to bite these little farts' faces off and stand roaring over them like a Cerberus.

Once in the room, however, the cart returned, all becomes instantly hotel perfect. Paul and I don't turn the TV on, only sit on parallel beds with our shoes on, speaking little, staring at the Constable-like print of Dorset or Devon, shifting our gazes to the window where snow is sliding past and an occasional pair of headlights glares in, then goes out. My sore back no longer hurts. Paul—balding, fat, musky, bespectacled in his "ALS Team Member" hoodie—for the moment gives no sign that he is afflicted by anything the rest of us aren't afflicted by. As advertised, there's a Denny's menu provided by Hilton management. We can call in, email or text for two "Grand Slams," which I can go next door and retrieve. In my duffel I've stashed away my Russki Stoli; and without attempting the ice machine, Paul and I share two plastic bathroom cups' worth—mine landing on my tongue, throat, and innards like a Brahms hymn to a grieving man, almost immediately requiring a second two fingers, as the cups are small.

Our room at once becomes dense and still and serene and smoothed. The banshee kids go quiet, reeled into their parents' rooms. Only a faint mechanical hum perturbs the wall behind my head—a pump or heating element or fan deep in the building's workings—white noise to summon sleep.

It is not bad, possibly it is even very good, to fit so easily into the nitch that the savviest thinkers—ergonomists and anthropologists employed by Hilton—have earmarked as right for me. So much better than being at odds with one's surroundings. It is all any of us would really like in such an untroubled moment—or in a thousand untroubled moments. Who cares if they're *really* untroubled or for how long?

I favor myself with a third Stoli, while Paul, who's no drinker, considers the Denny's offerings. The gold medallion of a yellow Caddie has swung up to our room window, then pulled away. I hear the scrape of a snow shovel and the whine of tires on ice, then laughter. A friend of mine in the Red Man Club believes every serious mistake he's made in life has come after a coupla drinks. Though still. Now could be another occasion for our "talk." The "hard things" discussion Paul's Mayo context therapist, Dr. Bogdan Čilić ("Dr. Bog Down"), believes will make cruel and certain death far easier—if we can just face the music. (What better setting for it than a Hilton in Sioux Falls?) Dr. Bog Down's list of hard discussable topics also includes— and we can both answer: 1. Does dying have a bright side and possibly make other things better? 2. Will it be funny or sad when we die? 3. What are our worst secrets we won't want to take to the grave? Possibly there will be moments—when I'm not three vodkas ahead—when these questions will seem more apropos. Though my son might enjoy them if he knew they gave me the creeps.

Paul has dozed off with the plastic Denny's menu on his belly, his glasses on, his right paw curled in as if his disease means to draw him into himself like a flower going to sleep. Which is not how it works, of course. Still, asleep across from me in the other bed, he doesn't look like somebody awaiting a bad fate. Only sweetly and slightly preoccupied.

"See something you'd like?" I say, assuming he'll answer as he used to when he was a child, and I came in his room to say good-night and switch off the light, and we'd talk trickily through his gauze of almost-sleep.

He is silent. Water circulates through pipes behind walls. A woman's muffled voice says something that sounds like "Rembrandt. It's always Rembrandt with you." Then someone—a man—laughs raucously, joined by someone else—a woman.

"I'm good," Paul says. Not opening his eyes, he takes a full but labored breath, lets it slowly out as if it was his last. His right hand experiences a visible quaking. His head rocks back and forth like a blind man's, keeping time with something audible only to him.

"Are you okay, Bergie? You should eat something." For some reason I am almost whispering.

"Do you think if we lived in an ancient civilization it would die out because we aren't smart enough?" His voice is thin and reedy.

"Yes." It's true. I've thought that. "I could score you a pecan waffle," I say. Once, he knew a joke about pecan waffles. I remember only the punch line: "And damned if he didn't eat the whole thing."

"Who are the people you'd like to live forever?" he mutters, his drifting mind making him happy.

"I don't know. Most of them are probably dead already."

He breathes a heavy, now-unimpeded breath. I hear a dog yapping outside, then a heavily bundled man passes our window, a snow shovel on his shoulder. He does not look in at us.

"I'm sorry to tell you, Mr. Bascombe, but you're suffering from an acute case of hypochondria," Paul says. "There's little we can do for you." I don't know what he's on about; but it's all right, since it pleases him.

I say, "I think you have a cute angina."

He instantly cocks an eye. This is one of his all-timers, shared even with his mother, which she howled about. I get high marks for remembering it now, when it almost fits—which is all we ask. "When I die, Lawrence, will it be after a brief illness, or will I have battled courageously?" A smile flickers into one corner of his mouth.

"That's up to you."

His body gives a little lurch. He makes a soft "ooof," as if something hurt. "Ooooh . . . boy. That again. Up to me. I'll just rest my eyes a while."

"You do that," I say, and let him slip away into his haze of dreams. Dinner, we're leaving behind.

EIGHT

In sleep's shallows I half-hear engines starting, car doors slamming, voices outside. "Oh, yeah, right. He'll put a quick stop to *that* happy horseshit." My head is under my pillow, as Paul has snored all night—not usual for him. I have closed the heavy curtains to blanket the light. Sounds say it's morning. Travelers getting going, laughing about the weather, talking about the president of the United States, who's as usual putting a stop to something I approve of.

Paul, I am aware, is not in the room, though I'm not majorly concerned. If he wants to manage and can manage, he should manage. Again, I do not have to watch him every minute and can take my time to lie in bed and listen. The wild children are up pounding the spongy Hilton hallways, giggling about something "Felicia" has said that she shouldn't have. It fits into the dream I was dreaming—of Sergeant-Major Gunnerson coming to our house on New Bemidji Street dressed as a white-coat doctor, telling me I needed to close on the house or someone will take it away from me. Mike Mahoney is at this dream's margins, doing what it isn't clear.

Last night, when Paul had drifted off, I wandered down to the lobby bar for a glass of Pinot Grigio and a peek at the bar menu—which turned out to be mountain-oyster shooters, which must've contributed to my dreams. Seated on a bar stool, I struck up a chat with a handsome Black lady lawyer more or less my age, headed off to her Zeta Phi Beta reunion in Rapid City. She still worked *of counsel* for a "significant" corporate firm in Chicago and seemed rich. We both agreed that "service" was in a dire state in America, where once "the guest was god." We wished it was better. Though she allowed that four hundred years of colonialization, plus frequent epidemics and world wars, plus a culture of greed and inequality, could probably bring good service back. I tried changing the subject to the iffy prospects of the Democrats in the long term. But she didn't care to talk to me further and left without saying goodbye. I paid for her Metropolitan and went back to the room. It's hard to do the right thing at all times.

We are now half-way to Mount Rushmore—most notional of national monuments, and thus most American. Now would be the predictable moment for me to fail of resolve, suffer misplaced regret and resignation, to cloud things and cause myself not to fully participate, but also to not abandon our plan, thereby ruining it. This I must avoid.

For this reason, and in a spirit of economy, adaptability and focus, the Crow Creek Hunkpati Oyate Indian reservation must be crossed off our itinerary. Likewise, Elvis's motorcycle (which is probably a fake). Also, the Minuteman Missile museum, Wall Drug, the world's largest pheasant statue and the Tractor Museum in Kimball—none of which I care about anyway. Only the World's Only Corn Palace remains worth our time, since Paul won't be able to resist it, and it's only sixty miles away. How much lighter on its feet the world would be if we only understood that precious fuck-all we do on any given day makes much difference in either the long run or the short.

When I make it to the lobby, pushing our gear in Paul's wheel-chair, the room is bustling—whole families, flight crews, kids in jammies, truckers, some white-helmeted, oil-well-roughneck types with per diems rich enough for a Hilton, are pounding down the continental breakfast. Paul is slumped in one of the bright-red lobby chairs where guests wait for the airport shuttle, which is just pulling up now at the entry, full of flight attendants and pilots. Paul's face is blotchy—he hasn't shaved (he can't very well). His comb-over is tufted on one side, there's toothpaste on his front and shampoo fuzz in his right ear. He's dressed in another of his sweatshirts—Genius at Wrok—in big red block letters. He's trying to manage his *USA Today* and having a hard time turning the big pages.

"Armadillos carry leprosy but they don't die from it. I guess you knew that." He has one earbud cord dangling across his shoulder. His Bluetooth has stopped working. He has also mis-placed his cell-phone holster and has to keep his instrument in his coat pocket.

"Did you eat anything?" I want to get us going and not fritter.

"I had a yogurt parfait."

I notice the unfriendly Black lawyer lady from last night, checking out at the front desk, pulling an expensive pink roller bag. She sees me behind the luggage-stuffed chair, and Paul musing over the *USA Today*. She raises a skeptical eyebrow but gives no other sign of having seen me before.

"I read in here . . ." Paul makes a clumsy try at folding the newspaper page with his less functioning right arm, then lets it fall ". . . there's such a thing as a crime-scene restoration com-pany. Did you hear about it? It'd be a good pick-up for the company—I think." He means Gormles Logistics 3.1 Innova-tions, his former employer. He fingers the shampoo tuft in his ear but doesn't seem to acknowledge it. It's regrettable I never got to expose Paul to Mike's scheme for farming private neighborhood intel. Now aglimmering.

"Are we ready?" I have his parka laid over the duffels in the wheelchair. The lady lawyer strides past, heading for the automatic doors. She's got up in a chic, black ankle-length quilted coat and sensational black quilted boots with gold heels and gold buckles. The flight attendants notice her and share an admiring word.

"I saw myself in the bathroom mirror," Paul says. "It wasn't good. I look like shit. I need to lose some weight." He's struggling, using his cane, to lever himself out of the chair, half-pushing against the armrest, his tongue bottom extruded. He breathes hard through his nose. "It's the Stockholm Syndrome in *this* fuckin' place. I don't want you to leave me *here*." Half up, he's looking around.

"Okay, then I won't." I step forward and grapple his forearms, which are flaccid and trembling. I don't want to have happen what happened yesterday—a spectacle. Other guests are watching us here the same way, but pretending they aren't. The lobby TV is sounding off about the impeachment, which has arrested some people's attention.

"What makes women attractive? Did you ever think about that?" Paul says, as I'm elevating him.

"Yeah. I've thought about it a lot. Just step sideways, son." I'm moving backwards, bumping his chair's foot cleat. Music (unidentifiable) is buzzing out of his dangling earbud. A bit of yogurt is tucked into the corner of his mouth. "Do you want to walk or sit," I say. He is up and not that shaky. He grunts when he realizes he's standing and semi-stable. Close to my ear, he says, "You said last night death was like a lightbulb going out." He is not talking about women being attractive now but about dying, while also trying to walk—which is good. I am clutching his arm.

"I said I *hoped* it was. I haven't died yet. Neither have you."

"Yeah, but it isn't," he says and plunks his cane hard down onto the Hilton terrazzo and lurches. He's dropped his USA Today where I can't reach it. "It's a fucking rheostat. I'm on a dimmer." We're moving toward the sliding front doors just as a Frontier crew trails in from the van, fresh from Denver. They shift to the side and offer us understanding smiles. "Spills and chills," Paul mutters. It's what he calls his walking forays, which are not so bad today.

Out in the startling South Dakota winter air, vehicles in the lot are moving, murmuring ahead of their exhaust streams. The lady lawyer idles past in a black Tesla (which very much resembles a Buick Regal). There's no new snow build-up and no wind. With luck the Dodge will come alive. My sore shoulder has re-ignited with a dull muscle stab. Dark words—"rotator cuff," "Tommy John," "full joint replacement"—enter the mind. Just when my son most needs me.

Paul is looking all around as if he hears something. In only his sick suit, he's freezing. He needs his coat. I'm not doing this very well.

He says, "So, is here like *the real west*?" I'm getting the Dodge opened.

"I guess," holding his arm and working the key in the lock that's possibly frozen. The Hilton van moves off from the drive-thru, bound back to the airport. "How do you like it *this* far?"

Paul weaves in my grasp like a building. I'm jabbing the key in and out. "Aren't I supposed to tell you what I'll miss when there's no tomorrow?"

"Yeah, sure. Tell me now." The lock makes a companionable click, and I can haul back the door.

"It won't be this shitty place," he says, listing to the left. "I told you. I don't want to keep doing *this*. It's boring."

"What's 'this'?" My toes are unmovable.

"Whatever it is we're doing out here. Am I just a victim of my own success, Lawrence?" His lower lip is up onto his upper. In this way he suppresses a smirk.

"You're awesome." I'm moving him up into the truck's doorway, which he could probably do himself.

"Okay. Just so I'm awesome." With his left hand, knees faltering, breath funneling out, he pulls himself up. "I made a pledge," he says with difficulty. "I have to always be awesome, or else."

"Okay." I push his legs into the well. "Just don't fall out."

"Not if we're not moving."

"That *wouldn't* be awesome." I put his coat in his lap and close the heavy door snug against his body. He is in. I turn to go back for his chair, and we are on our way again.

———

UP ONTO THE INTERSTATE, WE ARE WHIPPED PAST BY THREE South Dakota state trooper cars, flashers whirling, sirens a-whoop. Followed by two white-and-orange Sioux Falls FD-EMS meat wagons, lights strobing. We go another three miles, then all is explained. An accident—at exit 364. Our stream of cars and trucks is being diverted by deputies off the highway down to Route 38 and the cornfields. This has just happened.

A pile-up is in sight on the other side of the highway where we angle off. A tractor-trailer, a Mayflower van, rests on its side smack in the middle of the right-of-way. Underneath its green and yellow trailer, a passenger car has been pancaked, windows exploded, air bags deployed, front end and engine driven back where a driver would be. The police have set flares and hung blue tarps over the car to shield all that's terrible from travelers inching past. Eastbound traffic is backed to the horizon. I think for an instant it is the Tesla, cruising on auto-pilot right into calamity, but I'm not sure. A small man in short sleeves and capless is standing on the pavement talking calmly to the troopers. He is the trucker.

And then, like a curtain drawn closed, we are diverted off, and in two miles—at SD 38—turned west again, along where there are fields and irrigation pivots, and most of the snow has vanished, as if we'd entered a new dimension. If you don't like the weather, wait ten minutes. (Though where is that not true?)

Paul, up to the time we're detoured, has been yakking on about how we are badly served by our major news organs. The *New York Times* in particular, he believes, provides too much news to allow reliable opinions to be formed about anything. Stories should be more pared down like *USA Today*, which I have always thought of as "newspaper lite," but he prizes. Not that I think he's entirely wrong. He cites a recent *USA Today* story about a man in India—an untouchable—who can't stop sneezing, has sneezed at least ten times an hour for the past fifteen years. "Which is twenty-eight thousand sneezes," Paul says, "I think *I've* got problems. All in 800 words."

Watching frozen fields, empty farmsteads, empty fireworks stands, hawks on fence posts, a deer on the roadside—Paul becomes silent, as if some subject he'd been keeping at bay has stolen into his brain. His leg and pudgy-warty left hand aquiver (which doesn't seem to bother him), he stares out at a passenger car left to rust on a treeless rise in the vast field. The Great Plains are not flat the way they're portrayed as being.

"Has Clary called?"

"This morning," I say. "I didn't call her back. She wants you to move to Scottsdale. She thinks I'm not up to this."

Paul says, "I'd rather move to Libya." A relief. Though do all reliefs have to be welcome? "Do you remember we used to go up to Michigan in the summer? That fancy club?"

"Yes."

"I was trying to think of something this morning. I know Ralph was there. But I don't remember him." His brother.

"He jumped off the float and I had to save him. Don't you remember that? Later we all cooked tube steaks on the fire."

"I remember *me* jumping off the float, and *you* pulled *me* out. I remember Ralph reading a book, but that was someplace else."

"You were only five then."

"So when did Ralph die?"

"Nineteen seventy-nine. You were six."

He's looking at me across the seat as if he hasn't heard me. "There's a cognitive part to Al's. Okay? I'm getting that." Out the window we pass a helmeted boy on a four-wheeler, blazing along the highway shoulder, half in the ditch, as if he's racing us. "It's too bad we didn't do this trip before," Paul says, paying no attention to the boy outside his window.

"This works for me," I say.

"Great." He now looks out at the boy on the ATV. "How old was Ralph when he died?"

"Nine. He was nine," I say. "1979."

"Strange," he says. "1979."

"A long time ago now."

"Too young." And that is all he says about his brother.

BEYOND FULTON, SOUTH DAKOTA, OUT AHEAD OF US, A YELLOW train headlight is winking like a spaceship, a string of ore cars extending behind out of sight. The light is moving, but seems not to move. Paul sniffs the way my father sniffed when he'd said something that might be naughty but might be serious, too. "I thought I was going to get to drive," he says. "I guess you were lying." He looks ahead, but is estimating my truthfulness. My word.

"You can drive. Any time."

"The gimp wants to drive. Let the gimp drive."

"Let the gimp drive. How bad can it get?"

"It can," he says. "Wait and see. Bridge freezes before road surface."

I take the next farm road, 286th Street (counting from where?), and head us out between the cornfields. The train we both see will pass our road a mile farther on, but farther than I intend us to go. It is eleven. A lonely moon rides in the northern quadrant. No one else is out here with us. Fields on both sides make a straight allée where Paul can pilot us. I stop mid-road, snap loose from my seat and climb out into the waiting elements, which are fierce. The roadbed gravel is frozen to the dirt, sparse cheatweeds on both sides flattened from when snow has covered them. There is no wind. Far up the road, an animal—a large canine—steps out of the weeds, looks toward us, then trots to the other side into the field.

"What the fuck was that?" Paul says, when I get around and pull his door open.

"A dog. I don't know. It's too cold to wonder."

"I'll go without my parka." He's futzing his seat belt and having trouble enough that I lean in and un-buckle him, which I know he doesn't like. "This isn't worth the fucking aggravation," he says, his mouth already stiffened by frustration. He glances at me irritably then out the windshield.

"You don't have to drive far," I say. "Just take us for a spin."

"Fuck spin. I can't even get out of the truck. And I'm freezing." He rocks side to side as if he wants to eject himself.

"Yeah, you can. I'll get you out." I grab his left shoulder and the blousy front of his Genius at Wrok sweatshirt and pull and turn him. It is the precise way I hurt my shoulder yesterday, and right away a hot dagger slices up my arm into my sternum like an urgent message. "You could probably help me," I say. It's easily zero out here. I'm wearing no gloves or cap, just my Bean lumberjack shirt and wool trousers I've had for forty years.

He is trying to get out, and I have a stout grip on him. His feet are on the running board. Though the running board is two feet off the hardpan, and if I drop him and we stagger backwards into the weeds, I'll damage myself and freeze us both to death before anybody finds us.

"This is a fucked-up idea," Paul says, still working to climb down, his right foot dangling, seeking earth, his heavy, rubbery body leaning into me until I'm no longer getting him out but holding him like a roll of carpet. "You're gonna to kill us both, Frank. I'm fucked up. This is bullshit."

My cheek is into his sweatshirt front. His left hand squeezes my shoulder, right into its pain nexus. The train horn blares as the engine clatters over the crossing a mile up the road. I look to the empty sky, searching for something to focus on as I hold my son. Not a wispy cloud is there. Not a soaring raptor. Not a DC-10 with no idea what's doing down here.

And then that is enough. More than enough. I maintain the frozen ground's purchase and push meaningfully, clearing my throat which is dry in the scalping cold. My fingers sting and rasp, my shoulder throbs like I've done something bad to it. "Just get the fuck back in," I manage, and shoulder Paul up and back, my foot sliding so that I almost pitch face-first onto the running board. My cheeks are smarting, my hands feel blistered, my knees gone loosey-goosey.

"What would you do if you lived out here?" Paul says, infuriatingly calm, as I'm trying to get his seat belt around him so he can fasten it himself. His right arm is twitching like he was shaking a martini. I'm nearly frozen solid out here.

"Just what we're doing now," I say, reaching across. "Fuck everything up. Get mad."

"What'd that idiot woman say about me?" The freight train—three orange BNSF diesels pulling an endless cut of coal cars—sounds off another crossing it passes into the distance. I hear the tantalizing clatter-clack of wheels over the sleepers.

"Who?"

"That bimbo at the RV place."

"We didn't discuss you. It's hard to believe, I know." I'm standing out in the road, angry.

"Bull shit. I'm always the topic of conversation. I'm fascinating to the world."

"What can I do to make you happy, son?" I thought this would be easy. A no-brainer. A piece of cake. It should be.

"I'm never going to get laid again, am I? And I have my dick wound." He is trapped in his seat, staring furiously into the windshield.

"What?"

"I was making progress with that girl in the library." He lets his breath disconsolately out. His right hand is still agitating, palm tucked like a crab's, his hair disarranged by our struggle. He is a sorry sight.

"I don't know anything about that. I don't know what you don't talk about."

"May-be-to-mor-roh, I'll faaaa-ind what I'm af-TAAAH." He's singing.

"Don't do that, son. Don't sing," I say. "I'm freezing to death out here." I am in fact shuddering.

"It's my fucking theme song, Lawrence."

"Don't call me Lawrence, asshole. I'm your father not your nurse. Like it or don't."

"What's not to like?"

"I don't know. You tell me."

"You're the greatest, Alice. Now close this pneumonia hole. If you're freezing, think how I feel. I'm barely alive."

"Okay," I say, then say it again. "Okay." Far across the vasty cornfield, whatever canine has crossed our road now stops and stares back at us, scratches its ear with its hind leg, then sets off trotting toward the crest of the field and is lost from sight. We've come this far. Done only this much.

———

IN MITCHELL WE'RE QUICK TO OUR BUSINESS—LUNCH AT THE Ole Conestoga Chuckwagon, where the menus are laminated color photographs of the food (Paul's favorite menu). The plat du jour is the Bison Burger, which he orders then can't pick up, so I have to assist in cutting, which he lets me do. It is unpredictable what will and won't bother him. Once again, he is more adaptable than I am, mostly happy to focus on what's in front of him. Negotiating his Bison Burger and fries with a spoon clutched like a dagger, he expounds on what excellent work human logistics has been for him. Achieving personal and public relevance is not a lot of horseshit, since not "working creatively" leads to loneliness and early death. Etc., etc. It might be a good moment to lighten the mood and talk about the joint anti-bucket-list activities we'll never perform because we'll both be dead. Eat poi. Dunk a basketball. Be a hero in a subway car. Hold a French passport. Take a picture of our asses on a Xerox machine. Paul, though, begins in on light pollution and vehicular ground clutter "out west," and how it fucks with bird migration—"Rainbows do the same thing." At this exact moment, the Black lady lawyer I tried to make dalliant converse with last night but who snubbed me, and who I feared had been flattened by the eighteen-wheeler—but clearly wasn't—walks in through the Ole Conestoga's doors accompanied by another well-turned-out Black lady of the same vintage (unquestionably her Zeta sis), the two of them headed for high times farther west. Several of the cowboy customers plus two state cops take note of them, then go back to their apple crumble. (Mitchell is on the Interstate; you get used to weird people.) The woman's small, lawyerly eyes scan the crowded room for a place, pass me seated across from my son, then return as if she might like to share our table or supplant us. I smile a pointless semi-smile, but make no welcoming gesture, and she moves on without acknowledging, for the second time today, that I exist. Though for me, who'd had her counted out, and whose name I don't even know, nothing more is required. Occurrences of potential human significance frequently, now, leave me in this lurch. Sidelined.

"Most insomniacs sleep longer than they admit . . ." I hear my son saying. "I have no trouble sleeping whatsoever."

"That's good, son. I wish I could make the same claim."

"Yeah," he says, leveraging a last Bison-Burger wedge toward his mouth, opened in advance. "It's tough, Lawrence. It really is. Yep. You have my sympathies."

And that is lunch. Easy in. Easy out.

———

MITCHELL PER SE HAS LITTLE TO OFFER THE DEDICATED traveler—*except* The World's Only Corn Palace. We stage a short reconnoitering drive through the Mitchell "nice part," which includes the tidy-tiny brick and well-treed campus of Dakota Wesleyan—the Fighting Methodists—where I can easily imagine myself teaching (what, I'm not sure): The none-too-strenuous life-of-the-mind-on-the-prairie with evenings free for vodkas, plenty of TV, never meeting my neighbors, while romancing some sweet-natured divorcee who doesn't fancy the fast-paced lifestyle up in Pierre. I am tantalized, as always, by the dense life elsewhere, though smart enough not to breathe its fumes too deep. There are reasons so few people live out here. Settlers aren't called settlers for nothing.

"What's South Dakota famous for," Paul says, eyeing the older, stauncher faculty housing, quickly giving way to less staunch split-levels and ranches on postage stamps, most with plenty of gear—boats, cycles, snow machines, campers, atvs—cluttering their driveways. Minus winter's snow blanket, their affect is skimpy and insubstantial. Local election signage dots all yards. "Vote for Nepstadt. You Won't Be Sorry."

"George McGovern went to college here," I say. "They've got his museum right on campus." I've read this in my trip research.

"He was a doofus. Wasn't he?"

"We both voted for him. Your mother and I. We thought he'd win."

"Vote for Bascombe. You'll regret it as long as you live." Paul can't make his right knee be still and claps his hand on it, clearing his throat as a distraction.

"He would've made a good president."

"No more liberal claptrap. Build more private prisons." He's seen these signs on the highway. "You should be a professor of impersonal relations here, Frank."

"Maybe we could talk more. Not just tell jokes," I say. Which *I'd* like. I'm steering us out of the scratchy residentials back toward Mitchell's busy heart of commerce.

"If nothing's funny, nothing's serious, though. Right?" He looks at me.

"May be."

"I'm not worried about dying, okay? There's not that much to talk about."

"I guess not."

"I'm not in denial, are you?

"I might be," I say. "Sorry." I *am* sorry.

"You do the talking then. I'll tell the jokes. You're pathetic."

"Okay," I say. "I'll try to do better."

———

ALL SIGNS LEAD US TO THE CORN PALACE. I AM IMMEDIATELY IN recharged spirits in a townscape that includes a Mega Wash, a Kwik Phil, a Corn Trust Bank and Siouxland Oral Surgery. The expansive brio of business the day before Valentine's—a holiday born of business.

"I'm thinking about getting a tattoo," Paul says, watching Mitchell's pedestrians, frozen at eleven degrees, their pace quick into and out of stores. "I have to hurry up on these things now." He looks around at me, licks his lips as if his mouth is dry. "I want to get a bull's-eye over my heart. That'd be great, don't you think?" With his good hand he adjusts his sequined yarmulke, his doctor gift, which he's put on after we left the Conestoga. Meddling with it forces him to bite his lower lip for focus. Today is another good day to be Jewish.

"What about a mermaid? Or a dragon?" I say.

"And be a dipshit, no thanks. It has to be practical. Do *you* know exactly where your heart is? People try to shoot themselves in the heart all the time. But they miss, and then they're fucked up."

"Are you planning to shoot yourself?"

"I don't have the nuts for it. So no."

I'm turning us into the Corn Palace parking, where it's crowded with vehicles and families hustling across the lot to get in. "If you find your nuts, let me know, okay? I want to be somewhere else."

"Your heart's in the wrong place anyway, Frank." He purses his lips, wipes his nose with his sleeve, and looks moodily out at the noon-time traffic clutter.

———•———

THE CORN PALACE, WHEN I GET PAUL INTO HIS CHAIR AND shoved around to the front of the building, is gratifyingly as I remember it as a ten-year-old know-nothing. Though it is also *merely* as I remember it—early fond memories stoked by the glamour of life newly met, dimmed by time's passage. Often not a detriment.

Conceived initially by stolid, melancholy Lutheran town fathers with a mischievous streak to be a festive, if Kremlin-esque, homage to Demeter set down in the middle of town, the Corn Palace was always, even a hundred and forty years ago, an architectural curio. (Why would we want two of them?) Serving as a weird, frontier-days civic center, the entire Palace exterior—several 50 by a hundred foot walls—was literally clapboarded in corncob "art" to make giant, rustic panoramas promoting solid chamber-of-commerce, business-friendly, municipally uplifting themes. "75 Years of Prairie Progress." "The Noble Red Man." "Lewis and Clark." "Homesteaders' Faith." When my parents brought me in '54, on our way to Mount Rushmore, the year's theme was "Dakota Boy Returns," featuring great corn depictions of a grinning, accordion-wielding Mr. Welk and the

Champagne Orchestra (who actually performed while we were there and people danced inside) and which my mother liked and I sorta did, though my father, a determined non-dancer, stayed in the lobby smoking cigarettes and contemplating the Red Scare, which my mother and I didn't care much about.

As a youth, I deemed the Palace definitely the most flamboyant of human-constructed amazements—corncob minarets, corncob squinches, corncob Moorish arches and corncob "Russian" roof onions—plus corn entablatures featuring farmers clog-dancing, farmers singing, farmers farming, and Mr. Welk mincing around, pretending to lead the band like Paul Whiteman. On exiting back outside into the hot, soil-fragrant Dakota summer's eve, I recall thinking I'd made a first contact with the magical union of the unquestionably hay-wire with the inscrutably wondrous. Here, with materials found right under their feet (corn), hapless clodhoppers had built a Taj Mahal better (they thought) than the real one—since theirs was here on Main Street, and nobody needed to go to Agra. Billy Graham could stage a prayer breakfast here—and did. Tennessee Ernie could sing "Sixteen Tons," Jack Benny could play the violin. Presidential ballots (Grover Cleveland and William McKinley) could be cast. The art league could hold its spring outing of local genius, and the Mitchell Fighting Kernels could shoot hoops. Every last bit of it as American as the FBI. Which is why my son should see it—since connections between the heartfelt and the preposterous are his yin and yang.

As we approach the street entrance, tourists are streaming in and out of the Palace under the old movie marquee, some taking selfies, smirking and wisecracking about the Palace being a joke only they truly understand. This season's theme is a "Salute to the Military"—the huge Palace facade showing corn renderings of our Marines on Suribachi, our Air Force dropping the A-bomb on Nagasaki, our sailors on the ill-fated USS *South*

Dakota—casualty of Guadalcanal—as well as ranks of corn soldiers saluting an enormous corn stars-and-stripes. Many out here are veterans and are standing at fierce attention on the freezing sidewalk, saluting the big corn tapestries and having their pictures snapped by loved ones. To them this is the final measure.

"What the fuck *is* this?" Paul says, as I'm aiming his chair toward the bank of outside doors.

"It's hard to describe," I say. "It's my surprise."

"No shit," as I wheel him straight inside into what is, in essence, a dim-lit, old-style, odiferous theater lobby, unmodernized since my visit sixty-six years ago.

The big shadowy foyer is blessedly warm, and furnished with playbills of the many famous acts that have graced the auditorium stage, which lies beyond the lobby's rear doors with red-velvet curtains, which is where all the visitors are headed. There's a dense, lurid feel inside here of something not-quite-nice being made public, which I sort of like. Paul's gaping around as if he doesn't think anything's particularly strange, taking in photos of the Dorsey brothers, the Three Stooges, Crystal Gayle and Pat Boone, as well as The Great Commoner and right-wing huckster William Jennings Bryan who retailed his "Cross of Gold" speech here in 1900. Liberace is pictured at a white concert grand with candles, wearing a white tux and his trademark venereal grin.

Despite an Excedrin Extra-Strength bought at the Conestoga, my shoulder is back to aching, and it'd be okay with me if we left right now—before Paul's interest fades and we're stranded in treacherous no-place/no-time, which the Corn Palace lobby suddenly seems a breeding ground for. The risk of plunging into no-place/no-time with my ailing son is a constant to be confronted and subdued. How do we end up where we end up, when all our intentions are the best?

"Maybe we oughta take off," I say lamely.

Paul cranes around at me incredulous, zipped into his Chiefs parka, under his yarmulke, which I wish he'd lose. He is likely the only Jew in the Corn Palace today. "No way," he says. "You brought us. This is better than Disneyland—where you never took me anyway."

I'm pushing his chair toward the plush curtains and the inner-sanctum auditorium beyond.

"I always offered," I say. "You never wanted to go."

"You didn't mean it," he says. "Clary and I both knew it."

"My parents didn't take *me* to fucking Disneyland," I say. "They took me here."

"And when *I* feel despair, I read the great Russians," Paul says pseudo-dramatically, his hand twitching, his speech not entirely crisp.

"What's that supposed to mean?"

"It means *and* and *but* are the same, Lawrence. You're way behind. Keep pushing."

———

I WHEEL PAUL IN BETWEEN THE VELVET CURTAINS TO WHAT-ever is beyond—possibly treacherous. But to my happy surprise, the sanctuary of The World's Only Corn Palace is not what it was in 1954, when I danced with my mother alongside a hundred and fourteen waltzing Dakotans. Then, the "big room" had been fitted out as an old-fashioned gymnasium with a basketball court and wire windows, but with a stage on one side and balcony-seating for spectators. (We danced on the gym floor.) Now, all inside has been re-fangled into a corn-themed gift boutique, though the black scoreboard and game clock still hang at the south end, and the Fighting Methodists and Fighting Kernels no doubt still tilt on the parquet. I'd feared a ghostly inner chamber of memento mori—visiting the zoo and finding the white Rhino has died.

Like me, there's nothing my son thrills to more than the anomalies of commerce. The gravestone company that sells septics, the pet supply that offers burials at sea, the shoe store that sells baseball tickets. The "Palace Corn Boutique" spreads over the entire arena/performance venue/polling place; a Macy's of corn-themed crapola. Plastic corncob key-chains, plastic corn door-stops, corn picture frames, corn fly-swatters, corn back-scratchers. Plastic corn church-keys, corn sunglasses, corn toilet paper, corn billfolds, corn cowboy hats, ballpoints and tooth-brushes. All of it precisely what Paul Bascombe is put on the earth to seek, be deeply interested in and mesmerized by. I could not have been more prescient. I am for the moment saved.

"This is out*standing*," Paul says the moment we're in, hoicking his chair out ahead of me, scooting his wheels with both hands toward the racks, islands, endcaps and standing displays packed with corn essentials of a lifetime. The big room is full and a-hum with enthusiastic shoppers—burly, middle-age long-marrieds, men (and women) in leather biker gear on their way to Harley Heaven in Sturgis, college-agers of assorted ethnicities and hues, as well as the entire manifests off the "Pennsylvania Dutch Heart-land Tour" buses I've seen idling in the lot—off for a winter outing on the cheap, as if South Dakota in February is the Grenadines.

I'm immediately eager to get out of Paul's way and stand to the side against the stage apron and take in the shopping buzz, steps below where Patti Page sang "The Tennessee Waltz" in 1950. Paul has attained an instant grasp of things from his chair, and gone shoving and backing and sidling through the aisles, nudging the odd oldster in the Achilles, slicing between two slender Black Americans to get closer looks at corn-themed sweatshirts, tractor caps, rodeo belts and license-plate frames. He keeps an eye out for me and occasionally holds up a box of corn-flavored toothpaste or mouthwash—I offer back a knowing nod to which he gives me an even slyer, more knowing nod. If everything I ever admired in the world were to be housed in one place for my choosing, would I (I wonder) want any of it? The answer is—possibly.

"If this place didn't exist, you wouldn't invent it," Paul exclaims, navigating his chair over to me, eyes snapping behind his glasses, yarmulke still in place over his bald spot. Both his feet are working in their wheelchair stirrups. "I'm the only one in a wheelchair," he says. "Did you even notice?" He has grown younger.

"I wasn't paying attention," I say. Though I was. He is. We're standing close to the bustling till, manned by startling blond Mitchell amazons on high-school flex time, all wearing yellow Corn Palace T-shirts. Every register is doing ferocious business.

"I need to live here," Paul says, exultant. "I'd come every day." He's bought something I can't make out. Possibly a corncob shoe horn. "I didn't know what to buy," he says. "They have a cornhole game. But I've got one already. I just got these." I see, in his lap, a cellophane sleeve of yellow caramel corn, and from his parka side-pocket he produces a plastic-wood picture frame with "Corn Palace" "burnt" into the phony wood on its bottom panel like with an old wood-burning kit from my childhood. The word "Paul" is at the top, while down one vertical side of the frame is printed the list of extollable personal traits observable in all *homo sapiens* named Paul. This, he hands to me with the same sly-fox smile. In the frame's glass window is a cheap-paper color photograph of another "Paul," who turns out to be a sloe-eyed, vaguely Latinish, bushy-haired, handsome surfer-boy with full, girly lips and a leering, too-toothy smile. *This* Paul "is capable of learning great things," "is someone full of contentment," "gives a shoulder to lean on and shares himself," "is an enlightened person," and "is very dedicated."

Customers are shoving around us. Another tour-bus-full is coming in. It's hot and growing airless in here with the tills spitting receipts, dinging and whirring.

"Okay," is the best I can say about Paul's picture.

"Do you like it?" He is elated that I'm stumped. "He's the son you never dared dream of."

"Great. Okay," I say.

"This list describes me perfectly. Don't you think? 'An enlightened person.' 'Very dedicated.'"

"I guess. Maybe you don't need to buy that."

His eyes dart and sparkle in their orbits. "It's for you. It's a memento." He clears his throat of something his throat doesn't want to turn loose of.

I say, "I'm okay just with you."

"I bought it. It's excellent," he says.

"I don't want it. It's creepy. *You're* kinda creepy, in fact."

"Why'd we come in this fuckin' place if you didn't want me to have fun. I'm *having* fun. Why don't you lighten up and bite my ass."

"Okay. Yeah. I will." The shopper crowd is too much around me here—inducing a swirly sensation like vertigo, a neuropathy, a seizure, another TIA—all four at once. I feel my face go cold. Why wouldn't it? Death by Corn Palace.

Paul stares up from his chair, his moist, pink mouth trying to work up a grin but failing. "You're not croaking on me, are you, Lawrence? That wouldn't be fair."

"No," I say. "That's right. It wouldn't be." My face and hands are back warming already. Just a brief malfunction. Possibly I do have episodes. I feel the flatness of my two feet on the varnished boards where I once danced. They will still hold me up. "Can we just get out of here?"

"Sure," Paul says.

"I don't want this fucking picture."

"Too late. It's coming with us. You don't get to choose everything."

I take a vengeful grip on his wheelchair handles. "I know," I say and commence pushing then turning then angling my son across the floor toward the doors and the red curtains, through which are passing new visitors in stupendous spirits about everything in the world being made of corn. "I know," I say again. And I do. "It's okay," I say. And it is. We're headed out.

———

CLARISSA BASCOMBE IS CALLING (AGAIN) JUST AS WE REACH THE truck in the Corn Palace lot. As usual she wants to know (and dictate) everything. I am still slightly dazed.

"Okay. Where are you two?" She is in a hurry. A huffing Heartland tour bus is off-loading more jolly winter voyagers for the fun inside. I'd prefer talking to her not in Paul's presence, but there's no way. On his side of the front seat, he is holding his "Paul" picture, still in his yarmulke and Genius at Wrok sweatshirt, looking impatient, his right arm quivering.

"We're in Mitchell, South Dakota, sweetheart. We visited this amazing corn palace. It's the only one there is, to my knowledge. We're in the car now. Or the Windbreaker, to be precise. We're driving to Mount Rushmore today."

"What for?" Dogs are barking as always in her background. She's in the kennels. Then the sound of a heavy door closing, after which is silence. "Did you hear me, Frank?"

"Yes. To see the presidents. It was his idea." Paul pooches his lips and leers evilly at me. Our conversation pleases him because it is tricky and ironical and about him.

"When can I see him? Is he all right?"

"I'd say so. He has ALS. So he isn't perfect. But he's okay."

"Tell her I have sixty dogs and cats and am living in squalor," Paul says. "She needs to come get me. I'm a prisoner." This pleases him more.

"Did you hear that?" I say.

"What? No. You sound weird. Are you all right?"

Paul says, "Today's National Get a New Name Day. I'm changing mine to Ted Ramsey. Or possibly Gus Blaine. No Gus, no glory."

"Paul says he's changing his name, sweetheart."

"You're not taking care of him at all, that's obvious. Is he taking his Riluzole? This isn't good for him. Is he finished at the Clinic?"

"Yep. All finished. He's taking his Riluzole. He can still swallow. I'm doing okay with this."

"No, you're not. Stress is extremely dangerous. He needs all kinds of support now. He's got the fast-acting kind. Are you driving back to New Jersey?"

"We might go on to Custer's Last Stand. It's right down the road," I say. "Seems appropriate. Then maybe Kamloops. We have to talk about it." I *am* talking strangely. I don't know why. My daughter can churn up deranging effects in me. I don't much like her, if truth were told.

"He needs to come to Scottsdale, Frank. Right now. I can come out there. Or up there. It isn't very far, is it?"

"Probably not, no."

"We have access to a jet from Cookie's father. You can come back with us."

"That'd be great, sweetheart. But this is okay right now."

"I know a lot more about this now, Frank. I did an online course. It's really complicated."

"Yeah. I know. I'm glad you did a course. Was it at Harvard? I'll call you in a day or so. How's that?"

"You're scaring me. Both of you. You sound strange. I think I'm going to call the police."

"I wouldn't do that." Two men off the Heartland bus have noticed our Windbreaker rig and are having a good har-dee-har about it, giving us the thumbs-up, as if the camper box might be loaded with circus clowns.

Paul says, "Ask her if she knows the difference between a cornet and a trumpet,"

"Let me talk to him."

"He'll be glad to talk to you, won't you son. She wants to talk to you." I hand Paul my phone. His eyes are gleaming. He's still holding his "other Paul" picture and has to push it under his not-quite-working right hand.

"Hi," he says. Immediately he goes serious. Her truckler. Apple-polisher. Brown-nose and lickspittle. It is she he longs to please. "It's okay," he says. "Yeah. Yeah. It's fine." His voice no longer thin or elevated, his bad hand agitating at the end of his gray sweatshirt sleeve. With him, she has—and always *has* had—the power to alter things. And not always for the best. "I can see that," he says. "No, he's not. I will. You don't have to do that. It'll probably happen. No, not now. I'm sure. Yeah. Yeah. Yeah. Okay." He hands me my phone across the console. "I fixed everything," he says and produces a knifey smile of connivance and underhandedness. "She promised not to be a lesbian anymore."

"Hi," I say, back on the phone. "See, he's fine."

"He's not fine," Clarissa says. "He needs a new team of doctors."

"He had those at Mayo," I say. "They didn't fix anything. He's at least happy with me. I know more about this than you do."

Outside in the Corn Palace lot, someone dressed as an ear

of bright yellow South Dakota corn is greeting voyagers off the bus, all of them delighted and giving high fives to the corncob, taking selfies and pretending to dance with it on the freezing pavement. Paul is watching, then looks at me with deepest contentment. Nothing can make things all right. But here is a remnant of how life was once. A small mercy. A frolicsome corncob.

"All right, forget the police," Clarissa says. "Will you promise me, Frank, that whatever you two're doing, when you finish, you'll let me come get him and try to help him? You can come and stay. I'm not the worst person in the world."

"No. You're probably not. I'd rather live in Libya than Scottsdale, though."

"Fine. But will you promise?

"Tell her I hope to die before I lose all my hair." He is entranced by the corncob capering and cavorting along beside the bus passengers, dancing with them around the corner toward the grand entrance and the "Salute to the Military."

"I can't promise anything, honey. I'll try. Okay?"

"I'm his sister, you know. No matter how you feel about me."

"I feel great about you. And so does Paul. We both love you. Very much. We're just here in South Dakota today."

"Don't forget to call me Ted Ramsey," Paul says, forgetting Gus Blaine.

"I'm having a hard time dealing with you, Frank."

"I know. I'm sorry. I'll try to keep you in the loop." Another usage Paul adores.

"Okay. Tell him I love him, please."

"Your sister loves you, Ted. She said so."

"Tell her I'm filling my cooler from the ice machine," he says. "And *that's* the *way* it is in the loop. Loop. Loop."

"He says he loves you, too."

She is already off the line. Not waiting to hear his answer.

———◆———

NORTH OF THE MITCHELL CITY LIMITS WE STOP FOR A HALF-
hour at a weedy, lakeside, snow-scabbed, one-table picnic area to
eat our caramel corn and project our trip on to Rapid City, a distance of two-seventy-five, which, I've estimated, gives us time to
drive up and preview the presidents' visages on Mount Rushmore
before *officially* visiting tomorrow—Valentine's Day—following
which we will stare together into the cave-of-winds which is the
rest of life and how we will negotiate it. I believe in strategic pre-
views. Much can be salvaged if ironclad plans prove unwieldy.

However, since we departed Minnesota, and I set aside my
duty as time manager, I have miscalculated the time-distance
differential. It is now one thirty. Gaining an hour for Mountain
Time, we will not possibly reach Rapid City in fewer than four
hours, by which time night will have fallen and the mountain
gone dark. Still, we will get there.

Beyond the skimpy picnic ground, "Lake Mitchell" stretches a
mile across and twice as long, frozen hard as tungsten. In summer
it would be the playground of water skis, jet boats and party barges.
Mid February, though, the lake's skin is speckled with ice shan-
ties, snowmobiles, cars driven onto the ice, a hockey rink ruled
off near shore with skaters playing two on two. A few solitary
cross-country skiers are visible plodding along. And all around in
the sky, seagulls—from where who knows? Oversize lake villas
dot the far shore, making a kind of prairie Riviera for local bank-
ers, car dealers and John Deere franchisees. At the north end is a
links course where, with little snow, duffers are taking the front
nine in yellow carts. On the highway behind where we've stopped,
there's a Kiwanis sign and a plaque commemorating fallen trooper
Snediker, who died close-by doing his duty. Plus, signs for a pizza
place, a sign soliciting clean fill, a sign for an antique car rally last

summer, a sign saying we are in Packer Country, a sign saying this is Trump Country. And beside the picnic area, an untended cemetery with metal lettering above its arched entrance. Heavenly Rest. A single scraggly whitetail—a doe—stands among the grave markers, studying my car.

"Do you think I got sick because I'm weird?" Paul says. He's been serenely watching activity on the lake. He's forgotten about Ted Ramsey and Gus Blaine. I have begun watching the deer in the cemetery, wondering if I could be buried here. Or would I have to live here first? Possibly this cemetery is decommissioned.

"I wouldn't say you're weird enough to make yourself sick." Which is true. Having Al's has made his strangeness less strange. He can *act* weird, but at heart isn't very.

"I'm getting worse." He's ditched his yarmulke. His hair is slicked to his scalp like a cap.

"What makes you say that?"

"I don't connect things that well in my mind anymore. It's just one thing, then another thing. *You* connect everything."

"Not really. Most experiences don't seem like other experiences to me. You're just overthinking." He did this as a child. Morbid illness, though, can skew anyone's state of mind.

He says, "I'm sure my Functional Rating Scale's dropping."

Functional Rating is the ever-descending step-ladder of loss. The capacity to turn in bed, to climb stairs, to write with a pen. Later still, to breathe. Each forfeiture represents four points from a picture-perfect 48. His score is definitely falling. So is mine. Though the apparent congruity between ALS and being seventy-four is a prime example of how analogy deceives—as Aristotle knew. Having ALS might as well be comparable to how a turtle seeks the sea.

"I haven't noticed," I lie, about his FRS score.

"I feel like I'm more nervous in public. I didn't used to be. I guess, if I'm not getting better I have to get better about getting worse."

"It's the key to happiness," I say. "Most people never discover that."

Beyond the rusted cemetery fence and the grazing deer, I have not seen—but see now—the Art Deco marquee of an abandoned drive-in movie, CLOSED and "PSYCHO" COMING SOON, still block-lettered on. A few skeletal hoardings remain, but nothing's left of the projection house and concession stand. Six black cows are eating weeds and thistles where love cars parked in the dark. Mitchell once had plans for expansion out here, but elected to leave well-enough alone. Many's the time in the realty game, I've witnessed a young Lebanese go-getter open his lifelong dream of a falafel stand on Route 1, immediately enjoy his lot filling with cars, then lose his burnoose by opening three others he couldn't run as well as he could run one. A smart man knows when enough is enough.

Our caramel corn now seems less a good idea, and I take the half-empty cellophane out to the refuse barrel and drop it onto a car battery and a broken umbrella. Paul and I then sit for a time and spectate the ice huts on the white lake, the skaters, and the snowmobilers out for a pre-Valentine's careen, etching rainbow curves across the ice. Two people have brought a catamaran skimmer-craft out from a house on the far shore and rigged it with a jib, which propels it skittering and clattering across the lake plain and perilously onto one sled. On our side, there seems to be no wind, but on the lake there's plenty. Where the wind is, where it goes and will go next, is again the thing one needs to know.

"I wish I could skate," Paul says, watching. "I could be the goal."

He might mean goalie, but he might not.

"Your mother and I used to skate when we first knew each

other," I say. "Right in Rockefeller Center, where I was working. She was good at it. No surprise." I didn't need to mention his mother. I've managed to skirt the subject more or less unscathed. But mentioning her comes naturally.

"What're you getting out of all this?" He looks at me.

"A lot," I say. "I wanted us to do something we'd never do otherwise." Little Krista's sage counsel. "Sometimes I decide not to do things just to be *not* doing them. So, I wanted us to *do something*. I don't really know how to deal with you. Or if I even *am* dealing with you." What his sister said to me.

"So, is this a relationship now? Is that it?"

"Yeah. Sure. Good enough. Don't you think?" Far out on the lake, the water-sprite catamaran attempts an arc-ing glissade onto its skimming edges and goes over, spilling its two passengers over the ice like toys. They're quickly up. Mishaps are part of the fun.

The deer I've been watching saunters out the cemetery gate up onto the asphalt highway and stops where any passing cattle truck would pulverize it. Another deer—also a doe—is still in the cemetery calmly eating, unaware it is now alone.

"I wish you liked Clary." Both his knees are gently twitching in unison. His jaw is clenched. Being with me *is* perhaps stressful.

"I like your sister fine. I love her. Which is easier. She's a Republican."

"You don't know that."

"She says she is."

He clears his throat. "She probably is."

"Are you sorry to be released from the Clinic?"

"Why? I told you. I've taken on a life of my own. Isn't that what I'm supposed to do? For a while anyway?"

"You've always had a life of your own," I say calmly.

"Do you worry how I'll make out if *you* died?"

"Why do you want to know that? No."

"I just thought about it. What're you going to do when *I* give up the goat?"

"I don't know." Putting both hands on the steering wheel at high noon. "Get my *own* goat, maybe."

Far out on the lake, the two sports in the spilled-over ice sailer are up skirmishing around. A snowmobiler has circled back to give assistance. They're all waving arms and laughing. Sun gleams off the picture windows of the trophy homes on the far side. No one is visible among the ice shacks, inside which the Pete Engvalls of the world sit fishing, sipping schnapps and silently smoking.

"Do you think it's better to die fast or slow?" Paul asks. "Did I ask that before?"

"You did." Ten times. Al's patients all think about this. In the uncertain certainty of their lives, it is one of the attention-grabbing variables.

"Okay." He is like his mother who said "okay" to mean many things. Okay *no*. Okay *I heard you*. Okay *Yeah-No*. Okay *Okay*. The first deer has ambled safely out into the barren cornfield, just as a white pickup slams past heading toward North Dakota.

"Present mirth is present laughter is my motto," I say, as if that was an answer. "It's probably not worth worrying about."

"I'd like fast," he says. "But I'm not always sure."

"We should probably go," I say. "We're gassing ourselves out here." The truck is idling.

"We're not really going anywhere, are we?" He looks at me and smiles, his right hand aquiver. He licks his lips, which are shiny.

"We're going to Mount Rushmore," I say. "In this very Windbreaker."

"I was never a prime physical specimen, was I?" He moves

his crippled right hand off the armrest and onto his knee, as if to demonstrate what a physical specimen he is not.

"You were always a great athletic supporter, " I say to please him. We are both talking about him in the past tense—though here he is still.

"Did you know Ann had a girlfriend in the home?" I'm backing us up onto the highway. We must return to Mitchell to re-find the Interstate.

"Of course," I say.

"Do you have a problem with that?"

"None whatsoever." I did *not* know this and doubt it's true. He is making things up, which is his way of advancing interesting conversation. I am making something up because Ann is deceased and cannot hear me. Though if she'd had a "friend" other than me in her late days, I'm happy. Love extends far. "Do *you* have a problem with it?" I say, easing us away.

"No," he says almost privately, as if we have this in common. "It's the upside of the downside." I have no idea what this might mean. "Did I ask you what your favorite bodily function was?" His slate eyes gleam, his claw hand twittering.

"You did. I was given another chance to choose. I'd said hiccuping." And farting.

"So, what is it?" He is keen for this. "This better be good."

"Laughing."

He shakes his head vigorously. "Laughing's *not* a bodily function. Laughing's a learned response to stimulus. Choose better."

"What's your choice?" I say.

"I don't know," he says. "I don't have one."

"Laughing will have to do us then," I say to him. And so it will.

NINE

Once one has glimpsed the limits of one's existence, it snatches one back from the dream of endless possibilities we once thought were ours—comfort, idleness, taking things lightly.

I read this in the middle of last night, seconds past 2:46, in the Hilton in Sioux Falls, my son deep asleep in the matching bed. Often when I wake at that hour I think how far I am from my first waking—2:46, Biloxi, 1945—and marvel at the life in between; full of comfort, idleness and taking things lightly. Old Heidegger was only writing about being human (albeit German), but he has hit on a fairly accurate expression of my and my son's situation together upon the nation's great middle swath. Our human dilemma is not as unique as you might think, but akin to everyone's. Which means being old *really is* like having a fatal disease, at least insofar as I'm no more ready than my son is to give up on comfort, idleness and taking grave things lightly. In this, at least, we find common cause.

———◆———

PAST EXIT 230 OUR HIGHWAY SUDDENLY OPENS WIDER AROUND into movie-size western panoramics. Rolling wheat prairies and what by spring will be alfalfa hay; second-rate buttes and craggy outcrops, mournful cattle groupings on frozen, treeless, domeless terra firma. New dead animals dot the roadside—jack rabbits, badgers. A coyote. An unlucky antelope. Signage now is for Wall Drug, the Indian reservation, Elvis's shrine, a dinosaur park, a petrified forest, the Minuteman Missile museum and the Badlands—all of which I've decided we cannot bother with.

At Oacoma, where the Missouri River passes beneath the highway, we stop for gas at a mammoth truck stop—acres of 18-wheelers huffing and growling across a vast concrete veldt, their drivers disappeared inside for a Red Bull to get 'em to Chicago. Paul goes in by himself on his tripod cane. I am not invited. Though in ten minutes he's wobbling back across the windy tarmac like a movie zombie, stiff-legged and stumping, declaring the truck stop—LOVE'S—to be "way better" than the Corn Palace because of its choicer array of impulse offerings. He's brought back a Mount Rushmore photo book: *The Story Behind the Scenery—A Life-Changing Patriotic Experience*—text written by one of Charlie's Angels. This he considers prizeable. He's bought a new T-shirt that has "Proud To Be An Apache" on the front. Last out of his LOVE'S sack he produces a scarlet and gold baseball cap with scrambled eggs on the visor and "Semper Fi" crusted in gold on the front. "You have to wear this now," he says, pushing it at me with a bitter smile. We're out by the pump island, where it's ten degrees. Paul feels I don't claim credit due for my year-and-a-half undistinguished USMC "career," circa 1968—derailed by a case of pancreatitis (misdiagnosed as Hodgkin's disease) which landed me in a Navy hospital and after two months earned me a discharge and a train ride back to Ann Arbor. Free of having to kill or be killed, an actor of deeds not done.

Paul knows this saga well but for some reason (perverse) insists I was a bona fide Gyrene, should don the colors, fly the standard, know the password and the handshake of America's fighting elite, etc. Whereas, I don't want to, would feel even more fraudulent than usual on an average day. Plus today it reminds me of Sarge-Major Gunnerson, my nemesis.

"Go get your money back," I say. "I'm not wearing this." The Dodge is topped off—a cool 70 bills. A gas hog but necessary to get us to Rapid City.

"Thank you for your surplus," he says, teetering on his cane, his loony comb-over lifting in the frigid breeze whipping the truck plaza expanse. "Aren't you a big patriot?" He is struggling to keep his face muscles working in unison.

"You don't know anything about being a fucking patriot." I take the Semper Fi cap—he'd never make it back inside—and squeeze it into a tight crumple. It's cheap and stiff and wants to spring back into shape, but I stuff it in the Love's trash barrel beside the pump before it can.

"Oorah," Paul growls—with difficulty. "Isn't that what all you morons say?"

"I don't know."

"What does it mean? 'Oorah'?" He is unsteady against the side of the Windbreaker. "Is it some Indian thing?"

"Yeah. It's some Indian thing. You got it."

"Oorah!" Heaving, hissing semis are pulling past us, revving up for the Interstate. Heat from their engines briefly warms us. "Oorah!" Paul mugs a serious face though he's a shit-for-brains.

"Why don't you get back in the goddamn truck. You're gonna die out here."

He swivels round, bare-headed, to check if someone might be behind him. It is instinctive to him now. A world of perils. Holding onto the camper's back end, he directs his feet where he wants them to start going, still holding his paper sack. "Oorah," he says. "The war cry of the feral douchebag. I'm freezing my stones off out here."

And we are off again on our way west.

———•———

PAUL GOES INSTANTLY TO SLEEP, EARBUDS SOCKED IN HIS EARS, glasses on the dash, right hand clutched in his good left one for protection. I notice he's bitten down the nails on both hands—something I've missed. The back of his right hand also bears an ugly staining bruise—possibly incurred in sleep when his extremities move on their own.

At exit 163 we fall back from four o'clock to three, and not long after I pull us into a scenic overlook from which the Badlands stretch south in devolving, corrugating shadows. Due west, a mural of snowy mountains rises into view possibly a hundred miles away, a quivering sun sinking below a dark green sky, peaks sharpening in silhouette. There is Wyoming.

I climb out and walk to the rock wall that separates me from empty space. No one is here but us. Paul has roused. I've invited him to get out so we can take a selfie with his phone, and he can offer commentary about the Badlands not being all that bad. In the remnant sun it is oddly not so cold. For a moment he opens the truck door then stays in, looking undersized in the seat, in his Genius sweatshirt with its toothpaste stain. I come instead to him, and we snap our picture side-by-side, him in the doorway, me leaning in smiling—though he does not. A picture of two men in a truck.

"I lied about Candice," he says, once I'm back in the driver's seat, his right knee agitating.

"It was an interesting story. That's all dreams ever are," I say.

"I don't have to tell the truth anymore if I don't want to," he says, pulling his parka around him. He's cold. "The truth's about the future. So I can say whatever. It doesn't matter."

"She's a babe, though." Referring to the regal Candice, my heart-throb from her Steve McQueen days in *The Sand Pebbles*. 1966.

"Everybody knows she is."

"How do you feel right now?" I say. "Do you feel bad in the Badlands?"

"I feel super," he says. "I feel like I'm fighting the sky, and I'm winning. I'm a change agent." This, I suppose, I understand. "One-third of Americans over forty-five are chronically alone, Lawrence. That's *your* problem. You're a chronic loner. You need to get out more."

"This is as 'out' as I can get right now," I say, the Badlands all around us.

"This doesn't count," he says. "This is your job. You're the caregiver. Airline pilots don't think they're on vacation."

I smile at him in a way meant to be visibly patient while conceding he is an asshole. I *am* his caregiver and will be 'til his end, and am not so bad at it.

"What's my magic number?" He makes his mouth tight and pinched as a pink prune.

"I don't know, son."

"Zero. I don't have one. There's no tomorrow."

"That isn't literally true," I say. "Okay? There *is* one. It's tomorrow."

"Are steeple jacks all named Jack?" It is yet one more of our classic oldies from long-gone days, when he was an odd boy who would grow up someday to join the ranks of the normal—which didn't happen.

"Are civil servants always civil?" I answer. "Is real estate more real? Do pigeons speak pidgin English?"

"Are dare devils really devils?" It makes him smile wonderfully, sitting here in the late-afternoon South Dakota cold, idling and taking grave things lightly. He is not always an asshole. We can go on toward our destination now, whatever is beyond the Badlands.

———•———

THE NEW TIME ZONE MAKES US GAIN GROUND FASTER—OR seem to. There are few cars and semis now. Everyone has arrived where they're going and can claim a well-deserved rest. We pass classic western *built* landscape—bull auctions, Get Out of the UN billboards, Indian trading-posts and roadside remembrance crosses with bouquets. (As if the Interstate is a place you come to die.) There are scarcely towns at all—land and sky merging at a far distance, stitched across by a jet commencing the polar route. Paul sleeps with Anthony Newley in his earbuds. And I, for just these moments, become unaccountably happy. At the Clinic, under the doctors' vigilance, everything was of confounding consequence, requiring concern. (Though nothing I could do made a mouse fart's bit of difference.) Now though—driving—my son asleep, there is little I need do of genuine importance; only pilot the Dodge into the evening as if alone and free to think a thousand uncontested things, many of them pleasurable: that I am on the road to La Jolla and the stony, ever-summery cliff-side veranda of Dr. Flaherty, where we will take strong drink (two or three), sit on chaise longues, talk into the evening hours of the life that's passed and what parts might still be for the taking. There's nothing fraudulent about such flights of fancy. Why, otherwise, would we indulge them all the time?

Occasionally Paul wakes, flutters his eyelids behind his glasses, peers at the scenery—ever-craggier extrusions, floating fields soon to be sown, farmhouses, barns, stately silos—land, land and more land. Possibly he has only been zoning out so as not to broach hard subjects—which I don't want to broach anyway.

"How long does all this go on?" sleepily blinking at the horizon. He means *all of this* around us. Where we are.

"'Til we see the flagship of the Polish navy, I guess."

He doesn't respond.

"Do you know George Sanders' last words?"

"No." Why does he know who George Sanders is?

"'I'm soooo bored.' Right? I can sympathize." Then a moment later, "I don't like it that you can get any license plate style you want. It makes policing a lot harder." After which he returns to some version of sleep.

For a time I turn on NPR, something I normally never do since I hate the honied, insolent voices. Only I can't find a sports call-in out here in the middle of nowhere. This afternoon, there's a story from Penn State's Sensory Evaluation Center. A statistically appreciable virus is being watched at the CDC in Atlanta, which can cause—if you're unlucky enough to contract it—dramatic smell and taste distortions in ordinary humans. Coffee smells like garlic; peanut butter and feces both smell like burning rubber. All meat tastes putrid. There are podcasts, training kits, support groups and therapists in thirty languages, aiding sufferers to regain "sensory integrity." "I'd give anything to smell real urine again," a woman in Hershey PA, says. Rumor is the virus started in France, but it's not 100%.

Another story from the Census Bureau references the world's fastest growing population segment to be citizens age 102, though no one's lived past 115 since 1968 except a lady—also in France—who's made 122. "Predictions are," the Census people say, "the future more than anything will resemble the present, since it's all about health span not life span." To which I shout out "Whoever believes that wasn't seventy-four." Paul opens a googly eye, then ups the volume on whoever's he's listening to now—John Denver. There is other news. Kirk Douglas—never one of my favorites—has died at 103. Ditto one of the original Chordettes. As highway background noise none of this is as gripping as last night's NBA scores.

As we pass the National Grasslands Center, a hundred miles out from Rapid City (2 hours), I'm now beginning to brood that Mount Rushmore might be only one more empty "activity," like the Spam Museum or Elvis's Harley—of no consequence to anyone when it comes to the real business of making living vie with dying in real time. Just motions to go through. Possibly I am fraudulent *here* (again) for not realizing and doing more and better—a feeling not unfamiliar to me.

When I lived in my fancy beach house on the Jersey Shore (circa mid-nineties)—a glass & board & batten multi-decked architect's write-off on the sands—often I would stand at the deck-railing of a warm-summer's morning, watching a father and children on the beach; offspring doing what offspring do when they're alone with Dad at the seaside. Build castles. Dig to China. Bury each other neck down. While the father stares off, reads a newspaper, talks on his phone, often in business attire. Now and then the children would raise an appeal—that he notice a delicious detail of their castle, built with only a tiny spade. The father would re-direct his gaze, say a word, hike up his pants legs, squat for a closer look, offer an assessment. But then stand again, as the children returned to their pursuits, and stare out at the ocean's sparkling palette toward a distant freighter, a windsurfer, a charter craft riding at anchor. "I'm going through the motions *here*. I should be *there*," his posture and gaze declared.

"I could be heading toward a new horizon, a different sunrise. Yet I'm here, on the continent's edge with my wee ones, doing what life has ordained. It is not sad, not fraudulent in the least. Though, yes, there could be more, or other."

All the while I was thinking—mug of strong coffee steaming on the deck rail—"I know the hollow in the heart that is longing and longing's opposite—doing good because you want to do good and are a good man in spite of what you know is true of you. Yes. Happiness can still be yours, ole chap; since happiness is not a pure element like Manganese or Boron, but an alloy of metals both precious and base, and durable."

———————◆———————

ON AN INCREASING NUMBER OF BILLBOARDS I'M NOTICING splashy advertisements for the Fawning Buffalo Casino, Golf and Deluxe Convention Hotel—an entertainment subsidiary of the Wahpe-Mippa-Conji tribe of American Indians, lying somewhere out ahead of us. It's no place I'd ever think of setting foot, since I hate risking money. People believe selling real estate is a version of gambling. But as a professional, I can tell you—it's not if you do it right.

The lighted billboards all show a big cartoon face of a grinning, liver-lipped male with bulging eyes and a Jimmy Durante schnoz, tossing hundred-dollar bills in the air like confetti, and below it a "crawl" listing casino attractions to enjoy while you're losing all your money. There's a "Rolling Stones All-Native" cover band in the Circle-the-Wagons supper club. Exotic Entertainment in the Counting Coup Lounge. Ugly sweater, wet T-shirt and best-butt contests every weekend. A "gigantic" indoor waterslide. A "world famous" Tahitian Buffet. Plus,

"Lifestyle Enrichment" classes, a writers workshop, a mortuary science job fair, Tai Chi instruction, and a "How to Live in the Present" seminar taught by Native psychologists with degrees from South Dakota State. Plus, "Loose Slots" and Valentine's room rates for lovers—which my son and I are not but might pass for. There's also a free shuttle to the "The Monuments" every two hours, which appeals to me, since I'm not sure the Windbreaker makes the climb if the weather turns against us, which it could.

Of course, of course, of course. The Fawning Buffalo is not an inspired choice. There *are* no inspired choices for us now. Yet at this moment of almost-arrival to our destination—arrivals are always departures—*some* choice is what I want. In the spirit of Krista's injunction that my son and I do things we'd never do, a night in the Fawning Buffalo might move our needle off of where, I worry, it now lies—close to life support.

Paul has roused and is silently observing the frozen, darkening pampas shooting past. It is 5:21. Sunlight glistens salmony pink off the prairie, revealing it to be a solid ice sheet to the horizon, where winter sky is still blue high up. Possibly I've been speaking my thoughts out loud, which I often do now without realizing. "Did you know Valentine's is also National Organ Donor Day," my son says calmly.

"Are you contemplating auctioning off your parts?"

"No." With his left hand he tugs at his white earbud cord and lets both buds fall in his lap and taps them with his hand. "Do you know that I do *not* suffer erectile dysfunction? You'd think I might." He fattens his cheeks. Last light has silvered the highway ahead of us.

"Your dick's not connected to your brain," I say. "It does its own thinking. Great literature's mostly about that."

"Whatever." He clears his throat, which he's done more today. "Do you think someone would marry me? I've been wondering about it."

"Somebody'll marry anybody. Look at me."

"I'd be a catch, don't you think. I'm pretty rowdy in bed."

"You'd be a colorful catch, that's for sure," I say. Which is true.

"You talked in your sleep last night. I'm sure you don't know that." He steals a look at me. In the shadows his lenses catch the last sun like tiny diamonds. He is smirking. "It wasn't very interesting. It was just weird."

"Why don't you spare me." I don't need to explore this now.

"Do you want to know what you said?"

I decline an answer.

"You said, 'Those are cheap Chinese sunglasses. It's why you're a fucking liberal.' How weird is that? What's that about?"

"I'm confident I never said that."

"You did. You also said, 'Same shoe size, same scars, same overbite.'"

"I don't remember. I'm not responsible."

"Where *are* we?" He gazes toward the far mountains, inky in last light. Rapid City has materialized twenty miles ahead of us—a small galaxy of twinkles in the wintery evening. I've gotten us off at exit 78 and onto SD 44 following signs for the Fawning Buffalo. It's unlikely Paul's been inside a casino, much less one owned by Indians. These places are supposedly established by the tribe to rake in tourist dough in repayment for centuries of pillage perpetrated against their ancestors by my ancestors. I can't blame them.

"We're going to try something. It's different." Up ahead, a halo of misty gold frosts the sky, evidence of a big sign.

"I think I see the Northern Lights," Paul says.

"It's a casino. It's gonna be great." Another giant, sensationally lit sign showing a dejected-looking buffalo kneeling cravenly before a scantily clad man who might be a Native American, rises ahead with its marquee screaming "Valentine's Special! Everyone's a Winner. Pale Faces Welcome." Miles of parking, mostly vacant under lofty LED lighting, extends toward a hotel-ish structure where most windows aren't lit, though there's a grand entrance with lights streaming into the night like a hospital emergency room. A solid barrier of snow piled up from previous storms encircles the lot, along the back of which is a row of RVs not unlike ours where the employees must live or sleep. I see more Heartland buses parked in front and a small fleet of Fawning Buffalo shuttles for transporting customers to Mount Rushmore in the morning. I can't see where a golf course is. Nothing seems to be going great guns, though it qualifies as something I would never do and therefore should. It's at least more original than a Hilton Garden, which Paul has pronounced the Stockholm Syndrome.

I pull into a space close to the bright-flashing entrance. A scattering of casino patrons is trading out and in—mostly men in boots and hats and cowboy gear from the local oil-rigs, eager to lose their day's pay.

"Gambling's for morons." Paul's been waiting to say this.

"You don't have to gamble. There's a lot going on."

We both stare at the illuminated entrance as if orderlies with gurneys might suddenly dash out and snatch us. Over the bank of revolving doors, there's another events crawl announcing what's happening inside *right now*. A "Warriors All-Male Revue For the Ladies" and "The Epic Return of Midgette the Wood Chipper" in the Counting Coup Lounge. The battle of the Kiowa punk bands on the Little Bighorn mini-stage. The "South Dakota Past Management Association" is holding winter seminars in multi-purpose room 'J', while in multi-purpose room 'B' we could attend an EBITDA tribal brainstorming session. Mixed use is the theme of the day, even for Indians.

"You know, I don't need to live a whole lifetime in the time I have left," Paul says to me.

"No. Me, either."

"If you fucked your life up it's on you."

"I haven't fucked my life up. I think a casino's a novel idea, that's all. It's different."

"*I'm* taking care of *you* now, aren't I, Lawrence? You've lost your executive function." He has a hard time getting "executive function" out, which causes him to look away toward the casino's flagpole as a diversion. Old Glory and an MIA banner hang at half-staff (I don't know why. Kirk Douglas?), the pole anchored to the middle of a concrete fountain that in summer would showcase "dancing waters," but is iced over now.

"You're not taking care of *me*." I could answer that we're taking care of each other, but this is not true. We are mostly alone. I already feel abysmal, and we're not even inside.

"Do you feel trapped being with me, Lawrence?" He gets these words out distinctly enough. Speech loss can happen fast with the bad kind, but then come back.

I say, "No. I'm all set." All set. Another of his favorites.

"Okay. Just so you're all set."

"Can we go inside. I'm frozen out here." The temperature on the events marquee announces it to be minus 5.

"It'd be better to do this in the summer," he says. "I already said that."

"Yeah. I guess. Probably."

"Too bad," my son says. "Among the other too bads."

Then we are piling out for the casino.

———◆———

PAUL REQUIRES HIS CHAIR, HIS DUFFEL BAG AND HIS METAL BOX with Otto inside, as if he intends for Otto to perform once we've checked in. I pray not.

Entering the Fawning Buffalo grand entrance is not that different from entering the Mayo Clinic—a day and many miles behind us. The rotunda lobby—done up in north-woods ambience—is busy but not *very*. Sparse car numbers in the lot tell the story. In a year the whole place could be gut-rehabbed into senior living or down-graded to a vertical mini-storage, the big lot chain-linked and padlocked.

The glowing but un-crowded lobby opens out directly to a cavernous, murky, low-lit gaming pavilion, a sea of slots where only a handful of players perched on stools are goosing the machines, sipping free margaritas and smoking (health laws don't apply in here). Poker, roulette, bingo, and dice pits are far in the rear and out of action. A gray haze drifts out into the lobby, around the sides of which is the "Naughty Spot Gift Boutique" with a red neon sign, and a few other unpatronized storefronts—a Condom and Tattoo Station, an exotic bakery, a Crafts Centre with a window of baskets and knock-off tribal trappings for sale. Wide, shadowed hallways flow toward the Tahitian Buffet, the Circle the Wagons Stage, the convention facilities and multi-purpose rooms. There's no sign of a water slide. Nothing here is living up to the billboard hype. Possibly it never did. Tom Jones is singing strenuously over everything. "Whoa . . . whoa-whoa-whoa-whoa-whoa."

This time, I'm manning the luggage cart, and Paul is managing in his chair, geekily looking around as if seeking something specific—once again zipped into his long-boy Chiefs coat and watch cap. There are no bellhops, and the security personnel—impassive, beady-eyed, body-builder types (both genders) in gold sports jackets with Fawning Buffalo crests and curlicue earpieces

(they could be Italians) are paying no attention to us. Other sur-
veillors, stationed at video screens in the basement *are*, of course.
My immediate problem now is to decide, under what are already
becoming less-than-optimal prospects, whether to push ahead
and get us a room, or fold my tents. The Fawning Buffalo is not
what I bargained for without knowing what I bargained for. Except there's a chance—if we stay, don't gamble, fill our bellies at
the Tahitian Buffet, find front-row seats for the Wood Chipper,
avoid the writers workshop and the Native Rolling Stones—we
could end up swapping unique life experiences over breakfast
with a visiting past-management family from Aberdeen. Something we'll look back on and laugh like monkeys about. Or is it
already so dismal here we'll end up sorry, with too little time left
in my son's life to look back on anything. There is only *is*. I'm
trying, but don't seem to be doing this very well either.

The long reception desk is constructed of giant shellacked
timbers, with moose and elk heads, stuffed beavers, enormous
trout and walleyes mounted on surrounding walls and ceiling
surfaces. An authentic-looking birchbark canoe big enough
for twenty braves is suspended over everything right out of the
rustic rafters. Such fixtures must come from a casino-supply in
Paramus. On the PA, a sultry female voice breaks in on Tom,
shouting "A-nu-*ther* win-ner." The sound of coins loudly gushing
through a metal chute can be heard, while inside the gaming pavilion sirens sound, lights flash, a virtual crowd begins shouting
and woo-hooing. None of the slots players look up. Casinos may
not be the attractions they used to be.

The clerk manning the reception is unaccountably a tall,
handsome Sikh in a sky-blue turban into which his beard has
been roped upwards. An Indian of another tribe. As I walk over,
I'm not certain what I want to ask—detailed instruction about
what I'm supposed to do now, when signs seem unpromising.

A better question would be, *why is a Sikh here?* "Yes. Hello. Sir. Welcome. What shall I do for you?" This man affords me an enormous, white-incisored smile of unperturbed propitiation. He senses I sense I don't belong here. His long fingers have perfectly polished and sculpted nails. His work uniform is the same jacket with the same buffalo crest the security detail wears, only his is bright green for good luck. Possibly he sleeps in one of the RVs outside and commutes home weekends to his family in Nebraska, where Sikhs have it better.

"I'm wondering maybe about a room," I say, reluctance seeding my voice. "Just my son and me." I gesture toward Paul in his wheelchair, stranded in the middle of the lobby, looking slightly discomposed.

"Absolootely." This man's name tag states he is for some reason, "Allen." Likely a graduate of the hotel school at Michigan State. "Will that be two double beds? We have a Valentine's Special For Lovers. We can offer that. You are AARP or Triple-A?"

"Yeah. All of it." On the wall behind him hangs an immense eagle head-dress displayed in all its feathery glory, and below that a black silhouette of a Glock 17 with the dark warning "DON'T BRING THIS IN HERE!!!" Worth knowing.

"Will you need the wheelchair-accessible?" Allen smiles apologetically.

"Maybe. Yeah."

"I'll just need to see your ID and a major credit card. If you don't mind. I can upgrade you to a suite with twin waterbeds. They're very nice."

"No. That's okay."

"It won't be extra. Only ninety dollars." Another apologetic smile as he fiddles with his computer screen.

"My son wouldn't like it. He'd think a waterbed was stupid." Though he might not.

"Ahh, yes. He is entitled."

"He certainly is. I'll tell him you noticed."

"Please." Another smile, this time of glowing satisfaction.

"Let me talk to him before we sign the papers."

"Yes. Best to consult. I understand." Nodding his concern.

From his wheelchair, Paul is watching an elevated bank of TVs above a taxidermied wolverine doing combat with a taxidermied coyote over a taxidermied rabbit. One screen shows a loop of the slots pavilion in grander days, laughing, gambling customers of all shapes and sizes having the time of their lives. Another shows a Japanese League baseball game in action the Hiroshima Toyo Carp hosting the Tokyo Yakult Swallows and banjaxing them 9 zip. A third shows a traditional ceremony in which young Native men dance around a pole with leather thongs poked through their skin. The last is showing a championship cornhole tournament from Las Vegas, which has captured my son's full attention. He hasn't shaved in two days, and encased in his Chiefs regalia and in his chair, he again looks like an indigent the casino security would need to keep an eye on.

"This bean-pole geezer from Cincinnati's running the goddamn table," Paul exults. "The guy's a fucking artist with a beanbag." A long-armed, grim-faced drink-of-water in a bright orange shirt plastered with sponsor patches is just this moment lofting his bag toward the waiting orifice and disappearing it straight in—sending the Vegas crowd into ecstasy and provoking from the beanpole Tiger-like fist pumps and bizarre knee spasmings. "Air fucking mail! Game fuckin-A *over*!" Paul grins up at me, eyes behind his glasses wide with what could be misread as vengeance. "He opened up a can of instant whip-ass!" The picture switches to a young, rubber-faced woman in a polka-dot dress, signing the event for deaf cornhole fans across the globe.

"They'll give us the Valentine's suite," I say.

Paul's mouth—he can't completely control his lips, which are parted—works itself into a cock-eyed rictus, which may only be confusion. All his normal face configurings are slightly out of whack and may never be completely in whack again.

"It stinks in here," he says. It's true. The lobby is clouded with a fug of cigarettes and men's rooms and solvents you don't notice 'til you do. Casinos probably all smell this way.

Just exiting the slots pavilion are, I notice, three middle-aged women of color—all in pastel pantsuits with fancy coordinated track shoes, as if they've done their shopping at Dick's. Their hair is done in similar shining, molded, race-less ways, and they've been drinking, gambling and laughing—exactly what they came to do. The middle one is the Chicago lawyer from last night in Sioux Falls. If we take the Valentine's suite, possibly I can buy all three of them Metropolitans, while Paul uses the wheelchair ramp at the titty bar. Again, I don't have to be with him every minute. The lady lawyer glimpses me—her tracksuit is a pristine pale pink—her shiny cheeks fattening involuntarily. No, no, no-no-no. No drinks with me. No harmless jollying. No taking the edge off. No teasing, inter-racial banter. Fun doesn't have my name on it. Arms linked, they head off toward the free buffet before sneaking into the Warriors Revue.

Paul's knees are agitating under his coat. It's possible he's hurting. I'm never sure. "This place is the extinction vortex," he says, looking embittered. "How'd you fuckin' find it?"

"*It* found me. I was just thinking about a lap dance at the strip club. It might be a hoot. It'd be your big chance." I smile at him—not a mirthful smile, but one of concession. We're nearing an end of something, I can sense. A barrier we might not can pass beyond. This place shouts that out. He knows it.

More coins go whooshing through the chute on the public address. "A-nuh-ther win-neeeeer," the sexy girl-voice triumphs.

More simulated cheering and woo-hooing. The Sikh has disappeared from behind the registration. It's nearly six. Possibly he's taken a dinner break in his RV. A mug of strong tea. A smoke. A check-in at home.

"You couldn't get a lap dance in a fucking wheelchair," Paul says spitefully, both hands fidgeting. His knees, too. "Plus I've got a wound."

"I'm betting you're wrong. The Wood Chipper could get creative for you."

"I'm progressing. Okay, Frank? It's the word that means its opposite. I *progress* to spiritual enlightenment. Then I *progress* to stage four pancreatic cancer." He is irate. And embattled.

"I hadn't thought of it that way, I guess."

"Yeah. It's bullshit. *You* are."

"Okay. But we *can still* get the Valentine's suite. I'll order you up exotic room service. I'm sure it's available." I mean this.

"You're an asshole."

"Why am *I* an asshole? Life's a journey, son. You're on it." I'm willing to piss him off if I can't make him happy. Though I wish I could. He is quite a conventional, unadventurous man when you come down to it. Like me.

"It's not a journey to here," he says savagely.

"Okay."

"Where's Mount Never-more? Are we going there or not?"

"Tomorrow. We're there. Almost." More coins spitting down the chute, more cheering. "A-nut-ther win-nuuur!" Tom Jones breaks into "Delilah."

The handsome Sikh has already returned, looking refreshed and smiling toward us, radiating encouragement for the suite and the waterbeds. He doesn't care that Paul and I are arguing. Fatherhood is a battle in any language.

"I think we should stay here," I say, knowing he won't.

"*You* can fucking stay here. I'm calling an ambulance." His eyes are menacing, his claw hand jittering at the end of his red Gore-Tex sleeve. I've defeated him without meaning to.

"Okay." I smile—sorrowfully. The other defeated party.

"Okay what?" The idea of an ambulance, I know, appeals to him.

"Okay. You win. We can get outa here."

"About fuckin' time. I don't have forever like you do."

I look around the smoke-smeared lobby with its hokey north-woods motifs, its tall, polite turbaned man behind the desk. It is not really all that shabby or sad. A few upgrades in lighting and ventilation, a crowd of real gamblers drinking, laughing and letting it all happen, would make a difference. As with much else, we disparage and give up too easily.

TEN

Rapid City—late drive-time/early-dark—a brash street-light ribbon of too-wide streets, too-long traffic lights, too-loud pickup trucks, and franchises in quadruplicate (four Walgreens, four Midas Mufflers, four Wells Fargos). Billy Idol and Billy Ocean (whoever they are) are headlining the Civic Center "Rites of Spring" double-bill, followed by *The Lion King*. Psoriasis and back pain are on citizens' minds here and on billboards ("Is Psoriasis Affecting Your Life In Many Places?" "Back Ache? See Doctor Spine"). There's even a HoJo's, though it's only an orange-roofed "inn," not the venerated budget eatery where Ann and I split the fried clams and a tuna-melt, plus a dish of butter crunch with separate spoons.

Much in town is given over to Rushmore branding (the mountain and monument are a quick twenty-five miles down Route 16). Rushmore Gastroenterology. Rushmore Dialysis. Rushmore Optical. Rushmore Stump Grinding. Rushmore Waste. Rushmore Ford, Chevy, Hyundai. No one who can isn't cashing in. Why be here otherwise?

What causes places to be awful is always of interest, since places can be awful in myriad ways—though you sense it the moment you step off the bus. It's never the air quality or the car-truck congestion or income differential or racial mix or number of parks, miles of bike paths and paved jogging trails, a developed waterfront, access to public transit or a thriving art scene. A town can be on this year's "best place to live and raise a family" list—alongside Portland Maine, Billings Montana, and Rochester—and be wretched. It's about yawning streets, deathwatch stoplights and the aggregate number of used car lots. It's about whether the biggest buildings are parking structures, whether there's a satellite "downtown" off in the distance, relegating old downtown to skid row. It's about how fast new "loft" projects pave over old cow pastures, and how the older malls are faring and whether new-car dealerships look like Ming pagodas. A month of plying Rapid City's wide arterials—as Paul and I are doing in search of a Hilton Garden or a Courtyard Marriott—and I'd be buying a used Isuzu and heading off to anywhere but here.

Tonight, though, we're shit out of luck—even for an awful place. Three Hiltons, three Marriotts, four Holiday Inns, plus assorted Days Inns, Motels 6s and 8s, and the HoJo's. All full up. If I'd prevailed at the Fawning Buffalo, I'd right now be in the Tahitian Buffet, a couple of free Stolis to the good. Never let your son decide things.

Jeff, the courteous young, gap-toothed clerk trainee at the Hilton Homewood, informs me the town's fully booked—for the state high-school oratory contest. "Bigger than the state basketball tourney and the rodeo." Entire extended families travel from as far away as New Effington to hear their offspring deliver memorized speeches on pre-determined topics. This year's is "Why Do Americans Believe in Democracy?" (A good question I'd like to hear the answer to.) Things get spirited in the evenings, Jeff says, when parents of the winners and losers show up in the hotel bars. Citizens apparently take oratory seriously in The Swinged Cat state—though you wouldn't know it from McGovern's performance in '72.

Jeff—who's fresh-faced and Adam's-appled, a farm product from nearby Owanka and an alum of Black Hills State in Spearfish—tells me we're at least in luck monument-wise; "the Monuments" always open the week of Valentine's—weather permitting. For unclear reasons stretching back to the '30s, when Washington's face was unveiled to an awestruck world, tourists have made it an occasion to visit the shrine on Valentine's, alert apparently to astral affinities between Valentine's and four dead presidents. Heidegger would appreciate this, since he deals in unexpected connections all day every day.

Good man Jeff (Hansen, the family name) is generous enough to call around to some "nicer sister properties," including the competition. But no dice. Arrivals without rooms are sleeping in RVs behind the TravelCenter of America. (Not an option for us in the Windbreaker). However, he says, his mother's brother Harald owns an "older place a bit out of town" in the direction we've just come from—the Four Presidents Courts—a down-at-the-heels joint I spied as we passed, and chalked up as a rendezvous for insurance salesmen and their secretaries. Also, the same type of no-tell motel where I skived off with my college girlfriend Mindy Levinson of Royal Oak, and where we jollied the daylights out of each other for four dollars a night. Gone are those days. Gone, those sites and delights—so I thought.

Smiling young Jeff makes a call right from the front desk at the Homewood, gets through to Uncle Harald, says there's a "coupla good guys here" in need of a place to "bed down." Could he help us out? (How he knows we're good guys is anybody's guess. He hasn't seen Paul.) There's some small talk, then some nodding and grinning, followed by a thumbs-up with a done-'n-done wink. We're in. No need to thank anybody, it's what he's here for, everybody works together in these situations, come back when it's not so friggin' igloo-ville. And Paul and I are headed back out the wide, gawdy thoroughfare to the Four Presidents, which is close by a Tires, Tires, Tires, the Rushmore Auto-Suds, Rushmore Miniature Golf and Rushmore Custom Slaughtering. For a nickel I'd drive us straight back to the Fawning Buffalo. But that would be the wrong direction, and something tells me (an urgency I feel in my belly) that I have to get us going where we're going, and soon.

Paul, while I was in the Homewood, has gone—one and a half-handed—into his metal carrying case and hauled out his ventriloquist's dummy and propped him atop the case on the club-cab back seat, where I have to see his wooden face unnervingly in the rearview. As a youth ventriloquist, Paul mounted regular "shows" right in our living room on Cleveland Lane while he attended HHS, and his stepfather was at first recovering, then dying from colorectal cancer, and Paul became too much for his mother. In all these performances—I ultimately had to make him stop—he proved himself completely inept at keeping his lips still, wasn't skillful at working Otto's internal mechanics, and was really only good at making Otto "say" outrageous things he—Paul—believed were hilarious, and which sometimes targeted me or his mother or his dying stepfather Charley. (He never targeted his sister because he was afraid of her.)

My eyes are peeled now for the Tires, Tires, Tires or the putt-putt, while in the shadowy back seat, headlights are flashing past Otto's leering, bug-eyed face in the mirror.

"Otto's gotten into homonyms, haven't you, old bean?" Paul/Otto says. Sometimes Otto's a Brit. Paul gives me his trickster look and stifles a smirk. At one unlikely point, when he was sixteen, Paul believed a career lay ahead in which he would become a ventriloquist game-show panelist and make millions.

"Right you are, old turd bucket," Otto "says" in Paul's fragile falsetto, face averted to hide his trembling lips. The Dodge club-cab seat is a perfect proscenium.

"Do you want to get dinner," I ask. We're passing the Golden Dragon Chinese, vehicles outside but not crowded. Paul is a devotee of General Tso. I could go for pupu pork.

"Otto's talking. He only eats sawdust."

"Got it," I say and drive us on.

"What're your favorites, Otto?" Paul says squeakily, meaning homonyms. Otto's big, painted-blue eyes gaze luridly out of the dark—orange hair, hacking jacket and gloved balsa hands flashing in the traffic. "You and yew. Jim and gym. Feral and ferule. Horse and hoarse." Otto's lips do not move, only Paul's do. Paul considers himself to be "throwing his voice," but he's not.

"Anything else, Otto?" Paul is already hoarse-horse.

"Engine and injun," Otto "says."

"That's not a real one," I say. "Plus, it's racist." Up ahead under dimmer street lights, I see the Tires, Tires, Tires and the putt-putt, beside Rushmore Custom Slaughtering.

"Fuck you," Paul snarls. "It's real if Otto says it is."

I say, "Crypt and crip'd, new and g-nu, clause and claws. I'm just taking part in the fun."

"You're an idiot," Paul says.

"Two'll—tool. Dicker—dick her."

"Bite my ass and bite my ass," he says. "What's the most dangerous animal in South Dakota? You don't know."

"A leopard," I say. "Who cares? A prairie dog."

"Bison," Paul says. "More people are killed by bison than by rattlesnakes. You're a simpleton, Frank."

"What about Nude Jersey?" We are pulling into the motel lot—the Four Presidents Courts—a lone white rectangle with ten dark doors in a row and a dim-lit office window at the near end, where a pickup's parked.

"It's a coyote," Paul says. Otto's blue wall-eyes do not blink. He's happy for Paul to do all the talking. "Coyotes kill more people in New Jersey than brown recluse spiders. I knew you didn't know. You lack fact-based knowledge. You don't watch enough television."

"I do my best." We stop behind the pickup, which is a shambles of an F-150, girdled in rust, with stickers and decals and messages all over its wired-shut tailgate. "Dog is my co-pilot." "Nietzsche Was Right." "Don't Believe Everything You Think." "Jack Mormons Rock." "Biden." I'm wary of people who decorate their vehicles with their beliefs. They're usually the ones who disrupt planning board meetings and are always shouting about the system being rigged and everyone (but them) needing to be lined up against a wall, when ordinary, law-abiding citizens (me) are simply there to apply for a zoning variance. These people are not always Republicans.

"What're we going to do here?" Paul's voice is thin, and speaking makes him hock up something vile he swallows down. He's had a long day. So have I.

"We've got a room here," I say. "Think of it as a national heritage site. You'll like it."

Paul is turned around with difficulty, looking at the Four Presidents sign—a hand-painted rendering of the famous mountain with all four presidential faces painted in inexactly. Roosevelt's visage is larger than Lincoln's. Washington is facing straight ahead so that Jefferson looks like an afterthought. The sign is lighted only with too-small sealed beams trained down from the top, illuminating frozen ground more than the faces.

It's true Mindy Levinson and I stayed in precisely such dumps on our sex weekends. But that was fifty-five years ago.

"This looks like death's door." Paul's head is ducked, looking wizened and shrunk and slightly wretched. "It's a good place for me."

"You and Otto sit tight." I'm climbing out into the cold and the dim light from the sign.

"Otto says you start with a destination, but then you *end up* someplace."

"Otto can plan our next trip."

"When's that likely to be?"

Standing outside, the air smells stingingly of slaughter-house. A metal corral is visible in shadows across an alley. Two white-face cows stand together in the dark, staring not at me but at the slaughterhouse building. Tomorrow will be their day in history. Valentine's Day.

"I'm not doing great, Lawrence. Sorry." Paul's peering out my door, giving me an inquisitive look from within his parka. He hears himself. He seems to be nodding, possibly experiencing symptoms I haven't seen.

"You don't have to do great," I say. "Just put a cork in it." I don't know what to say better.

"Easy for you . . ." I shut the truck door before I hear his words and go shuffling toward the shadowy OFFICE.

———◆———

NO ONE'S IN EVIDENCE WHEN I GET THE OFFICE DOOR CLOSED. It's warm and close and ill-lit inside and smells like sour laundry. Something's cozy though, about cheap motel offices, as if owning a block of tourist rooms is all any person really needs.

"Okay. Yeah." A heavy, tussid voice (male) comes from rooms

back beyond an open doorway. Another door is heard to close. A video camera, bracketed near the ceiling is watching me in case I'm here to cause trouble.

The office walls contain old wire racks of vacation pamphlets and more personal-belief signage. "Alcohol Is A Good Servant, But A Bad Master." "Nothing Good Happens After Midnight." "Today Is the First Day of the Rest of Your Life." All true. There's also a mural-size sepia photograph of the Chicago lakefront, circa 1955, before progress wrecked it, and a framed publicity still of the old Sheffield gyrater Joe Cocker, arms swimming, mouth agape, as if he's hooked to an electrical socket. It's signed by Joe with a flourish.

"I'm watching the Winnipeg pre-game," the congested voice announces, still out of sight, moving with a heavy step.

"No hurry," I say.

"Hockey's a great sport. You ever play?" No one's visible, but we seem to know each other.

"Never did." I'm smiling in expectation.

On the glass-top check-in is a stack of "Is Hospice The Answer?" hand-outs. A distinguished white-haired gentleman is pictured, holding and smilingly cuddling a laughing, cherubic child. A grandson he's about to leave behind. Listed are frequently asked questions, with unvarnished answers. "What is Hospice's success rate at managing pain?" Very high. "How difficult is caring for a dying loved one at home?" Rarely easy. "Will Hospice abandon me if I don't transition in six months?" Usually not.

I leave these where I find them.

"Oh, yeah. You bet I did." The man not here, answering an unasked question. "Hospice pamphlets are free, by the way."

Harald, favorite uncle of Adam's-appled Jeff of the Hilton Homewood, leans in heavily through the narrow doorway to the back (PRIVATE! NO ENTRY!) and is a giant. Six-six, easy two-eighty, navigating on two metal canes that don't steady him enough, so he has to jab a big mitt on all passing surfaces. You'd think he'd be too big to play hockey. "Played up at Brookings. Played juniors in Medicine Hat. That was when you got put in just to fight. Not like now." The office has grown palpably smaller with Harald's presence in it. His breathing is audible and deep. Once he has been a big-featured James-Arness type—small nut-brown eyes with a full allotment of movie-star hair. His nose, though, bears a wide, dimpled *in*-dent from somebody's hockey stick. He is not at all old. With better mobility and luck he could be behind the help desk at Lowe's. I am smiling at him hopefully.

"Okay," getting himself squeezed down into a chair behind the check-in counter. He fits on bifocals and fingers a registration card. All is hands-on. No electronics. Probably the camera doesn't work, though he saw me reading the Hospice info. "You come down for the speeches?"

"No," I say. "My son and I are going to Mount Rushmore. Tomorrow."

"Uh-huh." He pushes a card up onto the glass. "Just fill this out." Harald's fist could hold twenty hockey pucks and still rain withering blows. Or once it could. I set about with the ballpoint provided. There is no mention of Jeff.

I say, "We'd like two double beds."

A fat white dog walks out of the back and stops in the doorway to stare at me. One of its eyes is clouded.

"Matrimonials only," Harald says. "I'll give you the bridal. It's got a door in between. It's a hundred." He breathes mightily. My own presence in the office hasn't changed anything.

"That'll be great." I finish writing and hand the card down.

"Need to come back in the summer."

"I know. We've got some special circumstances." The dog turns and walks back where it came from.

Harald stamps my check-in card PAID, using an ink pad. "Payment's in cash."

"That's fine." I have my card out but put it back. The Fawning Buffalo was ninety, including the Tahitian Buffet, the Wood Chipper and the shuttle. No reconsidering now. I produce the twenties.

Harald's movements are almost dainty. He fishes two plastic key fobs from under the counter and hands them up. "One's for the inside door. Check-out's at ten. My wife'll be here. It's number nine and ten at the end. Leave the keys in the room." I want to ask if there's someplace decent where we could order out. Paul isn't up to the Golden Dragon or an Applebee's. A small white refrigerator stands in the corner, a miniature Christmas tree on top, red, blue and green lights twinkling. Possibly there's something to microwave.

"Anything here I could buy to eat?" I cast a hopeful eye toward the fridge.

"Blood worms for the ice fishermen. That's who we get in the winter. Snickers and chips over there." He motions to a rack with a small assortment. "Where's Haddam . . ." Harald picks up the check-in card . . . "New Jersey."

"Halfway down the dog's leg." Six inches from his nuts. I don't say that.

"I was in Manalapan once. You been there?"

"I used to sell houses there. Not just Manalapan. Everywhere." I give Harald my courteous-customer countenance, offered through the years to thousands of wayward home-buyers.

"My sister got all balled up with a guy—Russian guy. Up to

no good. I had to go get her. He was taking full advantage. Not that some of it wasn't on her."

"Where's she now?" I say.

"Oh, she died." He actually smiles at me—at the wonder of it. Despite his too-big movie-star features Harald has a yielding, confiding face, as if life's had him wrong from the beginning. "Heroin. Not every story ends happy." He does not seem a man of decals and flaunting gestures; more a man of underappreci- ated priorities. Nothing, though, is ever out of character for any of us.

"I'm sorry," I say about the sister.

"It's why I got all the hospice stuff. They were good to her." Harald's rearranging himself in his chair as if he isn't happy be- ing there. "Just you and your son?"

"Yep."

"How old is *he*?"

"Forty-seven. He's got a neurological disorder. He doesn't walk great." I add this in case he might suspect something's fishy.

"We used to take our kids up. They got a kick out of the faces," Harald says. "It's all disable-equipped now. I have to pay attention to that. Probably not much open."

"That's okay."

"Where's the wife?" He's thought of his own wife and wants to mention mine.

"I don't have one anymore." I smile at him to let him know it's all right. Almost certainly there's a decal for my status. Not every story ends happy. Out in the gloom you can find some lights on. Shit happens. Harald is an optimist. A Biden supporter—unless it's a joke.

"I always thought I'd end up alone. And it'd be fine," Harald says, shaking his head at the wonder of that, too.

"I always thought I wouldn't," I say.

Harald begins, with effort, to get up, grappling one cane at a time. "Men and women are always wrong," he says. "Check-out's at ten. My wife'll be here. Did I say that?"

"Yeah. But thanks." Keys in hand.

"You'll do fine," Harald says.

"Great. I hope so." I have no idea what he means, but I'm counting on him being right. Then I am out the door into the cold again.

———————

DINNER TURNS OUT NOT TO BE A PROBLEM. PAUL IS SLUMPED IN sleep when I climb in with the keys—Otto eerily "awake" in the back. I drive us into town along the sodium-lit main drag—not knowing where I'm going—but then swerve into a Walgreens, where I lay in Vi-eeen-ahs, saltines, sardines, a small jar of kosher dills, Newtons, plus a six-pack of Dr Peppers, and two Coors long-necks for me—my mother's stand-bys for all family road trips. Walgreens now sells everything—sex toys to fishing gear to religious icons.

With Paul still sleeping, I drive us *back* to the Four Presidents and down to the last door—the two Herefords watching us from their enclosure. We appear to be the only guests. Someone—a small man in a large cowboy hat—is inside the bay of the Rushmore Auto-Suds across the street, giving his Silverado a going-over with the spray wand, cigarette in mouth, his wife inside reading a book. Harald's rusted Ford with its abundance of stickers is where it was; though the Presidents sign is turned off—Harald back in the back with the Jets game from Winnipeg. It is an unfraught winter night in Rapid City. If you lived here, you might feel semi-okay about it.

Paul wakes when I shut the motor off, looks around at the line of motel doors. "Is this really where we're staying?"

"The Carlyle's booked." I need to get him in the room and fed.

"I was dreaming of something being just out of my reach that had always been *in* my reach. I don't know what it was. Maybe I'm dead. Am I?"

"Not that I can tell." His spoken words are again not perfectly enunciated.

"I'm selecting my words now," he says. "That's why I'm so deliberate. Okay? They aren't flowing right. And I have a headache. I'm also cold."

"You have to be tired." I'm tired, and I'm in line for a beer with a vodka chaser no matter what our room's like.

"Do you think you care about all this more than I do?" He is facing forward as if he's concentrating.

"What's *this*?"

"Mmm. I don't know."

"I think *you* care more than I do," I say. "You should."

"Do you think my doctors worry about me?"

"Probably."

Off in the dark we now are a part of, I hear a distant siren, then the blat-blaaaat of a fire engine. Then a heavy truck accelerating, not far away. Someone is being helped somewhere. I wish it could be us. "Not to wear life's freshest feather," the poet said. There is nothing I can really deceive my son about now. Though I would.

"Are you disappointed I wasn't an Eagle Scout?"

"You weren't *in* the Boy Scouts. Scouts are a load of crap anyway. I hate camping out."

"You could still be disappointed."

"Nothing about you disappoints me." It is true.

"What if I get bad really fast?"

"I'll have you med-evac'd. Life Flight. No expense spared. Don't think about that, okay?" When he was fifteen and nearly lost his eye in a baseball accident, he was helicoptered to Yale-New Haven, after which he talked about helicopters for months. Even Otto commented.

"I haven't had a great run, have I, Frank?" He is not looking at me.

"No. But you've done okay." This is how he chooses for us to discuss our hard subjects—as things we don't say on the way to someplace more important. We're freezing in the truck. It's all fine.

"Do I piss you off?" He sniffs.

"Not right now. No. Just sometimes. Why?"

"You piss *me* off. This *all* pisses me off." He doesn't quite get 'pisses me off' right. More like 'miss-me-yof.' I cannot speak now. Only *his* words matter. His situation neutralizes mine.

"We should go inside," I manage in a clipped way. I'm shivering down into my thighs. Though Paul in his Chiefs greatcoat, Thinsulates, red watch cap and Genius at Wrok sweatshirt doesn't seem to be, though he said he was. In the rearview Otto watches us.

"Do you like The Eagles? Not the football team."

"They're okay." I've got our picnic-in-a-plastic-sack up off the floor.

"Did you know Tom Jones was knighted by the Queen of England?"

"Yes." I'm opening the door to the cold and the stinging cow fragrance.

"He's Welsh. Which is unusual."

"I know." I have to move us or we'll die out here and never see Mount Rushmore. Which would be a pity, given everything.

OUR ROOM—NUMBER TEN OUT OF TEN—IS NOT AS TERRIBLE AS I expected. A sizeable queen (the matrimonial), a compact escritoire-with-chair and plastic daisy-in-a-vase, should someone care to write a love letter. A tidy bath-shower with one towel and a single Colgate rectangle. An old dusty Carrier Super-Weather has been fitted through a hole in the wall—I switch this on since it's cold as outside in here. The flooring is death-chamber-green linoleum, and when I switch on the overhead, a death-chamber pall spreads to all interior spaces. It is, though, a decent facsimile of Mindy Levinson's and my love nest at the Silver Birches in Charlevoix and as such offers me the rarest sensation of homecoming, which would not have been true at the Fawning Buffalo.

I get our duffels inside. Paul's wheelchair proves too wide for the door, so I fireman-carry him in—perilous in the dark—which causes him to grunt and "ooof," as if being toted was painful. Even in his heavy coat, his arms and shoulders are un-resistant, so that leveraging him onto the bed isn't hard, though the strain reignites my collarbone, and for a moment renders me partially immobilized.

"Don't resuscitate," Paul says, heaped on the coarse bed-spread, his legs hung over the side, his good hand clutching the material as if that keeps him upright. "That's one of my epitaph choices. 'Nothing is enough' is another one."

"Fine." I'm out of breath and in scapular pain. The old Car-rier has gushed out a fine misting of dust but is semi-warming the room and giving it an unhealthy peach reek. "What else do you want from the truck?"

"Leave Otto," he says authoritatively. "Bring Paul-two-point-zero in. I want his picture where I can see it. He's my amigo."

"He's not mine," I say grimly.

"He *will* be some day, Lawrence. You don't have anything to say in this, remember?" My son and I stare at one another in this woeful little room—he truculent for want of anything else to be. As he's said already, being right doesn't count for shit. He's experiencing more than I can help with.

"When I wake up at night," he says, "I mostly don't know where I am. Or *who*. It's the best thing that's happened so far." He lifts his bad hand and whaps it into his palm—a gesture, I suppose, of applause. I have had the same experience. It is a kind of reprieve.

He says, "Do you think it's more authentic in the west? Or maybe *I'm* more authentic?"

"I just thought we'd have some laughs. I already told you. You're plenty authentic."

He looks up at me in the death-chamber luminance. "You mean laughs like 'Want fries with that?' 'Still workin?' 'Ready for the check?' 'You done?' That kind of laughs?"

"Yeah. Along those lines."

"My nerves really are quitting, don't you think?"

"Maybe. A little. We'll see."

"I'd still like to get laid, though." He's looking around the room. "Do you think this place is that kinda place?"

"I don't think so." What would Harald say if I came tap-tapping at his door. "The casino was your best shot."

"It's never too late, though, right?"

"Let's hope not."

My son lies back heavily on the stiff counterpane of faded bridal roses, and breathes a shallow breath in, then a shallow breath out. "Oooh . . . shit," he says. Not "Oooh, boy." Both his knees are lightly jittering. Possibly he will go to sleep before I can feed him. What I expected of our day I can't remember now.

Paul begins breathing fuller, early-sleep suspirations as if nothing was out of reach. His fingers twitter, his knees have stopped agitating. He looks like a bundle of clothes dropped from the sky.

I step out into the cold parking lot. The cowboy in the hat has finished cleaning his pickup and driven away, the light in the wash bay left on. Tires, Tires, Tires has a cyclone fence running its perimeter, and is—I see—a second-hand place. I hear a semi winding gears streets away. The Herefords in their pen have settled in a far corner, making one dark shape against the bars. Aloft, the sky offers the diminishing moon and a wild map of stars I know nothing about. My wife Ann knew all the constellations from years of outdoor sleeping at the Huron Mountain Club. When we were young, she was forever on about "The Bull," "The Water Carrier." "The Twins." It all seemed to me a pastime for those who feared being alone. Paul liked to lie on the ground and "see" his own constellations to frustrate his mother. "The Meerkat." "The typewriter." "The rutabaga." "The pig's pizzle." When I feel most in need, I can loose myself to the freeing incomprehensibility of all that's up there. Though in my heart of hearts I know that when we look toward deepest space what we're hoping to find is its limits.

I lay my hand on the Dodge's hood where it is warm but cooling. This could be a moment when a different kind of man might experience a long-dismissed re-regard for the afterlife; i.e., since death is irreversible, there must be a way around it. Though all I can think to do is call Betty Tran, beckon her voice from the spheres. (She shuts off her phone at eight to get her business accounting homework done. I don't need to say anything.)

"*Hi, it's Betty.*" (Singy-songy, suitably chirpy, which I love.) "*Hope you're having a super day. I'd love to talk to you. If you want to schedule an appointment, leave your name—if you're already a client—and your call-back number. Or if you're a new client, call Bethany Tran to schedule a new-client interview"* (something I never had to do) *"at 507-732-2961. Okay? Puuur-fect. Take good care now."* CLICK.

Perfect. Her tinkling voice out of the blue-black dome is really all I require. Though I admit, as I listened, the face in my mind's eye was Nurse Krista's from A Fool's Paradise, not Betty's at all.

———◆———

PAUL HASN'T MOVED WHEN I COME BACK IN WITH THE "OTHER Paul's" picture. The heater's turned the room toasty, though when I go in the bathroom there's an ice skim still on the toilet water and a decent-size ex-mouse in the bathtub. Hot water, though, is surprisingly working in the sink, and I leave the door open for things to thaw.

Room #9, when I get the communicating door unlocked and open, turns out to be cold storage—old motel furniture and appliances, cracked porcelain fixtures, venetian blinds—tumbled all over, much of it on the bed blocking the bathroom and the outside door. A spoiled sewer odor arises from somewhere. Nothing doing here. Which now means precisely what? *Not* to sleep in the Windbreaker and freeze? *Not* to sleep in the idling truck, trusting the exhaust to float away? There's no returning to the office. I need to be near in case my son gets up for the john, which 'til today he's managed, but now seems risky—emergency rooms, Mexico-trained doctors, Filipino nurses, medi-vac-for-real. On top of ALS.

I sit on the escritoire chair at the foot of the bed and finger out Viennas and crackers and drink a beer. Which proves not half bad and reminds me of my parents—the three of us seated at a roadside turn-out on Pensacola Beach, the two of them smoking and staring moodily at the lustreless Gulf, talking quietly about their own parents, while I drank root beers and calculated my chances for sports stardom. Which were nil.

I break into the fig-less Newtons, sit eating, and drinking the other beer, and simply look at my son, as I did two nights ago, when he was asleep at his computer and Tiger was re-winning his fifth green jacket. It is not that I watch him to detect features I haven't detected five hundred times. I stare only to certify that he is here and I am here, his still-shod feet no more than a yard from me, his breathing peaceful in spite of all that's broken inside. What otherwise can I do?

Which unexpectedly releases me to crawl onto the stiff bedspread beside him—once I've turned off the ceiling light. I leave the bathroom lit, the door ajar and, with a twinge in my scapula, peel off my parka and shoes. Years ago when Ann and I were becoming unmarried after our son Ralph's death, and she had relegated me to our basement on Hoving Road, Haddam, until our divorce "came through," I slept in my clothes every night, as if I needed to be ready to confront whatever opponents there were to my and Ann's surviving love. Sleeping in my clothes induced the most gratifying sensation of preparedness. Cavemen slept this way. Firemen. Lighthouse keepers. Pullman porters, neurosurgeons and air traffic controllers. Nothing would catch me neglectful at my station—a fire, a break-in, someone else's nightmare, a child crying, a wife crying, myself crying. I would be vigilant. My wife never understood my need to be so ready in those disordered days—among the legion of facts she didn't choose to credit yet could have.

Lying listening to the Carrier wheeze out dry and peachy zest, I think surprisingly of nothing in particular. Not Mount

Rushmore or my fears for it. Not what Paul and I will importantly do after—or not. Not about hard conversations we might never have. So many things that seem important on any given midnight are just dropped into our minds needless, while we await more vital instruction.

Though what I *do* think about as I lie beside my son in the dark, feeling his dense presence, is the strange event that befell me just the other week, and which I revisit often as if it held a secret. I had driven to Trader Joe's in the Thousand Lakes Mall to purchase a box of couscous. Paul likes couscous mixed with roasted root-vegetables and hot Italian sausage, and doesn't care any longer if he can taste it. When I walked in through the hissing Trader Joe's doors, I was as always instantly dazzled by the aroma of fruit and viand and by the human hum of shoppers filling baskets with delicacies their hearts desired. Nothing draws a green line between oneself and the day's woes like the first, rich effusions of the mega-market. However, I had not advanced far beyond the orchids and the new tulips when I lost couscous entirely. That is, the word *couscous*. I'd had it twenty seconds before, as I mushed across the frozen parking lot. But on hitting the humid indoor weather of Trader Joe's, couscous vanished like a star going out. I perfectly well remembered an "eat-today" avocado, a jar of Norwegian herring, a container of spiced baba ghanoush—which I was also there to buy. But couscous had suddenly entered deep space. This was not at all like my global amnesia episode because the word *had been there*. I remembered its existence—just not what it was. Standing stock still beside a rack of under-ripe limes, I experienced an icy sensation—of captivity; of being walled off. Losing a word when you've possessed it only seconds before has about it what must be the aura of death's absorbing, hollow perplexity.

What I did and quickly to escape captivity, was set off the

way a fisherman sets off to stalk a lunker bass he can't see but knows is there—only with a sterner sense of urgency. If I could pass down every aisle of Trader Joe's, panic peeking around the sides of my calm, *when* and *if* I passed whatever was the item (and word) I'd lost, I trusted the sight of it would trigger my memory, and all would be saved.

Down I went along the canned goods. Up past shadowy soda shelves, chilly meats and deli offerings. I knew that what I sought came in a cardboard box, was possibly a "grain," possibly Mediterranean, likely ethnic, and for that reason shelved in "International" or "gourmet." Couscous never for an instant revealed its name. Though all at once my heart leapt. In "Italian," I passed then turned quickly back to a shelf of boxed risotto. Relief (mistakenly, of course) welled in me. Risotto. Here it was. I was under no illusion I'd "found" it or had come upon it because I "knew" it was here. I had merely blundered onto it by searching until nothing was left that it wasn't. All of which had taken me twenty minutes. My viyella shirt was sweated-through under my parka. I knew my reaction had been exaggerated, but I felt as if I'd survived something dire, the way survivors must feel, having descended to their most makeshift of animal impulses. And the pure chance of it wasn't lost on me. I had not so much located my wits as learned to get along with a smaller portion of them.

When I got back to New Bemidji Street with my Trader Joe's bag (I'd remembered the avocados, the herring and the baba ghanoush) I decided not to expose my son to my muddle-headedness on grounds he might become destabilized, himself, just by hearing about it. He was using his walker and had emerged from the Kalbfleische hall into the kitchen where I was setting groceries on the counter. He was wearing his yarmulke and a green "I Break For Tilapia" shirt.

"Did they run out of couscous?" he said, teetering.

"What do you mean?" I looked at him wondrous, then down at the box of Lundberg risotto as if it were a death warrant bearing my name.

"You got risotto," he said. "It's never any fuckin' good. It tastes like wall-paper paste."

"I like it," I said. (I don't.) "Your mother made it really well." (She didn't.) "You probably don't remember." (He couldn't.) "They *were* out of couscous." Impertinent, impoverished word.

"*You* eat it, then," he said. "I'll order General Tso online." He began scraping around with his walker, back down the shadowy hallway. "What makes an old man look old?" he said, his back receding.

"I don't know," I said. "You tell me."

"Nose hair. Ear hair. Red ankles. Confusion. They never lie."

"Okay," I said. "Okay. Thanks."

What other crucial signs, I wondered then—and now in bed beside my son, wonder again—must I be missing as these eventful days file past me?

Through the old Carrier's rasp and grind I hear the sound of a train gaining momentum somewhere near in the winter darkness. It is eight p.m. at the earliest. I am over-alert to sounds. I've placed the depressing "other Paul" photograph on the writing desk, where I make it out in the light escaping the john and where Paul will see it when he wakes. I try hard to slip the day's anchorage, setting my mind free to float. Seeking-seeking-sikh-tahitian-marriage-colloquium-ram-dodge-psycho-coming-soon-I'd-like-to-be-the-goal. As always, it brews its magic, thoughts loosing from what's lurking in shadows. Couscous. Couscous. Tumbling, tumbling, slipping, slipping . . . Peace, peace, peace, peace, peace . . .

"I liked the Corn Palace. It was strange. Are you going to ask me what I'll miss?" my son says as plainly, unslurringly as if he didn't have a fatal disease. I am awake again, but he is deep asleep and talking. His breathing deepens. He turns toward the window, over which I have drawn the curtain to block the streetlight.

I say, "That's good, son. I'm glad." He will not hear me.

"It's a dry cold, of course," he says. To which I answer nothing. Let sleeping dogs lie. And sons.

It is much too warm in our bridal bower. Though I can manage on top of the covers. I am again slipping, slipping. His sleep begets my sleep—the rapture of sinking below walls surrounding us. Further and further and further into ocean-y ease that will end—or not—with daylight, when all will be new.

———

AT 2:46 I AWAKE. THE ROOM IS A SAUNA. I GET UP AND TURN OFF the wall unit and consider stripping off my clothes, though soon it will be cold again. I hear noises in the parking lot—metal clanking, men's voices laughing, a cow lowing, a bottle dropped on the pavement. More laughter. I go to the window but see only the Windbreaker's hulk in the shadows and Harald's white dog walking past, the car wash still lighted but no one there. I hear clanking again but do not elect to investigate. There is nothing to be alarmed by. It is Valentine's Day.

———

AT SEVEN-THIRTY, PAUL AND I ARE UP AND MOVING. IT IS LATER than I expected without really expecting. My night's sleep in the Four Presidents matrimonial—fully clad, beside my son—has been restorative.

We *are* in need of sustenance. A belly-buster breakfast

before our ascent. I've seen a Big Jack's Rancher's Café on the boulevard into town. Paul has awakened more mobile than when he went to bed. He's shed his slept-in clothes without help and undertaken a tub-shower, naked and oblivious, shuffling into the bathroom, bare feet cautious as an octogenarian, his bad hand out for balance while I come and guide his shoulders from behind, propping him on the sink and running the shower to warm—he doesn't like it hot—then helping his wobbly legs over the tub gunwale and seating him on the tub floor with water hissing onto him, and partly onto me. This has not been a facet of my care regime, but it is a facet this morning. When he is dressed and in his heavy clothes it is possible to think he is not worse. But on the bath-tub floor—without his glasses, his flaxen, translucent hair wet so he is almost as bald as he would become if he lived on for twenty years, his flesh blanched, his penis injured, his arm bruised with his shunt welt, his knees scuffed—he looks improbable. Which he tries to ignore, as anyone would. Though what he does not know and wouldn't like to hear is that sitting in the tub, soaping himself with concentration, he is the image of his mother and me together—her strong chin and forehead, my small nose and thin but shapely mouth. His slate eyes are his mother's, his modest ears with scored lobes and his mandible, bear the Bascombe imprint. Parents should pay heed to how their genes will pair up in the physiognomical sphere. We two, though, were too eager to get on with life, come what may. Which *does* come.

From beside the tub, I pull him onto his feet with the scratchy towel half around him—it is warm in the little bathroom, and he is not shuddering. He permits me to dry most of him with the exception of his abraded, sensitive part, which he manages with his left hand while I hold him against the sink and he murmurs "Uh-huh, uh-huh, uh-huh." He is heavy and light at once. Again his demise may be far in the future, but death is our cohort in this tiny space, our faces side-by-side in the clouded mirror.

I dry his hair and under his arms, down his thighs to his instep, my neck damp from the shower. He smells of Colgate. "How do you feel?" I say. Both his knees have begun agitating. His milky lips are pressed into a line of concentration.

"Like I'm taking a shit in public."

"I understand."

"Is my dick big enough? I'm really hung, aren't I?"

"Enough. Yeah."

"I suffer fools well, too, don't I?" He does shudder then, up and down his wiggly corpus. His left hand grips my shoulder right where it hurts. I'm in no fear of falling, but he is.

"Did you have me in mind as the fool?" I say, holding him.

"I don't have anybody in mind," he says. "It's my attitude since I got Al's. It makes me not be pathetic."

"You're way ahead of me," I say.

"I'm not ahead of anybody. That's clear to the naked eye. I could die of something else."

"I know." I'm navigating him through the bathroom door. He's lurching. Buck naked to the naked eye.

"That'd be great, wouldn't it? Get Al's and die of tetanus."

"That'd be great. Yeah." At the bedside his knees buckle, but he can still pilot them.

"You'd probably be relieved," he says with effort.

"Yeah. Think of the money I'd save."

"Is it Valentine's today?" He leans then sits on the matrimonial.

"National organ donation day," I say. "You get the heart."

"Did you buy me a card?"

"I did." I didn't. I only bought Betty one. But I'll find him one before the day's over. I need to get him dressed and on our way up the mountain. I'm not sure how, but somehow.

"I bought *you* one in the truck stop. It's raunchy as hell. You'll love it."

"Great." I'm down going into his duffel while he waits on the bedside in his altogether, feet on the linoleum, head slumped as if he's given up hope.

"I was thinking of the things it'd be impossible to live with. Do you have a list?"

"I keep a different list." I'm getting his socks on him. His feet are clammy and hard, his ankles bony and hairless.

"You want to hear mine?"

"I'm dying to."

"One is a colostomy bag. That'd be the pits. One is a permanent vegetative state. One is to be the Butcher of Bergen-Belsen. I couldn't think of any more. Al's isn't on the list. I already have that."

"Good." I'm staring at his feet, sheathed in gray and blue over-the-calf Thinsulates that reach his knees. It's all he has on.

"Al's is a piece of cake."

"I'm happy you see it that way." I take his feet in my hands as if to warm them.

"Okay. Then tell us how do *you* see it, sir?" An air microphone is being held down for me to speak into. He is Ted Ramsey, the *News at Six* guy, interviewing me on my life and caregiver experiences to date. How do I feel that my son has ALS? What goes through my mind when I really think about it? How will I explain it to my other children? Without his glasses he is peering at me with mock intensity. He is himself, no matter who he's mimicking. His round face, though, is again a composite of mine and his mother's. A face she loved.

"It's a piece of cake," I say, to confirm how I see it. He stares down with his frown of manufactured seriousness. It's I who's naked now and don't quite understand what I'm doing. What *we're* doing. I think I am only trying to get him dressed.

"That's not very original. Want me to sing a few bars?"

"No, son. Don't sing right now. Let me get your clothes on so we can get going."

"May-be-to-mor-row, Ah'll fah-ind what I'm *af-taaaah!* You don't know what's good, Lawrence."

"I know. I've never been skilled at that." I go again into his duffel bag for his longies. It is I for whom something has become out of reach. I wish I could say what that something is. Possibly this now is how it feels to hold nothing in reserve.

———

AS I'M GETTING OUR BAGS INTO THE WINDBREAKER, I SPY A woman outside the motel office. Undoubtedly Harald's wife, beginning the day shift—clearing out the pay-by-the-hour-truckers and their "girlfriends" from the all-night bars. Mrs. Harald, who's wearing a man's plaid shirt over a dress-and-trousers combo, is having an animated conversation with a uniformed policeman whose brown-and-white cruiser has its headlights blinking but not its blue topper. I have no business with Mrs. Harald. Keys left in the room was the deal. I have also experienced a brief but untimely episode of vertigo after getting Paul dressed and myself showered. (I almost took a header in the tub.) I've done 2 minutes of lie-down-sit-up therapy with my son watching. And my dizziness has mostly gone away. Though, as often happens, I'm now seeing the world as if I were watching it in a movie, everything slightly outsized, color saturated and out of kilter, as if whoever's filming the world is himself impaired.

Paul is still in the room, dressed in a new, clean sick-suit—

his "That's Not Funny!" sweatshirt and sweatpants, his parka, a dopey red Chiefs Stormy Kromer cap and Swiss ortho shoes—listening to Tony sing "I'm the Funny Man" through his earbuds. Mount Rushmore (I've checked on my phone) is a half hour from the motel on good days.

Of which today is surprisingly one. Overnight, the eye-aching cold has been pushed aside by a spirit-restoring "warm front" attributable to the jet stream, El Niño, the simoom, sunspots and other things, including the Trump-certified climate hoax. Morning light has become aqueous and milky as April Fool's, and the thermometer's approaching 40, making a difference to everything. School-bus riders, tradesmen in pickups, insurance brokers off for the office, all radiate a more hopeful outlook. The parking lot asphalt's damp and puddled, with crusts of iron-colored snow melting in the curb gutters as vehicles queue across at Rushmore Auto-Suds, their drivers grabbing a chance to get the salt and shit off, since tomorrow will probably be different. One man and his spindly daughter are out playing the putt-putt, which is opportunistically open. If you don't like Rapid City weather, wait *five* minutes.

I decide to hand over my room keys in person, as I can let Mrs. H.—assuming it's she—know room 9, which I've paid for, is non-operating. She's finished her conversation with the RCPD cop and is stopped, staring at the freshly clouded skies and street activity. The white dog from last night is sitting beside her.

"Hi," coming across the puddles, passing a red Escalade with Minnesota plates and a Trump sticker, parked in front of #5. The dog watches me, stands and takes a step forward, then sits down again. A positive sign. "We're down in number 10," I say. "My son and I. We're checking out. I'll just give you the keys." I'm all Valentine smiles on Valentine's morn. My vertigo is wearing off but not entirely. I still see the world in Technicolor.

Mrs. Harald—again, if it's she—is a tall, smiling, round-faced, thick-torso, short-waisted, long-armed female, who at some past time might've made a choice between a point-guard scholarship to Grinnell, or big Harald on a mission to Hastings and Medicine Hat. Her destiny is the opposite of Betty Tran's. Like Harald, she does not seem the likely proprietress of a rum dum motel. More a high-school gym teacher who subs in math.

"I was thinkin' 'bout you two," she says in music beamed straight from north Alabama (or at least east Tennessee). This, I didn't anticipate, or the big southern-belle smile of considerably white and large teeth. Southernness goes with body shape in my experience. Muscly, tall, long-armed, short-waisted is not one of them. "Howz-at son of yours doin'?" She offers a practiced "warm" look reserved for children, dogs and oldsters. It is an alarming accent, not one I'm able immediately to respond to. All southerners seem to me to be "putting it on." I will divulge nothing of my own long-fled Dixie lineage, and hope her accent doesn't stoke up my old worn-away one. Though it can happen. "Harald said you said he was a little puny." Mrs. Harald has on green rubber gloves and is probably bound for our room. An industrial-size broom is leaned outside the office door beside a plastic pail of astringents, rags and sponges. The door to the office stands open. I can see the twinkling Christmas tree from last night. It's just as well to intercept her before she encounters Paul in his Chiefs uni, and he encounters her.

"He's not really sick," I say. "He has a motor-neuron disease that affects his mobility. He's fine."

"Good-ness gra-cious," she says. "By the way, Harald forgot number 9 was out of commission. I've got a twenty-dollar refund for *you*. I hope you didn't sleep in that mess." She plucks the twenty from her man's plaid shirt pocket. She means this to be transacted now. As if a principle's involved.

"I didn't," I say. "No need to refund anything."

"Oooh, yes," Mrs. Harald says. "Have to be honest and forthright." She smilingly-forthrightly forks over the twenty, and I honestly-sensibly take it—with satisfaction for not being gypped. "J'you hear anything last night? Out in this lot?" Mrs. H. rolls her eyes at whatever it might've been. Something maybe funny.

"I heard metal clanking and some laughing. It was around 3. I didn't see anything."

"Tha-a-at's about when it was. You coulda made a citizen's arrest out here. Some buckaroos backed a trailer in and carted two beeves outa the pen over there. That Indian cop's hot on their trail, though. He thinks it's boys he played football with on the rez." This entire conception pleases her. Filching doomed cows as a prank. Nothing she takes too seriously.

"Now you two're going to have a fine time up on the mountain," Mrs. Harald says, nodding like a C of C booster. She knows all about us from Harald. "You'll *think* they're too small at first—the faces. But you'll get used to 'em. In Tuscumbia, Alabama, where I grew up" [bingo!] "we didn't have anything like a Mount Rushmore. If you needed a sight to see you had to go to Stone Mountain and whatnot. Which we did frequently." She wrinkles her large nose at a thought of Stone Mountain and those luminous days. "My sisters and cousins are loyal to the soil down there. But I like it out here, though. I like the grandeur. How old is your son?" I'm yet to return her keys.

"Forty-seven," I hear myself say, as if he weren't forty-seven and I'm lying. Mrs. H. seems like the best ole raw-boned gal you want to have be your cousin. But I'm willing to bet, after a couple of Crown Royals, she'll be laying the cordwood to immigrants, ethnics, socialists, elites, one-worlders, the UN, Kofi Annan and whatnot—and anybody else who fails to believe property rights outweigh human ones. If Mrs. Harald, who's quick-eyed with carefully plucked eyebrows, isn't a Sue or a Barb or a Bev I'll climb the Statue of Liberty and sing light opera. Mrs. H. has begun looking across the Four Presidents' lot at the Windbreaker, beginning to conclude—my guess—it's not all that funny. The Escalade is probably hers. Harald rates the junker with the decals.

"Today's Valentine's. Are you and your son celebratin'?" Nothing, happily, about the Windbreaker.

"That's our plan." I'm holding out the key fobs. Mrs. Harald is wearing low-top Keds of a pale lime hue which she no doubt wore in Tuscumbia—before she met Harald, and they eloped. Life can be easy to plumb—at least you can believe it is.

"We used to drag our kids up there," she says. "We thought it was educational. But they didn't much care. It's too bad y'all didn't come in the summer. Today's not bad, though." She pronounces 'didn't' in strictest Alabama cornpone style. 'Dit-n.' I stare at her, forgetting to respond about the quality of the day. "So, I'm a big yoga nut," Mrs. H. carries on. "Sometimes I go up there and set out my mat and greet the sun like an Indian. It was sacred for *them*, of course. Then I come back down here and resume life again. It adds to the experience." She toggles her head side to side and smiles her high-school smile—the one that made Harald sweep her off her feet all the way to Medicine Hat.

"I'm sure it does," I say.

"There's no tellin' where we end up in the world, is there?" I hand her the two keys, which she drops in her flannel shirt-pocket.

"No, there isn't." The two of us being exhibits A and B.

Mrs. H., with a dexterity only women possess, folds her two hands inward and pulls her flannel shirt sleeves down onto her gloves, which are possibly damp and chilled. The white dog stands and stares down the list of motel rooms as if it's heard something.

"I'm Patti, by the way. With an 'i'. Like that old TV show."

"Frank."

"Like that *other* old TV show."

"Right," I smile at her.

"And where is it you're from? New Hampshire?"

"New Jersey."

"Which is where Harald went to save poor Star. Which is his sister. Or was."

"He said."

"He was craaazy-crazy about *her*. If you're looking for break-fast, by the way, Big Jack's Rancher's pretty good. Though it'll be fulla the speech people today, I'm 'fraid. Sometimes I'll go hear the orations if they get a good topic. Last year they had 'Define Courage.' Which was good. I didn't know courage can be measured. It just needs to have something to work against. Like fear. Which was kinda interesting."

"Courage in the face of nothing doesn't seem worth measuring, I guess," I say.

"I guess that's right."

We are now doing what Americans do—holding a conversation that is not a true conversation yet manages to forge a connection. I am possibly wrong about Patti of Harald and Patti. Eyebrows and shifty eyes aside, she is conceivably the soul of tolerance and has never in her life uttered a word which meant something else. It's enough, on a spring-like morning in a motel parking lot, to conduct an earnest but inconsequential exchange with such a stranger.

Patti's phone chimes underneath her shirt. But before we can figure out more to say about courage and its ancient antagonist, fear, she says "Uh-oh." She has her frosted pink phone in her hand, but "uh-oh" isn't about that. "Would that be your son?" Patti says, offering a concerned look. She is looking past me.

Paul Bascombe is just this second exiting our room in his red long-boy coat. It *would* be my son. Though exiting is not exactly what he's doing. He is walking, but with one arm raised and one arm out ahead in the direction of the chrome ram's-head hood ornament of the Dodge, which I've parked too close to our door. Paul has his "other Paul" picture—"Loves to keep everyone laughing"—with him, but is losing his grip on it and actually lets it drop to the damp pavement, then steps onto it with a crunch. I am already going toward him down the motel sidewalk, saying (too loud), "Hold it. Goddamn it. Hold it." Patti is behind me saying "Lemme just call you back, sweetheart." Paul has failed to negotiate the curb step-down outside our room and launches straight into the truck front and down in a partial face-plant with the bumper—though his left hand hits first and keeps him from a total braining. "Good lord," I hear Patti say. "This man's poor son fell right down and hit a truck bumper."

"Can't you wait, you dimwit," I say, again too loud, down on my knees in a melt puddle. I grab the thick shoulder of his parka, as if he could fall again. He is also on his knees, supporting himself with one hand. He's knocked his glasses and cap off, and is extending his defective hand toward the cap as if he fears exposing how much hair he doesn't have. I am still seeing events saturated as in a movie. If I stand up too fast I might fall down myself.

"No," Paul says to my question about dimwits waiting. He expels air out his nose as if being on the ground is difficult. He has his glasses back on but not his cap.

"Did you brain yourself?" I'm touching his cheek and forehead, expecting blood.

"No," Paul says again. "I skinned my fucking hand."

"Are you all right, sweetheart? Is he okay?" Patti looms, peering down with consternation, still wearing her green gloves and holding her pink phone.

"Yes," Paul says spitefully. "I'm fine. Who're you?" He rares around at her, then upon seeing her begins trying to get up.

"It's all right, hon," Patti croons. "We'll help you."

"I think he's all right," I say. Pine-Sol reeks from Patti's gloves, plus a tincture of something sweet. Perfume she's wearing. I'm trying to re-right and re-stand Paul from my knees, but can't get leverage. One of his knees is wobbling, and his right hand is making movements like a child scribbling with a clutched pencil. He has incurred a red mark square in the middle of his forehead, right where a Muslim would contact his prayer carpet.

"Here, sweetie. I'll help." Patti's squatting and getting her long, strong arms under Paul's middle and standing up with him while I pull myself up on the truck front.

"This is the complete shits," Paul says.

"I know it is," Patti says. "It really is." Then he is up, and I am up. We are both disordered, both wet from the pavement. My shoulder is shooting what feels like hot liquid through my scapular process (thankfully, not the cardiac arrest side).

"I broke my fucking picture," Paul says.

"It'll be fine," Patti says. She's holding him, and I'm holding him. Paul is unsteady as if he could fall again. His lips are compressed and pale, but also pulsating as if it's his mouth that's in charge of him. The pink spot on his forehead isn't bleeding. He still smells of soap.

"I think we should get in the truck," I say. Paul's narrow eyes behind his glasses find me and blaze away, rejecting my being in charge.

"You sure?" Patti says. The corners of her mouth fatten to indicate she thinks this idea is crazy. "You can go right back in the room. It won't be any charge."

"Get the picture," Paul commands. He is looking around as if seeking to discern where he is, still willowy on his two feet. "I'll be fine. Okay?" he says to no one.

"Okay, hon," Patti says. She stoops and with her glove-protected hands, picks up what she can of the picture frame, the glass of which is poleaxed. "Other Paul's" insipid beach-boy face is muddied and torn where Paul has clobbered down on it. (Good.) "I trip on that ole curb twice a day," Patti says. "I need to get Harald to paint an orange stripe. This picture's not much good anymore, honey. I'm sure he'll get you a new one." She looks at me (the *he* in question) and makes a half-smile of half-assurance. Her lime Keds are wet-toes from the puddle.

Traffic is thickening out on the main drag. An immense truck transporting cylindrical hay bales lumbers past. A cop car slows, its lone occupant giving us an undecided look. At this moment, out the door of room 5 steps a tall, very thin man in a straw cowboy hat, boots, jeans and a tan shearling. He's carrying a leather attaché and has his mirrored sun-shades banded around his hat crown. Guys who wear sun-glasses this way are invariably assholes. When he sees our small assemblage in front of the Dodge, he turns back inside. I hear a woman's voice, then laughter, then the door closes.

"We'll get him another one," I say about the smashed picture. We *won't* get him another one. "Let's just pile in now."

"Let's just pile in now," Paul says brutally. I'm moving him, my left hand under his right arm, his feet operating independent of each other, knees bent to try to stride but staying locked, his left arm held out as before when he busted his face.

"I'll sweep this ole business up," Patti says. "Y'all both show a lot of courage. If you want to come back here tonight, that'll be great. I'll give you room one, which is nicer. I'm making Cupid's Delight, which we always have on Valentine's. Our son's coming up. Y'all'll get a kick out of him. He's a rodeo clown—a real one. He lives in Casper. Today's Harald's sixtieth, too. He's a Valentine's baby."

"Okay. Thanks." I'm getting the Dodge door open and my son around it and turned toward the seat. The inside air is chilled. I should've started the truck earlier.

"My hand hurts, and I can't control my fucking feet," Paul says, reaching for the hand grip on the windshield post.

"Yes, you can," I say. "Shift your weight. I'll push you." I *am* pushing him—his pillowy butt, his still-muscled thighs straining, straining. The door to number 5 opens again. The tall man's head, now without the hat, pops out to take a reading.

"Who's that?" Paul says as I'm pushing. The man closes the door again.

"You can meet him later," I say.

With his bad hand Paul loops his wrist through the inside hand-hold, manages a foot up to the running board, grasps the seat back with his good hand, and I push him forward and up like a sack of rocks. I fear he might fart more or less in my face where I'm close to him, helping him, and well in Patti's earshot—not that that matters. Miraculously he doesn't.

And then he is almost in. I give another grunting upwards lift, ignoring everything but what I'm doing and doing my best to do. And in he sags. At which point nothing else matters. We can leave. Our bags, including Otto, are in the camper.

Patti's been watching. She's observed our Florida plates and smiles at me through the passenger-side window as if we're not really from New Jersey, but who cares. I'm stretching to get Paul strapped in.

"If you two're goin' up there, you have to remember some-thin,' okay?" Patti comes around the open door, holding "Other Paul's" clutter, earmarked for the trash.

"Okay." I'm stressed. Paul frowns out at her as if she was an alien he wishes would evaporate. Do I hear *south* in my voice? I hope not.

"I know we all have to do what we have to do," Patti says. "But we don't always have to do the precise right thing for the precise right reasons *all* the time. Okay, Frank?" She pyramids her dark eyebrows as if she's imparting sacred truths anybody'd be crazy to ignore.

"Yeah-no," I say, distracted. Patti believes her genius is to read other people and know them better than she has any right to on the strength of zero first-hand experience. Most southern women believe this about themselves. Marrying one must be avoided at all costs. Poor Harald. The Valentine baby.

And of course she's wrong! Dead wrong! Should I *not* care that I'm doing what I'm doing and why? Or how I'm doing it? With my only son? Is that *ever* true? To not care and not do my best now could spell defeat for everything, first of all for our mountain ascent this morning, where my only asset is my good intention. She probably also has views about Paul's "courageous fight." I should let her ask him if he feels courageous, "battling" his opponent Al's, fighting the good and noble fight, so that one day soon, yes, he'll die but only after a valorous struggle against inconceivable odds. He'll laugh in her face, possibly fart, then tin her ears about little-known pressings from "Tony's" discog-raphy, and how KC's reprovisioning of their 'O' line in the face of age attrition is determining a possible run for the Lombardi—though alas he won't be around to see it. I have said little on the subject; but I am moved by whatever it is my son *is* at this drastic intersection of life. There *should* be a word for *that*—I wish I knew it—for what he is, a word that can be inserted in all obitu-aries to help them speak truth about human existence. Though whatever that word is, "courage" isn't it.

I simply stare at Patti, holding open the truck door in the eerily liquid morning breeze. No Cupid's Delight for us, no eve-ning with the birthday-boy discussing courage, the river that flows north, and how it's never understood. No wonder she thinks it's perfect that her son's a rodeo clown.

Just then the tall drink of water in the shearling and the hat again steps out of number 5, followed by a young, lanky blond woman in tight jeans, flip-flops and a halter top, carrying a backpack over one shoulder and a puffy green camo parka under her arm. The cowboy clicks open the Escalade with his remote. Lights flash. He's paying heed to no one and seems to have not a second to waste. The young woman herself is in no hurry. She pauses in the springlike airishness of morning, looks to the sky and at the Four Presidents' sign, runs her fingers through her long locks, which are freshly washed and uncombed. She seems about to say something for all of us to hear, but just laughs a happy, childish giggle that lets anyone know she's young and the day delights her. The cowboy is inside the car, saying something—obviously to her, though she isn't aware. The Escalade, I see, is riding a donut as its left rear tire. Paul and I are gawking at the girl, though Patti can't be bothered.

"Remember now, when you get to the monuments," Patti says happily, "those faces up there'll look small when you first see 'em. But you'll adjust. Or *they* will." This is her joke for wan-derers like us. She steps back, smiling, as I hoof it around to the driver's side. It is my weakness to wish that all exchanges end with a *bon mot*. A valediction. I have no *bon mot* for Patti, dispenser of traitorous, toxic wisdoms. No *mot* will have to do.

Patti turns and says something to the girl who's laughed so

sweetly at her surprise at the day—Valentine's Day. I hear the girl say, "Yes, ma'am." I shut us in and get the Dodge noisily cranked. A faint memory of minty car deodorizer floats in the cold cockpit.

"Who's that woman?" Paul asks. "Some friend of yours?"

"No. She's not."

Patti smiles, waves a green glove at the two of us. I wave back through the windshield. And we are off and well-off.

BIG JACK'S RANCHER'S CAFÉ—A MULTI-WINDOWED, BUILT-OUT diner with a giant white Stetson perched on top—is jam-packed as predicted. Breakfast at Jack's is a tradition for oratory families down from Bowdle and Mobridge. The sign on the street recommends the Valentine's Special—maple scrapple and *kottbula med cluck*—a cinch to bring the yokels running.

Fortunately, Big Jack has anticipated the crowds with a drive-up window out back, and a lighted "trail-riders" menu featuring precisely what Paul Bascombe wants for his breakfast—a shrimp basket. I opt for the "Tried 'n' True" bacon-and-fried-egg sammy on Texas toast. With our boxes, we drive back onto the wide boulevard (Omaha Street) and pull into the lot at a Black Hills Bank branch, ready to dig in.

In the truck seat, Paul deftly manages his shrimp one-handed and seems to have forgotten his Frankenstein dive at the Four Presidents. His head bump red mark is already fading. Possibly he's more inured to falling than I know. I may also be becoming—if I ever was—not as qualified to take care of him. Once again, I may have gotten *used* to him being "this way," and not noticed how well-inscribed are his losses, and that there is no ascertainable *way* he *is* now—or *is* for long. Even on days when he is so little worse as to seem better, he is worse. Conceivably I should be driving him back to Mayo for "follow ups," or shouldn't have brought him at all. These thoughts beget a downdraft of defeat inside the truck—almost of mourning. The inevitable fatherly defeat of everything you do—even if your son doesn't have Al's. Before I started into Heidegger, I read around in avuncular old Trollope—who really *is* a hoot. In his *Autobiography*, Trollope notes there exists in life a sorrow so great that sorrow becomes an alloy to happiness. This—in my assailed happiness here in the bank lot—is an alloy I know.

Paul has already ceased with his shrimp, which he's declared tastes "oddly plant-based." One shrimp has fallen on the truck floor, where he ignores it. Possibly he is not swallowing as well now; and because he can't taste much, eating one thing is like eating all things. His breakfast, however, has turned the inside of the Dodge into one great flourishing fried shrimp—oleaginous, dense and assertive, the fetor of all that's fry-able in the world. He clears his throat and cranes his short neck around to force down what he's chewing, then stares out at the bank, whose flagpole flies only old glory, flitting and flicking at full stem in the spring airs—a collar of bright snow around its base. In a month, crocuses will prosper here. Rapid City, from what I see of it, is a worse place in daylight—soul-less splat of mini-malls, tower cranes, franchise eats, car purveyors and new banks like this one where we're enjoying breakfast. Once only California looked this way. Helen Keller could sell real estate here, but eventually need to leave.

"I'm tired of people asking me why I'm not different than how I am," Paul says for no particular reason and clears his throat again, swallowing down the last of his words. 'How I am' comes out 'how-Ah-ham.' "They're stupid."

"Who does that? I never do."

"Yes, you do. You do it all the time. You always have. Since, 'ah wuz liddle.'" He clears his throat with even more difficulty, which confers some relief.

"I've always admired your independence." I say, carefully closing the slotted top of my Tried 'n' True box. "But I'll look into it."

"It's too late." Big sigh. Pause. "Do you want to know where I am on the Kübler-Ross scale?"

"Not so much. But okay."

He pauses, knees pulsating, right hand trembling. He extrudes his mealy tongue bottom, then the spasm leaves him. "I'm stuck on *escape*."

"Okay. If escape *was* one."

"It *should* be. They need to add more levels. Five isn't enough. I'm the expert, right?"

"Okay."

He waves his maimed right hand at two children —a boy and a girl, both under eight—dressed in spring-pastel party clothes, being taken hand-in-hand into the bank by an elderly man in a brown whipcord suit, western hat and boots. The children have waved first. They are off to a party in the bank, given by the employees. The man is their grandfather, the bank's president. It is Valentine's Day. The children are excused from school, etc., etc.

"This is your version of a do-over, isn't it?" Paul fires a feral look at me.

"What're we talking about?"

"May-be-to-mor-row," he sadly sings. "Frog-get-it."

"Do-over what? Do you think I'm making up for lost time with you? I'm not." I'm glaring daggers back at him. "I thought we could come out here and experience the same thing the same way for once. I guess I was wrong." I am fighting the battle of the situations again. His and mine. They are not congruent,

though they can sometimes seem to be. I try to stifle this awareness but rarely can—when something's funny. Caring takes us
only so far.

"You like to think about things a long time, don't you Frank?"

I am annoyed, so he wants to change the subject, which I'm
glad to do.

"No," I say, "I really don't. I trust dumb instinct, then fill
in reasons. Like everybody else." I reach and take his reeking
shrimp basket off his lap. It is ten o'clock. "*I'm* like everybody
else, and so are you."

For a moment I watch sturdy westerners leave and enter
the little glass bank cube, a spring in their step, a swell in their
hearts for the prosperity they're contributing to everything in
sight. Few of them notice us. Though soon they will—in a rig
like this one, two men alone spending too long in a bank parking lot. And from Florida. The older one gets the more one sees
the world through police eyes.

The lot is now filling up. The digital sign out on busy Omaha
Street boasts free checking with a dollar ante. Rapid City has
come alive for Valentine's. Positioned between the lot and
the street are trash receptacles shaped like the original bank
building—a solid-serious, columned Greek revival pile dated
"1876." I climb out and toss our breakfast boxes. The sun is out,
sparkling crazy on the glass bank windows.

"Do you want me to give you your Valentine now?" Paul says
when I'm back in—concentrating hard, as if words are again not
flowing. He's thinking them, then saying them. Though he is
smiling his tricky insider smile, which makes one cheek twitch.

"Okay," I say. "I'll have to give you yours later. It's in the
duffel." I will give him the one I meant for Betty, less the two
hundred bucks.

Paul has already produced a pink envelope from his parka

pocket. It is pristine in its bland pinkness and is slightly bent. "It got mooshed when I fell down," he says. For some reason he hands it to me with his claw hand which he can't entirely control, so that I hold his wrist to take the card. His stricken hand drops like a hammer into his lap. "Open it," he says, cheek still twitching, his head not all that steady on its spindle. He clears his throat again and swallows. "I got it at the truck stop. It's not traditional." I open the envelope with my finger as my knife. The card's outside says "A South Dakota Valentine" inside a boxy outline of the state. When I open it, here is revealed a bright yellow heart made entirely of actual corn kernels, underneath which is printed "It may sound corny, but I love you. Happy Valentine's Day." Paul has not signed it, for obvious reasons.

"*Okay!*" For the second, possibly the third time since we've been on our excursion, my eyes turn bleary, though not enough to need to wipe them. "This *is* great. Thank you." It is not raunchy as hell.

"I bought two of them just alike," he says, his face grown intense with satisfaction. "I lost one. I was going to send it to Clary." He breathes in and holds it.

"We'll get another one for her. She'll love it."

"Fuck it," he says. "It's the thought that counts."

"Correct." She *would* love it—if not at first, then later. I'm sorry she won't be receiving it. Conceivably, many things will not happen again—though what do I know about last things, including my own. It *is* the thought that counts.

We sit for a long bestilled moment and observe the city's traffic gliding along the spring-dampened boulevard. With noises all but silenced inside the truck, traffic becomes soothing; like a movie with no threatening elements to elevate the heart rate. Trucks and cars, cars and trucks, more trucks, more cars. The quilted sky. An empty cattle trailer. A bank's courier. A delivery van for French pastries. A hearse (without a customer). A snow-plow, blade up. An entire mobile home. Benjamin Franklin Practical Plumber. A white stretch limo with pink balloons bus-tling in the breeze. Across the way, beside a busy Jiffy Lube, the public library is open, its digital sign, which matches the bank's, reminds us "Poetry Reading Tonight. Bring Your Valentine." In the diffuse light, vitreous swimmers are doing laps across my vision. My eyes have dried, but still are stinging.

"I guess we better go on up there," Paul says, meaning, I understand, our destination. His warty bad hand and both knees are trembling.

"Great," I say.

"Can anybody go?"

"Non-citizens included. I have a senior pass."

"We don't always have to be doing the right thing, right? We just need to keep me pacified."

"That doesn't always work. We need to do the right thing sometimes."

"What hasn't killed you yet doesn't make you stronger, Lawrence," he says, "it makes you sorry." Which means something to him, not me.

"I guess." I'm starting the Dodge, happy to be going.

"What're we going to do when we're finished up there?"

"We'll have to figure that out," I say.

"How're *you* feeling? I never ask you that. I should."

"I'm feeling fine." I smile at him, backing us out and around. "Thanks for asking."

"You're my favorite turd, Frank. Don't you know that?"

"No," I say, backing, backing. "I don't know that. But it's good to hear."

And we are finally, really almost there.

ELEVEN

On our way out of town, we pass the civic center, where the oratory finals are in progress in a white, flat-roofed, brutalist structure, reminiscent of a minimum-security facility. Farm and ranch families from distant towns are loitering outside, waiting to go in for their kids to take part in the consolation rounds before striking off for the long ride home. No use to stay for the big awards tonight. Work's waiting.

Our highway south, once we pass the Rapid City limits, turns steep, mountain-sided and canyoned, following a half-frozen stream restored to life by the sudden warm-up. Businesses out this way are Rushmore-touro-centric. Rushmore helicopter rides, Rushmore Christmas village, donkey-trail adventures and reptile gardens. A Rushmore musket-shooting range and a drive-thru Rushmore ashram. All are shuttered, though a few are up For Sale, snow-covered cars abandoned in their lots, as if the owners had meant to come back but rolled the dice and traveled on.

Highway 16W—our road—begins climbing into sparser hardwoods, bare tamaracks, ponderosas and spruces clung to the sheer rock sides. At one point we pass through an actual rain shower with hailstones clattering the windshield—nothing leaks—then just as quickly the road again becomes damp as spring, reviving the shrimp-basket aromas, the Dodge taking charge without strain.

Paul fingers through *The Story Behind the Scenery—A Life-Changing Patriotic Experience*, which he bought yesterday, the book propped on his thigh, his good hand flipping pages. He's shed his parka and looks sallow and calm in his glasses and cap and clean "That's Not Funny!" shirt.

For the first time since we left Rochester—only two days back—I am not fearing our trip will be a bust, so that everything can now approximate normal—the one thing of course it can never be. At least for this instant, though, I feel as if I'd waked from a night of troubled-sleep, tortures and devilings, when the future was unconquerable, only to discover as light pales the curtains that I can sleep another hour. I've read testimonials from airline pilots where these heroes fully admit there have been times when the nose of the big Boeing self-corrects toward the ground, yet because of lifetimes spent doing only one thing, they feel they can literally do no wrong, and thus can perform without flaw.

This experience has never been mine. I can always do wrong, and frequently do. Still, the closest I can claim to this rare psychic ether—when decisions make themselves and failure isn't a topic—is how I recognize myself to feel at this moment of our ascent. Once more, nothing feels held in reserve as I ply the old Windbreaker up the mountain's side, one micro-season to the next. God only knows how much better my life could've worked out if I'd found such a path when I was young.

———

WE PASS ON THROUGH THE MOVIE-SET TOWN OF KEYSTONE, where in summer at noon each day, the Marshalls Earp (plus

Doc Holliday) *again* gun down the craven Clantons to the delight of day-trippers to the Monument (the actual gun fight took place in Arizona, but no one cares). Most of Keystone is also closed. The Red Garter Saloon, the chainsaw art atelier, the Big Thunder Gold Mine. Only a sheriff's white SUV idles outside the Gripes 'n Grinds, the deputy inside having a latte on the house.

And then, 500 yards past the Keystone town line we're there. Or here. Or almost. We enter through the Mount Rushmore gates and start up the 10% grade, all plowed and sanded. The big Dodge—I find and successfully engage the 4-wheel just in case—gathers and roars along throatily. (Why doesn't everybody have one of these brutes?) We are not alone heading up this morning. Other vehicles, given the weather's dispensation have materialized. A swaying land yacht ahead of us has blue Kansas plates and a sticker that says "Kansas Is For Lovers?" Behind us, I make out a Chrysler minivan from Michigan. Paul and I, of course, are life-long Floridians, in mourning for Norm Cepeda.

"'High above the plains of the American heartland, a colossus rises to greet the expectant eye of the traveler.'" Paul is reading to me from *The Story Behind the Scenery—A Life-Changing Patriotic Experience*. "'It's a shrine to democracy. When we re-enter the heedless world there will be a fullness of spirit and a lightening of the heart that was not there before.' Do you think that's true?" He everts his lips, his right hand trembling, feet shuffling but not strenuously. Reading aloud somehow allows him to speak distinctly. Like stutterers who don't stutter when they sing.

"I couldn't say. Maybe." We're approaching the Rushmore entry kiosk. An elderly, camp-hatted park ranger is waving vehicles through and having rollicking exchanges with all the drivers. It is a day to honor the right to recreate, irrespective of gender, orientation or place of national origin. I'm ready.

"'No words are needed to appreciate it,'" Paul reads on, giving me his secret look, the one he gives me when signs say "Kids Eat Free," "Bottomless Coffee Cup," or "Voted World's Best Chili Dog." In a world that thrives on nonsense he is a strict constructionist. "It's lucky," he says. "I'm getting low on words." Some internal torque makes him curl his tongue over his upper lip, as if he might lose his balance right in the seat he's belted into. "So did your parents bring you up here in the forties?" Drivers ahead are having over-long confabs with the ranger, who's handing out Rushmore literature and pointing drivers up the forested road to parking. This far down it's not yet possible to see the faces on the mountain.

"In the fifties," I say. "They had a big argument when we were up here. My father for some reason told my mother about a woman he'd liked a long time before. My mother got irate. She assumed there'd been a baby involved. He'd be your uncle."

"Parks make people think they're doing something when they aren't. I love it. I could work in HL up here." He means human logistics. He's ignoring my story of my parents. He coughs deeply, twists his head to the side, then back the other way.

We're nearing the ranger, who's hee-hawing and shaking hands with the driver of an ancient, loud-pink VW camper, its rear hatch-door bearing both a Biden *and* a Trump sticker—to be on the safe side. This bus has a license plate from what looks like a foreign nation. It's bright yellow, and the driver's hand I see extended out the window is extremely black. For some reason I believe they are Africans, which feels like a positive sign.

"'The Presidents' faces are supposed to last a hundred thousand years,'" Paul reads. "'To struggle with hostile human nature to carve a record which will live on and be an inspiration.' Everything has to oppose something else, I guess."

"I don't think that's true," I say, easing us up to the gassy old ranger. "Some things you just do."

"I'm glad *you're* finally getting to do something, Lawrence. You're not active enough. This'll be good for you." It amuses him to say this.

"I do plenty." I take care of my difficult son, but I don't offer that.

Paul with his useable left hand—I see this—unexpectedly makes the sign of the cross over his chest, the way a mackerel snapper would. Although he does it in reverse, then puts his hand in his lap as if I hadn't seen him.

"What're you doing? What's that?"

"You make such a big deal out of coming up here, I thought it might be a religious experience. The librarian at home's a Catholic. She's always doing it. So if I don't come back, I want to be protected."

"I'm not making a big deal out of this," I say. "Don't be an idiot."

"O-*kay*. Looks like, you two've come a fur piece," the old gobble-neck ranger is now saying in through my window, which I've lowered. His eyes are merry and startlingly blue with no smearage in the sclera. Though the rest of his face is gaunt and rucked and bony under his ranger hat, with nicks where his morning shave hasn't gone perfectly. He exudes a widower's vacant cheeriness and is probably a fill-in today. He believes we've driven up from Florida. "Happy Cupid's Day and welcome to the Rushmore Campus," he sings out. He's holding a Park Service fold-out containing an aerial map but doesn't give it to me. I have my senior pass out and ready.

"Everything's a fuckin' campus," Paul says.

"We're free today," the Ranger says, loudly. "Valentine's Day.

315

You two brought the good weather with you. Thanks for that."
He is Ranger Knippling—a toothy old grinner.

"That's great, thanks," I say out the window. Chill mountain
air floods in—cold and dry but not biting.

"You should get *his* job," Paul says. "They let anybody do it."

"Now just follow right on behind the Titanic there, up to the
Lincoln Ramp." This is Ranger Knippling's side-splitter about
the 'Kansas Is For Lovers?' land yacht. He'll have one about the
Windbreaker for the next car. "We're only open to the Avenue of
Flags today. But that's a superb view of the Presidents for you."

"These guys aren't armed," Paul says.

"Okay, *there* you go," Ranger Knippling says, still loud,
folding his uniformed arms mock-officially. "Now I like *him*.
Where'd you find this guy?" He hasn't heard anything Paul's
said. His big flaky ears contain acorn-size Beltones, which like
all hearing aids don't work worth a shit.

"He came from under a rock," I say, beginning to up my
window.

"I-I-I thought-so. Well, that's good to know." Ranger Knippling gapes another grin at me.

"He reminds me of you. A lot," Paul says. "He didn't give us
a map."

"We don't need one."

We roar away up the winding hardtop, closing on the Kan-
sans and the Africans' pink VW. There's plenty of snow on the
roadside, but many plow hours have gone into rendering the
campus open to all. The Dodge has now begun to make grinding, axle-y sounds and is producing a hot-oil smell from the
heater vent. Which is worrisome. I will need to consult Pete
Engvall. Hertz or National would've been smarter. The convenience principle always ends up saving you money.

Paul is periscoping around as we pass hardy citizens walking up from Keystone in breeks and alpine sweaters and fancy boots, some with ski poles. He hasn't crossed himself again. Very little, in truth, fazes him. In his current state there are no potatoes other than small ones.

"Are you still worried about this being all fucked up?" He's waving at the hikers, then biting a wart on his finger.

"I'm pretty happy now," I say.

"I really want things to work out for you. Okay?" He cuts his eyes at me. He means this and doesn't mean it—the best of all modalities.

"Yeah. Thanks."

And then we are at the top of the entrance road—the Lincoln parking ramp just ahead, the Washington ramp farther on—closed, gated and mounded with uncleared snow. Paul is looking around but can't find whatever he's looking for. The Presidents' faces—not in sight from here either.

It *is* a campus up here. Modern and concrete and inert. The campus of a suburban community college or a medical arts complex, where all is about parking, traffic flow, ingress and egress—the Presidents only add-ons. We could be cruising the Ocean County Mall in Toms River.

"I don't see anything," Paul says, slightly slurring "see" and "anything," his mouth cracked open as if he's tasting deception.

"Holger horses. It wasn't like this in 1954," I say.

"It's like a fuckin' airport. I don't need to see an airport on a mountain." His legs are humming. A part of him, though, is enjoying this.

I drive us on into the Lincoln structure, where vehicles are parked and people disembarking. I pull across from the pink microbus with the yellow plates. Its doors are slid back and kids-of-color piling out—all dressed smartly in bright down coats and boots and gloves and Nepalese caps out of a catalog. Ditto mom and dad, who're talking and laughing and getting the kids—four in all—started in the right direction. The father is an enthusiastic, roundly diminutive Black man in a bright red parka, exactly like his kids. He notices the Windbreaker, where I've stopped across the parking aisle and says something that causes his wife, who's tall and slender and beautiful in a long wool coat—to look over at us. They both laugh, share a word, then head off, the kids running on ahead. Their yellow license plate says Alaska. Not Côte d'Ivoire.

In short order, I get Paul out and bulkily into his chair—retrieved from the camper box—and work him back into his Chiefs coat and gloves and Stormy Kromer. It's colder up here, and even colder in the structure where wind is tricking through the parked-car rows. In his chair, in his coat, Paul looks smaller, slightly womanish—not like his mother, more like a woman who has recently become a man.

"Did you celebrate Valentine's day when you were a kid?" he says as I'm pushing him. He has his bad hand locked over the armrest. I've strapped him in. His nose is running, but he can wipe it without help.

"No," I say. "I gave a girl in my sixth-grade class a valentine once, but I wrote something stupid on it, and I never did it again." I see that I'm limping, but have no reason to limp.

"We called it an 'excuse holiday,' at Hallmark," he says (again). "An excuse to waste money. Not something you'd celebrate." He clears his throat and makes a ghastly, chesty noise which causes him to press against the leather chairback.

"Are you all right?" We're out into the open cold, crossing a plaza toward a concrete colonnade modeled on something from East Berlin—friendless and bruising. An architect's salute to American patriotism. Mount Rushmore visitors are moving through the colonnade's arches—not many of us, but enough

that we can feel part of something. A row of new porta-potties—
Sodak Convenience—has been trucked in for Valentines and
lined up on both ends of the colonnade. Women left, Men right.
These are seeing use, since Rushmore restrooms aren't open.

"Do you have to go?" I say, hoping not.

"I'm not getting the bull's-eye tattoo over my heart," he says,
ignoring me.

"Why is that?" Pushing him on through the colonnade's
portal. The Alaskans are far ahead in the crowd.

"I don't need it now." No explanation.

Up ahead is another, smaller columned entry—wheelchair
accessible—flanked by more long Cold-War-looking concrete
buildings where in summer there'd be video screens for viewing
virtual Mount Rushmores instead of the real one (many Americans prefer this). With our fellow Rushmoreans, Paul and I shove
out onto another breezy plaza, the sky beginning to lower and go
gray, the air turning damp and chlorinated-smelling, pressing
on my cheeks. All of us—several half-habited nuns, a couple of
collared priests, some certifiable Indians, a couple of wheelchair
visitors, an entire grade-school class—are passing through the
second set of columns out onto what I guess is the Avenue of
Flags, where our view will be superb. Some of the oratory crowd
is here, along with oldie couples, a contingent of spindly Asians
wearing germ masks, plenty of beefy farm-boy types with undersized girlfriends. The Black family has scooted ahead and is
through to the observation area. A teenage blond girl in a red
sweatshirt emblazoned with "Speech! Speech!" is giving Paul the
fish eye, possibly spotting his gimpy hand, which won't be still,
though he is trying to hide it, tucking it under his other arm and
staring all around as if it was normal. I, of a sudden, again experience the grainy sensation which momentarily stops me: That
from some nearby piney steep, someone—a disgruntled park

employee, a loner teen—is readying to open up on us (it's always a he), having scaled the mountain and taken a position commanding the entire promenade and everyone on it. I don't *really* believe this. Though why would any sane citizen not consider it? Once, nothing made me feel as civically invested and endorsed as public accommodation. A treed city park. The M4 bus to the Cloisters. The observation deck above misted Niagara. Now I less willingly find myself in such places, and when I do I feel a pull toward the exits, the needle-y urge to hang back, to not go near the edge (of anything), eyeing all opportune sites from which to draw a bead on me. Again, I'm not legitimately afraid, only aware I might better be. If you're looking for an earmark of old age, it is this: being aware you're aware and having little or no control over what's going on. In this case, *life in the public sphere* being not what it used to be.

"Oh, wow," I hear my son exclaim, unexpectedly, which releases me, as I don't believe I've ever heard him say these words. I've pushed him (I'm still limping. Why?) out onto the wide-open Avenue of Flags, which—its flagpoles vacant—presents a long, spacious unmistakably martial esplanade—like a parade ground—beyond which (a sign says) is the Grand View Terrace and beyond that the "amphitheater" where the Mormon Tabernacle Choir and the Marine Band perform, and where summertime visitants can relax and hum along to "Ol' Man River" and "El Capitan," while gazing upwards at the granite colossus and feeling, I suppose, colossal. Who cares if everything's not open and available? (The amphitheater's off-limits today, blocked by Jersey barriers like Exit 8A on the Turnpike.) From out here, no matter his or her state of body—and around us are many varieties—all can stand or sit and marvel at the big mountain that is Rushmore and take in the four presidents' granitudinally white faces, gazing into vacant space.

"This is great. I love this," Paul Bascombe—*the* Paul
Bascombe—says. He is craned forward in his chair, fingering
his silver ear stud, eyes riveted with all the others of us, upon the
four chiseled visages. L to R—Washington (the father), Jefferson
(the expansionist), Roosevelt #1 (the ham, snugged in like an
imposter) and stone-face Lincoln, the emancipator (though there
are fresh questions surrounding that). None of these candidates
could get a vote today—slavers, misogynists, homophobes,
warmongers, historical slyboots, all playing with house money.

I cannot completely believe I've brought this unlikeliest of
moments about, and can be here standing where I'm standing—
with my son. How often do *anyone's* best-laid plans work out?
How often are promises kept and destinations achieved? I'll
tell you. Not very goddamn often. Buddhists profess all is the
journey. Abjure arrival. But what do they know? They're hiding
something, like all religions.

And yet. *Something* about the four presidents-on-a-mountain
seems not exactly right to me. Which was not my experience
in '54, when my parents stopped speaking to each other, and
I took the role of peacemaker/cheerleader, and all became as
monumental as expected and in fact awesome. But to me now,
though certainly not to most of us down here, 1,500 feet below,
gawking up—but definitely to me—the faces appear *entirely* too
small (Patti said you get used to it). Photographs, of course, are
made by drones, so they look bigger. But for grandeur they're not
a patch on Niagara or the Bierstadt valleys or the mighty Mississippi at New Orleans, or for that matter, the dunes in Seaside
Heights, New Jersey, which never disappoint. They're more kin
to the facsimile Parthenon in Nashville or the fake Monticello
in Connecticut. Or the Space Needle. *Something's* decidedly
measly about them, something bally-hooed which they're not
up to. The empty space between us and them is, to me, more

impressive than the faces. Plus, the great men themselves seem unapologetically *apart*, as if *they've* seen *me*, and *I'm* too small. I'm slightly embarrassed by them.

None of which I need to share with my son. Because, am I sorry to have brought us up here? Not if he likes it. I'll get used to it.

Around us spectators are, in their positivist ways, personal-izing and memorializing their spectatorship. The down-jacketed Alaskan-Africans (they may well be from Dallas) have unlim-bered fancy video gear they're training up at the faces, as if Lincoln might wink or Jefferson smirk. Others are employing their phones. The masked Asians are posing for group selfies and laughing about the whole thing. Many are standing, staring as if waiting for something—a signal, the mountain to rumble, lightning to crash, white light to engulf them. Most, though, are satisfied to pause, look, look again, walk about the wide avenue slightly self-conscious, letting eyes roam—conversing quietly with others, gazing warily up toward the mountain slopes, won-dering about the gift shop and why it's not open and if there's a restroom other than the smelly porta-potties. Theirs, I silently believe, is a cousin to my embarrassment, since anyone becomes self-conscious when all there is to do is look. On the Great Wall you can walk the footsteps of Ming emperors; you can ascend the Eiffel Tower (if you have the nerve) to its swaying finial. At Niagara, you can take a boat into the flume and thrill at the thought of being swept over the brink. But *only looking* has its emotional limits. "It's a real legacy," I hear someone say. "I come every year," someone answers. "Do they *do* anything?" a young bride says, plainly skeptical. "Cupid's wingèd arrow," her young hubby replies with a guffaw. "I don't see why you took me *here*. It's kind of a big nothing, *I* think," she says.

Up in front where people are stopped at the low concrete

wall, I see the tall, rangy Escalade cowboy with his mirror shades tricked around his straw hat like a car salesman. No sign of the attaché case. The blond girl is close beside him in her camo parka, as delighted as she was at the motel, pointing toward the presidents and laughing. The cowboy is as masculinely non-committal as possible. They have with them now a much older woman—as old as I am—in a thin blue coat and a blue beret, rubber ankle boots and carrying a big patent leather purse. She's speaking to the cowboy and once or twice patting his arm to keep his attention. About the cowboy and the girl, I have obviously imagined connections that are not correct, and am not sorry to say so. Humans remain humans—largely impenetrable to the rest of us.

"The head of the Sphinx in Egypt isn't as long as Washington's nose," Paul is saying. He is rapt and smiling, staring up. It is a smile in which I detect a flicker of nervousness. I don't know what about. I have lost awareness of him for a minute. Though he hasn't gone anywhere. Is still in his chair. "They put the faces up high so no one'll deface them," he says. "Originally the sculptor wanted to show to their waists. Like a men's store. But just the heads are better, I think." He is still sitting forward and has become, for just this special time, un-afflicted, with untroubled speech. "No one even got killed building it," he says. "Which is surprising since they used dynamite. I read all this in the book." He looks around to detect if by being silent I am amused by him—which he wouldn't like. His round cheeks are pink from the damp and chill, his mouth closed, almost clenched with exertion and pleasure. Much that he isn't saying is buzzing in his hectic brain. Behind his glasses his eyes are darting and alert. I am happy to have done one seemingly right thing for one seemingly not wrong reason. Any trip can be perilous once you commit to the destination, as we have.

"You think it's better than Sopchoppy, Florida and Whynot, Mississippi?" The old Flying Dutchman that never flew.

"Do you know *why* it's so great, Lawrence? Why I'll never be able to thank you enough?" Paul clears his throat with a guttural *growlf*, like a codger, then casts his head to the side. Which sets his knees shuddering. All that is happening has not cured him.

"Tell me."

"It's completely pointless and ridiculous, and it's great." His eyes are jittering and gleaming. "There's not enough in the world that's intentionally this stupid." He is smiling beatifically, as if he's experienced an extraordinary discovery and surprise. A confirmation. I'm merely happy to believe we see the same thing the same way for once—more or less. It *is* pointless and it *is* stupid. And if seeing it can't fix him, it can a little. "We're bonded," Paul says slyly, still smiling, gazing with complete awareness toward the presidents. I am his favorite turd.

"I guess so." My hands are on his wheelchair handles and smarting. I've left my gloves in the truck.

Someone near us—a hefty sweet-faced, red-haired farm girl in a blue sweatshirt that has "Tolstoy Speech Club" across its spacious front—says to her father, "Is the monument down here or up there?" She has a point.

"Why don't we walk around?" I say.

"Hugo Furst," Paul says. "I'll just ride."

And so we do. I push him farther along the Avenue of Flags closer to where people are congregated at the temporary Grand View Terrace boundary, talking and laughing, taking videos and snapshots, commenting about what being here means. Again there is little to do but look and *be*, and not grow weary or sad. The Escalade man and his companions have slipped away when I wasn't looking. The Alaska Africans have produced sandwiches and canned drinks and are gathered happily at the far end of the wall. Other visitors are talking to them, smiling and nodding, pointing up at the presidents as though to explain it all. Everyone is polite. The novelty of the day and the weather are more than enough to fill out an adventure. And it is good for the two of us to be part of something far away from our pressing subject; a positive, low-impact Valentine's day, easy to make the most of, since it doesn't have to come out perfect. Though I have not completely shaken the anticipation of something being about to take place—as if people might leave their wheelchairs and begin walking around singing. Possibly this is what crossing a barrier feels like. We're never fully aware of what it is or when it happens. But. If some stealthy marksman concealed high in the stony fastness chooses me among the innocents to pick off like a mountain goat, his timing won't be altogether wrong. I have done what I came to do.

Just now, as if propelled from the mountain itself, a helicopter—tiny—materializes down out of the marbled heavens, high-tailed and insect-like, and for all of us along the viewing wall, soundless. It passes on strings through the grainy air, tilts to starboard, seems for a moment to pause, then slides away, changes course and makes a dreamlike pass close to the presidential physiognomies, comes about again, tail swaying, makes a pass the other way, so that whoever's inside gets the fullest view up close. No one could pay me to do this, but I am impressed by the dare-deviltry, as the little whizzer works round toward the north, glassy cockpit bulb nose-down, then disappears back from wherever it came.

"Some goddamn Russian ga-zillionaire," a man near me declares. "Had to show us who's boss. Probably buyin' it."

"Trump already bought it!" someone says, which provokes approval, some laughs, fitful applause, plus someone—there are such people in all groups—who must go "Yaaaaaas! Go for it! Woo-hoo!"

✦

I HAVE NOW BECOME VERY COLD. HALF-TURBULENT, OYSTER clouds have descended as fog onto the Avenue of Flags. Many of our number are straying back toward the Lincoln parking structure, having neglected to dress warmly enough—indicating many are not from these parts.

Paul is still smiling strangely and uncharacteristically—the soft corners of his mouth unmoving. It might simply be he's cold, even in his Chiefs ensemble. His knees are working above his footrests, his bad hand clutched in his good. I've seen him jerkily cross himself left-handed again, as if to solemnize something only he knows about. He's watching up at the four distant faces instead of staring around the way he normally would.

"It's not really like any place else, is it? It's monumental without being majestic." There is no trace of disappointment, double or triple meaning.

"One person's majesty is another person's steak au poivre, I guess."

"They're like big puppets." He thinks a moment. "Do you have a romance or something about them?"

"No," I admit. The Black family is skittering past us, headed back to their pink V-Dub. Only a hearty few are left out in the open. A coffin-y breeze has worked its way down (or up) from some cold redoubt. If the Avenue of Flags had flags they would be stirring. "We should start back," I say. I'm turning him and setting us into motion. We have been here twenty minutes. I have driven two and a half days to be here not quite a half hour. It couldn't be better.

"What's our altitude," Paul says like a pilot. *Altitude*—the word—posing a small challenge to him.

"I don't know."

He swivels half around in his chair—belted tight so only his capped head rotates. He is biting the corner of his mouth with unsuppressed pleasure. "Do you think I reveal hidden virtues, Lawrence?"

"Yeah. I'll enumerate them when I'm not so fucking frozen." Which I am. A new wind swirls and swarms and changes its bearing, and all at once the air and sky between us and the almost invisible mountain are full of dancing snow particles. We pass two laughing pink-masked Asian girls indulging in a last Rushmore selfie. They are talking. Who knows what they're saying.

"What choices have we got now?" Paul asks.

"Choices for what?" Limp, limp, limp, limping.

"Oh, oh, oh, eee, eee," the Asian girls go tripping past in high heels. I need a pit-stop. Probably we both do. Snow is making my eyes crust up and stinging my ears.

"I don't know," Paul says. His glasses catch snowflakes on their lenses. "What we're going to do now?"

"Well." The backs of my hands are red and stiff and old-looking. "There's the oratory. There's a poetry reading. There's *The Lion King*. I can take you back to the Fawning Buffalo and see what shakes out. I know what I'd choose." I'm pushing him faster, wiping my eyes with my shoulder. "We'll figure it all out." We will.

"See Mount Rushmore and then what?"

"I don't know." Pushing, limping, pushing. "Things are always happening. We just don't know about them."

"I know about them," he says. He's shivering, I can see, and slightly ashen. His breathing may be shallow, his face is strained. "I know all about you, too, Frank. Don't I?" His Stormy Kromer cap is bobbing side to side in front of me in his chair as though to a song playing in his head, which may be the case.

"Maybe you do," I say. "Maybe it's not very hard. Do you still have a headache?"

His head nods up then down, then up, then down in agreement. We continue, as if all that seems to be the way it is at this moment, *is* the way it is. "What would you be doing if you weren't doing this," he asks.

"I'd be doing this," I say.

"Okay. Good to know."

"I haven't given you your valentine yet," I say. "But I will." Snow is all about us, caking on top of his red cap and in my hair. Cars are leaving up ahead. New weather is calling a halt to everything up here.

"You have to not forget about my hidden virtues," Paul says. "I'll tell you yours. And we can both have a laugh."

"We'll do that," I say. "You have a lot of virtues."

"Am I a change agent?"

"Yes. I'd say you are. Are you still fighting the sky and winning?"

"Yes. I'm not worried about *anything*," he says. "No complaints. Okay?"

"Right. That's good," I say. "That's good to know, too."

"In case you were wondering."

"I was."

"Do you think they'll remember me at the Clinic?"

"I'm certain they will," I say.

"Am I still a presence, do you think?"

"Very much a presence. Yes."

"That's good." Paul says. "I was hoping I was."

And we push on.

HAPPINESS

Relations, the great master says, never really end. But it is the task of the teller to draw—by a geometry of his own—the circle within which they will, happily or otherwise, appear to do so.

My son Paul Bascombe died —in Scottsdale—on Saturday, September 19th (International Talk Like A Pirate Day—a fact he would've enjoyed). One of his last wishes was to not die after dark, and by the luck of the draw he did not, but in the early afternoon.

Following our Mount Rushmore ascent, we stayed a night to have the Dodge fixed at a Tire-Rama, but failed, so that Pete Engvall had to be called to retrieve it—which he might or might not have done. My Honda remains in his care. Next day, we rented a National one-way at the airport, passed a night in the Fawning Buffalo, then drove on not to Kamloops but to the Little Bighorn—which Paul agreed he should see, and where I gave him his valentine a day late and a dollar short. Following which we turned south, never to return together to Rochester or New Jersey in my son's life. Not the Flying Dutchman Tour, but as well as I could manage.

To his surprise and mine he did not die of Al's, but of a

completely new disease we had hardly heard of when we visited the Mayo Clinic then struck off on our un-victory lap across the great American wilds, all the way to the assailable majesty of Rushmore, which he loved and felt represented an important barrier surmounted in his life. I truly don't know much about that, such as which barrier, and between what and what—though I have my ideas. These words are metaphors, in any case, and highly personal.

I was not literally with my son when he died, nor was his sister, though we were nearby. I was parked outside the hospital in my daughter's car—109 degrees, the AC blasting—listening to the Yanks beat the Red Sox at Fenway. And while I can't say whether my son exhibited extraordinary courage in facing his nemesis, death—intubated, gaunt, ghastly, livid, uncharacteristically afraid, possibly panicked—his death was not completely different from how he'd have died anyway, muscles no longer supporting breath, lungs in freshet, strangled in his fluids. I do not believe, as some would say, that he was "lucky" for death to come to him as it did—relatively quickly—only that possibly it was not as bad as dying from ALS, whose sufferers can live for years, lose all but their cognitive powers (which do not require muscles) then die as miserably and as surely as they would had they only lived a year—like my son. As I've said, I did not allow myself to wish or hope one thing or another. Many times, near the end, when Paul wanted to know my worst secret (I wouldn't say), it would have been that. That I did not wish he wouldn't die—since such a wish was pointless. Many times I tried to say to myself that Paul evidenced a strong "life force." But I do not even think that was correct. Life force is only another metaphor—a euphemism for the same kind of wishing. Whereas continued existence is mostly luck. Or it's genes. Or it's something we'd find out about in a hundred years, if we were going to be here.

I will say for Paul, that though he died in a "facility," the way his mother died and no doubt I will (unless I'm hit by a truck full of golf carts), he died fundamentally unchanged, dedicated to being himself and giving life its full due—skeptical-seeming but not skeptical—much like the handsome little boy from long ago who kept pigeons in a coop behind our house in Haddam and sent them off each night in hopes of getting messages to his dead brother Ralph who, he thought, lived on Cape Cod—messages about how things were going in the diminished life he'd left behind, and where we were all sad.

In his final week in the Klaus and Helga Simmonsen Wing of the Carefree Medical Center (a location not lost on him) Paul sent notes to me via his care team. One message stated that on reflection he had not gained much from our trip across the nation, but that we *had* achieved something we'd set out to do, which was good per se—though it was too bad Mount Rushmore couldn't have been closer. He also asked me if I maintained a working definition of what *good* was—which surprised me, since all his life he'd seemed enviably non-absolutist about most things; reconciled to life's primarily offering only contingencies, bemusements, sly looks, and the unexamined way being all there is—at best, a momentary stay against confusion. I thought about this question for a while, then gave him the definition I still largely believe—the Augustinian one—that good is the absence of bad, that happiness is the absence of unhappiness. I added that the poet Blake believed good was only good in specifics—which is what we had experienced and enjoyed together on our trip. Details. To his question of what did I fear most, I told him the truth: That my biggest fear was not a real fear but an elder fear, a fear that I had *not* done all I in fact *had* done—with and for him; that everything had been a dream, every day and deed, a dream from which I would wake up to find . . . what? I didn't

331

know. Possibly only that I had outlived him—though I didn't tell him that. I wrote all this on a yellow legal sheet which required being sanitized before it could be read to him, since he could not hold a page by then. His nurses told me he was able to raise one thumb up.

For his final question—all were not equally interesting—he asked me again if I thought he possessed hidden virtues. And here, I may have let him down, since he would've liked a list either of riotous traits or profoundly serious ones—that he had a bigger schwantz than his hands, height and shoe size foretold; that he could've been a great ventriloquist with more encouragement from his parents; that he possessed a rare gift of changing every room he walked into for the better. Possibly I lacked the requisite light heart at the moment we had this virtual exchange, because I only told him he was a patient and independent person, was not a complainer, although he did not suffer in silence; that he had a good and unusual sense of humor, was witty, was possibly a better ventriloquist than he got credit for; that he had once been a good swimmer. And that I loved him—which was not literally a virtue.

On the Saturday he died, the Wolverines were not playing, but the Chiefs would play the Chargers the next day and win—which he unfortunately missed. On that morning, his sister told me—the two of them had been having "amazing" talks in the months he was in her house—that Paul's death, which we'd been told to expect, mirrored the decline of America's morals and influence in the world, and that his death was a significant symptom. This I hated to hear, since it seemed to steal his death from him, which I told her. She is a Log Cabin Republican (what could be worse for a father?). And even if I could've considered what she said (I didn't really understand it), I could not agree with her. No one's death is a symptom.

All of which was in my thinking there in the car, waiting for Paul to die—a disjointed chorus of imaginings, mostly death-inspired but in no way reconciled by death. I wondered whether dying was a means to communicate—which I'd read in a novel. And if so, what was being communicated? And whether dying frees something in us? Paul had insisted it did not. I wondered if nearness to death quickens the present for a magical time? Possibly. And whether dying illuminates one's essential self? Again, I do not believe I have an essential self, though if I have one it is always on display. I wondered, selfishly, if death inevitably revealed how Paul thought about me—his father—who cared for him 'til his end. But this I will never know. Sitting masked in my daughter's red Rover, in the eucalyptus-abundant hospital lot, listening to the Sox lose to the Yanks and drinking a toast to my son from a plastic flask bought for this purpose and moment, I decided that if death *is* a means to communicate, the message is about life; that the most important thing about life *is* that it will end, and that when it does, whether we are alone or not alone, we die in our own particular way. How that way goes is death's precious mystery, one that may never be fully plumbed. Again, all I feel I know is that when Paul departed his life, I did not depart mine.

IN THE END, PAUL DID NOT DONATE HIS BODY TO SCIENCE OR TO the Mayo Clinic *or* elect that it be composted or sprinkled from a small plane or buried at sea off Sea-Clift, New Jersey—all outcomes he talked about. His advance directive made no mention of how he should begin the reconstitution phase. His sister and I, faced with the difficulties surrounding his quarantine, agreed to have him impersonally but respectfully cremated (for $925) in nearby Surprise, Arizona, by an interfaith crematorium run by friendly Basques, a formality we were not allowed to attend, but could, if we chose (I did, his sister didn't) have recorded on Zoom, a link for which I have on my laptop but have yet to visit. It's impossible for me not to look at the world in terms of what Paul would've found hilarious and what he would've found boring. This may be his legacy for me. And while cremation would likely not have been his first choice, he would, I believe have loved *himself* going down the rails, through the Hadean doors to the flames—as seen from the comfort of a laptop, preserved forever as a keepsake.

A day will come, Clarissa and I have agreed, when we together will transport half of Paul's cremains to the cemetery in Haddam and inter them beside his mother and his brother. No bagpipes as per his wish; epitaph to be determined; a small notice placed in the *Haddam Packet*. The remainder of him we'll transport to the Huron Mountain Club (Clarissa inherited the family membership but never told me) and with more ceremony than I devised for their mother a year ago—possibly a true celebration of life—commit Paul's other half to the dancing, morainal waters of Ives Lake. All of this assuming such a day comes for any of us. Until then I keep Paul's ashes with me in a lacquered Chinese box the Basques provided as part of the "package."

Clarissa has observed, uncharitably—she is full of small uncharities; although in the long plague months when Paul was alive, I clearly out-stayed my welcome by remaining near my son—she's observed that Paul's life had just begun when it sadly started to end. Which I told her is also wrong, since the same can be said of anyone who dies wishing he or she could enjoy another day alive. When they had their amazing talks, she said she finally "discovered him," and that he was "a surprisingly real and complex whole person." As if for forty-seven years he had been less than a full entity, waiting only for her notice to render him plausible. For a smart woman—she is forty-five—she often thinks and talks in clichés and rarely sees through to what's dazzling in life. These qualities, of course, work well in the business world and possibly in psychoanalysis—of which she's had a god's own plenty. But they leave much of life unrevealed. Again, she is a Republican, and believes more money's to be gained by rendering life less interesting.

⁙

SINCE THE WEEKEND BEFORE COLUMBUS DAY—INDIGENOUS Peoples' Day, a holiday that celebrates me as a native American as much as Cochise and Jay Silverheels—I have been living the life of a temporary boarder in the guest accommodation (the stylishly appointed basement level) of Dr. Catherine Flaherty's privet-hedged, understated, Italian-fieldstone and pantile "Cliff House," once owned by the actor Leo G. Carroll, who played Topper on TV. Catherine's house sits high atop sheer rocks above the Pacific, with widely running verandas, passion flower'd pergolas and stone retaining walls fronting the sea— pretty much the way I fantasized it almost a year ago, the morning I learned my son had ALS, and she pulled strings for him to come to Mayo. I told her in that phone conversation—I was in the crowded Detroit airport—that I loved her and hoped one day to cross her threshold, ready to put my long-postponed money where my long-postponed mouth was. (Or, as my son would've said, "put my monkey where my mouse is.")

Catherine (who does, in fact, like to be called Kate) looks precisely as I remember her and hoped she would; a bit beamier than when I met her and she was a Dartmouth sportswriter intern, but golden skinned still, honey-haired (not natural, she assures me), brilliant of tooth and nail, given to smiling broadly and widening her dark eyes as if I'm always saying something shocking when in fact I rarely am. The truth is, the woman you loved long years ago but somehow failed to seal the deal with, but have gone on imagining that a sparkling day will dawn when you'll return to make good on a thousand unkept promises— that woman hasn't waited for you, if she's given you as much as a single thought. Catherine (Kate) has a perfectly acceptable goodly swain to occasionally share her bed and evenings with (not *live* with; "God, I don't need *that* aggravation"). I have been in basement-residence a month now, and I and the swain get on passably well, like shipwrecked survivors on a too-small raft. If I'm invited up for drinks, he and I easily launch into earnest, inconsequential elbows-to-knees conversations about sports, the real-estate market, the long view for bitcoin in the Eurozone— things he knows about and I know a little of. And all is fine. He is a lanky, vigorous seventy-odd with a heavy jaw, small, complacent mouth and a blond forever cowlick—a Williams man (Arsen 'Tap' Tapscott) retired from acquisitions-legal at the La Brea Tarpit Museum. He still does competitive open-ocean outrigger racing, drives a green Cayenne, and stands faithful guardian over his wife Mazie, who suffers frontotemporal dementia and hasn't had a clue who he is in a decade. He met Kate through Catholic fund-raising connections and slips down on weekends when his daughter can drive from Oxnard to stay with the mom in Pacific Palisades. I have no wish (nor hope) to supplant good man Tap from his enviable perch. He and Kate are like jolly dinner-party partners who flirt over the caviar and blinis, then go home separately—an equilibrium fragile yet sturdy, founded not on the old woogledy-woogle, but on a life-view of conservatorship, moderate Republican convictions and a late-dawning appreciation that the Latin Mass "really makes a kind of sense." I have never talked to him about Paul; though I'm sure Kate has—which explains as much as needs to about my lingering presence here. "Oh, just an interesting man I knew once long ago." The fate of many.

Of my time here, there is not much to say. From having looked after my dying son for ten eventful months, I am at ease with the remaining central life question of "What is my project now? What am I actually doing?" It is never an untimely question, as the answer almost always surprises you.

Catherine has afforded me great assistance in this odd time of my life—if not the love interest I'd dreamed about. She's been able to get me in to see the periodontist, Dr. Yih, as I finally wore a hole clean to the pulp of my bicuspid, requiring an implant—which I can attest is all but painless and a good solution. She has also arranged for me to read for the blind right here in La Jolla, as I did for decades in Haddam. There is always a need for practiced readers, and there are more than enough blind people to go around. Catherine believes, as a "physician-of-faith," that this is a better means of giving back than joining a dreary "grief group" of moaners and wailers. These people often declare themselves to have PTSD rather than admitting they're simply finding fellow-feeling from a rag tag group of lonely sufferers in a Church of Christ basement. It's like personal trainers at Planet Fitness making a claim to be essential workers.

Reading for the blind—which I do on Tuesdays and Fridays—takes place in a fake-adobe, Mexican-colonial community-access bunker, twenty minutes' walk from Catherine's house at 1830 Spindrift Drive. Reading is mostly a matter of going through the major news items in the morning's *Union-Tribune*—excluding the right-wing editorials and obits. This can take sometimes three hours. Though the station manager has invited me to bring in personal readings for his "Book Nook" feature on literary excerpts. I've so far brought in one "classic"—the droll opening of *Bleak House*, where fog covers everything; but also some out-takes from fresh contemporary novels I've lately begun to read as I once did as a young writer on the way up and quickly down.

These up-to-the-minute literary-fiction choices are ones I admire and thoroughly enjoy reading to blind people who would never know anything about them otherwise. These young writers, I've found, are all brilliant; keenly astute at knowing and saying precisely *what* causes *what* in life. What causes our lusts. What causes our guilts. What causes our disquiets and despairs. What causes joy. What causes tragedy to be tragic and comedy comic, and how these two are joined. When you think about it, isn't that what anyone wants to learn from literature, since knowing such data can initiate for you a practical understanding of true happiness?

This was the trick I could never perform when I was in my own scribbler period in the late sixties, though in my defense I never believed I needed to write about these subjects. The cause of most things was pretty obvious, I thought. Lust was natural and guilt was caused by lust, which then caused disquiet and despair, and none of it was funny. All I needed to do was simply take an interest in what I could make happen next—after lust, after disquiet, after despair—without worrying in the least about causation. I'd once read in a book about writing that in good novels, anything *can follow anything*, and nothing ever *necessarily follows anything else*. To me this was an invaluable revelation and relief, as it is precisely like life—ants scrabbling on a cupcake. I didn't see I had to speculate about what caused what. And truthfully, I believe it to this day. Witness my son's relentless assault by ALS, which as far as the best medical science understands, poses a near complete mystery. Yes, we see it happening. But nothing specifically causes it or specifically doesn't cause it. It just happens.

I have not, I should say, returned to the old Nazi Heidegger and will not now. There is something to be said for reading long, dense books you don't understand in order to wall yourself off from the world's meanness and arbitrary unfairness. Occasionally in Heidegger I would get a glimmer of something interesting—e.g., what human existence really amounts to. But then my mind fogged over like the Thames in *Bleak House* and off to sleep I went—if often badly dismayed. I've realized Heidegger makes life—which is already hard enough—ever so slightly more difficult by always positing something confining and unknowable just when I desire to feel free for a moment of airy, well-earned ease and clear-sightedness. Which is to say, not walled off. Not walled off anymore, ever. My son, I feel sure, would want this for me.

On my suburban walks to the radio station (my limp has mysteriously disappeared) I have plenty of time and inspiration to think about the character of my life project. We undervalue the suburbs, even the richest, most unwelcoming of them, by believing they can't facilitate such inquiries and by facilitating them hasten the spirit to take flight. I fully enjoy my walks along the curving, manicured, palm and bougainvillea-lined side-walks, past the asset-class dwellings hidden behind boxwoods, brick walls and dense bamboo curtains. The left side of Spindrift Drive is built a few feet higher than the right, to preserve the all-important view of the crystal Pacific. It is a glitzy, coastal version of those deep-monied, century-old brownstone neighborhoods you find in Cleveland and Pittsburgh, but which in California means houses that last only fifty years, then get torn down and replaced by new-generation citizens with different values and calibers of money, intent on making their own spirits soar. All of which signifies that value resides not in the people or the houses, but in the ground and the faith it inspires. Which I find encouraging for the future in a kind of Ozymandian way that maybe only realtors understand.

In these weeks of restorative, non-conjugal stay-cation and self-busying, I have discovered that my narrative, to my surprise, is not a sad man's narrative, not resigned, in spite of events. I sleep soundly, eat sensibly, am gastro-intestinally reliable, maintain a decent blood pressure for my age, and worry almost not at all. When, late of an autumn evening, Catherine ventures downstairs to my lair, bringing a bottle of frozen Stoli and something she's fixed to munch on, and we set up side-by-side on her Icelandic musk-ox couch to watch Netflix—the Swedish police procedurals are the best—I find I'm as gratified and as nearly happy as I've known myself to be. (Actually, I wish she would change her mind, throw the suitors—or suitor—out, and give me more serious consideration. But she will not.) And yet, if long ago I'd snared the golden ring and we had wandered off together forever, so that all that did and didn't happen in the in-between real-time was erased and life was only us, we would almost certainly have ended up on a commensurate couch somewhere, drinking commensurate vodka and bingeing on three episodes of *something*, before adjourning to separate cubicles for long, un-perturbed and dreamless sleeps. Similarly, when I contribute my small "rent payment" and walk her twin Lurchers—green-plastic eco-crap-bags tucked in my belt— down to the Pacific overlook so they can do their business and sniff around the fenced-off steps, now deemed hazardous, and where I sometimes see a rainbow in the sky, I realize that even in that wished-for alternate life, this is also what I would be doing. We can look too closely at life. Careful un-close looking is as much full immersion as I can stand anymore. Ending is hard,

I heard an anchorman say on PBS last week. He was talking not about the ending my son endured—about which there can be no disagreement—but about how tactically and artfully we cross the landscape ahead, once the next to last barrier is exceeded. Okay. Ending's hard, I thought. But it doesn't have to be all *that* hard.

This evening, standing by my lonesome outside on Catherine's sun-shot Italian, hand-glazed brick terrasse—thinking as always that I am not facing west but east, and having an early glass of North Coast rosé—I have, I believe, experienced my second episode of global amnesia. Humans are approved for only one of these per lifetime, so take what you will from that. I had just been thinking of whether I would go claim my belongings in Rochester (or not) and travel back to New Jersey—which seems a strange place to me now, even if I return to my job, let Mike Mahoney commodify my house, and move myself into (I can't think more than to say . . .) someplace else. I hear voices in the house—Catherine teasing and laughing at the dogs. Glasses and silverware and ice are tinkling. But I realize—just as I did before when I tried to take the garbage out twice at home—that some time has clearly passed without my knowing it. The weather is mostly the same here, the setting sun a liquid ball plumped upon the horizon and a fixture in California that never changes. But the sun is now gone. The air cooler. There are pale stars. A sliver of opalescent moon. Where did *I* go? And for how long? Five minutes? An hour? I remember what I was thinking. About Rochester. And Haddam. And about my son Paul's life and his death, and whether that combination of thoughts could sponsor some fresh claim on the present for me—even though the present does not seem such a secure place. I think of other things that might be of importance to me and that I might've been musing about: Can grief be defeated, or merely out-lived? How can I ever achieve complete immersion in earthly life? What is the greatest happiness? I can't, I realized, find whatever I'd been thinking during the passage of time I've clearly lost. It is not forgotten, but paved over, as before. Vanished. But to ponder this further is, I think, like longing for an afterlife only because so much of day-to-day existence can be drastic. I hear my name called. "Where *are* you, Frank? I'm coming. I have something you're going to like. Something very different and new." I turn to see who it is. The empty time I've missed has gone quietly closed from both sides. "Okay," I say, "I'm ready for something different." I smile, eager to know who is speaking to me.

ACKNOWLEDGMENTS

Kristina Ford helped me with her fullest engagement to write this book. Without her wisdom, intelligence, patience, perseverance, wit, brilliance, and love from beginning to end, it would simply not have happened.

Many, many others—cherished editors, agents, publishers, translators, physicians, teachers, colleagues, and friends—played crucial parts in this book's coming to be. I celebrate your generosities with great gratitude. You and I both know who you are.

—RF